Gratify

Katelyn Taylor

Playlist

hate u love u by Olivia O'brien
Chasing Cars by Snow Patrol
Supermarket Flowers by Ed Sheeran
Look After You by The Fray
Earned It by The Weeknd
Under The Influence by Chris Brown
Fetish by Selena Gomez, Gucci Mane
Say You Won't Let Go by James Arthur
See You Again by Wiz Khalifa, Charlie Puth
We Are Broken by Paramore
Stay by Rihanna, Mikkey Ekko
I Never Told You by Colbie Caillat
Thinking out Loud by Ed Sheeran

Copyright

Published by Katelyn Taylor

Cover by To.All.The.Books.I.Love

Edited by My Brother's Editor

Gratify is a work of fiction. Names, characters, incidents, and places are used fictitiously. Any resemblance to real people or events is coincidental.

Gratify Copyright © 2023 by Katelyn Taylor

Trigger Warning

This book does contain several triggers that could be harmful to some. Please prioritize your mental health first before proceeding.

Triggers are but not limited to:
    Loss of a parent/parents
    Graphic violence
    Trauma bond
    Explicit language
    Explicit sex scenes
    Cheating (Not between the MMC & FMC)
    Depression

If you're still with me, then buckle up, you're in for a ride, and yes, I mean the fun kind.

Dedication

To anyone who has ever been shamed for loving the age gap trope, they are clearly the problem because this shit is hot.

Foreword

Gratify
grat·i·fy
(*verb*)

1: to be a source of or give pleasure or satisfaction to someone/yourself.

Prologue
Atlas

I'll never forget the first time I heard the story of Atlas. I was a freshman in college, and it was move-in day. My best friend Paul and I had just finished getting our room set up when he crashed, literally, into a tiny woman with oval glasses, unruly blonde hair and bright blue eyes. I practically saw the sparks fly between them in the Ballard dorm hallway. I knew my best friend was done for then and there.

When we introduced ourselves and she heard my name, Emily's eyes lit up with excitement as she began to tell us the story of Atlas, which took at least forty-five minutes to do so. He was a Titan, a Greek god that came before the Olympian gods we learned about in school. When the Olympians overthrew the Titans, all were banished to Tartarus except for Atlas. He was condemned to stand at the western edge of the earth and hold the heavens on his shoulders.

I always thought my mom picked my name because she heard it in a movie when she was pregnant with me and liked it. That's what she had told me anyway, but I liked the idea of being named after a Titan, even if he suffered a life of having the entire world on his shoulders, literally.

It was fairly spot on to how my life was growing up, so it suited me. With a deadbeat dad and a mom who was sick off and on my whole life, I'm not sure I'd ever known what it felt like to not have the world on my shoulders, or at least my own world.

Paul's interest in Emily's story didn't waver once. He was hooked. When she finally paused to take a drink of her water after explaining that she was majoring in Greek mythology, big surprise there, we shared a look. The look on his face was pure shock and awe. A look of adoration. It was a look that told me my best friend was totally fucked and he knew it too. He was gonna marry this girl and I knew after less than an hour that we would all be best friends for the rest of our lives.

Chapter 1
Andromeda

My fingers drum against my jean-clad thigh as the bus moves down the road. Brighton, California to Oregon State University is almost an eight-and-a-half-hour bus ride. Would have only been five hours if Dad had just let me borrow the car. Before I could even finish asking for it though, he was giving me the old "I don't like you driving that far by yourself" speech. I understand where his level of protection is coming from, but I'm eighteen. I'm graduating in a few months, and my boyfriend is currently an entire state away.

Theo and I met practically as soon as I was born. His dad has been my dad's best friend since they were in elementary school. They met Mom in college, and they have all been best friends ever since. Theo and I grew up together, literally, next door. Atlas bought the house across the street shortly after I was born.

Theo and I have always been best friends, spending countless hours either in the back of my mom's classroom at Brighton University, where she teaches Greek mythology or at our dads' work, Kane Architecture. Atlas is the CEO and Dad is the CFO. They started it together just out of college, and it's turned into a thriving architecture and design company. Theo and I are going to be interning there this summer and I'm honestly so excited. First, because I want to be an architect one day. I've had a passion for it ever since I was a little girl. I even used to draw designs of what I wanted my dream house to look like, some still hold up residence in Atlas's study. Second, I finally get to spend all the time I want with my boyfriend.

We have been officially together for three years now, but I've loved Theo Kane my whole life. When we finally crossed the dreaded friend zone, I had just started my freshman year of high school while Theo was a junior. It was the day before the homecoming football game and one of Theo's teammates asked me to wear their jersey. He was a senior and totally gorgeous. Theo never saw me as anything more than basically a sister, so I said yes.

All it took was one look at me in Thomas Randall's jersey to have Theo snarling. He stormed up to me and demanded that I take it off. When I asked him why, he said, "Because if my girl is going to be wearing any man's clothes, it's gonna be mine," before he cupped my face and pulled me in for the most breathtaking kiss that I've ever had.

Turns out he had feelings for me just as long as I did but didn't know how to bring it up. When we officially got together, our parents were surprised, with how close they are, I don't doubt they discussed that scenario ever since the both of us were born.

My mom told me the story of Andromeda and Perseus almost every night before bed growing up, promising me that one day I would find my Perseus. When Theo and I walked into my house holding hands and smiling at each other like we were each other's world, my mom hugged me tight and said, "I told you that you'd find your Perseus."

I can't help but smile as I look out the bus window, varying shades of green passing me by in a blur as we come into town. Excitement swirls around inside me as I get closer and closer. Finally.

He doesn't know I'm coming, I wanted to surprise him. When I talked to him about coming home for spring break last week, he said that he had a test Friday afternoon and wouldn't be heading home until late Saturday afternoon, so I thought it was perfect to come and surprise him.

I haven't spent a ton of time at Oregon State yet, so I'm anxious to get there. I always planned to go to Brighton, it was all my parents ever talked about growing up. I was practically raised there, and I even got my acceptance letter already. Theo always planned to go there too, but senior year he changed his mind. Our parents think it's because he was just being rebellious, but I know he just wanted to do something for himself, live life on his own path. I respect that and I'm excited to join him next year. These last two years have been the hardest on our relationship since he's been away. The distance is exhausting, honestly.

I know that his dad is a hot-button topic for him and anytime I try to talk to him about it, he shuts down and closes me off. So his father is usually the last thing we talk about. Same goes for his mom. I don't think Theo has mentioned her in over five years at least.

Growing up together, I was there through it all. I know that Theo's mom essentially not wanting him hurts him more than he wants to let on. She walked out one day and never looked back, never having an ounce of interest in knowing Theo. I know that because he somehow dug up her information and quietly reached out to her when he was about fifteen. When he knocked on her door he was greeted with a young boy who couldn't be older than seven before his mom stepped into the doorway with a baby on her hip. It broke him.

He snuck into my room that night and cried for hours. I sat there quietly and ran my fingers through his hair as he let it all out. He never told his dad or my parents, they would have just stopped him, and once Theo Kane sets his mind to something, nothing will stop him.

I smile as we finally reach the stop for OSU. I grab the small bag that I packed and stand, walking down the aisle and off the bus. Anticipation thrums through me as I slowly start making my way to Theo's dorm.

A guy holds the door open for me as I step inside the short hallway, my sneakers softly squeaking against the linoleum floor as I come up to Theo's room. I know that he usually sleeps in on the weekends and since it's still morning, I'm sure he's still asleep. So, I gently grab the doorknob and push the door quietly, thankful it's unlocked. Smiling with excitement, I step inside the room before I instantly freeze. My eyes blink rapidly but my brain is frozen.

In front of me is a toned ass, an ass I'm very familiar with, thrusting over and over again as a soft voice begins to chant "fuck" while he moans, "Goddamn, Miranda."

His dark-brown hair is longer than I remember. Then again, I haven't seen him since he left for school in the fall, unlike last year when he came home often because he said he couldn't stand being away from me any longer. I guess he didn't feel the need to come home now that he was *coming* in *Miranda*.

My brain takes several moments to finally catch up with the sight before me as it all sinks in. Son of a fucking bitch. Theo is still pounding away at the slut beneath him like he doesn't have a care in the world, which sends the shock that previously overtook me away as rage courses through my veins. I reach over to his dresser and grab the first thick textbook I see before I wind back my arm and huck it at him. Unfortunately, I miss the back of his head where I was aiming as it connects with his bare back.

"You fucking son of a bitch!" I scream as he quickly turns around.

His eyes go from irritation at being interrupted during his midmorning hump to shock and then fear. He scrambles out of bed quickly, glancing down at the naked brunette in his bed before quickly covering her with the blankets, like maybe I won't see her now or something.

Fucking idiot.

"B-baby," he stutters as he reaches down and grabs the pair of boxers at his feet, pulling them up quickly as he speaks. "I didn't know you were coming."

"Clearly, looks like you were about to come yourself, though."

"Baby?" Miranda scoffs from under the covers before she pushes them down and looks at him with disgust. "You have a girlfriend?" Rolling her eyes, she quickly slips out of the bed, throwing on the dress on the floor before walking past me, a disappointed look on her face.

"I'm sorry, girl. I didn't know. For what it's worth, this was the first time, but he's been chasing after me all year."

My heart cracks at her words. All year? He's been trying to cheat on me all year? Oh my fucking god. My eyes begin to water as I quickly blink back the tears and give her a shaky nod. Not her fault my boyfriend is a fucking dog, I guess. Now I kinda feel bad about calling her a slut in my head.

She slips out of the room before I turn to him. His face is full of regret and desperation. He looks ready to beg for me to understand but I have nothing to say to this fucking asshole. So, instead, I shake my head with disgust and turn on my heel.

"Wait! Drama, baby. Please. Let me explain. I swear to god it isn't what it looks like. She was—"

"Was what?" I snap as I whirl on him, my body beginning to vibrate with anger and maybe a touch of humiliation.

Theo hasn't even bothered to get dressed, chasing me through his dorm's hallway in just his boxers. I can smell Miranda's vanilla perfume wafting off him and it instantly sours my stomach. He runs his hands through his hair as he shakes his head.

"I'm sorry," he says, his voice cracking. "I fucked up. I've been lonely and—"

I laugh bitterly through the tears that have begun to drip down my face as I shake my head.

"You've been lonely? What about me? I've been fucking lonely. Only difference is I chose to remain loyal. Don't worry though, Theo. You don't have to feel bad about sneaking around on your girlfriend anymore. You don't have one."

He reaches out to grab my elbow, but I quickly step out of his reach before taking off in a sprint down the rest of the hall and out the building. I don't stop running, scared to look back and see that he is following me. I don't want him to see my tears, to hear my pain. He doesn't deserve it.

When I'm several miles down the road, I finally slow down enough to take several deep breaths. My hands shake as I pull out my phone, my fingers unsure of who to call. My initial instinct is to call Atlas. He's the easiest option, the one who would pick me up, no questions asked, but I just caught his son balls deep in another girl so that option is automatically out. I could call my mom or dad, but knowing them, they'd probably storm into Theo's room and cause a huge scene and as satisfying as that would be, I don't want them mad at Theo. He may be a son of a fucking bitch, but he needs my parents.

So, I made the decision, sending a quick text before mapping out the bus route to my escape.

———

"He's such a little shit. Don't waste another tear on him, sweetheart. Trust me, no man is worth it," my aunt Alyssa says for probably the tenth time over the last week.

Aunt Alyssa is my mom's younger sister. So young that she is only eight years older than me. She's that typical fun-loving aunt that parties a little too hard but to be fair, she is twenty-six so that's normal, right?

I texted Alyssa last week to see if I could stay with her over spring break after being humiliated and left heartbroken by someone who I thought was my best friend and the love of my life. Obviously not, because boyfriend or not, a friend would have never put me through the pain that he did. Ever. He's texted me constantly, begged for me to talk to him, to which I ignored each and every plea until they eventually stopped.

Mom called me that evening when Theo came home, alone. I told her that Aunt Alyssa was having a crisis and needed me. Unsurprisingly, my mom didn't question me past that. Alyssa's been known to be a touch dramatic. She's definitely the most drama centered member of our family which is surprising since I'm the one with the literal nickname "Drama."

Alyssa lives in a nice condo in downtown Portland. She's a marketing manager for some granola bar company that she always brags "is thriving." I've been here a few times, usually with my mom and usually after she gets her heart broken after swearing up and down that she found *the* one after a date or two. Then a few months later, she is back on the hunt and falling in love all over again. She loves to fall in love. She does it quickly and without too much concern for the future, but the good thing is that when it doesn't work out, because it usually doesn't, she has an excellent rebound rate. That's where the Libra in her shines the brightest.

"The only shitty thing about you and Theo breaking up is that now that fine piece of man known as his dad won't be around as much." She pouts as she sips her wine while we eat dinner.

That's something that Mom and I joke about a lot. Mom swears up and down that Alyssa sabotages these relationships because she is waiting for Atlas to notice her. She's been in love with him since she first met him when she was seven years old and swears one day they will end up together.

Despite her confidence, I've never seen Atlas give her more than a polite smile. Not even close to the amount of attention she is used to getting from the male species. Who could blame them too? My aunt has the same blonde hair that me and my mom do but instead of having a modest but perky C-cup like me, she got her boobs done and is a full DDD. She also lives in the gym and probably has like a twenty-four-inch waist with a total bubble butt. She's every man's wet dream. Every man except Atlas Kane. I think that's honestly why she is so obsessed with him. He's the one man she can't put under her spell.

"It's not like me and Theo breaking up is going to stop my parents from hanging out with their best friend of over twenty years," I say dryly.

"True. They are like The Three Musketeers. Atlas still isn't seeing anyone, right?" she asks not so subtly.

I do my best to suppress my eye roll as I look up to my aunt. Her pale-blue eyes a stark contrast to the bright-green ones I inherited from my dad as I shake my head. A look of satisfaction spreads over her face as she settles back into her seat.

"Good. If things go according to plan by the end of this summer, Atlas Kane is going to be mine."

"What do you have planned?" I ask with a cocked brow and a dry laugh.

She gives me a devious smile as she smirks over her wineglass.

"I'm coming down a week early for Labor Day. Plenty of time to properly hook him."

I snort and shake my head as I finish the Chinese takeout we ordered. My mom is picking me up in the morning. I was going to ride the bus back, but they said that I had done enough bus riding across the states.

I haven't told them about me and Theo yet. I'm not sure why. Maybe I'm just too embarrassed that I wasn't enough for someone who swore that I was everything. Maybe it's because I don't want my parents to hate someone who is basically another son to them or maybe in a weird way, I'm trying to protect Theo. Even if I'm super fucking pissed with him, I still care about him. Just because he is okay with hurting me doesn't mean I feel the same way.

Chapter 2
Andromeda

"You've been awfully quiet over there," Mom says as she glances over to me before facing forward again.

I glance away from the window to look at her.

"It's early," I say lamely.

She nods. "Tell me about it. I got up at four in the morning to come pick up my daughter because she decided to reroute her little road trip several hours away from where she was supposed to be," she says with a look that tells me she didn't buy my story as easily as I thought.

"Aunt Alyssa needed me." I shrug.

My mom raises an eyebrow. "Since when does Alyssa call you instead of me when she is going through one of her meltdowns? And I seriously doubt that was the reason. I didn't see a Ben & Jerry's pint in sight. So, want to tell me the real reason you didn't come home with Theo like planned? Your dad nearly had a coronary when he showed up without you."

I blow out a long breath, deciding to just rip the Band-Aid off.

"Theo and I broke up."

My mom's eyes round, flicking over to me before going back to the road.

"What? What do you mean? When?"

"Shortly after I got there," I mutter under my breath.

"Honey, why? Are you okay? What happened?" she rapid fires.

My throat begins to tighten as images of him thrusting in and out of the gorgeous brunette flashes in my mind. The words die on my tongue as embarrassment washes over me.

"I don't really want to talk about it, Mom," I say softly, my voice breaking off at the end.

She gives me a sympathetic look as she nods and squeezes my knee lovingly.

"Well, that makes a lot more sense. Atlas says Theo has barely been out of his room all week. Then he just up and left this morning without even saying goodbye."

I bite the inside of my cheek and nod as I look out the window, and the rest of the car ride passes by in comfortable silence.

———

One Month Later

It's been a month since Theo and I broke up. He still tries to text and call here and there but I refuse to even look at his messages for longer than it takes to delete them. I don't care what he has to say. I'm still hurt and nowhere near ready to talk about it. Maybe I'll never be. Maybe I can just avoid him and the topic of him for the rest of my life.

I wish.

Unfortunately, we are having a barbeque at our house today and of course Atlas is coming over but even more unfortunately, so is Theo. Atlas somehow talked him into coming down for the weekend and I've done a remarkable job of avoiding nearly everyone since he got to town, but I guess all good things must come to an end.

A heavy knock comes from my door before I shout, "Come in."

My dad steps in, his bright blue Hawaiian shirt tucked into his khaki shorts. He always thinks it makes barbecues more festive when he wears Hawaiian shirts. Like it makes it a luau or something. I love my dad, but he is such a dork sometimes. I mean, he double majored in economics and finance, enough said there.

Sometimes I don't know how he and Atlas are best friends. Where Dad is a $20 Supercuts haircut, dorky Hawaiian shirts and thick-rimmed glasses with a clean-shaven face, Atlas is perfectly styled black hair, form-fitting dress shirts and chocolate-brown eyes with 20/20 vision and enough facial hair to call it a beard. They are total opposites and yet they are practically inseparable. My mom always teases that if he hadn't met her, he and Atlas would probably be together by now. I couldn't see it, though. Atlas is way out of Dad's league.

"Hey, kiddo. Food is ready." He smiles.

I nod as I set my English paper to the side and stand up from my bed. I go to walk by and out the door when he stops me.

"You know you can talk to me, right? And your mom. About anything."

I glance up to my dad, more than easily reading between the lines.

"I'm fine, Dad."

"We're worried about you, sweetheart. You and Theo were together for a long time, not to mention knowing each other since birth. It's got to be hard, and we want to be there for you. If having them over here is too uncomfortable, say the word and I'll send them home."

I shake my head. "It's fine. I'll deal."

Dad narrows his eyes at me. "I know Theo hurt you. I can see it on your face. I'm more intuitive than you think. Just tell me what happened, and I promise, godson or not, I'll rough him up a bit."

That gets a smile out of me, causing Dad to smile in response.

"You wouldn't hurt a fly."

He shrugs. "You're my baby girl. I'd do anything for you."

I smile a little bigger this time as I look up at my dad before wrapping my arms around his stomach.

"I appreciate it, even if you would no doubt lose that fight." I smirk as we make our way out of my room and down the stairs.

"Psh, you better watch yourself, kid. I'm a force to be reckoned with," he says as he kisses his bicep, or where I would guess a bicep should be.

The Clarkes are studious while the Kanes are physical. Our idea of a fun Friday night is a rousing game of Scrabble, which I'm proud to admit I come out the victor more times than not. As long as Atlas doesn't play with us.

Theo and Atlas both played sports in high school, while my parents were getting near-perfect scores on their SATs. Not to say Atlas or Theo aren't smart, I mean, Atlas is an architect and Theo got a 1410 on his SATs. I got a 1550 and my parents were thrilled but try to make me squat anything and I'll be on my face. We're just different. It also probably plays into the fact that my dad, mom, and I are all Capricorns.

I adjust my glasses that have shifted on my face when I threw my hair into a messy bun as we make our way outside. When we step onto the back porch, my dad walks over to the outdoor dining table where my mom is setting down the last few side dishes. Atlas is sipping a beer as he walks over to me and pulls me into a side hug.

"Didn't think we'd see you today," he comments casually, though the meaning behind his words weighs heavily on me. It's not his fault his son is a lying, cheating asshole. I've been avoiding Atlas like the plague just as much as Theo. Maybe more so since he's been around more often.

I glance up to those rich chocolate eyes and give him a sad smile. "Sorry."

He shrugs before giving me a small smile.

"Don't be, I'm glad you're joining us."

I nod as I turn to see Theo's eyes on me, they are dim in their normal hazel color and sad. I fight the urge to look away quickly, refusing to look weak as I maintain eye contact before taking my seat as far away from him as possible. I don't miss the subtle wince his face makes at the action, but I honestly don't care.

When we finally break eye contact, I look to see Atlas watching us with a slightly narrowed gaze, like he is trying to fit the puzzle pieces together, but they aren't fitting. Sometimes I really hate having a godfather who is a Taurus sun and Scorpio rising. He has all of the great characteristics of a Taurus, like being kind, generous and hardworking combined with the intense, passionate, and controlling traits of his rising. In this case, once he wants to get to the bottom of something, he won't stop...ever.

Thankfully before Detective Atlas can comment, Mom and Dad sit down, and we all dig in. Dinner goes by fine. Mom and Atlas carry most of the conversation, talking about Atlas's latest project that he is working on while Dad moans in appreciation over the food. Swear to god, moans. At the dinner table. Have I mentioned that my dad is a total dork? Because he is. Completely.

Atlas turns to me before his eyes flick to Theo.

"Are you guys looking forward to starting at the firm? I've got piles of grunt work lined up for both of you."

"Gee, thanks, Dad," Theo mutters sarcastically, his eyes flicking to me briefly after.

I swallow before speaking. Dammit. I hadn't even thought about the fact that both Theo and I were supposed to be interning with Atlas this summer. Add it to the quickly growing list of things I am not looking forward to. Like school. Hours away with only one person that I know. A person I can hardly tolerate right now. Spectacular.

"Yeah, it'll look incredible on my resume. Thank you again," I say.

Atlas brushes me off as he nods and takes a sip of his beer.

"Of course, it'll be good for you guys. Get some work experience under your belt."

I nod but don't say anything more before my dad moves to clear the table. I stand to help him, grateful for the distraction. We quickly clean up dinner and I'm heading back up to my room, hoping I can slink away when a hand catches the crook of my elbow.

Dread seeps into my stomach when I turn around to see Theo standing in front of me, his fingers tightening their hold as he looks down at me. He's only a few inches taller than me. At 5'10 I rarely feel intimidated by someone else's height but suddenly I feel two inches tall next to him as flashes of the last time I saw him play in my mind.

I squeeze my eyes shut, shaking my head as I turn to the side.

"Let me go," I say evenly.

"Baby, you have to hear me out. I need to apologize."

My eyes open at that as I yank my arm free of his grasp and push him back a step, jabbing my finger into his chest as I do.

"Do not ever call me 'baby' again. How dare you, Theo! You can't just corner me and demand me to hear you out. Guess what, I don't want to. Hence the ignored texts, phone calls, and social media messages. I'm done, we're done. End of discussion, okay?"

"I didn't want it to be like this," he says as he runs his hands through his hair. "I didn't want to hurt you."

I laugh bitterly as I shake my head.

"Well, then you probably shouldn't have stuck your dick in another girl. That would have been a sensible start."

"I know. Fuck, I know. I'm sorry. I fucked up. It was a mistake—"

"Apparently not, Theo. According to her, you've been 'chasing' her all year. One of you is a liar and call me crazy, but I'm gonna go out on a limb and guess that it's my cheating ex-boyfriend."

"Don't call me that." He winces.

"What?" I scoff.

"Don't call me your ex-boyfriend. This can't be it for us, we've been together for years, known each other our whole lives. This isn't over between us, Drama. I fucked up. I get it, I do, and I fucking hate myself for it. You have no idea. I—"

"Why'd you do it then? Why did you chase after her? Is she even the first? Have there been others?"

"No! God, no. I just, I don't know. I felt like we were drifting apart. She's in a few of my classes. We have mutual friends. I wasn't chasing after her. We would just hang out, and yeah, she's pretty but—"

I hold my hand up to stop him as I shake my head.

"Alright, that's enough. I don't need to hear about how you fell for her, honestly. I'm good."

He grabs my hand, lacing his fingers with mine as he pulls me a step closer to him.

"No, that's it. Don't you see? She was a distraction, a speed bump. I've only ever loved you, Drama. I thought, stupidly, that I was missing out somehow. I sat back and texted you at parties while all my friends were out there dancing, partying, and hooking up. It's dumb, I just—"

"Wanted to know what it was like to be single?"

He looks at the ground and shrugs sheepishly.

"Well, you got your wish. You're single, Theo. Go ahead, get out there. Party, dance. Live it up. Fuck as many people as you want, God knows I'm going to."

I throw that last little dig in because I just can't help myself. Hooking up with a stranger is the least appealing thing I can think of, but I hate feeling like the victim here. I may also be a little bit of a petty bitch when I'm hurting. Sue me.

I turn to walk away when Theo's hand slips from my fingers to my wrist and he squeezes.

"Don't say that," he grits between his teeth.

I roll my eyes and scoff. "Or what? You can't do anything to me, Theo. You've hurt me about as bad as anyone could, and I don't have to listen to you. We aren't together."

"Stop fucking saying shit like that!" he shouts, his tone angry but his face panicked, like if I keep saying it then it will become real. Like the jackass hasn't picked up on the fact that it is already as real as it gets.

"That's enough!" a thunderous voice barks.

Goose bumps spread across my body as we both turn to see a broad figure standing in the hallway. Atlas takes several steps toward us until he is only a foot away. He is standing to his full height, towering over Theo with his 6'4 form.

"We're talking," Theo snaps back, more irritation in his tone than before.

"No," Atlas corrects. "You're done. You are going to release Andromeda's wrist, let her go to her room and then we are going to have a long fucking talk. I sure as hell did not raise a son who puts his hands on a woman when he is anything less than pleasant and I sure as *fuck* didn't raise a son that raises his voice with a woman."

I see a flash of defiance pass across Theo's face as he stands up a little taller. At 6'o Theo is still tall but not compared to his dad. Atlas recognizes the defiance and his eyes narrow slightly. My stomach twists in anticipation, wanting nothing more than to be out of this situation.

"Now," Atlas rumbles lower than before.

The sound sends a chill down my spine, and it must do the same to Theo because in the next moment, my wrist is free and I'm hightailing it out of there. When I reach the stairs, I glance behind me to see Atlas walking Theo out the front door, a hand on the back of his neck like he is carrying a puppy by the scruff as they leave.

I rub my wrist as I make my way upstairs and into my room before shutting the door. I didn't realize how much his hold was hurting until Atlas said something about it. Glancing down, I see that the skin is slightly reddened. Theo has never been aggressive with me, not once. Even now I wouldn't necessarily take it as aggression, more like desperation. Clearly his dad wasn't having it, though.

Whatever. I'm officially done with this day.

Chapter 3
Atlas

I drag my twenty-year-old son by the scruff of his neck like he's a goddamn puppy. I'm doing my best to keep my temper in check as we cross the street and push open our front door but I'm struggling. What the hell is the matter with him?

The minute the door shuts, Theo shoves away from me and I allow him to as I cross my arms over my chest.

"What the fuck was all that?" I ask with a raised brow, my jaw clenched.

Theo rolls his eyes and lifts his mouth into a snarl.

"None of your fucking business. I was—"

"Hurting Andromeda," I interject.

His mouth is open like he's about to continue as his brows dip slightly. His shoulders sag slightly as his head turns to stare at the wall to his right.

"I didn't mean to. I'd never."

"I know, which is why I intervened. You need to calm down, you two can talk things out later."

Theo lets out a bitter laugh as he runs a hand through his hair.

"Yeah, sounds like that's not gonna happen if Drama has any say in the matter."

I keep my face blank as I stare at my son.

"And why would that be, Theo?"

His eyes come up to mine, blue just like his mother's. For just a second, I see my little guy again. The one who looked up to me like I hung the moon. The one who said he wanted to be just like me when he grew up. The one I taught how to ride a bike and fish. Not the moody teenager turned adult that he's been for the last five years or so. As soon as I saw a glimpse of that boy though, he's gone in a flash as Theo's eyes harden and he gives me a terse shake of his head.

"Stay in your lane. You mind your business, and I'll mind mine."

He turns on his heel and heads up the stairs before I can say anything else. His bedroom door closes with a sharp slam that has me blowing out a breath and walking toward the liquor cabinet.

Christ. It's cliché to say I pictured my life going a little differently than it did, but it's the truth. Paul, Em, and I had plans to move away from Brighton after graduation. Em is from Cincinnati whereas Paul and I grew up just outside of San Francisco. We didn't know where we wanted to go, we were down for anywhere really. Though of course Em was partial to Greece. But life didn't exactly go according to plan.

Paul helped me drink the weekend away when I first found out that I got my one-night stand pregnant our sophomore year at Brighton U. Then along came Emily. She sobered us up, slapped me behind the head and told me to get my shit together and step up to be the best dad that I could be.

I was used to responsibility anyway, I practically raised myself while caring for my mother, going to school and working as much as I could in between. It wasn't until she passed away just before I went off to college that I felt a small amount of relief, which sounds fucking terrible, I know, but true. Then Theo was born, and I realized that up until that moment all the previous responsibilities I had held didn't come close to what it meant holding that little blue blanket-wrapped baby in my arms.

I was twenty years old and fucking clueless but ready to do whatever it took to take care of that baby. It was ten times harder when Theo's mom decided she wasn't cut out for motherhood and skipped out on us when he was only two months old. I didn't know what the hell I was doing but Em and Paul were there to stand by me when I faltered. They are practically a second set of parents to Theo. Maybe better parents to him most days, if I'm honest with myself.

Pouring myself a generous drink, I grab the half-full glass of scotch before heading up to my office. I've got a ton of work I need to get to and a particularly straining job looming over my head. Typically one of our architects handles the initial plans and I'm on more of a consult basis at this point. But this contract is for Jonathan Michaels, an extremely particular and rich-as-sin businessman who is also the father of Trevor Michaels, one of the top quarterbacks in the NFL.

He hired us to design an add-on to his already expansive mansion. The property is several hours away but when he found out that I graduated from his alumni, Brighton University, he hired me on the spot. The job may be a headache but it's covering our entire quarter's metrics, so I'll manage at least when it comes to the business. Theo, that's a different topic entirely.

I talked to Em, and she said Andromeda hasn't opened up about why they split either. We are all completely bewildered by it. Em has been practically singing the wedding march since they first came home holding hands. I can't lie that I'm a little disappointed that they split on Theo's behalf. She was good for him, she grounded him.

Theo seems to be lost lately, bobbing around aimlessly with no clear direction while Andromeda has had her future mapped out since she was eight years old. It's easier for some than others, I suppose. And though yes, I love that Andromeda wants to follow in her father's and my footsteps, I wouldn't care what Theo wanted to do, if he would just choose something. He's going to be a junior in the fall and he's still undeclared, it's getting ridiculous at this point. I'm hoping working at the firm will open his eyes and help push him in the direction of what he wants to do with his life.

All I want is to see him happy with a plan for his future. Instead, he spent all of his free time when he was home with Andromeda or beating those damn drums in his room. Still hate Paul for getting him that set when he was fourteen.

My phone buzzes to life at my side. I reach for it, unlocking the screen before groaning softly.

Alyssa: Hey! It's been a while since I've heard from you. What are you doing tonight?

I try not to be irritated by Em's baby sister, but the girl can't take a hint. She's been infatuated with me since I met her when she was just a kid. Back then it was cute, but the amount of flirtatious messages I get from her is anything but cute. I've never even considered going there, and not because she isn't beautiful, Alyssa is very gorgeous according to traditional beauty standards. The reason I'd never go there is because I know if I even kissed Alyssa, she'd be moving in and planning our wedding. She's an all or nothing kind of woman like that. Andromeda says she's a Libra sun and Libra rising and that explains it all. I don't really follow astrology like she does though, so I'll take her word for it.

Marking the message as read, I toss my phone across the table and focus back on my work. Doing my best to push away the building migraine. I try to keep everything going, to run a healthy and growing business, be a present father and a good friend, but some days it's fucking exhausting.

I wish I could afford the luxury of taking some time off, but I have too much depending on me, too much riding on me to think like that. One day I'll be able to sit back and enjoy the legacy I've built, just not today.

Chapter 4
Andromeda

It's been months since I've seen Theo, outside of that weekend where things got heated before Atlas intervened. Theo came over the next day and apologized for his behavior. We talked a little bit more and I told him that there was no way in hell we were getting back together, and I wasn't even sure I could be his friend anymore now that there was all of this hurt between us. You could tell that my words upset him, but he accepted my choice.

Though I haven't seen him he has sent me the occasional video or meme that he knew would make me laugh. It's a weird transition period, honestly. I'm past the point of blinding anger and am more in the acceptance stage. I kinda get it, we really only know each other. I'd be lying if I said I never wondered if I was missing out. It doesn't excuse his actions but in a small way, I understand, I guess.

Still, I'm not sure how working together is going to go. Hopefully Atlas will have enough foresight to keep us on separate tasks, so the interaction isn't *too* much.

I'm currently cramming for my history final when a soft knock that I know belongs to my mother comes from my door before she steps inside.

"Hey, Drama. Still studying?"

I nod. "Whoever thought it was a good idea to push back finals to the last week of school should be pushed in front of a bus."

"Andromeda Nevaeh Clarke!" my mom admonishes.

I chuckle at her use of my full name before she does the same.

"I can't believe my little girl is about to be a high school graduate," she says as she leans forward and runs her fingers through my hair. I close my eyes on instinct. She's played with my hair ever since I was a kid and I've never stopped loving it.

"Who said you were allowed to grow up so fast?" she asks, her voice tightening as she does.

I open my eyes and smirk as I shake my head.

"I didn't have a lot of control over it, Mom. Sorry."

She shakes her head with a sad smile. "You'll get it one day. When you have a baby of your own, you won't even believe how fast they grow before your eyes. First, they're rolling over and then they're crawling. Pretty soon, they start walking and talking, and then the next thing you know they are in school. Then it's school plays and dances, first dates and prom and then they are about to graduate. In the next blink, you'll be off to college and, oh god, I can't even handle what comes after that," she says, her eyes watering over as she speaks.

I stand and wrap my arms around my mom, the smell of Marc Jacobs Daisy filling my senses. I inhale her scent softly as I hug her before I pull back.

"You act like you're never going to see me again," I tease.

She sniffles before chuckling. "I know, I'm sorry. I thought I had it together but god, you've grown into such an amazing young woman. Your dad and I are so proud of you."

"Thank you, Mom. I love you guys."

"We love you, sweetheart. Now, enough of this heavy crap," she says as she quickly wipes underneath her eyes. "We are meeting Atlas for dinner. Want to come?"

I grimace at that. My mom and dad dropped the questioning about what happened between Theo and me when I told them that we just needed some time to find ourselves. Atlas however did not. Maybe it's because he heard more than he let on when he interrupted Theo and me. Maybe it's because Theo told him something that tipped him off to more. Or maybe he just is better at sniffing out lies than my parents.

Either way, every time I've been around him since that barbeque, he's patiently watching me, like he's waiting for me to fess up. At this point, I don't think it would matter too much if everyone knew what happened between me and Theo but that's the same reasoning I have to not bring it up. All it will do is hurt Theo's relationship with everyone he loves and bring up something I'd rather forget.

"I'm not really that hungry, Mom." I shrug.

She frowns softly. "Honey, just because you and Theo aren't together, you know Atlas still loves you, right? You don't need to feel uncomfortable around him."

I do my best to give her a convincing smile as I nod.

"I know. I don't feel uncomfortable around him. I just want to make sure I do well on this final."

She gives me a smile as she nods like she doesn't buy it as my dad steps in and slips an arm around her shoulder.

"You know that acceptance letter to Brighton is probably still good. I don't think your mom has a single student that takes their schoolwork as seriously as you do. They'd be lucky to have you."

"Daddd, don't start," I groan.

We've had this argument more times than I'd like to count. I mean, I won't lie, a solid eighty percent of the reason why I committed to OSU instead of Brighton was because Theo was already there. But there is still the other twenty percent to consider and that was because I wanted to go to college and experience what it would be like to just be Andromeda Clarke, not Professor Clarke's daughter.

"I'm just saying, Brighton is right here, and I know several of your friends from school are going there. It might be a better fit. With you and Theo not together anymore, I'm worried about you all the way up at—"

"Jesus, fuck! Stop! I'm not going to fucking Brighton, I'm not going to change my mind just because of Theo fucking Kane and I don't need you to fucking manipulate me into doing what you think is best. Just back the hell off!" I nearly shout.

My parents stare at me, stunned. I'm a little stunned myself if I'm being honest. I rarely raise my voice and I definitely have never raised it to my parents. I'm the good kid, the calm one. I've never given my parents an ounce of crap and I guess I haven't been properly sorting through all of my emotions lately because I instantly feel regret.

Instead of freaking out and laying into me like any other parents would, mine just look at me with disappointment and sadness, like they know this isn't me. My dad clears his throat, standing a little more rigidly as he looks at me.

"We'll be back in a few hours, lock the door behind us."

With that, he turns and ushers my mom out the door who gives me a sad shake of her head before following him out. I almost call out to them to apologize, to explain that I've never felt so much unlike myself in my life, but I hear the front door shut before I can. Blowing out a heavy breath, I lift my glasses up before rubbing my eyes.

———

It didn't take much longer for me to finish studying for my final and I'm feeling pretty confident about my test in the morning. I decided to hang out downstairs and wait up for my parents. I hate feeling guilty. It's a gross feeling and I know I was out of line. My dad is the biggest teddy bear in the world, he didn't deserve for me to snap at him the way I did. Maybe I just need to come clean about everything. I think all of this bottling up is starting to get to me.

I'm currently binging *Peaky Blinders* when my phone buzzes.

Cassie: Hey girl! A few of us are hanging out at Grady's house and he keeps asking about you. You need to get your ass over here!

I roll my eyes as I text my friend Cassie back.

Me: Is that supposed to convince me? Grady smells like a sweaty gym sock and has slept with half the school.

Cassie: You're too picky. He has a six pack and perfect teeth, that's better than a lot of the guys in our school.

I snort.

Me: I think you need to broaden your horizons, babe.

Cassie: Maybe, but you need to narrow yours. You and

Theo have been broken up for over two months. It's time to get over him by getting under someone else!

She has a point, in a way, I guess. I'm sure Theo is seeing people by now, maybe even Miranda. I should get out there too, right? Still, I've gone to school with all of these kids practically my entire life and not a single one catches my attention. Here's hoping college is better.

I turn my attention back to the TV when a loud crunching sound echoes through the front window from outside. I immediately sit up, glancing through the curtain but don't see anything. Furrowing my brows, I pad across the hardwood to the front door, slowly opening it to peek my head outside.

We live in a cul-de-sac and are one of the last houses on the end next to the main road. I glance down the road, but I don't see anything that could have made that noise. Turning my head the other way, I gasp when I look at the four-way stop just down the road. A large delivery truck looks like it's plowed through what used to be a car before throwing it into a telephone pole.

It takes exactly two seconds to make out the entire scene and when I finally do, my stomach plummets to the floor and my heart drops. I'm tearing out of the doorway, my bare feet slapping against the rough asphalt as I stretch my legs out as far and as fast as I can. Several cars have pulled over and police sirens are already wailing in the distance.

Oh my god. Oh my god. Oh my god.

The closer I get to the mangled car, the more my body begins to seize. I do my best to keep my pace, but my muscles are giving way as shock settles in. The familiar maroon SUV that my parents have had ever since I was a baby resembles a crumpled soda can as the driver's side is completely wrapped around the telephone pole. The passenger side is crushed as well, probably from where the truck first impacted.

Oh my god. Oh my god. Oh my god.

A few people yell for me to stop as I make my way straight up to the passenger side where I see my mother's blonde hair through the now broken window. Suddenly, two large arms wrap around me, snatching me mid stride before hauling me into a strong chest and turning us away from the wreck.

"Don't look, Nevaeh! Jesus Christ, please, don't look," a rough voice sobs.

My body begins to shake uncontrollably as I glance up to see Atlas holding me tightly, thick streams of tears racing down his face.

Somehow the look on his face scares me more than seeing my family's SUV reduced to crushed metal and plastic. One look at his face and I know, within my gut, that my entire world has just shattered apart. That everything I thought was important, everything I thought I had, disintegrates right before my eyes.

My breathing begins to increase as my lungs beg for oxygen. I can't breathe. I can't breathe. This isn't real, it can't be real. A police car speeds onto the scene before the officer runs out of his car and toward us. He begins quickly talking with Atlas, but I can't hear the actual words. It all sounds like I'm under water, like I'm drowning. No. This isn't real, they are fine. They are alive and they need help!

Breaking free of Atlas's hold, I sprint the remaining distance to the car before brushing my mom's messy blonde hair out of her face. My eyes frantically run over her face only to find blank unblinking eyes staring back at me as red begins saturating her white shirt. Whipping my head over to what's left of the driver's side, I lose my stomach instantly. Bile splatters the asphalt as the image of my father impaled by the steering column burns itself into my brain until the end of time.

"Goddammit, Nevaeh!" Atlas barks before he is at my side, running his hand up and down my back as I continue emptying my stomach.

I rub the sleeve of my sweatshirt against my mouth before my head shakily lifts to make eye contact with Atlas, his normally tanned face completely devoid of any color as he looks at me with utter horror and devastation.

An ear-piercing wail slices through the midnight sky, sending a shiver running up my back at the sound of it. Several seconds pass before I realize the sound is coming from myself. My mouth is dropped open, my lungs burning as a pain like I've never known envelops me.

Th-they're gone...

Chapter 5
Atlas

Move-in day freshman year of college, I knew that Paul, Emily, and I were going to be best friends for the rest of our lives. I just didn't know that the rest of our lives would be cut so fucking short.

My vision blurs as I stare blankly ahead. I do my best to keep the tears at bay but fuck it's hard. The priest is rattling on, giving some drawn-out speech about how they are in a better place now. It's fucking bullshit, though. How the hell could anyone sit here and tell me that Paul and Emily Clarke are better off dead than here, by my side, where they've been for the last twenty-two years?

A soft whimpering to my left catches my attention. I look down to see the thin body huddled underneath my arm shaking uncontrollably as near-silent streams of tears cascade down her face. It's the first time I've seen her cry since that night. Andromeda was their whole world, and they were hers. How can we possibly be expected to go on without them?

I've known death and pain at a young age, but I've coped with it and made my peace. But it's a pain I wish Andromeda never had to know. I knew when my mom was going to die, I had time to say my goodbyes. Andromeda didn't. They were ripped away from her in a brutal way, and the worst part is she witnessed it.

She didn't watch as the truck ran the stop sign and t-boned their car like I did, she didn't hear Paul's dying words breathed to her like I did, but she saw the aftermath. She saw her mother, the woman who was the literal light to a room, cold and gray. She saw her father, the kindest and larger-than-life man anyone knew, practically severed in two by his own goddamn steering wheel.

I'd do anything to turn back time and hold on to her tighter, to make sure she never had to witness that. I fucked up, I let her slip away and I'll carry that weight with me for the rest of my life.

She won't talk about it. It's been nearly a week and she won't talk to anyone. I don't blame her, though. Whatever she needs, I'll do. I just don't have a fucking clue what that is.

On my right, Emily's baby sister, Alyssa, clings to me, sobbing much more dramatically than Andromeda. I know how much Emily loved her sister and in her own way, Alyssa loved her just the same. Glancing to my left, I see Theo sitting on the other side of Andromeda, his cheeks damp with fallen tears as he reaches out to hold Andromeda's hand. She tenses instantly before pulling away and burrowing further into my side.

I watch as my son's face crumples before turning back to face the priest. I know he's hurting over their breakup on top of everything else. He refused to open up to me and tell me why they broke up or what had happened. All I was able to really get out of him was that she ended things but I'm not stupid. There is more to the story. It's crazy how insignificant all of that has become in such a short amount of time, though.

Andromeda's tears seem to have dried out and her whimpers have quieted when the priest signals for her to stand and throw the first flower into each of the freshly dug holes. I watch as she lifts her chin in strength and pulls away from me, gripping the two red roses in her hands like they'll disappear if she doesn't hold on tight enough. She only makes it two steps before her legs buckle and she begins to fall. I'm behind her in a flash, scooping her up until she is steady enough to stand.

"I've got you, Nevaeh," I whisper into her ear. "I've got you."

She sucks in a sharp breath through her teeth before she nods firmly and attempts to stand taller than before, but I don't release my hold on her waist as we walk together to the matching holes in the ground. It's been a week since our world crumbled apart but it feels like it's only been hours. The pain in my chest has yet to subside, the twisting of my gut hasn't eased no matter what I do. I can't think about any of that right now, though. Andromeda needs me.

She needs me to be strong, to be her anchor, her protector. I'll easily push my own pain to the side to take on hers. I'll do whatever it takes to see her through this. It's what Emily and Paul would expect of me. I'll gladly take the burden on my own shoulders. For her. For them.

———

The reception is at Paul and Emily's, or I guess now, Andromeda's. In their will they had everything go to her so the house is technically hers and with the large life insurance policy they had thanks to Emily's over preparedness for everything, it will cover the house, Andromeda's college and then some on top of the large savings account they held. Who really gives a damn about all that though when you are suddenly left orphaned?

I offered to host the reception at my house since I figured Andromeda didn't want to deal with all of those people in her space, but she didn't respond one way or another and when Alyssa got into town and said that we could do it over there, I didn't push. Now I wish I had. It feels wrong to be here. A place that for nearly two decades has felt like a second home, suddenly feels hollow and cold.

People are milling about, chatting as they eat the platters of the food that Paul's parents picked up from the store. They got here yesterday, and it wasn't until I hugged his mom that I felt like it was actually real, that my best friend was gone. They are sticking around until Andromeda graduates in two days as well as Alyssa, though they've all opted to stay in hotels. They are all giving Andromeda space. I'm not sure if she's asked for it or if they just assume she needs it but at the end of the day, I think it's wrong.

She's eighteen years old. She just lost her parents, and the rest of her family is staying away from her like she's got the fucking plague. She's grieving, she isn't contagious.

My eyes skate over the busy living room where Alyssa is sobbing loudly, making large dramatic hand gestures as she eats up every ounce of attention and sympathy she's getting. Don't get me wrong, I know she is sad and hurting but she has always been like this. She's always in the spotlight, always needing others' validation and approval. Emily constantly worried about her because of it, she hoped that she would grow out of it, but the woman is twenty-six and if anything, she's worse.

I notice that Andromeda isn't in the room, I didn't see her in the kitchen where a few others are lingering either. Frowning, I slowly make my way through the house, looking for any sight of her when I run into Theo coming down the stairs. He shakes his head at me.

"Don't go up there. She needs to be alone."

"Why?" I frown.

"She says she needs to get away from all the people. She doesn't want to talk, trust me."

I nod and clap my son's shoulder.

"How are you holding up?"

His face falls as he shakes his head again.

"I'm not. Like, I still don't get it, I guess. How can they just be gone? I keep waiting for Aunt Emily to come through the door with bags full of groceries so that she can make dinner and tell Drama and me Greek mythology stories or to have Uncle Paul lecture me about the importance of an IRA while wearing some goofy ass outfit. But they won't and..."

"I know," I rasp as my throat begins to tighten despite my best efforts.

He looks at me, genuinely, for the first time in probably years.

"I'm really sorry you lost them, Dad."

The sincerity in his words takes my breath away and makes breathing that much harder. I nod stiffly as I clap his shoulder once more.

"Thanks, buddy," I say before slowly walking up the staircase.

When I get outside of Andromeda's door, I pause. Maybe I should leave her alone. Maybe everyone else has the right idea and she needs space. Something in my gut doesn't let that thought settle for too long, though.

I knock once but no answer comes. I knock a second time, but still nothing. Blowing a slow breath, I contemplate just heading back downstairs but my stubbornness overrules it and I gently push the door open. When I do, I see her, lying stiffly on her bed, facing the ceiling as still as a corpse. The assimilation is too much for my head right now and I suddenly find myself desperate to know that she is alive and moving.

"Nevaeh," I say gently as I take a step toward her. She doesn't respond, which only ratchets up the fear inside me. It's irrational, I know. I've seen her blink three times already and I can see her chest rising and falling with her breaths. Still, I need more.

"Nevaeh, please. Talk to me," I practically beg. "Tell me you're okay."

Slowly, her head turns until it's facing me.

"Okay?" Her voice cracks. "No, I'm not okay."

She turns back to face the ceiling without another word. I stand there and glance down at the worn wood beneath my feet before I speak.

"Me neither," I rasp.

I watch as she glances at me from the corners of her eyes. Wordlessly, she scoots over until she is lying on the far-right side of her bed before she goes back to staring at the ceiling. I hesitate for a second before I sit down on the side of the bed and lie on the left side. We sit there in silence for several minutes. For so long I almost think she fell asleep until her soft voice speaks.

"It hurts so bad," she whispers, not to me in particular, more like she is speaking it out into the universe. Like she is admitting it to herself for the first time. I'm proud of her for it, it's words I've yet to utter myself, probably for the same reasons that she hasn't.

"I know."

Chapter 6
Andromeda

I stand in line, numb. I hear the faint sound of applause echoing around me, but it doesn't quite register. One step. Smiling faces surround me, eyes filled with excitement, nervousness and apprehension. Two steps. My head slowly moves around to take in the large stadium filled with celebrating families, all excited for their loved ones on what is supposed to be a special day. It doesn't feel all that special to me, though. Three steps.

Principal Martinez smiles at me as I take those final steps to close the distance between us. He hands me my diploma, smiling for a picture I don't care to have, briefly pausing for cheers that won't come. Okay, that part isn't true. Cheers do come. Aunt Alyssa is like a bull horn, she could be heard over anything. I also hear hoots and hollers coming from those who I know to be Theo and Atlas as well as some quieter ones from my grandparents. People are here for me, but there are two empty seats that make this entire stadium feel vacant.

Slowly walking down the stage one step at a time, I make my way out of the room instead of going back to my seat. What are they gonna do? Un-graduate me? I don't want to sit surrounded by the pitying looks I receive from my classmates or listen to one more fucking speech about how this is the end of one chapter in our lives and the beginning of another. I don't want a goddamn thing to do with this chapter of my life. I can tell from the first page that it sucks.

It didn't take long for my family to follow me out of the stadium. I rode over with Aunt Alyssa, so I lean against her car until everyone makes their way over to me.

"We are so proud of you." Grandpa Greg and Grandma Jackie smile as they hug me.

I do my best to muster a smile of my own but I'm fairly certain it comes across as more of a grimace. I hug Alyssa too before Theo and Atlas. I can see my grandparents holding their phones expectantly, probably wanting to take pictures but I'm honestly drained and I don't have it in me to pretend that I'm okay anymore. So, I kiss their cheeks, tell them I love them and to have safe travels before climbing into Alyssa's car.

Alyssa climbs in shortly after and it doesn't take long for her to start rambling on to me about the new guy she met on some dating app. No other way to grieve the loss of your sister than to hook up with a guy who works at a coffee shop, right?

When we get back to the house, Alyssa doesn't even get out of the car, instead choosing to say her goodbyes from the front seat. Everyone asked me after the funeral if I wanted to do a special dinner or something after graduation, but I didn't see a point.

I'm still not quite sure why I'm the only one who isn't doing okay. Yeah, they were sad at the funeral and stuff, but everyone seems to be moving on like the two greatest people in the world weren't stolen so selfishly and tragically because some fucking asshole decided to get behind the wheel after having three too many.

I don't get it.

It hurts to move. It hurts to breathe. Call me dramatic all you want, but up until now, I've never really felt true gut-wrenching pain. Part of me would do anything to make it stop, the other part of me is terrified for it to. At least if the pain is still there, the memory of them is still alive and well. Everyone else seems to have been able to forget them in a matter of days. Not me.

The only other person that seems to be hurting the same way I am is Atlas, maybe Theo for a distant third. Atlas just shows it differently. He has somehow mastered the art of wearing a mask, of appearing okay and functioning like the others but he hasn't been able to mask the pain from his eyes. Those dark-brown eyes are drenched in sadness and laced with pain. It's a look that perfectly mirrors the way the inside of me feels.

I toss my cap onto the kitchen island as I make my way over to the fridge, grabbing one of Dad's beers and openly drinking it instead of sneaking it like Theo and I used to. I wince at the flavor. It's so hoppy and bitter, but it was always his favorite. I've limited myself to one a day so far, terrified for the day that is coming soon when they will be gone, and a new pack won't appear after he gets home from work one day.

Moving to head up to my room, I pause when I see a bouquet of Ferrero Rochers sitting in a vase on the coffee table that definitely wasn't there when I left for graduation earlier. They are my guilty pleasure and I've never seen them displayed like this before. It's definitely better than flowers. I haven't been able to even look at them without physically getting ill since the funeral.

Slowly, I inch my way toward the vase like it's a bomb ready to go off. My fingers reach out and open the small card, my chest concaving in on itself as I read the written words.

They were with you today, Nevaeh, and they are so proud.
-Atlas

Next to the card is a small black box that is all too familiar. I slowly open it to reveal a charm of an angel's wings. Glancing down at the charm bracelet that has been attached to me since Atlas first gave it to me for my ninth birthday my eyes burn as tears begin to build up. God, I'm already so fucking sick of crying and it's only been a little over a week. I really hope the crying fades soon, I don't know if I can handle much more of waking up with swollen eyes and a raw throat.

The smell of burned rubber stings my nose as I look around for the source of the smell. My head whips around wildly but it's so dark. I can't see anything out here. It's like the stars have been erased from the night sky, the streetlamps burned out and lifeless until I'm left out here in the pitch black.

Suddenly, a light begins to glow to my left. It takes me a few moments to recognize it as the glow from the inside of my mom's SUV. My heart leaps in my chest as I stretch my legs as far as I can to close the distance between us. What is she doing out here in the darkness?

"Mom! Mom, what's going on?" I ask as I come up to the rolled down window.

Her head turns to look at me and she smiles. It's not a wide smile but a small soft one. I don't understand why she is smiling or why Dad is taking a nap in the driver's seat in the middle of the road.

"Mom, what are you doing out here? Come inside," I say once more.

Her smile stays in place for a moment before her mouth opens slightly like she is about to speak. Instead of words, though, a thin line of red begins to trail out of her mouth and down her neck, collecting into a puddle at the neck of her white shirt.

"Oh my god!" I shout.

I pull my sweatshirt off and lift it to wipe the blood away but when I look up the line has expanded before her head slumps forward. Looking down I see her blonde hair laying just outside of the window that I can now see is shattered, not rolled down. It's as if everything in front of me shifts on its axis.

Suddenly, Dad isn't napping, he's nearly split in two with the dash buried into his stomach, his eyes wide and lifeless. The SUV that looked in perfect condition crinkles before me until it's left barely unrecognizable.

"Andromeda! Andromeda!" a faint voice calls out.

My head whips around quickly but I can't find the owner of the disembodied voice.

"Help! They're hurt! Somebody help!" I shriek into the silent night sky.

"Andromeda!" the useless voice shouts again.

I don't need a distant stranger shouting out for the sake of it, I need someone to help me get them to the hospital before it's too late!

"HELP ME!" I scream as loud as I can even as my throat begins to burn from the use.

"Open your eyes, Nevaeh! Open your eyes!"

I blink as I look around me. What the fuck is that supposed to mean? My eyes are open, and what I see is fucking horrifying. I squeeze them shut, hoping that when I open them again everything will be back to normal. But as soon as I do, a sickeningly loud crunch echoes through the street. Metal on metal. Screams, of a woman or a man, or maybe both. Pain. So much pain.

I lean forward, gasping for breath desperately as I feel wetness covering my cheeks. My head pounding as my own scream deafens me. I'm in my bed, the light is on, and a fear-stricken Atlas is standing over me, his hands gripping the tops of my shoulders tightly.

"There you are," he breathes in what sounds like relief before he releases his hold on me and runs a hand through his hair.

My breathing is still labored as I do my best to get it under control when I glance to the side to see Theo hovering in the doorway, concern written across his face as he assesses me warily.

"W-what are you guys doing here?" I say breathily before my heart begins to slowly beat to a steady pace.

"We heard you screaming from our house," Theo answers as he takes a small step inside.

"Screaming?" I repeat, confused as I turn to face Atlas.

Atlas nods once before swallowing roughly.

"You were dreaming, weren't you? About that night?"

My stomach twists at his words and I give him a shaky nod as I wipe my hands down my face and blow out a deep breath. For a moment, I almost forgot that they were gone.

"Sorry. I didn't know I was screaming. I..." I trail off because I don't really know what else I'm supposed to say right now.

"You shouldn't be alone right now, Drama," Theo says as he takes another small step closer. "Can't Alyssa or someone stay here?"

I shake my head. "Everyone is moving on with their lives, I need to do the same, right?"

Atlas's eyebrows furrow. "No one is moving on without them, Nevaeh. We are getting by, barely, one day at a time. But it's okay to lean on people, you should lean on people."

"Well, the two people I would lean on aren't here, are they Atlas? I'm on my own now and it's best for me to get used to that."

His concern quickly morphs to irritation, maybe a hint of offense as he slowly stands from the bed.

"You aren't alone. You have a lot of people who want to be there for you, when you're ready."

"I'm fine," I snap a little too defensively.

Theo looks like he's ready to argue but Atlas puts an arm on his shoulder as he looks down at me.

"Okay. If you need to talk or just need some company you call one of us, we'll be here anytime, day or night."

Theo nods his agreement.

"Thanks, but I won't need you."

They both send me worrying glances before they slowly make their way out of the house. I run a hand through my hair before glancing over to my alarm clock to see that it's a little after two in the morning. I should get some sleep. Somehow I don't see that happening, though.

Chapter 7
Andromeda

The next few days are more of the same, despite how hard I try to keep myself together, though it's getting worse if you can even imagine that. For the last three nights in a row, I've been woken up to Atlas, Theo or both of them shaking me awake. Every single night I've had the same dream on repeat. It always starts off confusing and ends traumatically.

Both Theo and Atlas have tried helping me but how do you save someone who isn't sure if they want to be saved? Why should I be saved when they weren't? I deserve the pain. I deserve the guilt. Knowing that my last words to my parents were ones of anger and irritation alone will haunt me for the rest of my days.

Atlas has been coming by the house every day, despite my instance not to. Some days, he just drops off takeout before leaving me in peace. Some days he brings over the Scrabble board and encourages me to play. Though I think me snapping the board in half and tossing it into the fireplace conveyed the message that I don't want to play, not anymore.

My phone buzzes beside me, momentarily pulling me out of my grievous thoughts. Looking down at the screen I see that it's a text from Cassie. I haven't heard from her since graduation. She came to the funeral I think. She told me she did, I don't really remember much about that day, though. Like a dark painful blur.

Cassie: Hey, you up for a party? I'm heading to Europe next weekend so it will be our last chance to see each other before I leave for college!

I wouldn't say Cassie is my best friend or anything. She was a great school friend. We sat next to each other at lunch and assemblies, we went to dances together and sometimes we would hang out when Theo was busy. Still, we aren't close enough that the thought of her going to college all the way across the country at NYU bothers me. She's excited to go and maybe before I would say that I was going to miss her. Can't say I can even fathom letting another event or action control my emotions. What's left of them, I suppose.

My instinct is to delete the message and move on with the rest of my night. It's been my auto-pilot response for almost two weeks now but if I have to stare at these cream walls for another night, I might officially descend into a full spiral depression or complete madness. Maybe both.

Me: Where?

Her reply comes almost immediately.

Cassie: Oh my god, seriously? I thought for sure you would turn me down! It's at Aaron Simpson's house. Want me to pick you up?

Aaron is just down the road from me. At least I can just walk home whenever I feel like it. Probably the best-case scenario because I never liked riding with Cassie even before, she's way too careless on the road. Now I'm even more against it.

Me: I'll walk. What time?

Cassie: Meet you there at 9?

I don't bother responding as I toss my phone on my bed and walk over to my closet. I grab a black bodysuit and a pair of jeans before slipping on my Keds. I don't bother with makeup, and I don't do more than tangle my fingers through my hair. This is probably stupid, but in the moment, nothing sounds better than being released from the constant pain in my chest, or at least as released as some warm beer will allow me.

———

As predicted, the beer is warm, the room is hot, and the people are less than good looking. Any other night and I would have been out of here and back home in bed before they tapped the first keg. But there is nothing but an empty house waiting for me, and I have an ugly gnashing wound in my chest that I'm desperate to bandage. So, I walk up to the keg and pour myself another beer, allowing the hoppy flavor to run down my throat until the cup is drained once again. I can't help but cringe at the bitter taste, but the warm haze that soon follows helps make it bearable.

Pouring myself another drink, I feel a heavy arm rest around my shoulders. A foul smell enters my nose as I look up with hazy eyes to see Grady smiling down at me.

"I didn't believe Cassie when she said you'd be here tonight. How you doing?"

I shrug his arm off as I take a step back, only stumbling slightly as I do.

"Peachy, thanks," I say, a slight slur to my words to even my own ears.

He grins at me in a way that should probably make my stomach fill with butterflies. Instead, it churns in a way that has my head spinning. God, maybe I need to go home. Without a word, I brush past him as I stumble through the crowds. The minute the brisk night hits me, a long-awaited sense of relief washes over me.

I take my steps lackadaisically, whether by choice or due to the fact the alcohol has more than damaged my normal capability to walk in a straight line, we will never know. I didn't realize I was being followed until that familiar heavy arm draped around me once more, causing me to bump into the stranger to my right.

"Hey, where are you running off to?"

My head looks up to see Grady watching me with that same stupid smile, but for some reason, there looks to be two smiles now. Good thing I'm out of here. A guy with two smiles is definitely not my type.

"Home," I slur as my body sways.

"I'll walk you," he says as he hauls me back toward him.

I try to push against him because seriously, he honestly smells so bad, but my arms give way in protest, too weak to do so, or maybe too lazy to care. I stumble over a crack, my face heading for the sidewalk when Grady's arm catches me. Before I can say anything, he bends down and slings me over his shoulder like a sack of flour. My head lulls as my hair rains down around me like a waterfall.

I love my hair, it's so golden and thick. It's just like my mom's. One single thought and that churning feeling in my stomach is back, accompanied by a painful crack in the armor I've been surrounding myself in all night.

"Put me down," I say against his back, a little more clear than my previous mumblings.

He reaches a hand up and swats my ass, a deep chuckle rumbling through his chest as he comes up to my yard.

"I'll put you down when we get to bed, baby."

I open my mouth to tell him there is no way he's coming into my house when a loud bang rings out through the now quiet neighborhood. It takes me several seconds to recognize that bang was actually a car door being shut. My head turns to the side to see Atlas's car parked sideways in the street, a furious-looking Atlas flying out of the car and toward us.

Someone's in troubleeeeee.

"What the fuck are you doing?" he practically snarls at Grady.

"Who the fuck are you?" Grady asks, indignation coating his words as his grip on me tightens slightly as if I was his prized kill he was hiding from the scouring buzzards.

"I'm Andromeda's godfather. Now, what the fuck are you doing with my goddaughter tossed over your shoulder like a wet towel?"

"I was just taking her home. Girl is drunk off her tits."

"And how about when you smacked her ass when she was 'drunk off her tits'? Got an explanation for that one or should I just call the cops for assault right now?"

My world spins, one minute I'm hanging upside down and the next I'm facing the sky, my stomach fluttering as I free fall for what feels like ever. My back lands first against the damp grass, my head following for a close second as all of the air in my lungs is instantly taken from me. I blink hard, surprised not to feel any pain as my head turns to the side to see Grady holding his hands up in surrender as Atlas stares at me, his intense eyes practically drilling holes in me as they scan me for injuries from head to toe.

His head snaps toward a slowly retreating Grady as he advances on him. Atlas's large fist grasps a hand full of Grady's T-shirt before dragging him close to him. I watch as Atlas's shoulders rise and fall with what look like labored breaths.

"How old are you?" he asks.

Grady stammers before Atlas yanks me once.

"E-eighteen."

"Good," Atlas says before he winds back his arm and swings, his fist connecting with Grady's jaw.

Grady falls to the ground immediately but clearly knows better than to stick around. He scrambles to his feet quickly before he starts booking it back to the party. Atlas stands his ground for several seconds, ensuring Grady won't come back before he comes over to me. I'm now sitting up, leaning my arms over my knees.

"Nevaeh, what the hell were you thinking? I've been looking for you everywhere. I brought you dinner and you weren't home. You weren't answering your phone. I—"

He pauses his rant, shaking his head a few times before bringing his eyes back up to mine.

"Are you okay?"

I shrug loosely as I face the house. I feel warm fingers slide underneath my chin, forcing my eyes to come to his, concern shining deep in those rich chocolate eyes.

"Are you okay?" he repeats gently.

"No," I whisper hoarsely, emotion choking my throat as I shake my head and rest my forehead against my crossed arms.

Several seconds pass before I feel a hand rest against my back, moving in small soothing circles. He doesn't say anything and neither do I. What's there to say? So, we just sit in my front yard for I don't know long, hoping, begging, praying for I don't know what.

A do-over. A miracle. A new beginning. Or maybe a different ending.

Chapter 8
Andromeda

The next morning I woke up in my bed. I don't remember how I got here, but I guess it doesn't really matter. I'm sure Atlas carried me upstairs and I guess I'm grateful since hypothermia is very much a real thing. Maybe not necessarily in Northern California during the summer, but still.

I remember a few words being said last night, about how Atlas wants me to see someone, talk through things, but honestly what would that help? It's not like talking about the inky black thoughts plaguing my mind will make them any less all consuming. Then again, something has to give. I don't know. Maybe the problem is that this house has so many suffocating memories, every single memory.

They didn't die in this house, but they might as well have. There is no laughter or joy left in these walls. No delicious smelling dinners or noisy barbeques in the backyard. No cozy movie nights in. Everything is cold, hollow and bland.

I'm standing in the kitchen, looking blankly around the house. I don't even recognize the space in front of me. My eyes snag on the family picture that is propped on the hall table. It was my eighteenth birthday. My parents woke me up early in the morning and surprised me, driving down to my favorite beach just outside of San Francisco. We spent the day on the sand, laughing, eating and just enjoying being together.

My eyes water as I pick up the glass frame. We looked so happy, so perfect. Now it's all just a memory. Rage courses through me at the unjustness of it all. Why the hell do I have to live a life without them, and they just get to be gone? Why do I have to know this pain, this abandonment?

My fingers curl around the frame before I wind my arm back and hurl the memory at the wall, feeling an odd sort of satisfaction when I watch the glass splinter to pieces across the room. I turn to see the vase of Ferrero's that Atlas bought me for graduation. The gesture was kind, but it hurts too fucking much to look at it. I quickly pick the vase up and throw it against the wall, watching as a mix of dismembered candy, glass, and wrappers rain down the wall before piling on the floor.

From there, it's all a blur. I grab anything and everything I can, hitting, ripping and breaking it all to pieces. I want it gone. All of it. It hurts too fucking much. This house haunts me, these memories terrorize me. I need it all gone. Gone. Gone. Gone.

Time seems to blur and in the next moment an arm bands around my waist, hauling me away from my mom's favorite lamp before I can reach it. I fight back against the arm clawing and slapping at it like my life depends on it. A sharp hiss escapes the person behind me before they release me. I return to my mission, crossing the room until two large hands grab the sides of my face and twist me around.

My nostrils flare at the intruder. Can't I at least fall apart in peace?

Atlas towers over me, his hold firm but his face full of compassion and pain. He shakes his head softly, never breaking eye contact with me as he does.

"Nevaeh, what are you doing?" he asks lowly.

I do my best to keep my tone even, but I fail instantly.

"I need it all gone," I choke as a sob rips through me. "I can't do it anymore. Waking up alone in this house, walking by the same furniture, the same pictures. I can't take it. It hurts so fucking bad. I need it to stop. God, Atlas, why won't it stop?" I plead.

His eyes turn sympathetic as his hold on me tightens slightly.

"It'll never stop, Nevaeh. You'll just learn to live with the pain until you won't know any different."

I wince at that, hating his answer.

"I think you need to get out of this house. It's clearly not helping with your healing," he says gently.

"Where am I supposed to go?" I snap. "I don't have any family within five hours of me, I'm starting my internship at your firm next week and this place is paid for, rent free. It's logical to stay."

Atlas shakes his head as he breaks eye contact for the first time, glancing at the wall behind me for several seconds before looking down at me again.

"You can stay with us. We have more than enough room. You'll have your own space. Maybe if you are somewhere new, you'll be able to get a decent night's sleep."

I shake my head. "No. That's extremely generous but staying with my ex-boyfriend and his dad sounds extremely unappealing. I think I'd rather take the nightmares," I say, only partially exaggerating. I don't know if I can handle another night filled with gruesome flashbacks. I've reached the point that I'm terrified to close my eyes even for a few moments.

Atlas's eyebrows furrow as he looks at me, his firm grip on my face softening before he drops his hands to his side.

"I'm not just your ex-boyfriend's dad, Nevaeh. I'm your godfather. Eighteen or not, your parents trusted me to watch after you if anything ever happened to them. Something did happen to them. Something fucking horrific and unfair and painful, and now I'm here to own up to my responsibility and be here for you."

"Glad to understand the real reason behind all of your actions lately," I scoff as I roll my eyes and look away.

Atlas pinches my chin like a child being scolded as he narrows his eyes in irritation.

"Stop being irrational, you know that isn't the case. I'm here because I care about you. I'm worried about you. I'm not going to let you self-destruct. Do you have any idea what could have happened to you last night alone had I not been there? What he could have done to you?

"Your parents trusted me to watch over and protect you in their place but that isn't the reason I'm ready and willing to do so. And if you truly think that then you aren't nearly the intelligent girl that I thought you were."

I'm left speechless for several long seconds. I don't think I've ever had anyone talk down to me yet put me in my place all at once before. I want to argue, to tell him to fuck off and leave me alone, but the words dry up on my tongue. A sinking feeling begins to overtake my stomach as I think about kicking him out and spending the rest of the day and night in this house, empty, alone and hurting like hell.

When I look up at Atlas, I see a similar pain mirrored in his rich brown eyes. A hurt that is felt deep, one that he will have to learn to live with but never truly get over. Maybe it wouldn't be the worst idea if I spent a couple nights away from the house. Just so that I can hopefully sleep a little better. And you know the saying, misery loves company.

"Just for a few nights," I concede cautiously.

Atlas nods approvingly as he drops his hand and takes a step back, taking in the state of the room around us before looking at me.

"Whatever you want. Go pack a bag. I'll go make sure one of the spare rooms is ready for you."

With that, he turns and walks out of the house. My eyes trace over the ransacked room. I'm honestly a little surprised at the destruction I caused in such a short amount of time. I blacked out. I don't even remember ripping the painting from the wall behind the couch down but there it lays, frame broken, and canvas gouged. Mom had it shipped all the way from Greece. If she wasn't dead, I'd be the one in a coffin.

For some reason, that thought has me cracking a smile. Then a chuckle bubbles out of me before another and another until I am full on crying slash laughing. This is it. I've finally hit my breaking point. I've officially lost my sanity. I must have, considering I just agreed to move in with the Kane's. Temporarily or not, I think it's safe to say that I'm batshit crazy.

Chapter 9
Atlas

Stepping inside the house, I glance around to find the living room empty. Theo must still not be up yet. Making my way up the stairs to the spare bedroom, I stop at the linen closet at the end of the hall before grabbing some fresh sheets and pillowcases. Opening up the door, I pause as the stale air greets me immediately. I can't remember the last time anyone stayed in here. Maybe it was when one of Theo's friends came to visit last summer?

I quickly strip the old sheets and make the bed before grabbing a few of the miscellaneous boxes around the room that have somehow taken up permanent residence here. Glancing around, I frown. I never realized how blank this room is. The walls are a cold white, the carpet a light gray. There isn't any sort of décor except for some painting of a lake that I can't even remember where I got from. There isn't even a TV.

Regardless of Andromeda only staying here for a few days, I want her to be comfortable. I know a good amount of the reason she doesn't want to be here is because of Theo. So, I want to make sure that she feels like she has somewhere to escape when she needs it.

After seeing how uncomfortable she's been around Theo over the last few months and how timid he's been around her, I've questioned if having them interning together is really the right move. I've already decided that Theo will be shadowing more of the business side of things while Andromeda focuses on the design and planning side.

"What's going on?" Theo asks on a yawn as he scratches at his mop of a head before leaning against the doorway.

I look over my shoulder as I lift the last box into my arms.

"Andromeda is going to be staying a little while."

In an instant, the sleepy haze has suddenly been wiped from my son as he stands up a little taller, eyebrows raised in surprise.

"Here?"

I nod. "Yep," I say as I move past him, carrying the box down to the garage with the rest of them.

"Why?" he asks as he follows me down.

I set the box in the corner before I turn to face him.

"Because staying in that house all alone is getting to her. She's going to stay with us as long as she needs, and I need you to help make her as comfortable as possible. That means if she wants you to leave her alone, you do that. Understood?"

Theo scoffs before he rolls his eyes.

"You act like I can't be trusted around her. She was my girlfriend for over four years, Dad. I know her better than anyone."

"Yeah, well, since you have refused to be upfront about what ended said relationship so suddenly, I don't know what to think. All I have to go on is what I see, and what I've seen between you two over the last several months makes me feel the need to reiterate, she needs to feel comfortable when she's here."

Theo ducks his head, rubbing the back of his neck before blowing out a rough breath.

"Fine, whatever," he says as he turns and heads back inside.

I run a hand through my hair as I shake my head. I swear I wasn't as difficult as Theo has become when I was his age. Then again, there wasn't really anyone to be difficult for. I was on my own with a baby on the way at his age. I only had two people in the entire world that I gave a shit about and that truly gave a shit about me.

And now they're fucking gone.

That's probably one of the most painful parts about grief, the part I know too well. The pain comes in waves. Some days you're able to wake up and start your day and for a few moments, you don't even think about it. Then other days are debilitating, you can hardly fucking breathe.

It's only been a little over a week since Emily and Paul's death and I've been lucky enough to have more okay days than not. If I'm being honest with myself, though, I'm sure it has to do with the fact that I've been doing everything possible not to think about it. I've been going into work early every day, bringing it home to work on until late in the evening before I drink a few generous glasses of scotch before passing out in bed. Not exactly the healthiest coping mechanism, but it's been working for me so far.

At least I've had work to distract me, unlike Andromeda. No wonder she's beginning to lose it. Alone in her childhood home, suddenly orphaned, nothing but a house full of memories and a heart full of hurt. Hopefully the nightmares will stop if she's in a new environment, though that isn't all she will need to make it out the other side. Therapy will be key, or at least that's what everyone always told me. I've never been a day in my life, so what would I really know?

The doorbell rings and I straighten up from my spot in the garage before making my way to the front door. When I open it, Andromeda is standing there holding a small duffle bag on her shoulder, her posture seemingly rigid and uncomfortable. It's not like she hasn't been here a million times before. But that's just it, that was all before. She hasn't been here since she and Theo broke up, since her parents died, since everything changed.

"Come on in," I say after a few heavy moments, gesturing inside.

She hesitates for a second, glancing over my shoulder before looking at me. Understanding dawns on me as I nod slightly.

"Theo went back to his room, I think. We talked. He's going to give you your space while you're here. Whatever you need."

The tension in her shoulders seems to ease slightly as she nods softly and takes a step inside. I silently lead her to the room I set up for her. She glances around before setting her bag on the floor near the foot of the bed.

"I don't think I've ever been in this room before."

I nod. "It's usually just filled with random junk. We don't have any use for it so it's yours to do with what you want. We could decorate it, or maybe paint it at least? Give it a pop of color. Or—"

"Atlas," she says, cutting me off. "It's fine. I'm only going to stay for a night or two, just until the dreams go away."

I nod as I put my hands into my jean pockets. "Whatever you—"

"Need," she snaps sharply. "I get it, thank you."

An awkward few moments pass by before I rub the back of my neck.

"Alright, I'll leave you to it then," I say as I step out of the room.

I don't know what the hell to do or say in this situation. Emily was the one out of the three of us that always knew what to say. Paul and I were the fixers, if someone told us what was wrong or how to solve a problem, we would take care of it. Em was the instinctual one, though.

Fuck.

So much for being able to go the day without letting the grief seep in. I can practically feel it spider webbing across my chest, seeping into my veins like a plague that will never go away.

Chapter 10
Andromeda

I spend the majority of the day in the bedroom. I brought a few books, so I spent most of my time that way. I glance at my phone to see that it's a little after six. I should probably eat something. I never did get around to having breakfast or lunch. I heard Atlas's car drive away an hour or so after he showed me to my temporary room, so I know he isn't home. I'm not much of a cook, not like my mom was. Atlas isn't either and Theo can hardly boil water.

Considering the lack of capable cooks in the house I'd bet there are plenty of frozen meals or things in the cabinet that will do. So, I reluctantly open the door before heading downstairs.

I glance across the hallway where Theo's bedroom is. I can't even count the number of times we would sneak into there when our parents were downstairs having a few drinks over a football game or a barbeque. I've grown up in this house practically, as much as my own. So why does it suddenly feel so foreign?

Once I'm in the kitchen, I begin with the freezer, deciding that I'll just grab whatever is easy. My fingers begin shuffling the various microwavable options when a melancholy voice comes from behind me.

"Hey."

I practically leap out of my skin as I quickly spin to find Theo in the entryway to the kitchen. He looks timid, his shoulders slightly slumped, hands tucked into his pockets as his messy hair falls slightly into his eyes. I debate on ignoring him altogether but after a moment, I give him a cautious glance as I speak.

"Hey."

"Looking for something?" he asks as he gestures toward the open freezer door.

I shrug. "Just wanting something easy. I don't feel like cooking anything, and I didn't know what you guys had."

"I was just about to order a pizza. Want some?"

I hesitate for a moment before nodding. "Sure, thanks. Can you just make sure there are n—"

"No mushrooms," he finishes. "I know, Drama."

He gives me something between a frown and a smile before pulling out his phone and walking into the hallway. After a minute or so, the intro music to The Lord of the Rings sounds from the living room. It's both Theo and my all-time favorite. We've probably watched it a hundred times growing up. It's our comfort show.

The gesture feels like a peace offering, like Theo is leaving it up to me, which I appreciate. I've thought about him a lot over the last few days. As disappointed in him as I am and sad and still a tiny bit mad, I just don't have it in me to waste the extra energy hating him. I've got enough emotions I'm trying to sort through. I don't need to add another to the list.

So, I slowly make my way into the living room. Theo is sitting on the couch on the very right side already engrossed in the movie. He doesn't look up to me when I walk in, and I don't say anything as I sit down on the left side of the couch. We quickly fall into comfortable silence as we are sucked into the movie.

Before I know it, the doorbell is ringing, and Theo is getting up to answer it. He comes back with a pizza before setting it on the coffee table and opening the lid. For the first time since I sat down, he looks at me, gesturing for me to take the first piece.

"Thanks," I say quietly as I pick up my slice of supreme pizza.

He nods as he picks up a piece, taking a small bite before setting it back down in the box and turning to me.

"I don't want things to be weird between us, Drama. I know they are, and I know it's all my fault. I also know you don't want to hear my bullshit excuses or apologies so I'm not going to waste your time with any of that. But I do want you to feel comfortable. My dad is right, you shouldn't be alone right now, and you are always welcome here no matter what. I've been thinking a lot about interning at Kane Designs, and I think I'm going to opt out."

My eyebrows knit together as I look at him.

"What do you mean opt out?"

"Architecture isn't my passion, it's yours. I don't know what the fuck I want to do but I know that I sure as hell don't want to be stuck in a cubicle all day doing a bunch of math and drawing buildings."

I can't help but snort at his vast oversimplification of the job duties an architect performs from day to day.

"I think it would be best, probably for both of us, if I found a different job for the summer. I don't want to be putting you on edge and full disclosure, I don't want to be there," he continues.

I nod, it makes sense. Theo hasn't exactly been subtle about having zero to no interest in the family business, despite Atlas's insistence.

"What's your dad going to say to all this?" I ask.

He shakes his head. "I'm an adult, he can't make me do anything I don't want to do. Besides, I think he will agree that me not being there will be better for you right now, even if he doesn't understand why. That alone should be enough to get him off my back."

"So, I'm your scapegoat?"

Theo looks at me for a moment before he barks out a laugh. I can't help but chuckle softly to myself. God, it feels like I haven't laughed in months. How dismal is that?

"Kinda, I guess. Is that alright?"

I shrug. "It's your life, Theo. I don't want you changing plans on my account but if you need me to be your reasoning for not working at the firm, then whatever works."

He gives me a half smile as he nods for a moment before the movement changes, and he shakes his head.

"Fuck. I was such an idiot."

I raise an eyebrow at him. I'm nowhere near in the mood to get into this with him right now, or possibly ever. So, instead, I opt for an "Mhmm," before focusing back on my pizza and the movie.

We didn't say anything else for the rest of the movie. Once it was over we said brief good nights before heading to our rooms. In a weird way it almost feels like a bridge has been made between us tonight. One I'm not quite sure he deserves. Holding a grudge against one of the only people left that I've known my entire life because of a stupid but selfish mistake just seems petty, though. Life is clearly too short.

———

My eyes flutter open the next morning, bouncing around the blank white room in confusion. It takes me a few seconds to fully recognize where I am. It takes me another few seconds to realize that it's the morning. I slept through the entire night, no nightmares. I let out a sigh of relief as I run my fingers through my thick hair before reaching for my glasses.

It's Sunday and I don't really have anything planned. I haven't had anything planned for over a week now. I was supposed to start working at Kane Designs tomorrow and I'm sure Atlas expects me to take some time before I start the internship but if I have to spend even another week sitting around, overanalyzing and hyper-focusing on the broken remnants of my life, I'm absolutely confident that I'll lose my shit.

I open the bedroom door, planning on taking a shower when a smell instantly infiltrates my nose. At first it smells almost sweet, but it quickly sours into something burned or burning. I follow the smell down the stairs and when I step inside the kitchen, I see a plume of smoke billowing from a hot pan as Atlas stands in front of it cursing up a storm before yanking the pan off the burner and tossing it to the other side of the stove.

"Stupid fucking piece of shit," Atlas grumbles at the smoking pan.

"What happened?" I ask as I take a step closer.

Atlas turns to face me and for a moment, I freeze. I knew that Atlas was shirtless, I saw his bare back when I walked in, and I've seen him shirtless thousands of times. Both my house and his have a pool that we all frequented nearly every day in the summers. I've seen Atlas Kane shirtless countless times in my life, but I've never *seen* him shirtless until right now.

His shoulders are wide, muscles sitting on top of them like only athletes or people that live in the gym usually have. His chest is built and firm, looking like it's more likely made from stone than skin and muscle. My eyes trail down to his abs two, four, six...is that an eight-pack? I thought that they only existed in Photoshop.

Painfully aware that I'm standing here staring at my parents' best friend, my godfather for fuck's sake. I quickly drop my eyes as I begin spinning the aquamarine charm on my bracelet that Atlas gave me last Christmas.

Slowly, I raise my eyes to see that Atlas is thankfully not paying any attention to me, instead using a fork to poke at whatever he was attempting to cook. Well, at least I was the only one to witness my perusal.

What the hell is wrong with me? He's like forty. And he's my godfather! I never fully realized how absolutely ripped my godfather was though...nope. No. Not going there.

Brushing off the scandalous thoughts that were attempting to plant themselves in my head, I walked over to the stove to inspect the burned food. I wrinkle my nose at the offensive smell.

"What was that?" I ask.

Atlas turns to look down at me, frustration written across his face.

"It was french toast. I followed a recipe online to a T. I stepped away for like twenty seconds to grab a paper off my desk and when I came down it was practically on fire."

"Well, how much butter was in the pan?"

He shrugs. "Like a half a stick or so."

My eyes bug out at him as I look down at the scorched bread. And I thought I was a bad cook.

"Okay, first rule when it comes to cooking with butter, less is definitely more. How hot did you have the burner?"

Atlas frowns slightly as he crosses his arms over his chest. His arms flex at the movement and I do my best to hold his eyes instead of staring like I suddenly feel desperate to do so. Seriously, what the actual fuck is wrong with me?

"High, it's eggs, you have to cook them through."

I stare at him blankly because the brilliant man in front of me couldn't be this clueless, right?

"Medium high at most, Atlas. No one likes french toast that's crunchy on the outside and mush on the inside. You were on your way to that before you decided to just set it on fire instead."

His irritation fades a bit as he lets out a tired chuckle and runs a hand through his dark wavy hair.

"Well, I tried. Sorry, Nevaeh. I definitely can't cook like your mom."

He frowns at his own words, and I watch as pain flashes across his face briefly, but it's gone as fast as it came.

"C'mon, crack some eggs in a bowl," I say as I step forward and grab the loaf of bread on the counter.

Atlas quirks an eyebrow at me, those rich brown orbs looking at me curiously for a few seconds before he wordlessly does what I say. I walk him through the basics of making french toast. I stand by my statement that I'm not a great cook, but I know the essentials and french toast is my favorite, so I've had the process mastered since I was old enough to help my mom in the kitchen.

We work together quickly and soon we have a nice stack of perfectly golden french toast. We decided that we tempted fate enough today and passed on making any sides. Atlas and I both grab two slices of french toast and the bottle of syrup before sitting at the island in the kitchen. A few minutes of silence go by as we eat before Atlas speaks up.

"So, Theo called me while I was at the office last night."

I turn to him and raise an eyebrow. "Yeah?"

"He said that he spoke to you about everything first and you both decided it was best if he looked for a different job instead of Kane Designs this summer. Said he got an interview at the hardware store the next town over."

Way to spin that one Theo.

"Yeah, we just thought it would be too much living together and working together. Not that I'm planning on staying long," I quickly add on. "This is temporary."

Atlas ignores my temporary comment as he stares at me in that unyielding way he does when he is trying to get to the bottom of something.

"What happened between you two, Andromeda? You were together for four years and have been in each other's lives since birth. What could have possibly happened to the point where you two can hardly be in the same room?"

Once again, I feel the need to protect Theo and I honestly don't know why. It was one thing with my parents, they would have sided with me and taken their protectiveness for me out on him. But Atlas is Theo's dad. Sure, Atlas loves me too but he'll always side with his son, just like my parents would with me.

Still, it just feels like dragging up drama unnecessarily. I mean, maybe it isn't unnecessary to Atlas because in his mind, it's so terrible that we can't even put it aside to work together when in reality, his son just has no desire to work for him.

I shrug, choosing to keep my lips sealed once again. If he's going to keep pushing the issue maybe I should just have Theo tell him. It's his dad after all, why do I have to be the one to talk about one of the most humiliating moments of my life?

Atlas's eyes narrow on me, like he is trying to dig through my mind to find the truth himself. I quirk an eyebrow at him in question and he leans back into his chair, assumingly admitting defeat, for now. He grabs his plate and brings it to the sink before grabbing mine as well.

"Thanks. So, what time should I be there tomorrow?"

"Be where?" Atlas asks as he loads the plates into the dishwasher.

"The office. Tomorrow is the fifth. I'm supposed to be starting my internship," I say plainly, like I couldn't imagine why he would think any differently.

Atlas lets out a long sigh as he turns around to face me, arms crossed over his still-naked chest.

"Nevaeh, I think you need to take a little more time. It's only been less than three months. You're still having night terrors—"

"I didn't last night," I argue. "Not a single dream. I didn't wake up until a few minutes before I came down here."

His eyebrows raise in surprise as a soft smile touches his lips.

"That's good. I'm really glad to hear that. But still, I think it might be a little soon. You don't need to do the internship at all if you just want to take the summer to—"

"I need this internship, Atlas."

He sighs again. "I know, it's important to have job experience, but—"

"The job experience is inconsequential. I need it. I need something to do. I need something to take my mind off...everything. My parents are gone, and my friends from school are on summer trips, spending time with their families before they're off to college. I don't have anything but grief and it's suffocating. I *need* this."

A complicated look comes over his face as he watches me for a few moments before eventually nodding.

"Alright. If you're sure. You can always change your mind."

I nod. "Thank you."

"I'm leaving the house at six thirty tomorrow. If you're up by then you can ride with me. No sense in us both driving to and from the same places."

"I don't know if I can keep up with your workaholic lifestyle," I joke lightly, though I'm not one hundred percent joking.

Atlas lets out a half chuckle as he nods. "Whatever I don't finish by the end of your workday I can bring home with me."

I nod at that, since I'd never admit it out loud but I'm all too relieved to not have to drive to work every day, at least yet. I wasn't a super solid driver before since I never had a car, and my parents were usually too protective to let me practice. But now, I'm fucking terrified to get behind the wheel. My father was a great driver. Safe, cautious. I used to tease him for it, and even he got into an accident. If I could walk to work, I would. I'm more than happy to stay out of cars as much as possible for the time being.

Chapter 11
Andromeda

I pull at the black three-quarter sleeved blouse I have on as I adjust the height of my knee length white pencil skirt. When I woke up this morning, I decided that I needed to dress the part. Even if this is just an internship and Atlas has seen me in sweats more than skirts over my lifetime it isn't about any of that. It's about presenting myself to the rest of the business world. If you dress with authority people treat you with authority. Or at least that's what the motivation podcast I listened to last night said.

Looking into the mirror, I'm slightly taken back. I rarely wear contacts because tell me who actually enjoys wearing them, but today I decided to ditch the frames and try something new. Something different. I can't hate how much my green eyes stand out without my signature glasses. They seem brighter, bigger. Maybe I'm just not used to seeing myself without them, though. Either way, I like it, so I'll deal with the mild irritation for the slight boost in confidence.

I go minimal on my makeup, just applying my foundation, mascara, and a little bit of blush before spreading on a nice mauve lipstick. I keep waiting to feel the wave of excitement at this new chapter. When Atlas agreed to have me intern with his company back in the fall, I was so excited. To have an internship with Kane Designs on my resume was going to open so many doors for me and it didn't hurt that I knew my boss wouldn't be some sadist asshole. The shine of it all seems kinda dulled now, though.

Pushing down the growing ache in my chest, I practice my professional smile, noting that it looks a little too forced on the edges before trying again.

Better.

I grab my purse and toss in my things before heading downstairs. Atlas is already in the kitchen, pouring a cup of coffee into a traveler's mug before grabbing a bagel out of the toaster when I step into the room at six thirty on the nose.

"Morning," I say as I make my way over to the coffee machine.

Atlas turns to see me, surprise flashing across his face. Guess he didn't think I'd actually get up on time or maybe even that I would change my mind about starting today.

I move around him to grab a mug down from the cupboard before grabbing a pod and popping it into the Nespresso.

"Good morning," Atlas says after a moment before I grab the open bag of bagels and throw one in the toaster for myself.

When I turn, I see Atlas is still staring at me, almost like he's perplexed.

"What?"

His dark eyes blink twice before he shakes his head slightly.

"Nothing. It's just been a while since I've seen you without your glasses on."

I shrug as I grab my coffee before finding the matching lid. My bagel pops out shortly after and I quickly spread some cream cheese on it before turning to Atlas who still has yet to move. His eyes flick back and forth between mine before he speaks quietly, almost to himself.

"I never realized how bright your eyes are behind your glasses."

I nod, doing my best to ignore the flipping in my strange stomach as I do.

"Thanks," I say with a slight rasp.

Damn it. I gave myself a pep talk this morning and everything. I have to work with Atlas five days a week for the next three months. Whatever the hell flashed in my head yesterday and apparently this morning has to go. I'm living in his house for god's sake. The last thing I need to do is be lusting after...nope. Not even going to elaborate on that thought. Walking past him, I make my way toward the garage.

"Let's go, Bossman."

I don't feel him follow me for a few moments but eventually, his heavy footsteps sound from behind me.

We both slide into the car and just like that, the weird almost tension that felt like it was about to suffocate me in the kitchen seems to dissipate into thin air as soon as Atlas puts the car in drive. As we make our way through town he begins telling me about what projects he's working on and what my responsibilities will be for the next couple of months.

"Since Theo isn't going to be interning, you'll be mainly assisting me. Coming with me to meetings to take notes, going through client emails and sending me the ones that need immediate attention, things like that."

I nod as Atlas pulls into the parking garage of the office building before turning the car off and stepping out. I climb out of my side, grabbing my bag before I shut the door. I go to take a step forward when I slam into a hard chest. Startled, I glanced up to see that Atlas is staring down at me with furrowed brows.

"I was going to get your door," he says flatly.

My eyebrows raise. "It's the twenty-first century, Atlas. I'm capable of getting my door. Women are doing all sorts of things these days," I say with a small smirk.

Atlas rolls his eyes at me as he locks the car and turns to walk toward the elevator. I think I vaguely hear him mutter, "Smartass," but I can't be entirely sure.

We take the elevator to the eleventh floor before stepping out into a stylish lobby. The floors are dark shaded hardwood, the walls a soft cream color and the receptionist's desk in the middle of it all is wrapped in a shiny white and cream-colored marble.

A gorgeous woman who looks to be in her early thirties is sitting there to greet us. She has dark-hazel eyes with sleek black hair that comes to her shoulders. When she notices us, she gives us both a wide friendly smile.

"Good morning, Mr. Kane."

"Good morning, Cathy. Any calls this morning?" Atlas says.

"Dillon called to get final approval on the blueprints for the Fowley project and Mr. Abner called to confirm your lunch meeting tomorrow at one. I reserved a table for two at The White Pelican."

"Can you make it for three? Andromeda will be joining us. This is the intern I was telling you about, Andromeda. Andromeda, this is our receptionist, Cathy."

"Receptionist?" she mimics with a wrinkled nose. "I think I deserve a more prestigious title. What about, backbone of this company? Assistant to all? Superstar in every way? Underpaid for the insurmountable work I do?" She lists off with a mischievous twinkle in her eye.

Atlas cocks an eyebrow and smirks slightly.

"Are you underpaid? If I recall, you just got a hefty raise last quarter."

"There's never such a thing as too much money, Mr. Kane," she fires back with a smirk before shooting a wink over at me.

I can't help but laugh. Oh, I like her. Atlas shakes his head and rolls his eyes with a small trace of humor lingering on his mouth.

"Andromeda, Cathy will be able to help you get acclimated to our systems and how things run around here. As she so humbly pointed out, she's basically the super glue holding this place together. On top of the typical receptionist workload, she is also Dillon's right-hand woman. Dillon's our lead architect, you'll meet him when he gets back from Chicago."

I nod as I smile at her. "Nice to meet you."

"You too, hun. Once Mr. Kane is done giving you the tour, come find me and I'll help you get set up."

"Thanks," I say as Atlas nods his head for me to follow him. We walk through the office space where he points out the break room, copy room, bathrooms, and each employee's office. Since it's a smaller firm there aren't a ton of people that work here. He only has five architects on staff, each of whom has an assistant except for Dillon who has Cathy. Then there is Mandy who is the HR generalist and Dan who is the accountant/CFO in training. I know Dan because he used to work under my dad.

Guess he got a promotion.

After I fill out some paperwork with Mandy, I meet up with Cathy at the front desk. She helps give me access to their system and sets up my desk which is situated just outside of Atlas' office. She shows me how to pull up his calendar, go through emails and flag them for him and then a few more technical things that if I'm honest, I won't remember by tomorrow.

"It's a lot for your first day, I know." Cathy smiles. "I'm sorry. It'll get easier but it's kind of a sink-or-swim thing. I'm getting married in four weeks and I'm taking a three-week honeymoon, so you'll be managing Atlas and Dillon's schedules and emails while I'm gone."

I blink a few times at that but do my best to remain composed. Cool. Sink or swim it is.

"Well, congratulations on your wedding. I'll try not to burn the place down while you're gone."

She laughs at that. "Thanks, and please don't. I bust my ass to keep this place running, but I have faith in you. Atlas has been singing your praises for months and as nice as he is, he doesn't just hand compliments out so you must be worth something."

Atlas has been talking about me? For months? I wonder what he's been saying. I glance over to see that Cathy is watching me with a small smirk. Ignoring whatever is going on in her clearly mischievous brain, I rifle through the side drawer next to me, pausing when I see a small package of Ferrero Rochers. There isn't a note or anything like that but it's not like I don't know who left it there for me to find. I feel Cathy's eyes watching me carefully, but she doesn't say anything as she begins walking me through their systems.

After a few hours, she says that she's taking her lunch and invites me along with her.

"I'm kidnapping your assistant for lunch, Mr. Kane," Cathy says as she pops her head into Atlas's office.

He glances up from his laptop briefly, nodding before looking back down at his screen and typing away. She laughs and rolls her eyes as she loops her arm through mine and starts walking us toward the elevator.

"I swear, when that man gets into work mode I could do the Macarena naked, and he wouldn't even notice."

My brows dip and my stomach twists at that for some reason. Pushing it to the side I follow after her. We take the elevator down to the bottom floor where there is conveniently a nice little café. After we sit and begin browsing the menus Cathy clears her throat.

"So, how long have you had the hots for Mr. Kane?"

My eyes bug out of my head as I drop my menu and gape at her. I do my best to come up with a response but my brain misfires for several seconds before my mouth finally decides to start working.

"What? You're kidding, right? He's my godfather! My parents' best friend." I wince before I correct myself. "Well, late parents, but still."

A sympathetic look crosses her face as she nods.

"I'm really sorry for your loss. We all loved your dad. I still can't believe he's gone."

My throat begins to tighten as my eyes burn. I will not cry in front of my new coworker. Blinking hard once, I'm able to keep the tears at bay before giving her an appreciative smile.

"He was the best. Anyway, yeah, no, definitely nothing there."

"You sure?" Cathy tests. "I couldn't help but notice the daggers you threw at me when I mentioned being naked in his office."

I grimace, not sure how to verbally explain whatever the hell has been going on in my head these last few days. I shrug nonchalantly as I glance at the menu.

"So, it doesn't bother you to know that Mr. Kane and I used to be lovers?"

My head whips up at that, my eyes bulging as the small flame of jealousy I felt earlier increases to a near inferno. Cathy smirks like the cat who got the cream as she sips on her water.

"Liar. I've been with Jeff for three years. Although I can appreciate how hot Mr. Kane is, there has definitely never been anything more between him and anyone in the office."

I slightly relax at her words, but then immediately scold myself because why on earth did I get so tense so quickly in the first place? This is Atlas, the same man who taught me how to swim. He was there the first time I rode a bike, when I lost my first tooth. Hell, he was there the day I was born. He is about as unappealing to me as it gets.

I just have recognized how physically appealing he is. That's all.

"It's okay. Your secret is safe with me. He's gorgeous and a really great man. Not to mention the forbidden fruit and all that. Sounds steamy." She smirks.

I roll my eyes, doing my best to keep up my crumbling ruse.

"Gross. He's like forty. I'm eighteen."

"Age is just a number, hun. Love is love."

I narrow my eyes at her knowing smirk before choosing to ignore her. She's trouble for sure.

———

After lunch, Atlas has me come into his office where he shows me some of the back end of things that he's working on. I'm currently looking at some blueprints on his laptop while he sits at his desk and shows me the addition that he designed.

I've been doing my best to stay focused on his words, to absorb as much information as I can and file it away but ever since lunch my brain has been hardly functioning. When I sat down, I watched almost transfixed as Atlas undid the cuffs of his dress shirt before rolling the sleeves up to his elbows, exposing his corded forearms.

I could feel Atlas's eyes on me after a few moments and I pretended to be distracted by an imaginary piece of lint on his shirt that I quickly brushed at before returning my focus to the computer. Pathetic, I know.

The rest of the workday thankfully goes by soon. My head is spinning from all the new information that I'm expected to learn and as nice as everyone was, I'm definitely ready for the day to be done. Atlas asked me on the drive home how my first day was. I told him that it was a lot, but I thought that I would get the hang of it. He agreed that I'd be in the swing of things in no time, and we drove the rest of the way in silence.

When we get back to the house, I pause for a moment in the garage. I should probably go back to my house soon. It's time, isn't it? I haven't had a nightmare in two days. Hopefully it stays that way, and I really don't want to burden Atlas or even Theo. They need their space back and I need mine. My stomach sours instantly at the thought of returning to that cold empty home.

Soon. I'll go back soon.

Today is an unusually hot day for only being early June and now that I'm not in a nice, air-conditioned office I can tell. I decide to head up to my room and slip on my swimsuit. I just washed my hair this morning so I don't really want to get it wet, but I could definitely go for getting some tanning in.

I choose my emerald-green bikini and throw on my white swim wrap before grabbing my Kindle and sunglasses as I head downstairs. When I step outside I instantly freeze. My eyes are solely focused on the long, toned arms, cutting through the silky water of the pool like butter, stretching out as they push the large body through the water effortlessly.

Looks like I wasn't the only one who thought the pool sounded nice after a day of work. Debating on turning around and going back to my room, I decide against it when I hear the splashing stop and glance over to see that Atlas has spotted me. I give him a tight smile and a little wave as I walk over to one of the lounge chairs, setting down my Kindle before shucking off my wrap and lying down.

With my sunglasses on, I pretend to be looking at my Kindle but out of the corner of my eye, I can't help but notice that Atlas has yet to resume his swimming. Instead he is just floating in the water, almost completely still as his eyes burn holes into me. His jaw is tight, eyes narrowed. He looks downright pissed off that I'm out here. Is this his unwind time or something? Am I ruining that by being out here? God, this is why staying here was a bad idea.

I'm ready to get up and leave since I'm clearly upsetting him and ruining whatever it is he was doing but before I can a harsh sloshing noise of the water sounds before Atlas's body is out of the pool and striding over to the towel on the lounger near the hot tub to my right. He doesn't even spare me a second glance as he walks inside the house, dripping water as the back door practically slams shut behind him.

I get that maybe he wanted some time to himself, but did he have to be so rude?

Chapter 12
Atlas

Something's wrong.

I don't know what's going on. I think grief has finally started digging its nasty claws into me with everything it's got because it feels like I'm losing my goddamn mind.

I've known Andromeda since the day she was born. I was in the waiting room for fifteen hours, excited to finally meet my goddaughter. I've been by her side through skinned knees, first dates, and everything in between.

She's always been a pretty girl just like her mom, but it's like something has suddenly changed. Maybe it's the contacts or the new clothes. Or maybe I'm just going fucking insane because yesterday when Andromeda took off her coverup by the pool, the first thought that popped into my head was how goddamn sexy she looked.

Jesus, I'm going to hell.

I run my fingers through my hair, doing my best to banish the mental image of her tanned skin practically glowing in the mid-afternoon sun as she lay down on my poolside chair. I've been trying to forget it ever since yesterday but if anything, it's only embedded itself deeper.

The image of her back slightly arching, her barely covering bikini straining at the movement as she settled in to start reading has been etched into the deepest darkest part of my mind. A part that I didn't know even existed until yesterday. A part where salacious images of my fucking goddaughter play on repeat.

"Fucking hell," I curse as I squeeze my eyes shut while rubbing at my temples. What the fuck is happening to me?

Opening my eyes, I stare blankly at my computer screen, doing my best to focus on the blueprints Dillon sent me when a soft knock comes from my door. Andromeda pokes her head in, her soft blonde curls falling over her shoulders as she steps in a little more. Despite my best efforts, I find my eyes briefly wandering over her outfit. A tight black skirt that stops just above her knees and a sleeveless red blouse that looks professional in theory but clings to her soft curves like a second skin. My jaw clenches in irritation. Is she doing this on purpose? Dressing like this to mess with my head?

"Sorry to bother you, Atlas. I just had a question on—"

"It's Mr. Kane when we're at work," I snap, pure frustration practically oozing out of each syllable.

Surprise flashes across her face before irritation takes over.

"Sorry, *Mr. Kane*. I had a question on the proposal you forwarded to me but on second thought, I'll get Cathy's opinion."

She practically storms out of my office as quickly as she came in. Though I'm relieved she's gone so I don't have to look at her in that inappropriately tight outfit, I can't help but feel a ball of guilt form inside my chest at how I spoke to her.

Pushing it aside for now, I focus back on work and am thankfully able to get lost in it for a few hours. When I glance at the clock, I see that it's almost time for my meeting with Charles Abner. We have done several projects for him and he's a no-nonsense kind of man if not a bit of a prick. But he's a big client, so we all handle him with wide smiles on our faces.

I quickly print off the preliminary designs that I mocked up based on his initial request since he's old school and likes everything on paper and in person before grabbing my briefcase as I step outside my office.

Andromeda is at the printer skimming through papers when one slips out of her hand. She quickly bends down to grab it and of course, she just has to be facing away from me. Of course I would have to walk out at the exact moment that her perky peach-shaped ass is in the air in that fucking skirt. I feel the blood rush begin to my cock at the sight no matter how much I berate myself to not get turned on at the sight of my goddaughter on her knees in front of me.

Son of a fucking bitch.

She quickly gets to her feet, her heels clicking against the floor as she looks up at me.

"Are these for you?" she asks, holding up Abner's designs.

I nod. "Grab your purse, we're gonna be late," I say briskly, clearing the tension from my throat as I walk off, not waiting a second to make sure she will follow.

Part of me hopes she won't. Right now, I need space from Andromeda Clarke. A lot of it from the look of things. Unfortunately for me, she hustles and is next to me in a matter of seconds. We ride the elevator down together in silence and that silence is only broken when we climb into the car, and she asks where we're going.

"Shouldn't you know that? You are my assistant, after all."

Her eyes narrow at me as she turns slightly in her seat.

"What is your problem?"

I cut her a sideways look as I maneuvered out of the parking garage and toward the restaurant.

"What do you mean?"

"You've been snapping at me all morning. What's going on? It's my second day. I'm doing my best and you are quite frankly being a prick."

My eyebrows shoot up at that as I glance at her again.

"First tip to being successful in the workplace, you should avoid calling your boss a prick, especially to his face."

She scoffs as she crosses her arms across her chest.

"I call it like I see it. I'm not going to apologize for being right. So, what's your problem?"

Her attitude has my jaw clenching but confusingly my cock stiffening in my pants, even more so than when she was bent over a few minutes ago. I'd love nothing more than to beat her tight little ass red for being such a smart-ass.

FUCK.

I shake my head, choosing to ignore her. Mainly because I can't trust what will come out of my mouth if I do. Jesus, Atlas. This is fucking Andromeda. Andromeda Clarke. Paul and Em's daughter. Theo's ex-girlfriend. I've never had an impure thought about her a day in my life until twenty-four hours ago.

Now, it's like a pair of rose-colored glasses have been ripped off my face and I'm seeing her for the first time. I'm hearing her words like never before, watching her with a steadiness that I never would have even fathomed.

I need to let out some of this built-up tension, immediately. Anyone will do at this point. Just as long as they aren't the stunning blonde with bright-green eyes in my passenger seat.

Finally, we are pulling up to The White Pelican and handing the valet the keys to the car. Andromeda gets out behind me. We are quickly welcomed and shown to our table where Abner is already seated and looks to be enjoying a glass of scotch. It's probably the only thing me and the old bastard can see eye to eye on.

His beady eyes land on me as he nods his head in greeting, not bothering to stand up as I shake his hand.

"Kane, good to see you," he says in his usually gruff tone.

"Charles." I nod. "Thanks for meeting with me. This is my assistant, Andromeda. She will be sitting in with us today."

Abner's eyes run over Andromeda from head to toe, slowly pausing on her chest before he gives her a grin that can only be described as smarmy. He stands up, quickly adjusting his suit jacket as he takes her hand.

"Pleasure to meet you, my dear. Charles Abner," he introduces with a gleam in his eye like he is expecting a reaction out of her.

Andromeda smiles politely as she shakes his hand. "Nice to meet you, sir."

"Oh please, call me Charles." He winks before bringing the back of her hand to his mouth and pressing an excessively long kiss to the back of it.

I find my fists curling at my sides before I quickly shake them out. Andromeda does her best at keeping her smile in place, but I watch as it tightens at the corners and her eyes narrow slightly. Finally, she is able to extract her hand from his grip as she pulls away.

The table is set for four and I don't miss how Abner not so subtly pulls out the chair next to him like he seriously expects Andromeda to sit next to him. I quickly put my hand on her lower back, ushering her into the seat across from the empty one so that she could be as far away from him as possible.

The gesture doesn't go unnoticed by Andromeda who shoots me a small thankful look. Apparently, it doesn't go unnoticed by Abner either who shoots me a narrowed glare.

Pulling out the preliminary designs I hand them to Abner and dive right into business while Andromeda pulls out a small notepad and pen and begins jotting down Abner's comments, or more accurately, complaints.

I take them all in stride, nodding like some of his ideas are brilliant and pointing out why others won't be doable because that's not the way fucking gravity works. The man can run a multimillion-dollar hotel chain but can't understand basic physics.

The entire lunch, Abner found every excuse possible to catch Andromeda's attention. Whether it was boasting about his wealth or accomplishments and even going as far as trying to reach out and touch her, which I quickly intervened in every time. My normal irritation that I have during meetings with him has increased tenfold. The moment we had finally come to some sort of conclusion for now, I was paying the check and practically dragging Andromeda out of that place.

As soon as my fingers wrapped around the bare skin in the crook of her elbow, I felt goose bumps erupt over her skin. I glanced down at her curiously, but I didn't say anything. The air conditioning was set to high in the restaurant, but it didn't feel too cold. The heavy look in her eyes as she looked up at me though, had that dark part in my mind flaring to life, whispering salacious fueled thoughts that should never come to mind. At least not about Andromeda Clarke.

———

The feel of something wet and warm slowly wakes me up. I blink my eyes blurrily, barely half awake as I glance to see the moonlight shining in through my bedroom window. I'm about to fall completely back to sleep when a soft sucking noise captures my attention. Pleasure runs from the base of my spine to the tip of my cock as what I now recognize as a warm wet mouth tightens around me, taking me deeper down a slim throat.

Fuck. I can't remember the last time I've had my cock sucked. It's been too fucking long. My hands wander down to the mystery goddess, burying my fingers into a head of silky hair as she eagerly bobs up and down faster, running her tongue up and down the length of me as she does.

"Shit, yes. Just like that," I encourage lowly.

She hums around my cock in agreement, causing my balls to tighten at the vibration. Holy hell, where did I meet this girl? I try to remember if I went out last night and brought someone home, but nothing comes to mind. Not exactly surprising. Since Em and Paul, I've been drinking heavier than normal. Blacking out and bringing home a woman isn't all that out of character right now.

I'm surprised at how good she is working me over. I take the most gratification in giving pleasure but goddamn, receiving it like this is fucking amazing. I begin thrusting my hips, pushing deeper and deeper down her throat. The sound of her gagging sends an extra rush of pleasure through me as I quicken my pace. She adjusts her angle to take me deeper as her hair slips through my fingers and falls across her face.

Her smooth hands reach down to start massaging my balls and they instantly draw up at her touch. Holy fuck, I'm gonna fill her sweet little throat with my cum if she doesn't stop soon. I don't know if I said that out loud or if she's just a mind reader because she continues massaging my balls and gently dragging her soft fingers underneath them.

I feel the tingling in the base of my spine start and I know I don't have long. I'm suddenly desperate to see the face of my mystery woman. To watch as her eyes widen with surprise as I empty myself in her heavenly mouth.

When I brush the soft hair out of her face it takes me a few moments to make out anything but darkness. But when my eyes finally adjust and the moonlight shines just right, my heart drops at what I see.

Andromeda's full lips are wrapped around the head of my cock, her bright-green eyes looking up at me intently as she takes me deeper. Oh, fuck. I have to stop this. Push her away. Kick her out. This is so wrong. She shouldn't be here. Shouldn't be touching me like this. She shouldn't feel so good.

"Nevaeh," I choke out, hoping to god I'm wrong, hoping to god this is just some sick twisted hallucination, no matter how goddamn good her mouth is.

Her eyes give a seductive little twinkle before nodding softly as she continues sucking the life out of my cock.

Goddamn. What a good fucking girl.

What should have ended this whole thing becomes my undoing as my eyes roll into the back of my head my cock throbbing ready to come when a knock sounds at the door. I whip my head over to it before glancing down between my legs where Andromeda is...or was. Suddenly, she's gone, and the late-night moon has shifted into the morning sun.

"Atlas? Are you up? It's six forty," Andromeda's voice calls out through the door.

My head spins as it tries to catch up to everything. I reach over to grab my phone, my eyes bugging out of my head when I see that I slept in. I fucking never sleep in, ever. I never had erotic dreams about my goddaughter either, so I guess today is a day full of firsts.

I'm not just going to hell. I'm gonna fucking *burn*.

"I'll be ready in ten. Can you start some coffee?" I ask, doing my best to keep my voice steady when in fact my hands are shaking uncontrollably because what in the actual fuck?

"Already done. I'll make you some breakfast while you get ready," she says.

"Thanks," I rasp, running a hand down my face as I hurry into the shower.

I turn on the water quickly, doing my best to rush through my morning routine. But my cock has other plans. *I will not touch my cock to the thought of my goddaughter. I will not touch my cock to the thought of my goddaughter.*

Repeating the mantra continuously as I rinse out the shampoo in my hair, I reach down and give it a sharp tug, doing my best to get my suddenly raging hard-on to fuck off. The image of Andromeda's pink puffy lips wrapped around the head of my cock springs to life, causing a bead of precum to leak.

Goddammit. Fuck burning. I'm gonna be incinerated for this.

My hand grips my cock tighter, knowing it won't take much to get me there. I just need to get this shit out of my system and then I can forget it ever happened. I close my eyes, thinking about the vivid dream, the soft noises she made, the way her mouth molded around me like she was made for me. God, it all felt so real. Then mental flashes of her in that green bikini comes to the front of my mind and her in those tight outfits that she's been wearing around the office for the last week.

We haven't even been working together for a week and I can already tell it's going to end in disaster. Why do I say that? I'm currently stroking my cock in the shower to the thought of an eighteen-year-old fucking *girl*. Not just any girl, the only one I can never have. The one I should never want to have in the first place.

The bathroom door is suddenly thrown open just as I feel my balls begin to draw up.

"Hey, Dad. You in here?" Theo asks.

"Jesus!" I shout, quickly turning away from the glass shower door before Theo can see what I was doing. "What's the matter with you?"

"Sorry. I just wanted to let you know my work is sending me up to their Seattle location for the rest of the week. I should be back by Sunday."

"Seattle? For what?"

"They need extra hands with an opening, they are sending several of us."

It's hard for me to clear the fog clouding my mind enough to come up with a coherent thought. Funny enough having your son walk in on you jerking off to the thought of his ex-girlfriend is enough to send your mind scrambling.

"Awesome, Theo. Do I need to take you to the airport or something?"

"Nah, they are covering it all. Just wanted to let you know I'm not gonna be around for a bit."

"Alright. Text me when you get to Seattle."

"Will do," Theo calls out over his shoulder.

I lean my head against the tiled shower as the previously warm water cools down with a bitter chill as it pours over me. Just Andromeda and me at work and in the house all alone for a week.

Fucking perfect.

Chapter 13
Andromeda

When Atlas is finally ready, he takes the coffee and protein shake I made for him as I grab my own before we head out to the door. I was surprised when it was past six thirty and I still hadn't seen Atlas downstairs. He is usually an early riser, so him sleeping in was definitely not normal.

Nothing about Atlas seems to be normal lately, though. Or maybe I never knew him as well as I thought I did. He always came across as the caring respectful man that I've known my whole life. But after living with him for a little over two weeks and working with him for one, I can say that is definitely not the Atlas I've seen.

At work, he is constantly snapping at me or glaring. He looks me up and down nearly every day like my outfits offend him and he rarely ever looks me in the eye, like I'm not worthy of his eye contact.

I don't know what to think about the disrespectful attitude but as far as clothes I know I was dressing up a little more than everyone else and maybe I was coming across like I was trying too hard or something. This morning I decided to switch it up and just wear a nice pair of cream-colored trousers and a white blouse. Unfortunately the moment he stepped into the room he narrowed his sharp gaze at my clothes before shaking his head and storming toward his car. So I guess it doesn't matter what I do at this point.

At the house it's almost worse. He avoids me at nearly every turn. If I'm in the kitchen and he needs some water, he turns around and goes to the garage fridge. If he's in the pool and I go outside, he comes right in. It's like he can't stand to even breathe the same air as me. I'm finally to the point where I don't think I can handle walking on eggshells. No matter how much I don't want to go back to my house, I can't stay here anymore.

"I called a real estate agent," I say as we drive down the road.

Atlas's eyebrows furrow as he continues to look straight ahead.

"For what?"

"To sell the house. I can't live there without them. It just feels... wrong. I haven't paid it off with the insurance money yet and it's worth over two hundred grand what is owed on the mortgage, so I'll just take that money and some of my inheritance and buy a new house. Or rent for a bit before I go to college. I don't know yet."

The car is thick with silence for several seconds. At first I don't think he is going to respond at all before he gently clears his throat.

"I think you should hold off on any rash decisions until you go to college at least. You're still, trying to figure out how to go about your day-to-day without them and—"

"And nothing, Atlas," I cut off bitterly. "I'm not trying to figure anything out. My parents are dead and the one home I've ever known no longer feels like it. I'm staying in a house that I'm unwelcome in with someone who can hardly stand to be near me," I snap, accidentally letting the hurt in my words bleed through.

Atlas quickly turns on his turn signal, pulling off to the side of the road before turning the ignition off and facing me.

"What are you talking about? You think I can't stand to be around you?" he asks, seemingly baffled.

I can't help but let out a disbelieving chuckle. Is he serious?

"I *know* you can't. You're an asshole to me at work and you avoid me like the plague at the house. I get it, you opened your doors to be nice and out of some sense of duty to my parents, but you clearly don't want me here. And I'm honestly sick of feeling so displaced."

Atlas opens his mouth to speak but pauses, rubbing a hand down his face for a second before looking at me.

"Nevaeh, that's not it. It's just different. I can't be easy on you at work—"

I let out a scoff as I shook my head. "Oh my god, cut the bullshit. I'm the only one who gets snarly demanding Atlas. I honestly don't know what I did to deserve the treatment that you've given me lately but frankly, I'm tired of it. I was going to do this later but I'm quitting. I found another internship that has already accepted me at Prism downtown."

A look of hurt flashes across Atlas's face at my words as he thinks over them for a second before blowing out a heavy breath and nodding.

"I'm sorry, Nevaeh. You're right. I've been an asshole. I'm just trying to keep it together and I'm failing. That's all on me, not you. I don't want you to go, especially not to my competitor, but I don't blame you for wanting to leave."

He pauses as he lets out a dry laugh and runs his hand against his freshly shaven face.

"Guess I didn't do a great job at giving you a good impression of the job to begin with, huh?"

"Not terribly, no. You've always been nothing but nice to me, what's changed?"

He pauses for a second, his eyes scanning over my face carefully before I see the true pain behind them bleed through as he comes up to meet my gaze.

"Everything."

My heart aches at his words. He isn't wrong.

I hesitate for a moment before reaching my hand out and placing it on his forearm. He glances down at the touch before giving me a heavy look. After a few seconds, he lets out a heavy sigh as he closes his eyes. When he opens them, the pain and weight of everything clearly weighing on him seems to have disappeared, and that in-control mask is back in place.

Atlas starts the car again and turns back onto the road before he speaks again.

"I'm sorry. I'll do better," he says like a promise.

"You don't owe me anything, Atlas. You've done enough for me. You've done enough for everyone. When was the last time you paused for just a moment to do something for yourself?"

He glances over at me, his forehead creasing like he's trying to think of an instance before he shakes his head and faces forward.

That's what I thought.

When we get to the parking garage at work, I go to open my door when a heavy hand touches my knee. I look up to see Atlas watching me closely, a small amount of vulnerability on display like when he had pulled over.

"I don't want you to leave. I don't want you to stop working here," he says softly. "I can see how my behavior has come across like you are a burden or that I don't want you around but it's the opposite. Sometimes I want you around too much."

I'm stunned, frozen into place. Is he saying that he...I honestly don't know how to take that. Suddenly his hand feels heavier than before, warmer. Tingles are running up my leg from the contact alone as heat pools in my stomach.

I lick my lips and Atlas's eyes snap down to my mouth, tracking the action slowly. My breath suddenly stalls in my chest as I see Atlas's eyes darken. My heart is racing inside my chest as my stomach twists with anticipation. In the next blink of an eye though, the heat I thought I saw is gone, replaced with a warm if not familial look.

"I'll do better," he promises. "Just, hold off on making any big decisions for now, please?"

Nodding softly, I agree which causes him to give me one of his breathtaking smiles that makes my stomach flip. Oh god. He should warn someone before he busts one of those out. I swear, he never used to smile like that. I would have noticed.

I don't realize that I'm just sitting here staring at Atlas wordlessly until he speaks.

"Well, let's see if we can get through a workday without your boss being a 'prick' as you say," he says with half a smirk.

I let out a light laugh as I opened the door and stepped out. "I won't hold my breath."

Atlas chuckles as he locks the car and rests his lower hand on my back, guiding us toward the elevator. I do my best to ignore the sparks that fly up my back from the heat of his palm resting against the thin material of my shirt, but I do a terrible job. God what is happening?

––––––

Cathy and I have become good friends over the last week of work. She has been amazing at teaching me as much as she can before she leaves. We've had lunch almost every day together and on top of being awesome with helping me learn how to do the job, she is hilarious. She told me all about how she met her fiancé Jeff. Apparently, he was a client of ours and fell for Cathy the moment he met her. She also told me that she didn't give in to him for a while because of their significant age difference.

She was twenty-four, and he was thirty-seven. Despite her hesitance though, she fell for him hard and now they've been together for three years and are getting married this weekend. It's amazing how fundamentally crucial yet insignificant at moments time can be.

"So, this is what Dillon's schedule is looking like when he gets back. Since you'll be helping out both him and Atlas, I want to make sure you are well prepared. Atlas doesn't really need any management with his schedule, but Dillon is like a child. He will probably ask you seven times a day where he is supposed to be," Cathy says with a chuckle.

"I'm not sure how I feel about this Dillon character," I say with only a touch of sincerity. "Atlas says he is like his protégé, but you make him sound like my worst nightmare."

Cathy laughs and shakes her head. "No, no. He's great, you'll like him, and I have a feeling that he is going to love you."

"Really?" I ask with a raised brow. "Why do you say that?"

She gets a mischievous look in her eye before shrugging. Well that is a little unsettling.

After work is done, Atlas and I get in the car but instead of going straight to the house, he pulls into the grocery store.

"I thought we could make something instead of just getting takeout every night. My gym routine can't keep up with the carb intake we are going at," he says as he pats at his completely ripped stomach.

I can't help but laugh at that but nod as we walk inside. I quickly pull out my phone and go on Pinterest to see what we should make. It takes a little bit of scrolling before I find a recipe for lemon chicken and roasted asparagus that we both agree on. It doesn't take us long to get all of the ingredients and get the groceries back to the house.

Atlas insisted on carrying all the groceries inside and I wasn't going to argue with him, so I held the door open for him before he set the bags on the counter. From there we split up the tasks. Atlas preps the food while I cook it. Mainly because I don't trust him not to burn the place down like that poor piece of french toast.

"You're cutting the asparagus too high," I say as I look around his massive shoulders to see that he is making the asparagus spears appear more like asparagus nubs.

He gives me a mock glare before tossing an asparagus nub at me.

"Mind your business. I prep, you cook. That's the deal," he says, his lips twitching in amusement.

"Yeah, you're giving me a lot to work with."

Atlas lets out a short huff that sounds more like a laugh as he looks at me.

"Brat."

I smile at him sweetly, though it must not be very convincing because one of his eyebrows raise in suspicion, causing both of us to begin laughing.

"I'm sorry I offended your delicate male ego. They are lovely. I can't wait to eat these asparagus nubs," I say with that same cheesy smile.

Amusement sparkles in Atlas's rich eyes as he gives me a crooked smirk.

"Good girl."

The way his thick voice rolls over that word sends a shiver up my spine. The temporary euphoria I was feeling from the teasing and laughing has been amplified with two words alone. It's not like I'm not used to being praised, I've always been an overachiever and done my best to do a good job at everything I do. Hearing those words fall from Atlas's lips are something all in its own, though.

Atlas is staring at me quietly, his mind seemingly racing the way my own is. Though I would bet anything the thoughts are not even in the same hemisphere of what is swirling in my mind. Turning my attention to the chicken, I walk over to the other side of the kitchen and continue cooking our meal.

Twenty minutes later, we are able to sit down and eat our delicious, yet very small chunked dinner.

"Can I ask you something?" Atlas asks after a few minutes.

"Sure."

"Why are you trying to protect Theo?"

I'm caught off guard for a moment before I do my best to school my expression.

"What do you mean?"

"Don't play dumb with me, Nevaeh. You're too smart for that and I know you too well. Theo did something to end you two. Not sure if it was the full reason why you two broke up or if it was the straw that broke the camel's back but either way, he did something."

"Why would you think that? Maybe I did something?" I counter.

"Because of the argument I interrupted right after you two broke up. Because anytime he is around you, still, he acts like a skittish cat, constantly on edge. You weren't around for the weeks following your split, but I was. He was devastated, moping around the house, moodier than ever. He was acting like a man that had lost it all, not thrown it all away."

"Well, you got that last part wrong," I mutter as I take a sip of my water before mentally smacking myself. Why on earth did I just say that?

Atlas immediately latches on to my comment as he cocks his head to the side curiously.

"What do you mean?"

I let out a heavy sigh as I pushed my plate away and crossed my arms over my chest.

"Look, it doesn't matter. What's in the past is in the past. Neither of us wants to dwell on it, we just want to move on. Why do you care so much? Why can't you just let it go? Are you disappointed that we aren't together anymore or something?"

Atlas frowns for a moment, appearing to be in thought before he shakes his head.

"No. If I'm being completely honest, I think it was probably for the best. You guys were always great friends, best friends, but that doesn't always mean that you will be great in any other capacity. You two are different in a lot of ways that matter when you are in a relationship. You're driven, grounded. Whereas Theo is more of a free spirit, he likes to go with the flow, drift along, and see where life takes him."

His words hit me in a way I hadn't expected. I had never thought that Theo and I were incompatible, not once. But after months of being apart and taking a step back from it all, I see Atlas's point. Yeah, we always got along great and had things in common like favorite TV shows and food. But is that from our soul's compatibility or just being raised on the same traditions and habits since our parents were best friends?

"To answer your question, though," he continues. "I guess I don't have a good reason behind why I've been so insistent to know the truth. I think for me it's more about the fact that you haven't felt comfortable enough to talk to me. I used to feel like you would tell me anything. It felt like we had this trust, I guess."

I glance down at my lap for a moment. He's right. Atlas was always my confidant. When I knew my parents wouldn't approve of something or I needed advice, I would almost always go to him. He kept more secrets than I can count and was the sounding voice a lot of the times when my young self couldn't comprehend why my parents would do or say something. Maybe I've just been lying to myself, thinking that I've been avoiding the topic because I wanted to protect Theo. Maybe I've been avoiding it all because deep down I still feel embarrassed that I was made out to be such a fool. I think that is a bigger part of it than I originally considered because when the words slip past my lips, embarrassment instantly burns through me.

"He cheated on me."

I expect Atlas to respond instantly but he doesn't. Several seconds go by before I chance a look only to see him staring at me with a steady yet cold gaze, the fork in his right hand being clenched tighter than any utensil should ever need to be. His chocolate eyes burn a hole straight through me as his jaw flexes several times before he speaks.

"Come again?" he questions lowly, his voice gruff and tight.

"Before spring break, when I went to surprise him at OSU, well, I really surprised him," I laugh hollowly. "I walked into his dorm room to find him balls deep in some girl."

The corners of Atlas's eyes tense at that. "I didn't need to hear that."

"Yeah, well, I didn't need to see it, but I did. And it was awful. The worst part though was she said that he had been trying to hook up with her all semester. It wasn't a drunken mistake. It wasn't a lapse in judgment. He was actively trying to cheat on me for months before the girl finally hooked up with him."

Atlas looks equal parts angered and disappointed as he shakes his head at me.

"I'm sorry, Nevaeh. I'm sorry that my son treated you with such little respect. I'm sorry that he humiliated you, that he no doubt made you question your own self-worth in that moment and maybe after as well."

My chest lightly aches at his words. He's speaking the thoughts that I've never uttered to anyone but have thought dozens of times.

"But know this," he continues. "It was him, not you. He was the problem, not you. He is the fuck up in this, not you. You are a smart, kind, driven, beautiful woman and any man would be lucky just to have the honor to call you his. My son wasted his chance with you, and I can promise he will regret it for the rest of his life."

My stomach flips at his words as my breathing stalls slightly. Wow. I don't think anyone has spoken to me like that, well, ever. I open my mouth to say something, but my brain is stuck on his words.

Any man would be lucky just to have the honor to call you his.

Is it stupid if a small part of me hopes that he really means *any* man? Probably. Yes, definitely. I shouldn't have even thought that. Why the hell can't I shut these thoughts off?

Before I have the chance to say something, Atlas stands, grabbing my plate as well as his before moving into the kitchen. Probably for the best.

I stand up and join him and we clean up dinner and the kitchen in a fairly comfortable albeit heavy silence.

Chapter 14
Atlas

The next day is long, but the Michaels project is finally closed out which is good. My full focus has shifted to Abner's project, though I'm not sure how much of an improvement that is since I dislike him more than I do Jonathan Michaels. I tell myself that it's because he is a demanding asshole with unrealistic expectations and not because of the fact that he salivated over Andromeda like she was a delicacy. The thought alone has my fists tightening in irritation. I'll be more than ready to be done with this project as soon as humanly possible.

When we got home, Andromeda said that she was going for a swim since it's been so hot today. I nodded my head as I went to my room to change and get as far away from my pool as possible without being obvious. My next-door neighbor Dolores is a seventy-six-year-old widow who is probably the sweetest woman you'll ever meet. I mow her lawn once a week during the summer to help her out and I'm ashamed to admit that it's been two weeks now since I've made it over there.

I don't bother knocking since she keeps everything in the shed around the side of the house and her little ankle-biter dogs go crazy any time anyone comes to the front door. Normally I try to mow on the cooler days or a little later when the heat isn't so sweltering, but I could use the distraction.

Firing up the mower, I go to work on her lawn. I glance over at her garden bed as I pass by, noticing that it's looking a lot more run-down than it usually does. Maybe I should have a few bags of bark delivered, freshen it up a bit for her. She can't get out here as much as she used to anymore, unfortunately, but I remember ten years ago or so she would spend hours and hours working on making her garden immaculate.

It doesn't take me long to finish up, but it doesn't matter, my shirt is practically sticking to me from the heat. I peel the T-shirt off my back as I wipe my forehead with it when I hear the front door open.

"Have I ever told you how much I love you?" Dolores asks as she makes her way over to me.

I smile at her as I nod. "A time or two."

She grins as she hands me what I know to be a loaf of her banana bread.

"You know you don't have to do this, Dolores," I say as I take the bread, knowing she won't accept no for an answer.

She predictably waves me off as she shakes her head.

"It's the least I can do, Atlas. How have you been doing?" she asks as she casts a sad look over to the Clarke's house.

"I'm hanging in there. One day at a time."

She nods sympathetically. "That's all any of us can do. How's Andromeda doing? The poor dear."

My chest twists just at the mention of her name as I nod and blow out a soft breath.

"Doing better, I think."

"Good. I haven't heard her screaming in a while from those terrible nightmares."

"You heard her too?" I wince.

"Sweetie, I think the whole neighborhood did. Can't say I blame her."

"She's staying with me and Theo right now. I think it's helping."

"That's probably for the best. The loneliness is often the worst part." She smiles sadly. "Well, I've got to get inside. My damn faucet is leaking again."

"Let me take a look at it," I say as I start walking with her.

"Oh, no. You do too much already. Thank you, though."

"I insist," I say as I reach the front door, holding it open for her. "Just keep those rats you call dogs at bay, and I'll handle the faucet."

She lets out a laugh and shakes her head as she steps inside and leads me to the kitchen.

———

Once I tightened Dolores's faucet, she sent me on my way with the banana bread and an apple pie that she had just pulled from the oven. I tried to turn her down, but she insisted, and I knew better than to argue.

When I make my way inside the house, I look out the back window to see that the pool is empty, thankfully. I set the banana bread and pie on the counter, having faith that if it's in plain sight Theo will gladly take it off my hands when he gets back from his trip. When I turn to head upstairs, I pause and notice Andromeda sitting at the dining room table to the side.

"I didn't see you there," I say.

Her hair is still wet, probably from the pool but she's wearing a pair of shorts and a T-shirt as she sits in her seat staring at the Scrabble box that's on the built-in shelf next to the table. I don't think she heard me come in or that I just spoke to her because she hasn't broken her stare on the board game yet.

"Nevaeh?" I ask tentatively as I take a step closer.

Suddenly, her eyes snap away from the box and over to me, her eyes slightly glassy as she screws on a plastic smile.

"Hey, were you mowing Mrs. Reynold's yard?"

I nod as she smiles. "That was nice of you. I feel like you've been doing it forever."

I shrug. "Only since Larry passed away a few years ago."

She nods, a heavy silence weighing on us as her gaze travels back to the box.

"Do you want to play?" I ask, half expecting her to turn me down. She did all the other times I've offered over the last few months.

Andromeda looks over to me, her mouth partially open for a few moments before she nods.

"Okay, let me just jump in the shower. Want to set it up?"

"Sure," she says as she grabs the game and begins unboxing it as I head upstairs.

Once I rinse off and throw on a pair of sweats and a new T-shirt, I make my way downstairs to see the table all set up. I grab us a couple of waters before taking the seat across from her and grabbing my seven tiles.

"Ladies first," I say with a head nod.

She looks over her tiles before spelling *fiz*.

"Fifteen points," she says as she writes it down on the scratch paper she has.

I nod as I scan over my letters.

"Ax. Nine points," I say as I lay my tiles out.

Andromeda jots that down before choosing her next word. It doesn't take long to fall into a familiar comfortability. I can practically see the heaviness that seems to always surround her these days lifting with each word.

"*Fozy*. Nineteen points," I say proudly.

"*Fozy?* That's not a word."

"It is."

She shakes her head as she pulls out her phone and looks it up, Seconds later she looks up, scowling at me as she mutters what a stupid word that is.

"Don't be a sore loser, Nevaeh. I'm the best, it's understandable that you would feel undermined," I goad.

Her eyes narrow as she lines up *jiffy*. Happily jotting down her points.

I roll my eyes like I'm irritated with her even though I couldn't be more happy. This is the most I've seen her act like herself in months. For a little bit, I thought that this Nevaeh had died with Paul and Em. I'm glad she's still in there.

I'm running out of options, and I know we are neck and neck. I decide to just toss out what I have and throw out *icy*. Andromeda jots it down before looking at her tiles, pausing for a moment as she carefully lays out her words.

"*Gratify*. Fourteen points," she says, the room suddenly heavy with tension.

I've heard the word before, countless times. I've used it countless times, but something about hearing a word that is the literal definition of giving or receiving pleasure drip off her pillowy lips has my breath stalling and my cock stiffening.

Christ, what the fuck is wrong with me?

Neither of us speak for several seconds, our chests both rising and falling slowly as we watch each other, the tension between us sizzling to an uncomfortably all-time high. Fuck. I can't do this.

"I've got to jump on a call. What do we have for totals?" I ask.

My words seem to have shattered the lust-hazed bubble we inadvertently wrapped ourselves in and she quickly blinks before glancing down at the sheet.

"One hundred forty-eight for you, one hundred fifty-two for me."

I nod as I stand up, looking down at my phone like I'm expecting a call though I suspect she knows it's a lie. She does after all have full access to my schedule.

"Congratulations, Nevaeh. You got lucky," I say as I turn and start walking down the hall.

"Not lucky enough," she mumbles softly, so soft I doubt she knows I heard her. But the way my feet cemented to the ground the instant the words were uttered had me confident those words definitely slipped out of my goddaughter's mouth. Instead of turning back to find out what she meant or worse what I could do to change her response, I keep moving toward the stairs.

Chapter 15
Andromeda

The rest of the work week goes by a lot better than the first. Atlas doesn't bark at me or sneer at my outfits. He also doesn't avoid me like the plague at work. We've cooked something new every night this week. And although some have turned out worse than others (like last night's meatloaf which was more of a meat brick) it's been kinda fun. Relaxing, almost.

We also spend almost every night playing Scrabble. It goes back and forth on who wins each night, though he swears on the nights I win that I'm cheating.

It's Sunday today but it's also Atlas's birthday. Not like I would have known if I hadn't had his birthday memorized since I was a kid. It's exactly five months after mine so it's always been easy to remember. My mom used to always make him a German chocolate cake, his favorite and my dad would buy him a bottle of fancy scotch. Then we would all have dinner together just like any other night.

I picked up on it quickly that Atlas didn't like celebrating his birthday. He would smile and thank my parents, but you could tell there was a trace of sadness in his features. It didn't make sense to me when I was younger because why would anyone be sad on their birthday? Now I think I understand a little better.

His parents are gone, and he has no siblings. His definition of family started and ended with his best friends. On a day that he should be celebrating the beginning of his life and every year since then, he's left reflecting on how much he has lost versus what he has. Now that my parents are gone...I can only imagine how alone he must be feeling today.

I know he's home because his car is here, but he hasn't left his office ever since this morning. At around six at night, I finally knocked and asked if he had any requests but was met with the faint sound of typing on a keyboard and no response. I figured it was best if I just let him be, so I ended up heating up a frozen pizza that we had in the freezer.

Now I'm standing here, pacing outside of his office with a small, wrapped rectangle in my hand. It felt wrong to not acknowledge his birthday at all. Theo didn't get home from his work trip until three hours ago and he barely even gave me a wave before heading off to bed. I know that he's always felt that his dad is overbearing and too involved in his life, but he couldn't take two seconds to wish his dad a happy birthday? Tell him he loved him? Anything?

It didn't sit right with me, so I went across the street to my parents' house and grabbed a few things I needed. It was easier than I anticipated to walk in there for one of the first times in a while. Unsettling, most definitely, but the bone-crippling pain didn't set in immediately. It took poking my head into my father's office, seeing one of his signature gold pens lying on the desk for the hurt to take hold fully.

My father was practically obsessed with using exclusively these solid gold pens, I never really knew why, all I knew was that they filled his office and any junk drawer in our home. The sleek precious metal felt so familiar, yet so foreign at the same time. Before I knew what I was doing, I was slipping it into my pocket. It's just a pen and rather insignificant compared to many of his other belongings but for some reason, it gives me a small sense of peace having it in my possession. Like a small part of him is almost with me.

Now I find myself outside of Atlas's home office, too nervous to knock. What if he hates it? What if he's mad that I'm giving him anything to begin with? His attitude is so all over the place. I never know what version of Atlas I'm going to get these days. We just got into a place where I don't have to walk on eggshells around him and I don't want to mess that up.

Glancing down at the pretty bow wrapped around the gift, I decide to just get it over with, what's the worst that could happen? I'm trying to be nice and be there for him like he's always been there for me. If he doesn't appreciate it, that's on him, not me.

I raise my right hand and knock twice. There's no answer, so I try again. After a few more seconds with no response, I gently push the door open.

"Atlas?" I ask softly as I take a small step inside.

Instantly, I'm stunned at the sight before me. Atlas is resting his head in his hands as he slumps over his desk. Papers are strewn all over the place, his laptop haphazardly tossed to the other side of his desk and an empty scotch bottle is on its side next to a half-empty one. The heavy smell of the spicy liquor fills the air and with each step I take toward Atlas, the stronger it becomes.

"Atlas?" I question softly, starting to think that maybe he's asleep based on his lack of movement except for the slight breathing.

It takes a second before his head lifts just barely out of his hands, his glossy eyes gazing up at me as if confused as to where he is for a moment. He blinks hard before rubbing at them. It's the first time in a while that I really get a good look at Atlas, or maybe just the first time that I've really taken the time to notice him.

His hair has always been a dark black color but now I see the first peppering of gray at his temples. His skin was always perfectly tanned and smooth but fine lines near his eyes are suddenly there. I don't know if it's the result of the hard life he has had that is finally wearing down on him or if I've just never noticed these things until now, either way, it doesn't diminish his good looks. The man is still entrancing.

Those dark-chocolate eyes look up to me a little unfocused as his rough voice speaks.

"What are you doing here?"

I hesitate for a moment before I lift up the birthday gift in my hand.

"Everyone needs to open a gift on their birthday," I say as I carefully set it in front of him.

Atlas turns his attention to the black wrapping paper before his eyebrows furrow. I watch silently as he just stares at the present for several seconds. I'm ready to take the gift back when one of his large hands lifts from his lap, his fingers gently brushing across the red bow.

"It's not a lot," I say with a shrug as I cross my arms over my chest. "It's okay if you don't want to open it. I can take it back if you—"

I go to reach for the gift when Atlas's hands quickly grab the gift, tucking it into his lap possessively as he looks down at it before carefully undoing the paper. When the gift is unwrapped sitting in his lap, I hold my breath as his fingers still.

Glancing down at the picture of my parents and Atlas at their college graduation, I wonder if I made a mistake. It was one of my dad's favorites. He had it displayed on his desk at the house, it had been there ever since I can remember. I didn't know what to get a man who has virtually everything so I thought something sentimental would be best. Maybe that was the worst idea, though based on Atlas's lack of emotion.

"It was Dad's favorite picture of you guys," I whisper softly, trying to justify my action. "It was just sitting on his desk, and I thought maybe you would like to have it."

Unease seeps in as Atlas still doesn't respond, instead just brushing his fingers over the picture frame over and over again. After another minute or so, Atlas finally looks up at me. His eyes like glass, filled with unshed tears. This is only the second time I've ever seen Atlas cry in my entire life. He wasn't the emotional one, that title went to my mother. My dad was a close second, not Atlas, though. He was the strong one, the one who took everything on his shoulders with a nod of his head.

He squeezes his eyes shut hard, forcing a single tear to slip down his face before he quickly swipes it away.

"Thank you, Nevaeh. This means a lot."

I watch as the pain from his eyes slowly recedes, like he is physically forcing it down. I recognize the look from the mirror I stare into every morning. It doesn't hurt as bad when I'm here, though. At first, I thought it was because I just needed space from the memories but now, I'm wondering if it's just Atlas. Our pain blends together into a soothing concoction that helps ease the hurt inside me, at least for a little while.

Words feel useless right now, so instead I reach down and wrap my arms around Atlas's neck. He loops an arm around my lower back as he hugs me back. I don't know how long we stay like that but the ache that is almost permanently inside my chest eases a bit at the contact and it has me wanting to bury into this feeling and never come up for air again.

Before I can stop myself, I feel my mouth moving slowly against his smooth neck as I speak.

"It doesn't hurt as much when you're around."

His body stiffens before he eases away. Disappointment sinks into my stomach as I do the same, but I don't get far before Atlas's hold tightens on me once more, when my face is just above his. I watch as his eyes flick back and forth across my face, seemingly looking for something. I don't know what it is, but I wish I did. I'd do anything to know what's going on inside that head of his right now.

The smell of the freshly drank scotch and his cologne swirls around the small space between us and suddenly it's more intoxicating than any other scent I've ever experienced in my life. My stomach begins to flutter as I take my fill of Atlas, memorizing how full and soft his lips look, how deep his melted chocolate eyes are, how perfect he is.

Without meaning to, my tongue lightly runs across my bottom lip and Atlas's eyes snap down at the movement, his gaze tracking it steadily. The soft vulnerability that was in his eyes just moments ago dissipates as something darker, hungrier, takes over.

My stomach flips as my breathing stalls. This is a bad idea. I should move, go to bed. At least stop hugging him. Instead of doing any of that though, I lean closer and gently press my lips against his. The moment the softness of his mouth touches mine, sparks shoot through my body all the way down to my toes. My heart beats heavily as I slowly move my lips against his.

I can feel the thrumming of my blood in my veins, my heart pounding fiercely in my chest as the smoothness of his full lips brush against my own. The feeling of euphoria running through me is unlike any high I could ever describe. It's a weightless, empowering, soaring type of feeling. The kind that holds you in place, you can't move, you can hardly breathe. All you can do is exist in this moment.

I know I shouldn't be kissing him. This is wrong and taboo in every sense. Something has taken over me, though, and I can't stop. Maybe it's because it's Atlas, because this Titan of a man simply has this much power. Whatever the reason, I relish in it, feeling more alive in this moment than I've ever felt before.

When I dart my tongue out to brush against his lips, I realize that he hasn't moved since I initiated this kiss, not a muscle. Unsure of what to do, my adrenaline high ebbs as I slowly break the kiss, leaning back enough to look at him. His eyes are still darkened with what I took for lust, his muscles tight while his breathing labored.

After several heavy seconds, I go to speak but he holds a hand up, silencing me as he looks down at his lap, clenching his jaw tight before looking back up to me. All traces of desire are gone in an instant, replaced with pity and maybe even a hint of disgust.

Oh god. I misinterpreted the situation. He wasn't feeling anything except for pain over his friends and a bottle of whiskey. Then I threw myself at him...at my parent's best friend...who is looking at me like his own flesh and blood kissed him...oh god.

"That can never happen again," he says on a wince as he wipes the back of his hand across his mouth like the taste of me on his lips is the most vile thing he's ever endured.

I don't know why but the action hurts ten times more than his words. To my horror, my eyes begin to water as my throat tightens. Embarrassment has me in a choke hold to the point where I can't even speak. Shakily, I nod before I slip off his lap, turn on my heels and run out the door. Thankfully, Atlas doesn't call out to me or follow me and I'm able to hide in my room for the rest of the night.

Chapter 16
Andromeda

The next morning, I didn't ride with Atlas to work. Instead, I sucked up my fear of driving, got into my dad's car and drove myself to work. Theo was just coming downstairs to get ready for work when I did and he called out to me, but I was too focused on getting out of the house to respond.

I white knuckled it the entire drive and just about threw up when I finally made it to the office. I made sure to get up over a half an hour earlier than when Atlas does so that I could be long gone before he was ready for work so thankfully, I'll have a little time for myself. At least until I have to face him again and no doubt the full extent of my humiliation will overtake me.

When I get to the office, it's only me which I'm thankful for. I'm still trying to run different scenarios through my head about what exactly I'm going to say when Atlas no doubt questions me about last night. The only scenario I'm hoping for is that he was too shitfaced last night to even remember it and I can be embarrassed in peace.

Of course, he didn't want you to kiss him, Andromeda. He's known you since you were in diapers. Worse. He's known you since you were in your mother's womb. If he does remember, he's probably revolted by the thought of kissing you.

After I get my computer fired up, I'm walking over the blueprints

Atlas asked me to drop off to one of the architects, Keira, when I slam into something.

The papers go flying as hot liquid instantly singes my skin. I shout in surprise as I try to peel the searing shirt now soaked in what I can smell is coffee off myself as I look down at my previously white blouse. Perfect.

"Oh my god, are you okay? I'm so sorry. I didn't think anyone would be up here this early. I wasn't looking," a deep English accent says.

Glancing up from my stain, I look into a pair of light-blue eyes to see concern heavy in them as they look me over. I take half a step back to fully take in the stranger in front of me and when I do, my heart thunders. Holy shit. This has got to be one of the sexiest men I've ever seen in my life.

He looks to be in his early thirties or so. A dimpled smile slowly pops out as his perfectly styled blonde head cocks to the side slightly, watching me watch him. Oh god, I'm staring, aren't I?

"Sorry," I rasp, my throat suddenly drier than it was moments ago as I look up into those sky-blue eyes again. "I was looking over these," I say as I look down at the blueprints that are now ruined from the spilled coffee.

This morning keeps getting better and better.

The man looks at them and grimaces as he bends down and picks up what's left of the soggy papers before giving me a sympathetic look and tossing them in the trash.

"Probably best if you print them out again. I can do it if you give me the job number?" he offers with a kind smile.

"Wait, you work here?" I ask with furrowed brows.

He nods with that smile still in place as he extends his hand to me.

"Dillon Mathews."

"Oh, Dillon. I'm Andromeda."

Recognition flashes in his eyes as he looks me over like he's seeing me for the first time.

"The intern. Cathy's told me good things about you so far. If you're able to impress her, you must be something special."

His eyes twinkle the way he says special, not in a creepy way but in a way that oozes natural charm. I doubt this man has ever had to do much more than crack a smile to get his way with anything in life. He has this warmth emanating from him, this kindness. Like he is the type of guy who gets along with anyone. Then again, maybe that's just because of his jaw-dropping good looks and practically hypnotic accent. Either way, you won't hear me complain about him shooting that smile at me.

His smile begins to fade as his brows furrow when he looks at my stained shirt.

"Shit, I ruined your shirt. I'm so sorry. Do you have another on you?" he asks.

I glance down at the large dark-brown stain before grimacing and shaking my head. He nods.

"Follow me."

We take a few steps to my right before stepping into what I now know is his office. He walks inside and begins unbuttoning his white dress shirt. My eyes widen and I quickly turn my head to the side.

"Uh, what are you doing?" I ask.

He chuckles. "Fixing your wardrobe malfunction. As disappointed as I am that you didn't take the opportunity to check me out, I'm wearing a shirt under this."

I glance out of the corner of my eye to see Dillon smiling at me in a white tank top that has his toned muscles stretching against the thin fabric. He's holding out his shirt to me with that dimpled grin as I slowly take it from him.

"Since I can't promise that I'll have the same restraint as you, probably best if you change in the bathroom. Bring me your shirt and I'll have Cathy get it dry-cleaned when she gets in."

"Oh, no. That's okay. I can wash it after work," I say, dancing around his restraint comment because I'm honestly a little too flustered to respond to that.

"I insist," he says as he steps over to a side cabinet and opens it up, pulling out a powder blue dress shirt that matches his eyes almost perfectly.

"If you had an extra shirt, why give me the one you were wearing?" I ask with a raised brow.

He gives me a devilish smirk as he steps around his desk to face me, buttoning his shirt as he does.

"What would be the fun in that?"

My mouth drops open slightly before I let out a light laugh.

"You're going to be trouble, aren't you, Mr. Mathews?"

His bright white teeth sink into his bottom lip as he looks down at me before giving me a small nod.

"For you? You can count on it."

"In that case, I'll just go give Mandy a heads up about the inevitable harassment complaint."

A little bit of color leaves his face before I can't hold it together any longer and let a laugh slip. He laughs nervously as he rubs the back of his neck and shakes his head.

"I'm not so sure I'm going to be the troublemaker around here."

I shrug with a smile as I step outside his office and head into the bathroom. Dillon's shirt is way too big for me, so I decide to cross-tuck the bottoms of the shirt into my black trousers. They are high-waisted anyway, so it hides a lot of the fabric. It actually doesn't look too bad. I could probably rock this outfit on a normal day.

Picking up my stained shirt, I head back to my desk when Atlas suddenly comes storming in through the lobby, freezing when he sees me. He opens his mouth to say something when his eyes flick down to the shirt in my hand before examining the shirt I'm now wearing.

"What are you wearing?" he asks gruffly, a tone that bristles me instantly.

For a second there I forgot about last night. Based on Atlas's attitude it's clear he didn't and he's either not happy about it or not happy that I left without telling him. More than likely both.

"A shirt," I deadpan before stepping past him and making my way down the hallway.

"I have two eyes. I can see that. But it's significantly too big for you. Whose shirt are you wearing?"

"That would be mine," Dillon says with a carefree smile as he pokes his head out of his door.

"I ran into Andromeda, literally, and ruined her shirt. It was the least I could do."

Atlas frowns as he looks at Dillon before flicking his gaze back at me.

"I wasn't aware you two had met."

Something in his tone is off, he seems almost upset, maybe confused. It's childish of me but I can't help but poke at it a little bit.

"Oh yeah, we're old friends. Right, Dilly?"

Mischief sparks in Dillon's eyes and I can tell it's hard for him to keep it together with the impromptu nickname, but he does a good job of hiding it before nodding.

"Oh yeah, Andy and I are as thick as thieves."

"Andy?" Atlas asks, his tone thick with derision as he cocks an eyebrow.

I let out a laugh and shake my head. "Yeah, jig's up, Dillon. My friends and family call me Drama."

"I knew I should have taken that improv class my junior year," he says with a sad shake of his head.

I can't help but smile at him, but it doesn't last long before Atlas is interrupting.

"Did you drop off the Dawes blueprints to Keira?" he asks me curtly.

"No, sorry. They got coffee spilled all over them. I was just going to re-print them—"

"Don't bother," Atlas scoffs as he storms off toward his office, slamming the door shut as he does.

I blink a few times in his direction before turning to see Dillon staring in that direction with a shocked expression.

"Looks like the boss woke up on the wrong side of the bed, I suppose."

"Oh, is this not normal? I swear he's a moody prick all the time these days."

Dillon shrugs. "Cut him some slack. He just lost his best friends in a—"

"Car accident. Yeah, they were my parents."

Dillon's eyes round with recognition as sympathy floods his features. "Oh my god. I'm an idiot, Andromeda. I knew that too. I'm so sorry—"

"It's fine," I say with that practiced smile. "Anyway, I better go deal with all of that," I say as I gesture down the hall. "See you around."

"Give me your shirt, seriously. I want to."

I pause and look down at the silk material in my hand before back up at him.

"If you really want to, then you won't send Cathy out like an errand girl and you'll handle it on your own," I challenge.

Dillon smirks as he nods. "Scout's honor."

"You were a Boy Scout?"

"No, but if you don't tell anyone and it still counts."

I shake my head and laugh as he takes the shirt from me.

"I've got it. Have a good day, Drama," he says with a wink before striding back into his office.

Knowing that Atlas is clearly already in a foul mood and ignoring him will only make it worse, I lightly knock on his closed door.

"What?" he snaps.

Apparently he hasn't calmed down yet.

When I step inside his office, he's sitting at his desk in front of his computer. His eyes flick up to me instantly before he speaks.

"Close the door."

I do as he says before taking a few steps toward his desk where I pause and cross my arms over my chest.

"Look, I'm sorry about the blueprints. I'll re-print them and—"

"I don't give a damn about the fucking blueprints, Nevaeh. I care that I woke up this morning and you were gone, and your phone was off. I didn't know what the hell happened to you or where you had gone. It took me over twenty minutes to even fathom that you would suddenly drive yourself. Then when I arrive, you're laughing and flirting with another man while wearing his shirt."

I'm stunned at his outburst for a moment, and then one part of that rant sticks out more than the rest.

"Who should I be laughing and flirting with then?" I ask boldly.

"What?" Atlas grits with a clenched jaw.

"You said with another man, meaning Dillon. So, if I'm not supposed to be laughing and flirting with Dillon, who should I be?"

Atlas's chest begins rising and falling raggedly as he stares at me with so much intensity it sends goose bumps scattering across my skin.

"No one. You should be focused on yourself right now. You're going through a hard time in your life and—"

"No better way to get over something than to get under someone."

His heavy fists bang against the desk.

"Do not speak like that," he says with a tight jaw, eyes clenched shut before he gives me a near-murderous look.

I roll my eyes, not at all deterred by his attitude.

"Oh, come on, Atlas. Don't act like you think I'm an innocent little virgin. Your son snagged my V-card freshman year. If I remember correctly, you even walked in on us sophomore year. You pretended like you didn't know what we were doing but why else would I have been sitting on his lap in bed, my dress bunched up around my hips?"

The thin band of restraint keeping Atlas from completely losing his shit officially snaps at that. He is out of his chair and flies across the room until he is toe to toe with me. I feel his large hand wrap around my throat, but he doesn't apply any pressure. It's like he is trying to control me, not hurt me. Or maybe he's just trying to control himself.

His rich brown eyes are obsidian black, his nostrils flared as he bends down to eye level with me. I feel his warm breath fan across my lips as he speaks, instantly taking me back to last night.

"Don't say things like that. You're my goddaughter, I can't think about you in that type of position," he rumbles lowly.

My heart is beating out of my chest, my hands shaking at my sides, but I do my best to hide my nerves as I raise my chin a little higher just barely brushing my lips against his lower one as I speak.

"Don't want to or can't?" I whisper.

His jaw tics as his hold tightens just barely.

"Both," he grits out.

I run my tongue along my lower lip like I did last night and just as anticipated, he can't resist the urge to watch the movement, tracking my tongue like it's his very being for existence. I don't know what's going on here and I'm not sure I even want to know. All I can be sure of is that if Atlas doesn't kiss me right now, I'm going to combust.

As if he can hear my sinful thoughts, he whispers in a strained voice, "We can't."

"Says who?" I counter.

Uncertainty flashes across his eyes for a moment before I speak again.

"Kiss me, Atlas. Kiss me like you should have last night."

I watch his forearm flex as he lets out a ragged breath.

"It's not right," he says as he breaks our eye contact, not moving an inch otherwise.

"It feels right, though. You feel it too, don't you?"

Snapping back up to me, his eyes hold me in place as he stays silent. Telling me everything I need to know.

"I'm just asking for one kiss. I want to know what it's like to have you want to kiss me. To run your tongue against mine, to devour me like I'm—"

I'm silenced with the brutal force of Atlas's lips against mine. The kiss is more crushing and violent then I would have anticipated. I also wouldn't have expected how much I like it. Every first kiss I've ever had was soft and slow, sweet and gentle. Not this one, though. This is rough and passionate, carnal and sinful. My pussy throbs when Atlas's tongue dives into my mouth, not asking permission but forcing his way in, taking what he wants, how he wants it.

The hand not cradling my neck like my new favorite necklace reaches down and cups my ass, dragging me against him where my pussy grinds against his rock-hard cock. We both let out simultaneous moans into each other's mouths at the contact. My body lights up at his touch as his grip on my ass tightens while he uses me against him, rubbing and grinding us together as if he can't get close enough.

His mouth breaks away from my lips trailing hot kisses across my cheek and down my neck before freezing in the next second. Pulling back to look at me, Atlas's gorgeous face is twisted up into a sneer as he looks down at me.

"You will never wear another man's clothes again, is that understood?"

I nod quickly. I would promise anything right now to feel his lips on my skin again. I'd sell my soul right here on the spot to have no clothes between us.

Atlas runs his nose along my neck once more, an almost feral growl coming from his chest.

"I can't even smell your sweet perfume. All I smell is *him*. It's driving me fucking mad."

"I can take it off," I suggest breathily.

Atlas pulls back to look at me once more, his mouth ready to respond when his desk phone rings, causing us both to nearly jump out of our skin. We glance at each other wide eyed before looking back at the phone. I watch as the lust fades from his eyes and realization takes place. He slowly backs away from me, dropping his hands from me as he runs his hands through his previously perfect hair.

"Atlas," I say softly, causing his eyes to snap up to me.

His face is drenched in shame and disgust as he looks at me.

"Fuck, Andromeda. I'm sorry. I don't know what to say. I've never... fuck," he mutters as he covers his mouth with a clenched fist.

I thought that I had never felt true embarrassment until last night. Now I know that I was so wrong. Kissing Atlas Kane, having him really kiss me, touch me, own me in the corner of his office, only for him to shove me away like I'm disease ridden is worse. So much fucking worse.

Doing my best to swallow past the lump in my throat, I struggle to keep the tears at bay before I flatten out my untucked shirt. When did that even happen?

Without saying a word, I do my best to keep my chin held high as I walk straight out of the room only calling out over my shoulder once.

"I'll re-print the Dawes blueprints and give them to Keira."

Chapter 17
Andromeda

"C'mon Drama, you have to bring a date. There is an odd number of people at your table. Help the stressed bride out," Cathy complains with a mischievous grin that tells me she's full of shit.

I shake my head as I start the coffee machine for another cup before I look at her.

"First of all, I told you that you didn't have to invite me, we haven't even known each other for two weeks. Second, I'm not exactly in a place in my life where I want to be dating."

"Who says anything about dating? I think a good fuck is just what you need," she says with a casual shrug.

Yeah, can't say I disagree. Too bad I can't admit the only man that's truly caught my attention since Theo is his dad, a man I can't have. A man I shouldn't want to have. A man who very clearly doesn't want me. Or at least pretends not to want me. The raging hard-on he had on Monday after devouring my mouth speaks in complete contrast to his actions over the rest of this week.

Unsurprisingly, since our little spur-of-the-moment make-out session, he has gone back to avoiding me like I'm contagious. Which I guess I've been making easier since I've been driving myself to work ever since Monday. I'm still not totally at ease behind the wheel but it's getting better. Progress.

"What are you two lovely ladies gossiping about?" Dillon asks as he strides into the break room, that smooth accent practically rolling off his tongue as he does.

Well, I guess Atlas being the only man to catch my attention since Theo isn't totally true. Dillon is the quintessential standard of handsome. Pair his flirty and fun personality with that British accent and who wouldn't swoon? He's not Atlas-level sexy, but still.

"My wedding." Cathy smiles. "I'm trying to convince Andromeda to bring a date."

"Oh really?" Dillon asks with a raised eyebrow as he smirks at me. "Is there a waitlist for that position? Do I need to provide any references to apply?"

A laugh escapes me as I turn to face him fully, crossing my arms over my chest as I do.

"References? What, like other girls you've gone out with?"

"Exactly. They can attest that I'm quite the gentleman, an excellent dancer, and an exceptional kisser."

"Well, if they think you're so great why aren't you with them anymore?" I question.

He gives me a mock disappointed look as he glances down at his feet before looking up at me beneath his eyelashes.

"I'm afraid I was a little too perfect. They couldn't handle the pressure of being with such a nice guy and missed being neglected and mistreated."

I can't help but let out a snort as I smirk.

"Oh, I'm sure. What woman wouldn't miss that? Nice guys always finish last, right?"

"A proper gentleman always finishes last," he says with a flirty wink that has a fluttering racing to my lower stomach. I try to laugh it off even if mental images that are definitely not work-appropriate begin flickering in my head.

"Okay, please for me will you just go together, Dillon? This sexual tension is killing me," Cathy says dramatically but the smile on her face tells me she has never been more pleased.

Dillon looks at me with a smile that is much more sincere than the flirty one he was giving me moments ago.

"I would be honored to accompany you to the wedding of our darling Cathy, if you'll allow it, Miss Clarke."

I do my best to hold back my amused smirk as my eyes trace him over consideringly.

"Just as friends. I don't want things to get weird when you fall in love with me and I break your heart," I tease.

Dillon tosses his head back and lets out a melodic laugh as his hands clutch over his heart.

"Love, I'm afraid I'm already well on my way. Be kind to me, I beg of you."

I shrug as I grab my coffee and start back toward my desk.

"I warned you."

I'd be lying if I said I wasn't a little bit excited to be on Dillon's arm this weekend, even as friends. My dating experience outside of Theo consists of a few awkward middle school kisses and a few chaperoned movie dates. I still don't think starting anything with Dillon would be a good idea for a number of reasons, though.

The first is obvious, we work together and what would happen if things didn't work out? Sounds uncomfortable. There is also the fact that he is thirteen years older than me. It's not necessarily a problem but he's definitely in a different place in life than me right now. The more I think about it, the more I realize I'm not really in the same place in life as other eighteen-year-olds are in, so maybe it's not such a con. The last is the most concrete reason, my life is currently a dumpster fire.

With the pain I feel every day at the two empty holes in my chest, the sinful thoughts that I've been having about my ex-boyfriend's dad slash parents' best friend and even the lust-fueled kisses that we've exchanged, getting involved with someone, especially with someone as nice as Dillon only spells disaster.

———

It's Saturday and I just finished putting on my diamond teardrop earrings before I look at myself in the mirror. I decided to wear the satin emerald-green dress that I got last year when Mom and I went shopping in San Francisco. Just looking at it sends a twinge through my chest. I remember how her mouth dropped when I came out of the dressing room. She started to tear up, telling me how I didn't look like a little girl anymore.

God, I miss her.

Ugh, nope. Not digging that shit up right now. Pushing all of that down where it belongs, I stand up a little straighter as I fluff out my hair once more. A heavy knock comes from downstairs and my stomach flips for a moment in excitement.

Atlas already left this morning, or maybe he never came home. He's still refusing to speak to me unless absolutely necessary. I don't know why he thinks he can just avoid what happened between us. I mean, I guess he can since that's exactly what he's doing.

Whatever, I promised myself I wouldn't think about him today. My new friend is getting married to her soulmate, and I have a hot older man downstairs waiting to pick me up. Atlas who, right?

Grabbing a black shawl since it's an evening wedding, I toss my lipstick, phone, and keys into my clutch before heading down the stairs and up to the front door. Dillon is standing at the entrance, a crisp gray suit with a white dress shirt wrapped around him giving a wide smile as he looks at me.

"My god, who is the lucky bloke that gets to be seen with you?" he asks as he holds out his hand for me.

I place my hand in his and he lifts it above my head before encouraging me to twirl. I can't help but giggle, feeling ridiculous but also kinda sexy as he looks me over in appreciation.

"This guy I work with. His flirting was getting pathetic, so I thought I'd throw him a bone," I tease with a wink.

Dillon laughs as he brings his arm down, not letting go of my hand as he does.

"Your insults do nothing to me, love. My flirting got me this date, so I have no complaints."

"Not a date," I remind him.

"Agree to disagree." He smiles as an arm comes up behind me, sliding over my shoulders before a familiar voice speaks.

"Dillon? What are you doing here?" Theo asks stiffly.

Dillon's eyes flick down to Theo's arm assessing before letting go of my hand and giving him a friendly smile.

"Here to escort Andromeda to Cathy's wedding. How have you been? I haven't seen you around the office lately?"

"Been busy traveling for work." Theo shrugs.

He's been traveling again? For a hardware store? I feel like a jerk that I haven't really noticed Theo has been gone a lot lately for it being summer. Now that I think about it though, I rarely see him around the house. Sometimes I will go days without seeing him and we live together. Is he even coming home? I've been so wrapped up with Atlas and my grief that I haven't even been paying attention to my surroundings, apparently.

I glance up to look at Theo curiously. I can tell when he's lying, and he most definitely is right now. What are you hiding, Theo? Then again I'm not sure if I want to go digging around in Theo's secrets if I don't want him to dig into mine. Like the fact that I kissed his dad. And then he kissed me back. Maybe some secrets are better kept.

"Ah, good on you. Well, we better get going," Dillon says as he extends his hand for me to take.

Turning to Theo, I see him watching me with a concerned furrow of his brow. I give him a small smile before taking Dillon's hand and walking down the driveway to his sleek black BMW.

Dillon grabs the door for me, holding it open as I slide in before walking over to the driver's seat and starting up the car. He reaches down and pulls out a pair of aviators before sliding them on.

The ride to the venue is a bit of a trek since Cathy is getting married at a hotel on the beach off Highway 101. But between learning about all of Dillon's zodiac signs, listening to his horribly off-key singing, the stories he tells about growing up in England, and the flirty looks he sends me, it feels like it flies by.

Chapter 18
Atlas

I'm fucking losing it.

I've always been composed, collected. I've always been able to separate my wants and desires from doing the right thing. My entire life has revolved around others, their wellbeing, their happiness. It's the way my mother raised me, to care for others, and I believe it is my most admirable trait.

I don't feel very admirable lately, though.

The things I think, the things I fantasize. Shit, the things I've done.

I kissed Andromeda. Andromeda Clarke.

Paul and Emily's little girl. Theo's girlfriend, ex-girlfriend, whatever.

If I hadn't been in that room, I'd never believe me. Never believe that I could do something so horrifying, so selfish, so reckless. I need to be focused on keeping the company running smoothly after the loss of my partner. I need to make sure that Andromeda isn't drowning in her grief as I try to avoid the same. I don't need to be imagining what shade of pink her nipples are or how good her tongue would feel swirling around the head of my cock.

Goddammit.

This is exactly why I have to maintain as much distance from her as possible. Which isn't exactly easy when I live and work with her. If I was a prick, I'd ask her to move out. It would make things a hell of a lot easier. It would take away the slight urge that flares up when I know she's in the shower, alone, wet and naked.

Goddammit. Do you hear yourself, Atlas? You sound like a fucking perv.

I guess I am if I'm sitting here lusting after an eighteen-year-old. I'm forty-one for fuck's sake. I have no business thinking anything sexual about anyone with a teen in their age. Especially not someone that I've known since the day they were born.

When I'm around her, it's like I blackout. I'm not in control of my thoughts, of my actions. A thick red haze of lust takes over me and then the next thing I know, I'm shaking myself out of the fog, mortified at what I'd just done.

Shaking my head, I toss back the glass of scotch in my hand, letting the cool liquid run down my throat, leaving a sharp burn in its wake. I've probably had too many considering what a far drive it is back to Brighton, but I've got time to sober up since the wedding hasn't even started yet.

I glance out at the soft waves of the ocean rolling against the light brown sand as the sun begins to dip beyond the horizon. Of course, Cathy would have a sunset ceremony. She talked my and Dillon's ear off for nearly two weeks when she decided on it, telling us how romantic it was going to be. I'm glad to be here and help celebrate such a happy day for one of my best employees but god can that woman talk.

The other guests standing around the beach, sipping cocktails and mingling, begin making their way over to the empty chairs set up in front of the floral and fabric-draped arch. I glance at my watch noticing that it's only a few minutes until the ceremony starts so I decide to take a seat.

Dillon. That's a topic that I haven't allowed myself to think about too much since he's been back. Mainly because I like Dillon, he's a great architect and an even better employee. Paul really liked him too. He even joked a few times that if Dillon was a few years younger he would be perfect for Andromeda. I'm pretty sure he wouldn't have said things like that if he knew Dillon was looking at Andromeda the way I've seen him.

Really? Are you sure Dillon is the one Paul would have issues with how he's looking at Andromeda?

Shaking my head at myself, I push the nagging voice inside my head to the side. I've seen the way Dillon watches Andromeda. The way he always gets coffee as soon as she does even though he always used to have Cathy get him coffee. He even took an early lunch on Monday and went to get Andromeda's shirt dry cleaned and brought it back himself before dropping it off at her desk.

Thanks to my office door being left open after she stormed out, I saw it all and it had a nasty feeling flaring inside me as I did. I always liked Dillon, always thought that he was a good guy. But him being interested in Andromeda has me seeing things a little differently and I've decided the prick isn't as funny or charismatic as he thinks he is.

A woman in a tight-fitting green dress walks down the aisle toward the front. Her long lean legs stretch out as she walks gracefully in her heels through the sand. I can't help but let my eyes fall to her full ass that looks perfectly shaped from back here. Her waist dips in dramatically from her hips and I can only imagine the gorgeous tits she has to compliment that flawless body.

It's been a while since a woman has caught my interest. I haven't gone out in a few months. Not really sure why, I guess I've just been too busy to really put in any effort. If the beauty in the green dress doesn't have a date maybe she can help break my dry spell.

Unfortunately, a blond guy in a gray suit walks over to her before they both sit down. He slips his arm around her shoulders, officially shooting that plan in the face. Fuck, of course.

Soft music starts to play from all around us as everyone turns to watch the bridal party making their way down the aisle. Instead of doing the same though I'm stuck, frozen in place as my heart drops into my stomach. Are you fucking kidding me?

Bright-green eyes snag my attention, those familiar pouty lips parted slightly as she looks at me for half a second before returning her attention to the bridal party. I've never seen Andromeda wear that dress before. I definitely would have remembered, and that makes me feel like a disgusting piece of shit.

Shaking my head, I rub my fingers against my temples as I seriously contemplate leaving. But when I lift my head quickly and a lightheaded feeling washes over me, I know the scotch I downed earlier is starting to take full effect. So leaving isn't an option, at least yet.

Once the bridal party is at the altar the music changes before everyone stands and turns. Curiosity gets the best of me, and I stay facing forward to see who the douchebag with his arm around Andromeda's shoulders is since I didn't get a look before. My fists tighten at my sides when I see Dillon smiling down at Andromeda like she hung the fucking moon before they both turn to face the aisle.

This is going to be a long fucking night.

The ceremony goes by in a blur, or maybe it's the number of scotches that I've had that's making things slightly blurry. Cathy and her fiancé, now husband, exchanged vows filled with sentimental anecdotes, inside jokes and mentions that love knows no number or no bounds. It was cute and you can tell that the crowd ate up every bit of it.

I'm currently sitting at a table inside the hotel where the reception is being held. I debated on just leaving after the ceremony but something inside me wouldn't leave. Maybe it's because it doesn't feel right to leave her here with Dillon. What do I actually know about the guy outside of work? Not a lot and that doesn't sit well with me. Andromeda is my responsibility. I can't just leave her in the hands of a guy I don't fully trust just because I want to be anywhere but here.

I'm sipping on my freshly poured drink when a tightness squeezes inside my gut as Dillon leads Andromeda over to my table, his hand on her lower back as they take their seats across from me. I didn't even think about checking the seating chart to see where Cathy had them seated once I found my place. She is now officially on my shit list, right next to Dillon.

Andromeda notices me first, giving me a tight-lipped smile as Dillon nods and leans over the table to shake my hand. As much as I'd love to knock his hand away and ignore him altogether, I shake it instead, giving him a polite greeting before I focus back on my scotch. The rest of the tables begin to fill up as everyone waits for the newlyweds to make their grand entrance.

A soft giggle that sends my chest stuttering shakes me out of my head as I look up to see Dillon's head buried into the crook of Andromeda's neck, seemingly whispering something to her. Her face is red, her dimples deep as she tosses her head back and laughs.

He's not that fucking funny.

I lift my glass up to take a hearty swig when I see his left hand disappear from the top of the table and drift toward her leg. Without being able to stop myself, I set my drink down harder than necessary before shoving my seat back and storming over to their side of the table.

My hand reaches out and wraps around Andromeda's wrist before pulling her to stand. An unwanted but persistent spark raced up my arm from the contact.

"We need to talk," I practically growl before I briskly walk us out of the reception room and into the hallway.

Once we are through the doors, I drop her wrist like the touch has burned me as I begin pacing. I hear her huff and glance over to see her folding her arms over her chest like she always seems to do when she's irritated or entertained. Based on the sour look on her face I'm going to go with irritated this time.

Join the fucking club.

"What the hell, Atlas? You can't just yank people out of a room like a caveman. What is your problem?"

"You are!" I snap as I stop pacing and turn to face her, crossing the distance between us until my chest brushes against hers. Pushing away the desire that flares to life inside me from the barely there touch, I focus on my anger and irritation.

"What are you doing here with him?" I demand.

"Who?" she asks, confused. "Dillon?"

"No, Santa Claus. Yes, fucking Dillon," I sneer.

Her eyes narrow as she speaks. "Watch your tone when you speak to me. You may be my elder, my boss and my late parents' best friend, but you will not treat me with disrespect."

My chest heaves at her words, partially irritated by the nerve of her, but partially proud of her for standing up for herself. Blowing out a deep breath I squeeze my eyes shut for a moment before I feel some of the anger leave my body as I look at her again.

"Why are you here with Dillon?" I ask, softer this time.

She shrugs. "He asked if he could take me, I said yes. It's not a big deal. We're just friends."

I laugh hollowly as I shake my head. "You can't honestly buy that shit. He has a whole lot more than friendship on his mind when it comes to you."

"So?"

I scoff. "So, he's too old for you."

"Are you kidding me? Were you not at the same wedding ceremony as me? The one where a couple who is a true testament of love having no age spoke about it? If I'm interested in someone, their age is not my first concern."

"You're interested in him?"

"I am. I like him."

"You like him?" I grit out, practically in disbelief of what I'm hearing.

"Is there an echo in here?" she asks dryly as she looks around the hall like she's searching for the source.

"Watch it," I snap. "You can't date him."

Andromeda lets out a full laugh as she smiles in a way that definitely does not represent happiness before she turns her sharp green eyes toward me.

"Oh yeah? Why not?"

"I just told you. He's too old for you. He's thirty-one, you're only eighteen."

"You're forty-one," she points out.

I furrow my brows as I look down at her.

"This has nothing to do with me. I'm trying to protect you, Nevaeh.

He's a nice enough guy in the workplace but any man as old as him that's interested in a girl your age only wants one thing."

She shrugs, seemingly unbothered.

"That's fine. I'm not exactly looking for anything serious and trust me, there isn't a thing Dillon could try to take that I wouldn't willingly give him."

My fist balls up at my side as I do my best to breathe through my rising anger.

"I don't want to hear words like that come out of your mouth again. Understood?"

"Why?" she taunts with the trace of a smirk. "Is it because it gets under your skin? You don't like the thought of another man touching me? You don't like the thought of another man's hands roaming my body, grinding his hard cock against me as his mouth devours my own?"

I feel my pulse thunder in my neck as my cock begins stiffening in my slacks. I glance down at her full pink lips. Swear to god, I can still taste them. Still feel them. It would be so easy to take what I need. What I crave. To steal just one more kiss, to lose myself in their pillowy softness.

I see the need in her eyes, the lust heavily displayed across her face. She wants me, maybe as badly as I want her, though I can't see how that's possible. She doesn't know better, she's so young, so vulnerable. The things I could show her, the things I could make her feel. She'd never be the same. Neither of us would, which is why as much as my painfully hard cock hates me for it, I take a step back, shoving my deepest desires into the dark part of my mind where they belong.

"I don't want you dating him," I say steadier than before, firmer this time.

The want that consumed her face is gone in an instant as disappointment flashes briefly before indifference takes up residence.

"Well, you are definitely not my dad, Atlas. I can date, kiss or fuck whoever the hell I want. It's really none of your business."

Before I can argue that everything that has to do with her is my business, she steps away from me and makes her way back into the room. I contemplate going after her and not letting her leave until she agrees to never see Dillon outside of work again but deep down I know that won't work. She is one of the most stubborn women that I've ever met. The more I demand, the harder she will fight me.

So, I do the only thing I know how to do. I blow out a heavy breath, pull my keys out from my pocket and drive as far away from Andromeda Clarke as I can, at least until she comes home.

Chapter 19
Andromeda

Doing my best to put a smile on my face, I walk back into the reception room where I lock eyes with Dillon instantly. He looks concerned as his eyes run over me, so I smile a little bigger to ease his worries. It seems to work a little as his shoulders relax slightly, but the questions in his eyes don't disappear as I approach our table.

I slide down into my seat when he speaks.

"You okay, love?"

"Yeah." I smile. "Just Atlas being a nosey asshole."

He quirks an eyebrow at that. "I take it he isn't all that pleased that you're my date tonight?"

I pick up the filled wineglass in front of me, tossing it back before anyone can tell me I can't.

"Let's just enjoy the rest of the night, please?"

Dillon smiles and nods before slipping his arm around my shoulders like he's been doing most of the night. I lean into him a little more than I had been earlier. Don't know why. It definitely has nothing to do with Atlas thinking he can forbid me from seeing him. I'm not that petty.

Cathy and Jeff come into the room, all smiles and heart eyes as they look at each other and are introduced as husband and wife before moving into their first dance. My heart squeezes as I watch the way

Cathy smiles up at him while Jeff looks down at her adoringly. I haven't seen a couple that in love since my parents. I swear they loved each other more than any other couple in the world. I never thought anyone would have a love like theirs but the way those two are looking at each other gives me hope. Maybe it's not as exceedingly impossible as I thought.

A few couples begin joining the dance floor before Dillon stands up and extends his hand to me. I hesitate for a moment before intertwining my fingers through his. He walks us out to the edge of the dancefloor before resting one of his hands on my lower back and the other holding my hand as we begin gently swaying to the slow song.

"I'm really glad you came with me tonight," Dillon says softly as he looks down at me.

I smile as I nod. "Me too. I didn't think I would have as much fun as I have."

"You wound me, love," he says dramatically with a sad look before he smirks at me.

I smack his arm lightly as I shake my head and laugh.

"That's alright. I think that big ego of yours could use a little wounding."

He shrugs as he turns me for a spin as the music morphs into something a little faster.

"As long as you're the one doing the wounding, I won't mind."

The look he gives me sends butterflies rushing through me as he brings me back into his arms. Spinning and dipping me through the song. I'm definitely not an experienced dancer so thank God Dillon wasn't lying when he said he could dance.

We spend the rest of the night eating, dancing and sneaking drinks. At least I do the sneaking since I'm obviously not of drinking age. Dillon gave me a mock look of horror when I stole his whiskey and took a sip which had me dying laughing just as the music cut off for speeches. Only a few dozen heads turned our way before focusing back on the head table, but Dillon made sure to mercilessly tease me about it for the rest of the night.

The drive home went by fast. We just pulled up to the front of the house before Dillon shuts off the car, his eyes trained on Atlas's empty car next to us before he turns to face me.

"So how long have you been staying here?" he asks.

"About a month. I'll probably move back to my house soon or rent an apartment or something."

He nods. "It must be hard to be in that house all alone. Makes sense that you would want to be around people. You know if you ever need anything, someone to talk to, or a place to get away, I'm only a call away."

I smirk at him as I cock an eyebrow. "Oh, I'm sure you would be oh-so-willing to offer up your bed for a night or two."

Dillon barks out a laugh as he nods.

"For you? I'd be willing to invite you every night, but seriously. No strings attached. If you ever need anything, I'm here for you. Even if it's just to take your mind off things."

My throat constricts slightly as I do my best to swallow over the lump that has suddenly formed in it.

"Thanks, Dillon. That actually means a lot."

He gives me a kind smile and nods before his smile slowly fades as he looks over the dark house in front of us.

"I think the boss likes you."

I still at his words, my shock at his bluntness completely obvious as his eyes move to look at me. Laughing lightly, I do my best to shove the swirling feelings inside me to the side as I shake my head.

"Yeah, I don't think so. He barely tolerates me most days. You saw how he was tonight, how he treats me at the office. I can assure you, it's no better in that house."

Dillon tilts his head to the side as he watches me carefully.

"I'm not so sure about that."

"Trust me," I laugh hollowly. "I'm just a burden to him. He feels required to look after me for my parents. Nothing more."

He doesn't look convinced at my words, but he nods all the same as he raises a hand to brush a piece of hair out of my face.

"Good. I'm a pretty jealous man when I like a woman. And I most definitely like you, Andromeda."

My heart flips at the way my name sounds on his lips as I do my best to bite back my smile.

"I like you too."

A smile slowly stretches across his face before he leans forward and brushes his lips across mine, it's tentative at first, like he's testing the waters. When he feels my lips move against his though, the dynamic changes. His hands reach down to wrap around my hips as he lifts me out of my seat and over the center console into his lap.

Our lips never break contact as I feel Dillon's hands everywhere. The fire inside me that started in Atlas's office nearly a week ago ignites into an inferno as Dillon's fingers trail against my bare thigh. His lips move flawlessly against mine, his smooth silky tongue stroking mine like I'm the finest dessert.

The image of the last kiss I had flashes to the forefront of my mind, much to my annoyance. I do my best to keep that buried into the back of my mind as I try to enjoy this incredibly sexy man in front of me, but the strong possessive hold of Atlas's fingers wrapped around my throat, the dominating way he kissed me, the way every touch from him set me on fire is incomparable. No matter how good of a kisser Dillon is.

Hating myself for doing it, I break our kiss, easing back to see Dillon look at me with concern.

"Are you okay?"

"Yeah, I'm just not sure I'm really ready for...all of this," I say as I gesture around us.

He eases his head back against his headrest and nods with a soft smile.

"I understand. I'd never want to pressure you into anything. We go at your pace, okay, love?"

I smile and nod. "Thank you. I had a great time tonight."

"Me too, first of many, hopefully."

I smile and nod before awkwardly climbing off his lap and back into my seat. Dillon gets out of the car and jogs around to grab my door before letting me out. As soon as I stand he leans down and brushes a soft kiss against my lips. When he pulls away, he gives me a smile as he cups my face, his baby blue eyes twinkling in the moonlight.

"Try not to think about me too much tonight," he says with a wink before taking a step back.

Not able to hold my chuckle in, I roll my eyes as I start walking toward the house.

"I'll do my best!"

When I step inside, the house is dark and silent. Kicking off my heels, I rub the bottoms of my feet before making my way upstairs. My steps falter outside my bedroom door as I glance across the hall to Atlas's room. The lights are off, and the hallway is quiet. His car was in the driveway so he must be home. Hopefully he calmed down enough, so he won't be such a pain in the ass in the morning.

I look to the other side of the hall to see Theo's room looking just as dark and empty. Now that I think about it, I'm not even sure if his car was in the driveway. Where is he going to this late at night? Or maybe he's staying the night somewhere. Maybe he has a girlfriend. Why doesn't the thought of that send my stomach twisting?

Walking into my room, I step inside and toss my clutch on top of the dresser before closing the door. I go through my nightly routine before crawling into bed. I close my eyes, doing my best to let sleep take me, but the ache between my thighs from my little make-out session with Dillon is making that practically impossible.

It's been so long since I've had an orgasm I couldn't even tell you, and I'm officially fed up. Sliding my hand across my stomach, I slowly slip it beneath my pajama bottoms and panties. I close my eyes as I imagine a scenario where I didn't get in my head earlier. Where Dillon and I took it further, where he fucked me good and hard in the front seat of his car.

My fingers begin moving in quick strokes over my clit as I feel myself get wetter with each brush. I do my best to focus on how it all felt. His lips, his tongue, his hands running up and down my body as I sat on top of him. The mental image of his blond hair and blue eyes is sharp in my head but it quickly morphs before I can stop it.

Soon, instead of being in Dillon's car I'm bent over a desk, my skirt hiked up over my hips as a hard cock presses against me, begging for entrance. Turning my head over my shoulder I'm shocked to see a dark head of hair with chocolate-brown eyes looking at me intently as he inches inside me before slamming into me the rest of the way.

I feel my fingers begin to move frantically as I reach down with the other hand to fill the empty space as best as I can. It's not a cock, but it will have to do. I begin riding my hand, quickly banishing the image of Atlas bending me over a desk and replacing it with Dillon in his car. Sweet sexy charming Dillon with that delicious accent and soft lips. I bet he could make me come with the snap of his fingers. The way his tongue flicked against mine tells me that his tongue game would be strong all the way around.

My orgasm begins to build as my pussy starts pulsing around my fingers. I feel that familiar pressure build in my lower stomach as my thighs begin to shake. Just like before, my fantasy morphs and instead of imagining Dillon eating me out, the head between my thighs is dark. And instead of the tongue flicking against me being soft and skilled, this one is wild and passionate, near feral as it attacks me like a starving animal.

"Oh fuck, fuck, fuck," I mutter under my breath as my orgasm builds.

Those chocolate eyes snap up to me as his mouth continues to consume me and that right there is my undoing. The look of pure desire in his eyes, of total want. Not an ounce of disgust or pity in sight. Just need and hunger.

"Atlas!" I shout before I think better of it and muffle my orgasm, my pussy spasming against my fingers as I do my best to draw it out for as long as possible.

When my body stops shaking and my head stops swimming with the post-orgasmic high, reality sets in. I just touched myself to the thought of Atlas Kane. My ex-boyfriend's dad. My godfather. A man I've known my whole life. The sick part?

I feel fucking great about it.

Chapter 20
Andromeda

I cautiously open my door the next morning, holding my breath at the prospect of coming face to face with Atlas after last night. Will he know that I touched myself to the thought of him last night? It feels like I have it stamped across my forehead, in bold letters for anyone nearby to see.

Thankfully, Atlas's door is still closed, and the house is quiet, so I slowly walk down the stairs and into the kitchen. I'm just starting up some coffee when I hear the front door quietly creak open before snicking shut. I furrow my brows before peering around the corner to see Theo tiptoeing inside the house, a black T-shirt and ripped jeans on, his hair messy like he's run his hair through it a million times, and a nose ring that I've never seen before.

What the hell?

"Theo?" I call out in a soft whisper, causing him to physically jump in place as his eyes whip over to me.

"Drama? Fuck, you scared the hell out of me," he sighs.

Frowning, I fold my arms over my chest as I step out of the kitchen as I walk into the entryway.

"Are you just getting in?"

He reaches his hand up to scratch the back of his neck as he shrugs.

"Uh, yeah. Late night."

"Doing what?" I question.

He looks at me blowing out a soft sigh as he glances at the empty staircase before nodding to the kitchen. I nod and follow him in the direction, moving to the cupboard to grab him a cup of coffee. When I slide it over to him he gives me a small smile in thanks before he speaks.

"I met these guys at a bar off campus back in May. They are in a band and needed a drummer."

"No way? You are in a band!" I exclaim, softening my voice when I realize he is clearly trying to keep this quiet.

"Yeah," he smiles, true pride shining through. "The lead singer is kind of a dick, but he gets us gigs, which gets us exposure, so I'll deal with him."

"That's amazing, Theo. I'm so proud of you. What's your band called?"

"The Mudslide Men."

I blink at him a few times which earns me a laugh.

"Yeah, I felt the same when they told me. One of the things Jimmy and I fight over. It's all good, though. All we need is to get picked up by a label and they will rebrand us. So for now, I'm the drummer for The Mudslide Men," he says, holding up the rock on hand gesture before laughing.

I let out a laugh with him before our laughter subsides.

"So, that's where you've been going? What about the hardware store?"

Theo shrugs. "I've been going to band practice, doing gigs like last night. Dad gives me enough monthly allowance to live off and then some."

"What about when you went to Seattle to open that new store?"

His smile is guilty as he shrugs again.

"Seattle's annual grunge fest. It was epic. We got a lot of interest, even talked to a few labels."

"No way! That's so cool. Why haven't you told anyone?"

He reaches a hand up to play with his piercing almost nervously as he glances down at his coffee cup.

"You know how my dad is. He wants me to join the company, follow in his footsteps. I just want to make music, you know that."

I smile and nod softly. "I do, and I think you can make it one day, Theo. You have the talent. All you need is the right band, the right label, and you could make it."

"You really think so?" he asks, his eyes wide and hopeful.

Nodding to him, seeing more passion and excitement in his eyes than I've seen in years, I grin.

"Definitely, but you also can't keep this under wraps for long. You should tell your dad. He will get it."

Theo lets out a hollow laugh as he pushes off the island to stand up straight.

"Are you crazy? He will lose his shit on me. I've already been mentally preparing myself for the endless lectures that will come when he finds out."

"He just wants the best life possible for you," I say sympathetically.

He frowns. "I think you've been spending too much time with him lately, you're clearly blind to what a controlling prick he can be."

His words have me stilling, not sure how to explain that I agree I have been spending too much time with him, but not for the reasons he thinks.

"Well, what about school? It starts in two weeks," I ask, hopefully seamlessly switching topics.

"Kurt, our bassist, is a junior at OSU this year too so we are going to keep our gigs local during the school year, unless we get picked up or something. I mean, if we get a record deal I'm not going to not do it, you know?"

I nod, that would be a once-in-a-lifetime opportunity. He couldn't pass it up. School will always be there for him when and if he needed.

"What about you? Have you thought about what you are going to do?"

I shrug. "I emailed my advisor at the beginning of the summer to tell them that I was going to defer a year, but I've been thinking about switching to online if they'll allow it. The work at Kane Designs isn't too much, I think I could balance both."

Theo frowns. "Kinda sucks. I was looking forward to you joining me at school."

"I know." I smile sadly. "I just don't know if I'm ready yet. I don't know, I haven't really thought about it too much, I guess."

"Makes sense. Online is cool, flexible."

"Yeah." I shrug.

"Hey," Theo says softly. "Just because I'm going to be gone doesn't mean I won't be a call away. You need anything day or night you call me, okay? Even if it's to bitch or vent."

"Once I'm done with this internship I'm sure I'll have enough to bitch about," I tease.

Theo barks out a laugh as he nods. "I don't doubt it. You let me know if the old man treats you like shit, I'll drive my ass down here and knock him around."

"You think you could take him?" I ask with a cocked brow, remembering how his dad basically picked him up by his scruff when we got into it earlier this summer.

Theo looks offended as his mouth drops open. He sprints around the island, caging me in before beginning to tickle me. I squeal as he goes straight to my hips, my most ticklish spot, as he attacks me. I laugh and shout, begging him to stop before he finally does. We are both smiling lightly chuckling when he pauses to brush a piece of hair out of my face.

"I'll always love you, Drama. That means I'll always be here for you, you can tell me anything, no matter what, okay?"

There is something in his tone. Not necessarily suspicion, maybe concern? I'm not really sure and to be honest I'm a little too nervous to ask, so instead, I smile and nod before wrapping him up in a hug. I'm glad that Theo and I have been able to work past the heartbreak. Me more than him if the lingering of his hug is anything to go off. He respects my boundaries though and that's all I can ask for. I've already lost too much. I couldn't bear losing him too.

Chapter 21
Andromeda

Atlas avoided me all day Sunday after Cathy's wedding, which was fine by me. Theo and I ended up spending the day together, having a movie marathon and just catching up. He told me about some of the crazy stories that he already had from the couple of gigs he's done. When Atlas left the house, he took me to his room and played a few songs on his drum set. It was amazing to see how far his talent has come just since the last time I've listened to him play.

Theo had to leave for school the next morning, hugging me extra tight before he took off. He reminded me that if I needed him, he would drop everything and rush back here. Whether that was for me to have a shoulder to lean on or to kick his dad's ass for me. You'd have to be stupid to ignore the tension between Atlas and me in the house over the last two weeks. It's palpable. Theo naturally thinks it's because Atlas and I are butting heads. Guess he isn't totally wrong. We are definitely not seeing eye to eye on certain things.

Whatever. I'm honestly done. The emotional whiplash that man provides is too much. Space is best, so I really should consider moving out. I don't know what my next move will be, and I don't really care. Something just needs to change. This was supposed to be temporary, and I think I've more than overstayed my welcome at this point.

The next day, I'm working on a project at my desk that Atlas gave me when a familiar high-pitched voice hits my ears.

"Miss me, babe?" Aunt Alyssa calls out as she lifts her Gucci sunglasses to rest on top of her perfectly styled hair as she smooths down her satin deep V-neck blouse. My eyes run over her outfit, glancing down at her white designer strappy heels that stop just before her tight blue jeans begin. It's a Tuesday and she looks like she's ready to walk the runway in a 'casual way'. At least that's what she always describes her style as.

"Hey! I didn't know you were in town," I say as I stand from my desk and wrap my arms around her.

I haven't seen her since the funeral. I've only spoken to her on the phone once since then. She may be a little extra at times and overly dramatic, but I still miss her. She's the only family I have left on Mom's side.

"Well, I thought it would be good to pop in for a little visit. I have a bit of vacation time and figured I'd check on Atlas, see how he's doing."

My brows furrow at that and a small ache forms in my chest. She came all this way to check on Atlas? Not her niece? I watch as she fluffs her hair before turning to face Atlas's office. Disappointment squashes out any excitement that rose in me at seeing my aunt for the first time in months.

She opens his door without even knocking and I don't know why but something about that irks me. I follow behind her, trying to come up with a way that I can convince her to leave him alone since I know he has back-to-back meetings today.

"Alyssa, he's got a lot of meetings today. It's probably not a good time," I say as I find myself only a few steps away from Atlas's desk as Alyssa continues sashaying across the room before stopping next to his chair.

Atlas looks at me before glancing at Alyssa. He holds a finger up as he hits a button on his phone and takes it off speaker.

"Hey, Harry? Can I call you back? Something's come up. Alright, sounds good," he says before hanging up the phone and standing from his desk.

"Alyssa, what a surprise. Nice to see you," he says as he leans down and brushes a polite kiss on her cheek.

She gives him a megawatt smile before she leans in to place a kiss on his cheek too. The movement instantly bristles me, and I find myself narrowing my eyes at my overly eager aunt. Atlas doesn't seem too put off though as he smiles down at her.

"What brings you all the way down here?"

"Oh, I had some PTO to burn and thought I'd come and check on you. You haven't been responding to my text messages lately and I got worried. How are you doing?" she asks sympathetically as her perfectly manicured hand rests on his bicep. A hand I would very much like to claw off right now.

Wait. Text messages? Since when do they text? Why did I not know this? I always thought the feelings she had for him were unrequited. That's what she and Mom had always said. Is there more to this? Are they dating? The very thought of that sends my stomach rolling and my anger rising.

Atlas gives her a smile that is a lot less enthusiastic and plastic than hers as he shrugs.

"Hanging in there. We are just trying to take it one day at a time, right, Nevaeh?" he asks, his eyes coming to me.

The anger stirring inside of me ebbs slightly at having his attention on me. God, would you listen to me? How pathetic can I get? About as pathetic as my aunt apparently if her toddler-sized pout at losing Atlas's focus is anything to go off.

"Yeah," I say. "Atlas's birthday without Mom and Dad was different, memorable, but different."

A flash of something dark passes in Atlas's eyes. Hunger or anger. Maybe both? It's gone before I can even blink, though. He looks back down at Alyssa who has taken another step toward him, her breasts very intentionally brushing against his chest as she bats her eyes at him.

"I bet. I'm so sorry. Hopefully your girlfriend was able to keep you company?" she fishes.

Atlas rolls his eyes though he has a small smirk on his lips as he looks down at her.

"You know I don't have a girlfriend, Alyssa."

"Well, you never know. A handsome man like you could get snatched off the market in a flash," she says with a seductive smile.

Atlas laughs and shakes his head at her. "I don't know about that. It's been a while since I've even gone out."

"How about we change that? Tonight? Pick me up at seven?" she practically demands with a winning smile.

The amused smirk on Atlas's face strains as he looks at her. He opens his mouth, no doubt to turn her down, when she speaks again.

"C'mon, Atlas. Don't give me the typical bullshit that I'm too young for you. We are both adults here. I'm attracted to you, and I know you're attracted to me. I promise after one night with me, you'll hate yourself for making me wait so long," she says as she brushes against his chest one more time.

My stomach twists in displeasure when Atlas doesn't immediately turn her down. It's not like I've ever paid attention to their interactions too closely, but I can honestly say that I've never seen him look so tempted by her before. His eyes quickly cut to me, a look of confliction passing over his face before he looks down at her and nods.

"Seven it is. Where are you staying?"

A triumphant smile lights up Alyssa's face as she looks at him.

"Perfect. I'm staying at my sister's house, of course. Drama, can I have your key so I can go drop my stuff off? I'll give it back when you get home."

I open my mouth to tell her that place isn't home anymore. That I haven't stayed a night there in over a month. For some reason, though, I don't. Maybe it's the fact that I'm still processing that Atlas is going out with Alyssa, my aunt, tonight. It could be the fact that they made the plans right in front of me like I don't even exist. Wait, that's not true. Atlas looked at me before agreeing, acknowledging me before doing so, which makes it even worse.

It's not Alyssa's fault. She doesn't know that Atlas and I have been having these weird feelings between us over the last month or so. Atlas does, though, so my ire is completely geared toward him.

"Sure," I say, my voice coming out a little more strained than I intended before I turn on my heel and walk out of the office and over to my desk.

I hear Alyssa's giggling and some whispered words before Atlas lets out a throaty laugh that is like nails on a chalkboard for me. I grit my teeth together as I hear Alyssa's heels click clack behind me. Doing my best to wipe my face clean of emotion, I hand the key to her.

"Oh my god! Pinch me, I must be dreaming!" she whisper squeals. Yeah, whisper squeals. I didn't know it was a thing until now either.

"You've wanted a date with him forever," I say with forced enthusiasm.

"I know! I knew this top was a good investment," she says as she shimmies her full cleavage at me

"Anyway. I've gotta go. I need to find the perfect dress for tonight and squeeze in a wax. I've been dreaming about riding Atlas's cock since I knew what it meant and I'm definitely not doing it with stubble. See you at home!" she calls out over her shoulder as she sashays off.

I don't realize that I'm standing there with my hands balled at my sides, staring after her until a gentle hand touches my shoulder. I nearly jump out of my skin as I turn to face Dillon who has a curious smile on his face.

"You okay, love?"

"Yeah, sorry," I say as I shake my head. "What's up?"

"I was just wondering if you got that contract I sent you?"

"Shit, yes. I'm sorry. I haven't opened it yet, let me do that now."

He nods as he leans against my desk while I sit down and pull up my email.

"So, I've been wondering how long was the appropriate amount of time to ask you out again without spooking you? What would you say?"

"I'd say if I was going to get spooked, your bluntness alone would have taken care of that," I joke, not taking my eyes off my screen before I glance out of the corner of my eye at him and smirk softly.

Dillon chuckles as he shakes his head.

"I swear, I've never met a woman so hell-bent on giving me shit."

I look over the contract he sent me before grabbing the paperwork he will need to go with it as I hit print and turn to face him.

"You love it."

"More than I should," he admits. "So what do you think? Dinner? Maybe as more than friends this time?"

I hesitate for a moment, not wanting to lead him on when I've got someone else that seems to be stuck in my mind whether I like it or not. The same someone who is going out with Alyssa tonight, who looked almost excited about it. Why the hell should he get to stir up all of these unwanted feelings inside me, kiss me like the world was ending only to push me away and go out with my aunt?

No. I'm better than all of that. I deserve better than that. I'm looking at better right now as my eyes trace over Dillon's hopeful yet confident smile.

"Tonight, seven?" I ask.

Dillon grins as he leans forward and places a quick kiss to the corner of my mouth.

"It's a date."

———

I'm putting the finishing touches on my deep red lipstick as Alyssa adjusts the straps of her dress. She went out and bought a blood red velvet dress that clings to her curves like a second skin, leaving pretty much nothing to the imagination paired with a set of matching heels. If she would shut the hell up about how excited she is for tonight and how she can't wait to fuck Atlas, I'd say we were having a nice evening getting ready together.

When I got back to my parents' house and told her that I was going on a date tonight she was so excited. She said it was just like high school and dragged me into my room to help me pick out an outfit. Since I didn't have tons to choose from and didn't have the time or desire to go shopping after work like she did, I settled on a nice little black dress that I wore to homecoming last year. It's simple and understated but it hugs my hips in a flattering way and makes my breasts look a cup size bigger so it's good enough for me.

I was nervous about going back into my parent's house again for the first time in a while. I mean, obviously I've been in and out of here to grab things, but I haven't spent more than ten minutes at a time since I left to stay with Atlas. With Alyssa staying here I feel obligated to stay the night as well. It's been over a month since I've had a nightmare so here's hoping that streak continues.

A knock comes from the door downstairs while Alyssa finishes applying one more layer of her lipstick.

"Can you get that? If it's Atlas I want to make a grand entrance," she says, not even glancing at me as she stares into the mirror.

I don't try to suppress my eye roll as I turn to head down the stairs. I yank the door open with more attitude than I should, mainly because Alyssa has been slowly getting on my nerves more and more from the second she rolled into town.

Atlas is standing at the door, a nice sport coat and slacks on with a clean white dress shirt. He has a kind smile on his face that falters when he sees me. His mouth parts slightly as his eyes slowly make their way down me, pausing on my exposed legs for a few moments before making their way back up to my face.

"Where are you going?" he rumbles almost to himself.

I quirk an eyebrow at his tone before I speak.

"Out."

"Out? Where out? With who?"

"I believe I'm the lucky bloke tonight," Dillon interrupts from behind Atlas.

Atlas turns to face him which allows Dillon enough room to step through the doorway and inside the house before handing me a beautiful bouquet of flowers. They are gorgeous, but I still can barely handle the sight of flowers. Dillon doesn't know that, though and the gesture is sweet, so I paste on a huge smile and even dramatically smell them.

"This is so sweet. Thank you, Dillon," I say as I move into the kitchen to find a vase.

"Of course," he says as he follows me deeper into the house, Atlas on his heels like a shadow.

"You two are going out? Where to?" he almost demands.

Dillon looks at Atlas in an assessing way before turning to me and winking.

"It's a surprise."

I smile at that, and Atlas opens his mouth, probably to argue, when an exaggerated cough comes from behind them. Alyssa is posed dramatically at the bottom of the staircase like she is waiting for her picture to be taken as she gives Atlas her best fuck me eyes. Much to her disappointment, though, Atlas only lets his eyes wander over her for a second at most before he is turning back to face Dillon.

He misses the disappointment and irritation on her face at the lack of awe from her 'grand entrance', but I don't. Her eyes trace over the room before stopping on the flowers in my hand.

"Are those for me?" she asks hopefully as she smiles at Atlas.

Oh my god. She is so cringy it's painful sometimes.

"Uh, afraid not. I got them for Andromeda. Dillon Mathews," Dillon says as he extends his hand out for her to shake.

Disappointment is nowhere to be seen on her face as full-on irritation takes over. She barely touches Dillon's hand as she practically sneers at him.

"Aren't you a little old to be dating my niece?"

"My thoughts exactly," Atlas agrees.

"I'm not sure how that's your concern?" Dillon asks in a challenging tone that I've never heard him use before as he stares directly at Atlas.

I watch as anger passes over Atlas's face and I jump in before he can argue with him because honestly, Dillon is right.

"I'm eighteen, I'm an adult. Who I date is none of anyone's business but mine."

Atlas's eyes cut to me as disapproval weighs heavy in his eyes.

"The fact that your age still has a teen in it, speaks for itself," he says as he turns to face Dillion. "I would have expected you had better taste," Atlas says as he shakes his head.

"I think that's enough of that," Dillon says, the jovial flirty man I've come to know gone in a flash as a fierce protective man replaces him.

I do my best to control the building tears behind my eyes as my throat tightens. Screw him. Where the hell does he get off saying I'm not good enough for Dillon. That he should have better taste. Fuck Atlas Kane.

Dillon turns to me, his irritation melting into soft concern.

"You ready to go, love?"

I nod wordlessly, giving him a strained smile as I lace my fingers with his outstretched fingers. Without sparing Atlas or Alyssa a second glance, I hold my head up high and stride out of the house, not giving a second thought to either of them. They fucking deserve each other.

Chapter 22
Andromeda

Dillon ended up taking us to a nice little French restaurant in town called Bastille. The entire night he was sweet, funny and charming. At first it was hard for me to get into it, Atlas's callous words playing on a loop in my head for half the night. Dillon said that he was sorry that Atlas spoke to me that way and insisted that we not let an 'overprotective wanker' like him ruin our night. I couldn't help but laugh and from there on out we had a great night.

We are walking up the porch of my childhood home before we turn to face each other.

"That place was amazing. I think I'm officially obsessed with French food."

"It was good. You haven't had fine dining until you've eaten in London, though."

"Can't say I've ever had the pleasure. I've never even been outside the US. I want to start a bucket list, though."

"Well that is a travesty. We'll definitely have to correct that."

"We?" I ask as I tilt my head to the side with a smile.

"Oh, yes. I would be honored to be your personal tour guide. London, Paris, Venice, Santorini—"

"You've been to Greece?" I interrupt.

Dillon smiles and nods. "Spent a summer backpacking the

country after I graduated college." He pauses for a second before he continues. "Your mum, she taught a class at Brighton University, right?"

I nod. "Greek Mythology and History. She always said we'd all go to Greece one day. Never got the chance, obviously."

Dillon gives me a sad smile as he nods. "Sounds like you found your first bucket list destination."

"Guess so."

Taking a step closer to me, Dillon cups the bottom of my jaw with his hand, his fingers stroking my cheek gently.

"I really like you, Andromeda."

My pulse quickens at the seriousness of his words.

"I like you too," I say softly.

His mouth stretches into a soft smile as he closes the distance between us, brushing his lips against mine in a gentle gesture. Butterflies flutter inside my chest at the contact as I bring my hands up to wrap around his neck. Dillon deepens the kiss, his tongue gently sweeping across the seam of my lips before I allow him access.

We move together so fluently, so easily. His right hand comes to cup the other side of my face as he holds me like I'm the most precious thing he's ever touched. When the kiss breaks, Dillon rests his forehead against mine before grinning widely.

"I could definitely get used to that," he whispers, causing me to let out a chuckle.

"Good night, love."

"Good night, Dillon."

I watch as Dillon takes a step back and rubs his thumb against his lower lip, smiling at me as he turns and heads back to his car. I give him a small wave before unlocking the front door and stepping inside the house. The door is only shut for maybe ten seconds at most before a loud banging comes from the other side.

Frowning, I look through the peephole to see Atlas staring straight at it. Slowly, I open the door, finding Atlas braced against the doorway, his hands gripping the trim board tightly as his chest heaves with deep breaths.

"You let him kiss you," he rumbles lowly, his labored breaths increasing.

"What?"

His eyes narrow as he takes a step inside. The way his shoulders are bunched, his strides purposeful and strong have me stepping backward. Atlas matches me step for step though until I'm backed into the wall.

"You. Let. Him. Kiss. You," he grits between clenched teeth as he places his palms against the wall on either side of my head.

He saw? What, was he spying on me or something? I raise my chin a little higher, hoping that my defiance is clearly shown.

"I did."

His jaw tics as he drops his head to stare at the ground for a few seconds before he raises it again.

"Did you enjoy it?"

I don't have to think twice about my answer to that.

"I did."

Not as much as my kiss with you.

I make sure to keep that part to myself, though.

Atlas squeezes his eyes closed almost painfully so, like I've seen him do more times than I can count over the last month. He doesn't say anything for several moments, his mind seemingly racing.

"Did you and Alyssa just get back?" I ask curiously since the house is dark and she is nowhere in sight.

"Our date was over in forty-five minutes. Same can't be said for you," he sneers lowly.

Only forty-five minutes? Ouch. Alyssa is going to take that one hard. She spent well over double that just getting ready. Why does their date running so short send a rush of giddiness through me? That's incredibly insensitive of me.

Right?

"I guess Dillion's taste in women isn't as bad as you originally thought," I say with a cock of my head.

"I didn't say that," Atlas scoffs.

"You actually said that verbatim."

"I didn't mean it like that," he rephrases.

"It doesn't matter."

I turn to duck under his arm and head upstairs when a strong hand clasps around my wrist.

"Atlas, what the hell?" I demand as he begins dragging me out the front door and through the front yard.

"Seriously!" I snap. "Where are we going?" I ask as we cross the street before making our way up his front steps.

He doesn't say a word to me until we are through his front door. Once we are inside, in a flash, he spins on me, pinning me against the solid wood before his arms come to cage me in.

"What is happening to us, Nevaeh?" he asks almost on a plea.

"I don't know," I whisper as his head lowers until he is only centimeters away from my lips.

"I'm trying so fucking hard. I'm trying to be a good man, a good father, a good friend, a good godfather," Atlas strains, his resolve visibly weakening by the second.

"Stop trying," I breathe softly, watching as his eyes flick over my face rapidly.

In the next breath, his lips are on mine. Much like the other day in his office there is nothing sweet or gentle about this kiss. Where Dillon kisses me like I am something precious and treasured, Atlas kisses me like he has to. Like he'll starve to death if he doesn't have a taste. It's the most empowering and invigorating feeling of my life.

Atlas's tongue dives into my mouth, tangling with mine in a battle for dominance. I do my best to keep up with him, but Atlas's dominance far outweighs mine. His teeth come out to sink into my bottom lip, causing me to let out a gasp as a zip of pleasure runs through my body.

His hands are everywhere. In my hair, on my breasts, cupping my ass before he lifts me up into his arms. I wrap my legs around his waist as he moves us away from the door and begins moving deeper into the house. I pull away from the kiss, brushing my lips against his bearded cheek and working my way down his neck as I speak against his skin.

"Where are you taking us?"

"To bed," he rasps. "I've tried to be strong, to do the right thing, but I'm fucking done."

Atlas tosses me onto his bed, the overwhelming smell of him surrounding me as his down pillow comforter engulfs me before he climbs on top.

"You better hold on tight, Little Nevaeh. I'm about to fuck this obsession right out of the both of us."

"Please," I beg.

I watch in fascination as he reaches a single hand down and undoes his belt, tossing it to the side before sliding his slacks off and quickly unbuttoning his shirt. My mouth drops when I see him for the first time. I've seen him shirtless several times since living here and a ton before that, but I've definitely never seen him with no pants on. Oh my fucking god. No offense to Theo but he definitely did not get his dad's size.

"What are you thinking about, Nevaeh?" Atlas asks as his hands go to the hem of my dress, slowly inching it up my skin.

I physically have to swallow before I remove my eyes from Atlas's cock as I look into his dark eyes.

"I was thinking about how you and Theo are definitely not built the same," I admit honestly.

A dangerous glint flares in his eyes as his hand buries into the back of my hair, keeping a firm grip on me as he speaks. I lift my hips in response, desperate for some friction as my pussy throbs.

"Let me make something perfectly clear. You're never going to talk about you and my son again. As far as I'm concerned, you were never with anyone before me," he says as he yanks my dress up to rest just under my breasts.

"Not any *boys* from school," he practically growls as he grips my panties in his hand and peels them down my legs before tossing them to the side.

"Not Dillon fucking Mathews," he says as he slips a finger inside me, almost instantly finding my G-spot before rubbing against it slowly.

I let out a breathy moan as I bridge my back to encourage the movement. Unfortunately he pulls his finger out in the next moment as his grip on my hair tightens slightly to regain my attention.

"And definitely not my fucking son!"

Atlas wraps his hand around his cock stroking himself up and down twice before lining up against me as his eyes drill into mine.

"When we are behind this closed door, Nevaeh, you are mine. I'll do whatever I want to this beautiful body, understand?"

I nod quickly, my pussy practically pulsing in anticipation as I stare down at his cock only inches from being inside me. Atlas gives a little tug on my hair, pulling my eyes back up to him.

"Words, babygirl. I need to hear those pretty pouty lips tell me what I want to hear."

"In here, I'm yours. Do whatever you want, anything. Just touch me," I practically beg as I begin squirming underneath him.

"With pleasure, Nevaeh," he rumbles before thrusting inside me until he is buried to the hilt. My mouth opens in a gasp as Atlas groans in what sounds like pain.

"Goddammit! Your cunt is so fucking tight. I can hardly move," Atlas barks as his body stills for a moment.

"Am I hurting you?" I ask tightly as I do my best to adjust to his sudden intrusion.

A low chuckle rumbles through his chest as he makes eye contact with me.

"No, Nevaeh. You're perfect. Too fucking perfect," his rough voice strains.

Desire pools in my lower stomach at his words.

"You're pretty perfect yourself," I say breathily.

Atlas stills for a moment, staring down at me, his eyes intense on mine as he lifts a hand to cup my face.

"I'm the farthest thing from perfect, Nevaeh. If I was, I wouldn't be buried inside my goddaughter's cunt. I'm gonna burn for this but there is no going back, so we might as well enjoy it."

Before I can say anything, he rolls his hips into me, causing my eyes to go into the back of my head.

"Oh my god," I gasp.

He repeats the action, causing my toes to curl.

"Atlas," I breathe heavily as he finds a steady rhythm with the motion.

A familiar pressure is beginning to build in me already. There is no way I can be close, not yet. But I'm quickly proven wrong with one more roll of his hips, his pelvis coming down more than before to grind against my clit, sending me shattering apart in his arms.

"That's it, babygirl. Come on my cock. You're so fucking beautiful," Atlas praises as he coaches me through my orgasm.

When the pleasure begins to recede, Atlas looks down at me and smiles before pulling out. I go to ask him what he's doing when he flips us. In an instant, he's on his back and I'm awkwardly falling on top of him. Before I can completely fall, his hands are on my hips, steadying me before guiding me to his cock.

"Come ride my cock, Nevaeh. Show me what else this sweet cunt can do."

The steady way he watches me has me slowly sinking down on him, like a sailor being called to the sea, I can't help but go to him. The connection Atlas and I have been trying to fight for months now has been amplified in moments and an overwhelming desire to please him takes over me.

When I fully sink down on him, my pussy throbs at the familiar intrusion while Atlas hums a satisfied moan. Slowly, I start moving my hips, doing my best to find just the right angle and rhythm that will hopefully drive him as wild as he drove me.

"That's it," he encourages as one of his hands stays on my hips while the other reaches around to my lower back, encouraging my movements as he thrusts up into me. "Such a good fucking girl," he moans.

His words send a warm feeling spreading through my chest and my pussy as I continue to follow his instruction. Before long I don't need his guidance as my body takes over, pleasure sparking every movement.

"Oh god. Atlas," I breathe. "Are you close? I think I'm gonna come again," I whine, doing my best to fight the building pressure beginning to take over me.

"So come, Nevaeh. Let me see how gorgeous you are as you fall apart on top of me."

"But that's not fair," I complain. "I'll be ahead of you."

Atlas's movements falter for a moment as his head turns curiously.

His hands are massaging the upper parts of my thighs in a soothing way as he speaks.

"Ahead of me? Babygirl, if you don't walk out of here with at least three orgasms to my one, then I didn't do my job right."

"Three?" I gasp with widened eyes.

His eyes darken with lust as he nods his head slowly and forces my movements to continue.

"Your pleasure gives me pleasure, Nevaeh. Watching you fall apart is the sweetest sight I've ever been gifted. I want to see it again and again and again," he rasps, pulling me down onto him with each word.

"You're greedy for my pleasure?" I ask as Atlas basically fucks me from underneath me, my body practically a wanton mess as I try to keep my head about me while the pleasure from it all overwhelms me.

"Fucking desperate for it," he grits, pushing up into me once more, the head of his cock rubbing against my G-spot and officially detonating me.

I scream out my orgasm, my legs shaking, pussy spasming as I toss my head back in pleasure.

"Oh fuck, fuck, fuck," I whine as the orgasm tears through me.

I feel Atlas's cock begin to pulse and I know he won't last long now. Surprising me yet again, though, he flips us until we are on our sides. He's behind me, somehow still inside me as his left leg comes up around my own. I feel his hands trail up my bare side before his left hand comes underneath the fabric of my dress, pushing it up to expose my breasts while his right slips around to grip my neck.

His large hand holds me firmly, but without making it hard to breathe, while the other cups my breast easily, his thumb begins brushing against my nipple, causing my body to shiver against him.

"A-atlas," I stutter. "I can't. I can't."

"Yes you can, Nevaeh. You can do it."

"No," I say with a shake of my head. "I've never been able to come more than once in one session."

"Well, then we're already ahead," he says as his hips begin slowly thrusting. "Now be a good girl and give me what I need."

"I want to but there is no way I—"

"Shhh," he says as he places a gentle kiss to my spine, nipping at the skin lightly as his hold on my throat tightens slightly while his other hand moves from my breast down my stomach to rest over my pussy.

"Give me one more, Nevaeh."

His hand moves over to my clit, fingers rubbing tight quick circles over it that to my surprise, sends a zing of pleasure running up my spine.

"God," I breathe out as my head rests against his chest.

"Not God, baby, Atlas. A fucking Titan."

I can't help but smirk at that as he continues rubbing and fucking me.

"So modest, I see."

His hand cradling my neck gives a slight warning squeeze before his fingers reach my jaw, directing me to look at him over my shoulder. Once I do, he crushes his lips to mine. It instantly detonates me, again. I try to scream my release, but Atlas consumes it, taking everything from me as I feel his cock swell before a rush of liquid begins filling me up. He doesn't stop kissing me as he fucks me through his orgasm, his moans rumbling from his chest as his grip on my body becomes near punishing.

When we both come down from our highs, we are silent for a moment before Atlas places a quick kiss to the back of my neck as he pulls out of me. I feel empty instantly and miss him immediately. Don't know how I could since I'm fairly sure I'll already struggle to walk again tomorrow.

Atlas walks into the bathroom for a moment before coming back out with a cloth as he begins to clean me. I feel myself begin to melt into his bed as he presses the warm washcloth and wipes between my legs. Both acts are done extremely gently, and it has my mind whirling. Who the hell is this guy now? This definitely still isn't my godfather. But this isn't the man who made me come on his cock three times because he *needed* it. This guy is soft and sweet, and gentle.

Taking a chance, I slowly turn my head to glance behind me, where Atlas is staring at me softly, a look of peace on his face as he gives me a caring barely there smile. It's the most at peace I've seen him look in months. Hell, maybe even years.

"How are you feeling?" he asks.

I nod as I rest my cheek against the pillow underneath me.

"Good."

"Just good?" he asks with a raised brow.

I shrug softly, doing my best to hide my grin. "Maybe like a step above good."

His hand stops moving before pinching the sensitive skin on my thigh. I yelp in response as Atlas scoots up to lay down next to me, hauling me into his bare chest. I slip my bunched-up dress off before tossing it to the ground.

We lay there in silence for a while, skin to skin. I'm not sure what to say or what to do. I'm not even sure what to think. I slept with Atlas. No, that's not right. I got fucked by Atlas.

Did that actually just happen? I open my mouth, to say what, I'm not quite sure when Atlas's hold on me tightens.

"Shhh. Go to sleep, Nevaeh."

Not having it in me to argue, I close my eyes and quickly drift off into a deep sleep.

Chapter 23
Atlas

A soft yet sweet smell enters my nose as I slowly begin to wake. My eyes feel heavy as I try to place what exactly happened last night. I remember my date with Alyssa, hell what a train wreck that was. She spent the entire time conversationally bragging about everything good in her life while I obsessively stared at my phone.

Not really sure what I was waiting for. Maybe an SOS text from Andromeda, that she needed me to save her from her bad date. Maybe a call from someone else that she was in trouble or hurt. Anything, I suppose. No text ever came, though.

As Alyssa continued going on and on about herself, I was counting down the minutes until the date could be over so that I could track down Andromeda. I didn't know where to start thanks to Dillon being an asshole, but I was willing to call every nice restaurant in town if that's what it took.

At the end of the night, I walked Alyssa to her door and that's where things got uncomfortable. I saw the look in her eye when she leaned up on her toes to kiss me. The moment she made her move a feeling like an iron ball sunk into my stomach and had me gently but firmly pushing her away. She looked up at me with glossy eyes that made me instantly feel like a prick as I gave her a bullshit excuse about not wanting to rush things.

She still seemed put off but the sweet smile she gave me told me she semi-bought it so instead of arguing, she kissed my cheek and went inside. I jumped in my car and was about to head into town when I stopped myself. What the hell was I doing? Even if I could find them, what would I do when I got there? What would I say when I found them enjoying the date they both agreed to and seemed to be excited for?

Shaking my head, I stepped out of the car before locking myself inside my house. Unfortunately the plan to stay inside didn't work as well as I hoped when I heard a car pulling into the driveway across the street at almost eleven at night. I don't know what possessed me to look out my window and watch Dillon walk her to the door. Even more, I don't know why I stood there and watched as Dillon kissed her as if she was his to kiss, his to touch, his to have. My pulse was thrumming, my anger burning and vision practically blurring with the rage. In that moment, I wanted nothing more than to rip his hands from her flawless skin and beat the shit out of him.

Then the next thing I knew she was stepping inside her house, and he was driving away as my feet were carrying me across my yard and to the Clarke's. I remember my fist banging against the heavy door and Andromeda opening it, looking bewildered. I remember feeling overcome with lust when I saw her again in that black dress that made her legs go on for miles. Her lips were pouty and swollen and at first I didn't think I could find anything sexier than the sight in front of me. Then I remembered that it was Dillon that did that to her. Dillon was the last one to touch her lips, not me.

That thought broke something inside me. My resolve? My sanity? I couldn't tell you which. Maybe both. Whatever it was, it obliterated into a million pieces as I yanked her out her house, across the street and into my own. When my lips crushed against hers an overwhelming need filled me. It was like air had been breathed into my lungs for the first time in I don't know how long. Like my fingertips had slipped just above water desperate for help and she pulled me to the surface.

She did something to me that I didn't even think was possible. It was like she breathed life back into me. When I watched her fall apart in my arms, I knew right then and there that she would be my undoing if I let her.

I can't let her.

If I allowed myself to have her the fall out would be more catastrophic than I can hardly fathom. Not because I went out with her aunt last night, not because she is my son's ex-girlfriend. Not even because her late parents were my best friends in the whole world, my chosen family.

We could never be more than one night because I know that if I allowed myself to have Andromeda Clarke, I could never let her go.

I shake my head at that thought, glancing down to see the silky blond strands fanned out across my bare chest shift slightly as she makes a soft almost mewling sound before those bright-green eyes flutter open. My gaze travels over her slowly, momentarily caught off guard by this stunning woman curled up in my arms.

Memories of last night vividly come to the forefront of my mind. Images of me taking her the way I never should have wanted. The way I craved.

Last night was a release, a desperately needed one. I needed to fuck her out of my system, for both our sakes. Unfortunately, it doesn't seem to have worked. Instead, now all I can think about is what she feels like when I'm buried deep inside her, what she looks like with her head tossed back, mouth parted as she rides my cock until she covers me in her sweet cum.

Instead of fixing the mess I've suddenly found myself in, all I want to do is spend the day in bed ruining her for all men, giving her unsurmountable pleasure until she is nothing but a lithe body to bend at my will. Reality unfortunately brings me back from my unattainable fantasy when her soft voice speaks.

"Atlas? Are you okay?"

I don't know why, but the tone of her question strikes a nerve. It plucks at a memory, one I can vaguely recall of little Andromeda who couldn't have been more than eight years old, checking in on Em when she had just found out that her dad passed away. Her voice was so small, so tiny. We were all hurting over the loss, but the way Andromeda's voice barely whispered to her mother embedded itself into my memory forever.

This is a prime example of why I can never have her. I have too much of her as it is. I'm only allowed to have what I've already been given. What I took last night, it was never mine to take. Guilt begins burrowing into me as I drop my head against the pillow and look up at the ceiling.

I feel Andromeda's hand press against my chest as she leans up to keep eye contact with me despite my avoidance.

"Talk to me," she begs softly.

Against my better judgment, I glance down to see her staring at me with worry in those big emerald-green eyes. Her shoulders and chest are bare, reminding me of how she stripped off her dress last night before falling asleep in my arms. My eyes involuntarily skate over her creamy smooth skin, drinking in the sight of her pale pink nipples that sit perfectly on her full breasts.

I feel my cock harden at the sight and my mouth water, desperate to have them in my mouth, just once. It would be so easy to order her to crawl on top of me. To make her ride my cock again while I feasted on her beautiful tits. A dark voice inside urges me to do it, that it will only be one more time, that I've already fucked her once. Having her a second time isn't going to make or break anything.

It will though. My self-restraint is hanging on by a thread just from having her here, in my bed, looking freshly fucked and beautiful. I could lose myself in Andromeda until the end of time without a care in the world. I could, if I didn't care about what that would do to those around us, what that would do to her. She needs to focus on healing and moving forward with her life. If and when she's ready to start dating again, it definitely shouldn't be her dad's forty-one-year-old best friend.

The thought of how disappointed Em would be in me, how hard Paul would rightly kick my ass if they knew what I had done effectively squashes any salacious desires, bringing that nasty taste of guilt back in full force. I practically leap out of bed, striding over to the dresser before pulling on a pair of boxers as I turn to face the beautiful naked angel in my bed.

Fuck, no. Not an angel. Andromeda. Andromeda Clarke. Your son's ex-girlfriend. Your goddaughter.

That last one sends my stomach rolling which is probably exactly what I need.

"You need to go," I say evenly.

Her concern morphs into confusion.

"What?"

"You need to go. Last night was a mistake. One I hope you won't hold against me."

"Mistake?" she echoes. "What part of it was a mistake?" she asks as she slides out of bed, not doing a thing to cover up her naked body as she begins walking toward me.

"The part where you finally took what you wanted?" she asks with a step. "The part where you took what I wanted?"

Another step.

I feel my chest rising and falling with labored breaths as she stops just when her hardened nipples brush against my bare chest, causing a shiver to run up my back as she lowers her voice to almost a whisper.

"Or the part where you fucked me so hard I saw stars as you filled me to the brim with your cum?"

"Jesus," I breathe out as I close my eyes and shake my head. "All of it. It was all a mistake," I say with a newfound determination.

Hurt flashes across her face as she takes a small step back, slightly covering her breasts as she crosses her arms vulnerably. I hate that I'm putting that look on her face right now but it's best this way.

"I'm so sorry I took advantage of you, Andromeda. My head is a mess right now. It's no excuse but—"

"You didn't take advantage of me, Atlas. I wanted it, wanted you. For a while now."

I shouldn't respond, I should hold my ground and continue urging her to leave as quickly as possible, but curiosity gets the best of me.

"For how long?" My voice strains despite my efforts.

She shrugs. "Not exactly sure. A little after I started living here, I guess."

I swallow over the realization that she has wanted me for over a month. That she's slept in the room across from mine for over a month, thinking about me, wanting me. Has she touched herself to the thought of me like I've wanted to about her?

"Maybe that's the problem then," I voice. "Maybe we need to figure out other living situations."

Her mouth parts in what looks like shock as her eyes hold mine.

"You're kicking me out."

"No," I urge quickly. "I just think it might be best if we have some space. I think we need some time apart and we can't get that at work. Something is happening to us, something that can't happen."

She scoffs as she tosses her hands out at her sides.

"Newsflash, Atlas. It already did, the rag you used to clean your cum out of me with was proof of that."

"It can't happen again!" I snap as frustration begins to fill me.

What is the matter with her? She should be disgusted with me. Why is she being so difficult? Doesn't she see this is for the best? That I'm trying to protect her?

A hardness settles across her face as she turns and scoops up her dress from the floor.

"Fine. I'll start moving my stuff after work today."

I don't get the chance to respond before she is storming out of my room bare ass naked. I lift my hands up to my face, slowly dragging them down as I shake my head.

What the fuck have I done?

My shower takes twice as long as normal. I used extra hot water and extra soap. As if soap and water could erase the feel of Andromeda's lithe body against me. My cock was so pissed at me for kicking her out this morning it took nearly twenty minutes for it to finally get the hint that I would not be inviting her back into bed, ever, and I wouldn't be touching myself to the thought of her either.

When I get dressed and walk downstairs, the house is quiet. Andromeda's car is gone from the Clarke's driveway so it's safe to say she has already left for work. I decide to skip breakfast and stick with coffee before getting in the car and heading to work.

Goddammit.

Andromeda coming to work for me was probably the stupidest idea I ever had. Bringing her into my world, placing her just out of reach day in and out is the sickest form of torture imaginable. Especially now that I know what she looks like when she's getting railed from behind, or how her eyes roll into the back of her head when my hand slipped between her silky thighs. Or how she moaned in pleasure, practically arched into me anytime my hand slid around her slim throat. The power I feel, the control. I crave it when I'm with her. I can't seem to control much else except her in those moments. Her reactions are beautiful, her desires perfect.

Perfect for me.

Fucking hell.

When I get to work, I walk straight past her desk, doing my best to not even give her a glance as I step inside my office. It takes me an hour or so to get into things but I'm finally able to get some work done. I just hit send on my latest email to Abner about his urgent request for a meeting when my office door is pushed open.

I don't know why I expect it to be Andromeda. Even more concerning, I don't know why I *hope* it's Andromeda. Either way, it's irrelevant. Alyssa strides into my office like she owns the place, her designer heels eating up the distance between the door and my desk before she perches herself on the edge of it with a seductive smile.

"Good morning, handsome."

Her smile does absolutely nothing for me, but I don't let her see it. I can't lie. I only said yes to Alyssa yesterday because I couldn't stop thinking about Andromeda. I thought, what was a better way to annihilate all desires I could have for her, and she could have for me than if I started dating her aunt? Unfortunately, I learned last night that there is a reason I never gave Alyssa more than a second look over the years. We are just not compatible, at all.

"Good morning. How are you?" I ask with a polite smile.

"I'm good." She smiles as she leans closer, attempting to whisper but the high pitch of her voice hardly allows it. "I thought about you while I made myself come last night."

Normally, if a woman were to come tell me something like that I'd find the confidence sexy but coming from Emily's baby sister, it just makes me cringe? Alyssa is undeniably gorgeous, but I've just never been able to see her in that way. Any other man my age would be salivating at the thought of having her attention. Compared to Andromeda though...well, there is no comparison.

Fuck! Stop thinking about her. You shouldn't have anything about her to compare others to in the first place.

Not knowing how to respond to Alyssa, I give her a tight smile as I nod. Her face falters as she seems to grit her teeth before she shakes her head and tosses her hair over one of her shoulders.

"I came by to see if I could take you out to lunch."

I open my mouth to decline, to come up with literally any reason as to why I can't when Andromeda steps in, not even making eye contact with me as she speaks.

"I've got those numbers you were asking for," she says as she drops a file onto my desk.

Just because she doesn't look at me doesn't mean she misses the fact that Alyssa is in here perched on the corner of my desk. I watch as Andromeda gives her a forced smile and a nod before heading back to her desk. Alyssa wrinkles her nose at her before she looks down at me.

"What's her problem? Her date not go well or something?"

I glance down at the papers Andromeda left me as I shrug.

"Not sure."

"Whatever," Alyssa says with an eye roll. "There's a reason her nickname is Drama. It's always something with her."

That has me raising a brow toward her. What the hell is she even talking about? Paul and Emily started calling her Drama as a joke, because she was the most easygoing kid there was. She's always been calm, collected and never got caught up in all of the typical shit that teenagers do. It's cliché to say she's mature for her age but she actually is. If anyone is constantly dramatic, it's the woman sitting in front of me.

I can't say any of that, though. Coming to Andromeda's defense would only raise suspicions. Not like Alyssa has any reason to be suspicious of Andromeda and me. There's nothing to be suspicious of.

Except for the fact that I drug her by her arm across the street and fucked her tight cunt into my mattress until she fell asleep in my arms.

"So, lunch?" Alyssa asks again with a waiting smile.

"Yeah, let's go. I have to be back in an hour for a meeting."

"Yes, sir," she salutes as she giggles to herself before climbing off my desk.

I lock my computer and grab my phone and wallet before standing and walking out of my office.

"I'm going to run to the bathroom before we grab lunch," Alyssa says as she begins digging around in her purse as she makes her way to the bathrooms.

When I look away from her, I see Andromeda staring at me from her desk with a flat look.

"What?" I grit out, not liking the heavy judgment in her eyes.

"Are you fucking kidding me? You're going to lunch with her?"

I raise an eyebrow at her, doing my best to keep a look of casual indifference.

"We both need to eat, don't we?"

Andromeda lets out a hollow laugh as she shakes her head, turning her attention back to her computer.

"If you have something to say, spit it out."

Her eyes narrow at me before she turns in her chair to fully face me.

"Fine. The fact that you're going to lunch with my *aunt* when your cock still smells like my pussy is disgusting."

My eyes widen slightly as I quickly whip my head around to see if anyone can overhear our conversation. Thankfully the office seems to be fairly empty today. Turning back to her, my eyes harden on her.

"We are not discussing last night ever again. Is that understood?"

"Oh yeah, it's so easy to forget when my godfather fucks me s—"

"Andromeda!" I bark. "If you don't keep your mouth shut, I will fire you."

She scoffs. "Yeah, right."

"Try me," I challenge. "Last night was a mistake. One that will not be repeated. Go home. You're done for the day."

Her eyes are like slits as she glares at me before she shoves back from her chair to stand.

"Fine. I have to get a head start on moving anyway."

"That's probably best," I say as she grabs her purse.

She pauses like she's surprised at my compliance before her voice strains slightly.

"Screw you."

She rushes past me before making her way to the elevators. I don't know how long I stand there before a small hand wraps around my arm, shaking me out of my daze.

"Ready?" Alyssa asks.

"Yeah. Ready."

Chapter 24
Andromeda

I moved out of Atlas's and back into my family home that day. The nightmares have returned, not as brutally as before, but they are still there. They've changed now, though. They aren't the violent traumatic nightmares of how they died that night. Instead, the much more painful reminder of how great life was, how perfect it used to be now mocks me in my sleep.

Flashes of my mom making breakfast and my dad sipping coffee at the island as they chatted. Or their smiling faces turning to me as I come down the stairs. When I wake up, it's a stark reminder that those times have passed, the memories will fade but the remaining truth is that I'm alone.

Not totally alone, I guess. Theo and I have FaceTimed several times over the last week. It's a nice distraction to just talk to him about everything and nothing. I mean, usually he leads the conversation because no way in hell I'm shedding light on the soap opera that has become my life. Besides, I'm fairly certain that if Theo found out I slept with his father, he'd never forgive me.

Atlas has steered clear of me over the last few days, and I've made sure to stay out of his way. I don't want to turn my back on the company that my dad helped build but I'm starting to feel like I don't have a choice. Atlas is toxic. Or maybe we are just a toxic combination.

If he didn't want to fuck me, he shouldn't have. He doesn't get to fuck me and then treat me like shit. He doesn't get to be kind and sweet and there for me in easily the darkest part of my life and then kick me out of bed only to go to lunch with my aunt.

It's un-fucking-acceptable.

Alyssa called me after their lunch date. She gushed on and on about how interested and attentive Atlas was with her for seemingly the first time ever. I had to set the phone down while I finished packing my things because her words were physically making me ill.

When she was finally done, she told me that she didn't have time to come say goodbye to me and that she had to head back to Portland.

Good riddance.

I never fully understood why my mom and Alyssa had such a strained relationship. Alyssa was always the cool aunt, the fun one. I think I'm seeing the full picture now, though. She's extremely self-centered and quite frankly, obnoxious as hell. No wonder my mom could only handle her in doses.

Maybe I'm being a little hard on Alyssa, though. She had no way of knowing that I was developing a little crush, or whatever you want to call it, on Atlas. And I guess if you want to be technical about it, she has been head over heels for him going on twenty years now. But he clearly isn't interested, so why won't she back off? After their date she wasn't the one he fucked, it was me.

Yeah, but then he told you it was a mistake and spent hours alone with her the next day.

Rolling my eyes at myself, I practically stomp my way to the copier near the receptionist's desk since the one next to mine broke yesterday.

"Hey," a soft voice calls out to me.

I turn to see Dillon smiling at me, his blue eyes practically sparkling as he walks up to me.

Doing my best to push all of the bullshit thoughts inside my head, I smile at him. Dillon. We like Dillon. Sweet, funny, charming, non-douchebag hot and cold every five minutes, Dillon. Yeah, we like him.

"Hey. How's it going?"

"Good. I'm sorry I've been in and out of the office this week."

He has? Why didn't I notice that?

Probably because every spare thought lately has been about Atlas fucking Kane.

"I feel like I haven't really seen you since our date," he says as he takes a smaller step closer, lowering his voice as he does.

I smile at the reminder. That was a really great day. Oh my god. I haven't even reflected on the fact that I slept with Atlas *after* my date with Dillon. Is that considered cheating? I mean, we aren't exclusive or anything. No, I don't think it's cheating. It just makes me a terrible person.

"Yeah, I had fun," I say, doing my best to keep my smile in place.

He nods as one of his warm hands reaches down to take mine.

"I'd love to take you out again. I got tickets to a Seth Bishop concert this Saturday. Want to be my date?"

"No way? I love Seth Bishop. I've been following him since he started putting out his EPs when he still lived down in Alabama. I had the song *Aubrey* on repeat last year. How did you manage to get tickets? His shows are always sold out!"

"I have my ways." Dillon grins with a wink. "So, what do you say, love?"

"Yes, of course! I'm so excited."

"Me too." He nods before his eyes dart around us before leaning down and pressing his lips against mine.

I don't hesitate to meet him, letting the warm feeling from his soft kiss wash over me. It's not earth-shattering or all-consuming, but who says that a kiss has to be?

"What the hell is going on out here?" a voice snarls from behind us.

I break away from Dillon to see Atlas standing just outside his office, his fists clenched at his sides, eyes practically bulging out of his head as his chest moves up and down rapidly.

"Do I need to remind everyone that there is a no fraternization condition to your employment here?" Atlas practically growls.

Dillon lifts a disbelieving eyebrow, not letting go of my hand despite my trying to wiggle out of his hold.

"Since when?" he challenges.

Atlas's eyes narrow into thin slits as he holds his focus on Dillon.

"Since now, effective immediately."

Dillon scoffs but it's so soft that I don't think Atlas hears him. Otherwise I'm fairly certain he'd throw Dillon into the wall behind us.

"My office, now!" Atlas barks, his eyes trained on me before he turns and storms inside.

Not bothering to waste my breath arguing with him, I slip my hand from Dillon's as I walk down the hall and into Atlas's office. He's leaning against his desk, his head in his hands, fingers buried deep into that thick hair when I step inside.

"Close the door," he rumbles lowly, not bothering to look up from the spot that he is staring at on the floor.

I do as he says and stand there in silence, gearing up for a fight when he says something that catches me completely off guard.

"Crawl to me."

What?

"Excuse me?" I balk.

His head snaps up at me, anger like I've never quite seen before splashed across his face as he looks at me.

"Now. Believe me when I say I do not have the control or patience for your attitude Andromeda Nevaeh. Now get on your hands and knees and fucking crawl to me."

I want to resist him just on the simple fact that he ordered me to. How degrading? Still, there is a small bit of me that can't deny I'm curious. Why does he want me to crawl to him? What kind of satisfaction will that give him? What will it give me? I feel my legs slowly begin bending as I sink to the floor. The industrial carpet bites into my bare knees when my pencil skirt rises up, but I barely recognize it as I keep my eyes on his once I'm on all fours. I stay there for a moment, feeling completely confused, a little unsure and definitely turned on.

What the hell is this man doing to me?

"Crawl," he demands again, a lot less anger in his voice this time and far more heat.

I bite my bottom lip for a moment before I slowly stretch my hands out one by one as I begin crawling across the floor. Atlas never drops his eyes from me once as I cross the room before stopping a few feet in front of him. I pause, looking up to him for guidance.

"All the way."

The way the tenor of his voice fills the room sends a trail of goose bumps running across my skin. Slowly, I continue my pace until I'm face to face with his navy-blue slacks. My eyes aren't trained on his pants, though. Instead I'm left almost mesmerized as one of his hands rubs against his raging hard-on through the thin material.

I'm only able to look up just enough to catch his eyes as he looks down, flicking over to the elastic band on my wrist.

"Put your hair up like a good girl and open your mouth."

The low timbre of his voice sends a shiver running through me as I lift my hands, slowly tying back my hair as I look up at him for his next direction.

"Take it out."

Cautiously, I reach my hands out to his zipper, slowly undoing it before pushing inside past his boxers. I wrap my fingers around his thick cock, causing him to let out a sharp hiss. My eyes flick up to see a hungry look in his eyes as he nods silently.

Licking my lips slowly, I pull his cock out of his pants to free it fully before sticking out my tongue. I make sure to look up as I do, snagging Atlas's eye contact as I flatten my tongue against his head. Atlas bangs a fist against the top of the desk as his eyes roll into the back of his head, encouraging me to do it again.

"Fuck!" he grunts.

Smirking to myself that I can have such an effect on a man like him, I lower my head to start my tongue at the base of his cock before licking a slow line all the way to the top. His hips jerk in response before he brings his hands down to cup both sides of my face gently. I look up at him, getting lost in that stormy gaze as I practically hold my breath for what's next.

"I'm going to hell," he mutters under his breath before he pulls my face forward, forcing his cock into my mouth and down my throat until he bottoms out.

I gag on instinct despite doing my best to relax. Atlas lifts my head up to allow me to breathe before bringing me back down harder this time.

"Fuck, yes. Just like that. Such a good girl. Sucking my cock like you were made for it."

His words egg me on as I begin bobbing my head up and down, trying to take him deeper each time. I feel his fingers weave their way through my hair as he forces my head down faster and harder with each thrust. His head is tipped back to the ceiling as he leans back further while he lets out moans of approval.

Reaching up one of my hands, I slip inside his slacks to massage his balls, earning another approving growl as his hips begin to move faster. A rush of exhilaration runs through me, at the power I feel. I may be the one on my knees right now but make no mistake, Atlas Kane is at my mercy.

I feel his balls begin to draw up as I suck harder and faster, allowing my tongue to lash against his head as I come up high enough for air before sinking his cock back down my throat. Pushing him as deep as I can, I stop moving my head as I glance up to look at him. His head is now down, watching me like a predator watches its prey, his eyes practically on fire with lust, his breathing ragged, like he knows I'm about to ruin us both.

The other night was wild and hot and passionate, but it was also dark, discreet, and private. None of those things can be said about this moment.

Atlas opens his mouth, assumingly to say something but I make my move before he can speak. I swallow around his cock several times back-to-back, effectively sending him crumbling over the edge. He barks out a rough, "Fuck," before I feel his cum run down my throat.

I continue swallowing the warm liquid as it begins to fill my mouth. His body is trembling as I swallow him down whole and only stops when I drag my mouth up his cock, releasing him with a loud pop.

His chest is heaving, his eyes wild as he reaches down to my face, brushing his thumb against the corner of my mouth before pushing the drip of cum back inside.

"Good girls don't waste a drop."

My tongue greedily wraps around his thumb, desperate for the taste of him, the feel of him. Desperate for *him*. He groans as he tosses his head to face the ceiling once again for several seconds, clenching his eyes tight before looking back down at me. Just like before, all traces of lust have evaporated in a moment and that familiar look of regret has taken up residence.

You've got to be fucking kidding me.

Not wasting a moment, I scramble to my feet and turn to walk out of the office.

"Nevaeh. Wait," he says hoarsely.

"No!" I snap as I turn on my heel and storm toward him, pushing my finger into his chest as I do.

"I'm done, Atlas! You can't keep treating me like a fuck toy that you drag out whenever you feel like abandoning your morals for a few minutes. You say that you can't get involved with me, that my parents would be so disappointed in you. Well, if this is how you treat all women then you're fucking right. I'm disappointed in you, I'm disgusted with you, and I'm *fucking* done."

With that, I spin around and walk out of his office, slamming the door shut behind me. I see a few curious glances tossed my way around the office, but I keep my head down as I gather my things before rushing down the hallway to the elevator. I hear Dillon call out to me, but I pretend that I don't hear him. I can't face anyone right now, especially not him.

I jam my thumb into the button, leaning my head against the elevator wall. Only once the doors shut do I let the first tear slip down my face. God fucking dammit. I swear for being such a smart girl sometimes I can be so stupid.

Chapter 25
Andromeda

I don't go straight home. I can't. I already feel like shit and sitting around in a house haunted by memories will only make it worse. So, I spend the afternoon getting some groceries and some of my essentials that I've run out of. It's dark when I get to my house, and I fumble with carrying all the groceries through the door as I try to kick it shut behind me.

I'm hurrying to the kitchen to dump them on the island when I see a figure sitting on my couch causing me to scream. My bags of groceries are abandoned as I drop them in a rush and run to the kitchen.

Kitchens have knives. I need a knife!

"Andromeda! It's me, it's me," a familiar voice calls out.

In the next moment the living room light flicks on and Atlas is standing there, his tie loosened around his neck, hair messy like he's run his fingers through it a million times. My brain registers that a stranger didn't break into my house, but my rapidly beating heart hasn't gotten the memo that there is no threat. Maybe because it knows better than me that the biggest threat I've ever faced is standing right in front of me.

"What the hell, Atlas!" I shout in between gasps. "What are you doing here? How do you still have a key? Do you know how creepy that is? Give it to me now!" I demand.

"I needed to talk to you."

"So you break into my house? That was the solution?" I scoff.

"Well, I didn't have much of an option. You moved out of mine like you were never there and—"

"You're the one that told me to!"

"I didn't mean it, okay?" he snaps. "I said it, yeah. But it's not what I wanted. I didn't think you actually would. When I got home, and you weren't there I..." he trails off as he looks down the hallway.

"Well how the hell am I supposed to know that, Atlas? I don't read minds. I'll never stick around where I'm not wanted, and you made it blatantly clear that I'm not wanted."

"That's not true," he says as he continues to look anywhere but me.

"Oh? Was the whole you continuously pushing me away, kicking me out of your bed, out of your office, some type of foreplay? Wait, don't tell me. Those were mistakes and should have never happened in the first place, right?"

That gets his attention, and slowly his gaze comes to mine, a pain like I've only seen in flashes on full display as he looks at me.

"I'm sorry. I've been an asshole. I know that. I don't know what's happening to me, to us. One moment, I'm fine and the next I see you kissing another man and anger like I've never felt takes over me. I want to slaughter any man who has ever touched you, Nevaeh. Do you get how dangerous that is? How dangerous I am to you?" he asks as he takes a few steps toward me.

I don't respond, watching him carefully as he runs a hand through his hair.

"The way I've treated you is unforgivable. I recognize that and I can't apologize enough. You're under my skin and I don't know when or how you ever got there, but you're there. I promise though, I'm going to do everything I can to fix it, to make sure things go back to normal."

I laugh bitterly as I shake my head.

"What does that even mean? Nothing is normal anymore, Atlas. Our entire world has been flipped upside down. There is no more normal, it doesn't exist."

He frowns at that, pausing a moment before he nods.

"You're right. I just want...I need to make things right between us."

"Well not treating me like a pocket pussy is a good start," I snark.

Atlas grimaces at that as he shakes his head.

"How do you even know what that is?"

I roll my eyes at him. "I'm young, not inexperienced."

"Yeah, I could tell," he says lowly, a hint of heat in his words before he closes his eyes and shakes his head.

"Look, I just wanted to apologize. To try to put all of this behind us so we can get to a new normal. Since the day you were born, I vowed to look after you—"

"Well, you've done a shit job lately."

"I know and—"

"You know what, just go. Dillon's gonna be here any minute."

It's a lie and an unnecessary jab but it seems to have the intended reaction as the air in the room shifts on a dime.

"Dillon?" he questions slowly.

"Yeah," I confirm with my best I don't give a shit face.

I watch as his jaw clenches in irritation as he speaks. "I thought I made myself clear about employees fraternizing outside the workplace?"

"Oh, right. You said no hooking up with coworkers right before you ordered me to crawl across the floor and suck your cock like a whore, right?"

His nostrils flare as he looks down at me, his jaw clenching tightly as he speaks.

"Yes."

Rolling my eyes again, I shake my head.

"Yeah, well I decided that since you broke your own rule, it was null and void," I say before turning to the abandoned groceries on the floor as I begin slowly picking them up.

"I don't want you seeing him, Nevaeh," Atlas says like I didn't even speak.

"Yeah, well, I don't want you to be such a raging fucking asshole all the time. Guess we are both in an unfortunate predicament, huh?"

"Don't test me, Andromeda Nevaeh Clarke. I'm about three seconds away from bending you over my knee and spanking your ass raw," he says darkly.

I hate that a thrill runs through me at his words and do my best to squash any swarming desire sparked to life by his words.

"Just before you get what you want and then toss my ass to the curb, right? You know what, Atlas. Be a fucking man and take what you want or walk away if you can't. But don't be a coward and run just because you're scared of what comes next. You want me and you can't deny that. There are men out there more than willing to take what they want. Dillion for instance, or even your son. I could call Theo home, tell him I want to give us another chance, and he would be here in an instant on his knees begging for me."

I don't see it coming when he crosses the room in a flash and pins me against the wall. His arms are braced above my head, his face lowered to brush his nose against mine.

"Don't ever speak about my son or any other man on his knees for you ever again. You. Are. Fucking. *Mine!*"

I scoff and roll my eyes, despite his domineering presence. I see through his bullshit. Atlas Kane doesn't scare me.

"Since when?"

"Always," he promises lowly.

He closes his eyes, taking several deep breaths like he is trying to talk himself off the ledge before he opens those melted chocolate eyes and speaks.

"My entire life I've thought of everyone before myself. Done everything I could for everyone else. I've sacrificed a lot for those around me and I have no regrets, but I'm done, Nevaeh. I'm gonna be selfish and reckless for the first time in my goddamn life. I'm taking something for me and that something is *you.*"

My breath hitches at his words, my eyes frantically scanning his face to see the doubt or lies coating his honey-drenched words but all I find is raw passion, pain, and want. So much want.

"Don't say it if you don't mean it," I practically beg, my voice shaking as I do.

His hand lowers to cup my face possessively as he pulls back enough to properly look me in the eye.

"I mean it. You've officially broken me. Congratulations. I hope you're prepared for what's next because there's no going back now."

My heart flips at his words as I nod. "Please," I say softly.

His lips crash against mine in the next moment, his hold on me strong and steady. I feel the difference in the kiss alone. Before our interactions have been fueled by lust and repressed desire. They were desperate and reckless. Something is different now, though. As he nips at my lower lip before running his tongue over the sore spot a sort of promise settles behind it. Maybe it's naïve to believe that he won't run for the hills the moment his guilty conscience takes hold of him. But is it so bad for me to want to live in the moment? Even if we do crash and burn?

Suddenly, his hand drops before scooping me up from behind my thighs and carrying me over to the kitchen island. One of his arms reaches out, swiping the entire contents of the island onto the floor before laying me down. I'm still wearing my work clothes and Atlas takes full advantage of my skirt, hiking it up until it's bunched around my thighs, yanking my panties down in the process. He lifts the scrap of lace to his nose, inhaling deeply before pocketing them into his slacks.

"You smell like fucking heaven, Nevaeh. Fitting, don't you think?"

I go to speak but gasp instead when Atlas buries his head between my thighs. His tongue devours me, not wasting a second on being sweet or gentle as he consumes me whole. Pleasure sparks through me as his hands lift my thighs up to straddle his shoulders.

His soft beard rubs against the sensitive skin between my legs as he feasts on me like a starved man. I feel his tongue lick a long line through me before landing on my clit where he begins sucking and nipping as he slips two fingers inside me. Atlas Kane never does anything halfway. It's never just one finger, it's never easing into anything. No, instead he is finger fucking me like he'll die if he doesn't make me come on his hand.

My orgasm begins building as I grip the edge of the counter. *Oh god, oh god.*

Just as I'm ready to fall apart, his fingers withdraw, and his mouth pulls away. My head whips up to look at him, outrage filling me as I see him wearing a cocky smirk as he slowly sucks on his fingers, taking his time like I'm not spread eagle on top of my parent's kitchen island.

Slowly, he backs away from me, his eyes on mine as he moves to the fridge.

"Where are you going?" I ask.

He doesn't say a thing, just holding my gaze as he puts his hand under the ice maker, pressing against it to allow several cubes to fall into his hand. My brows furrow as he makes his way back to me. Ice? What the hell is he planning to do with that?

He sets the handful of ice down on the island beside me, only holding one cube as he brushes it against my hip bone. I shiver at the contact, a chill running through me as he draws a slow line from one hip to the other before tracing over the seam of my thigh.

I feel myself spasming in anticipation, each chilled stroke of the ice building my anticipation higher and higher until he is hovering just above my pussy. His eyes come up to me, a challenging look in him as he slowly runs the cube through me, never pushing in fully as the icy chill sends my system into overdrive.

Goose bumps cover my skin as Atlas continues teasing me, tantalizing me with the cube until it's a melted puddle. I feel his hand rub over my clit, giving it a small pat before grabbing another cube. This one he doesn't tease me with. Instead, it goes straight against my clit. The motion has my back bowing and my hips bucking. Fuck!

Atlas somehow is able to hold my squirming body down as the quickly melting ice cube rubs against my swollen clit. I feel my toes begin curling as my body shakes, whether from the cold or pleasure, more than likely a mixture of both.

As the chill of the ice continues moving in tight circles against my clit, I feel Atlas's hot mouth on my pussy in the next moment. I gasp in surprise as the drastic difference in temperature overtakes me. The warm silkiness of his tongue running over me like I'm a fine dessert while the frozen cube puckers my skin, pushing me right to the edge. It's like heaven and hell. Fire and ice. And with one more stroke of Atlas's tongue across me, I shatter apart, screaming out my orgasm as I come on his face.

His tongue doesn't relent, licking and sucking me ravenously until there is practically nothing left. When my body finally stops shivering he pulls away, licking at his lips like he's desperate for another taste.

"A-atlas," I say through my labored breaths.

"Yes, babygirl?" he rumbles lowly.

"I swear to God, if you don't fuck me right now, I will kill you," I practically snarl with desperation.

A low chuckle rumbles from his chest as he gently removes the ice cube and begins undoing his belt.

"No need to threaten me. I'm happy to fill my sweet girl up. Is that what you need, Nevaeh? Need to get stuffed full of my cock?"

"Yes!" I practically shout as I rub my thighs together, desperate for some kind of relief.

A hand suddenly comes down and slaps the sensitive skin against my thigh, shocking me and causing my legs to fall open.

He tuts as he takes his cock out, stroking it up and down slowly while he holds my gaze.

"Don't you know that I'm the only one that can give you pleasure? When I'm done with you, even your own touch won't be enough. Catch your breath, Nevaeh. I'm about to fucking ruin this pussy."

Atlas pushes inside me with one thrust, causing my back to bow off the cool countertop as he does. He takes advantage of it, looping his arm underneath, yanking me into him where I can't escape. His thrusts are wild and savage as they deliver equal amounts of pain and pleasure that I'm starting to realize is that largest factor that sends me over the edge for this man.

His large hand traces up my bare thigh, trailing over my bunched-up skirt before cupping the front of my pussy.

"Who does this pussy belong to, Nevaeh? Is it Dillon's?" he asks almost ferally.

"No!" I gasp as his cock rubs my G-spot.

"Is it my son's?" he grits.

"God no!" I swear as my orgasm begins to build.

"Then whose is it? Who owns this greedy little pussy that's just desperate to be fucked hard and raw?"

"You! You, Atlas. It's yours, I'm yours!" I shout as his arms around me tighten slightly.

"Right answer, babygirl," he says as his hand slaps against my clit, hard enough to send my pussy spasming against his cock as my orgasm tears through me.

I feel his cock swell before his warm cum coats my walls, emptying every last drop deep inside me. The feeling of being completely full of him, our mixed orgasms has me riding a high that I didn't know was possible.

Instead of pulling out immediately like last time, he leans back to look me in the eyes before lifting his hand to brush the hair in my face away. A tender look passes across his face as he leans down and kisses me. I melt into the touch before he slowly draws away and rests his forehead against mine.

"Let's go home, Neveah."

Chapter 26
Andromeda

I woke up the next morning expecting to be in my bed. Yesterday had to have been a dream. There is no way that actually happened.

But the sleeping giant behind me tells me that it wasn't a dream and the deliciously sore ache between my thighs confirms it. I reach over to the bedside table where I dumped my phone in a rush as Atlas chased me into his bedroom and fucked me two more times before we finally fell asleep.

Shit. We're already late. I roll over and shake Atlas softly, but he doesn't move an inch. I'll let him sleep for a little longer, but I at least need to get into the shower. I try to slide out my side of the bed, but thick arms wrap around my stomach and haul me back into a hard chest.

"Where are you going?" he mumbles into his pillow.

"I need to get in the shower. We slept in, seems to be a habit of ours," I say with a small smirk.

He cracks an eye open to look at me as he holds me tighter.

"We're not going into work today."

"We aren't?"

"Nope. I've noticed that you need a little more one-on-one training."

I let out a laugh and shake my head. "I don't think our clients will see that as enough reason to miss meetings and deadlines."

"If they saw what you looked like with your naked cunt bent over they would," he counters with his eyes still closed.

My cheeks flame at his words. I'm definitely not used to the things that can come out of this man's mouth. I press a kiss against his nose before I can psyche myself out of it. His eyes open at that and my breath stalls in my chest because I know what comes next. Before I can see the confliction or self-loathing, I scoot out of his hold and rush to the bathroom. I hear him call for me, but I ignore him as I climb into the shower.

The warm water is soothing against my skin as I close my eyes and let it pour over me. I'm only alone for maybe a minute before Atlas steps behind me, wrapping his arms around my stomach and lowering his head to press a kiss against my bare shoulder.

"What's wrong, Neveah?"

I blow out a steady breath, doing my best to keep the emotion out of my voice as I speak.

"I'm just not ready for the bubble to pop."

"What bubble?" he asks against my skin.

"This one," I say as I stare at the wall in front of me. "The one that we are safe in, where we can be together without guilt or doubt or any other ugly feeling that I want nothing to do with. In this bubble, I can be yours and you can be mine and it's just...perfect."

His hands go down to my hips before they gently turn me until I'm facing him. I look away from him as I feel a tear slip down my face. Dammit.

His hand cups my chin, his thumb quickly brushing the fallen tear away as he lifts my face up to meet his gaze. Those deep chocolate eyes are thick with concern as he looks at me.

"I meant what I said yesterday, Neveah. I'm not fighting this anymore, I can't. The bubble isn't going to pop because we aren't in a bubble anymore. This is real, *we* are real."

My heart soars, so badly wanting to believe him but terrified that the rug will get pulled out from under me.

"It's okay," he says softly. "I've treated you terribly. I don't expect you to blindly trust me. I'm going to earn it, I promise."

Blowing out a soft breath I nod as he comes down to give me another kiss that takes my breath away. When we break apart he takes a handful of body wash before running it up and down my back, tracing over every inch of my skin. The gesture is surprisingly tender, heartfelt. It has feelings burrowing their way into me, despite how stupid they are, despite how dangerous they are. I'll never utter them out loud, though, so what's the harm in them. Right?

———

Once we finish showering, we get ready for work. After we cleaned up last night, he had me pack a bag for the night before informing me that we were moving me back into his house, into his room this time. I asked him what we would tell people and he said that no one needs to know right now. That we can keep this between us for now, which I'm relieved about, honestly. I'm still trying to wrap my own head around us. I can't imagine having that conversation with my grandparents or Theo...oh god, or worse. Aunt Alyssa.

When we left the house for work, I was walking to my car when he grabbed my hand and yanked me back to him. I went to ask him what he was doing when he practically dragged me over to his car before opening the door and ushering me inside. I smirked but didn't argue.

We are just pulling into the parking garage as he lets go of my hand for the first time since we got in. A small pang of disappointment runs through me at the loss of contact as we get out of the car before walking over to the elevator door. We can explore whatever this is behind closed doors but like we both agree, out in the open not so much. Despite the logical side of my brain telling me this is for the best, the emotional, I'll admit needy at times, side is overly disappointed. I give Atlas a small smile as he lets me step inside first, but I don't think I mask my disappointment well.

Turning to cage me in with his arms against the wall he looks down at me, concern heavy in his deep eyes.

"What's wrong?"

"Nothing."

"You're a terrible liar. Now tell me the truth," he says with a barely there smirk.

I let out a short laugh at that as I shake my head.

"It's stupid. I just, I liked holding your hand," I say with a small shrug before looking away, suddenly feeling so immature and childish.

I liked holding your hand? Seriously, Andromeda? You want him to see you as a woman but you're pouting over him not holding your hand to work?

"Hey," he says as he turns me to face him. "I do too. How about tonight we order in instead of cooking and I'll hold your hand the whole time while I eat your delectable cunt?"

Excitement rushes through me as my eyes flick down to his mischievous grin. I can't help but smile and nod at that.

"Don't tempt me with a good time," I tease as the elevator door opens.

Atlas moves away from me quickly but subtly as he shoots me a wink before turning and striding out the door and down the hallway. A smiling Cathy is at the desk to greet us. She says good morning to Atlas before looking at me, a curious look passing over her as she watches me.

"Hey! You're back already. How was the honeymoon?" I ask, trying to hopefully brush off any suspicions she has if the thoughtful look on her face is anything to go off.

"Beautiful, wish I didn't have to be back. So, what was that?"

"What was what?" I ask casually with faux-furrowed brows.

She gives me a deadpan look as she folds her hands under her chin.

"Oh, is that how we're gonna play it? We're acting dumb? Okay then. I definitely didn't see the boss crowding you like he was the big bad wolf, and you were just an innocent little piggy up for slaughter."

"Shhh," I say quickly as my eyes whip around our surroundings, thankful no one is close enough to hear her big mouth.

She has a brow cocked as she seems to be waiting for me to explain but Atlas and I just talked about how we should keep things under wraps so she's out of luck. I slap on a look of indifference as I shrug and head down the hall to my desk.

Once I set my things down and scoot my chair into my desk I peek out of the corner of my eye through Atlas's open door to see him watching me with a secretive smirk. He shoots me a wink when he catches my eye before turning to face his computer. I can't help but smile as I do the same. We are really doing this.

Holy shit.

I'm just scanning over the first email in my inbox when I feel someone come up and stand next to my desk. Turning with a smile, I find Dillon watching me with a sweet smile. My previous grin fades in an instant.

Dillon. Shit.

"Hey, how are you doing?" he asks.

"Good," I nod, my tone lacking the usual enthusiasm even to my own ears.

Dillon's eyebrows dip for half a second before they rise again.

"I'm really looking forward to tomorrow. What time should I pick you up?"

A loud slam startles me as Dillon and I both look to see Atlas opening and shutting his desk drawers aggressively before writing angrily on a piece of paper. Dillon turns his focus back to me, that hopeful smile still in place.

Dammit, this is gonna suck.

"I actually wanted to talk to you about that. I'm not going to be able to go."

Disappointment colors his features as he takes a half a step closer.

"Why? Something come up?"

I grimace as I turn to face him fully. "I'm just not ready for...all of this," I say as I gesture between us.

"I don't understand, I thought we had a nice time the other night? Did I misread the situation?" he asks, seeming genuinely confused.

"We did and I like you but with my parents passing and the only relationship I've ever had ending in fiery flames I just don't know if I'm ready to date."

It's the coward's way out. I know it but what was I supposed to say?

Sorry, Dillon. I like you and you're sweet, but you don't send a white-

hot need pulsing between my thighs while you bury yourself in me from behind?

Yeah, I think I'll pass, thank you very much.

He looks at me sympathetically before nodding. "I understand. We can take stuff slow for now, just friends, okay? Just because you don't want to date doesn't mean you can't come to a concert with a friend?" He smiles softly, clearly still hopeful.

A snap now comes from Atlas's office. This time when I peek around Dillon I see Atlas staring at us with a murderous glare, a pen broken in two on his desk, ink everywhere yet he doesn't seem to care about that right now. His eyes are narrowed on the two of us instead, his nostrils flared as he sits there silently. If I wasn't partially loving how riled up he's getting about Dillon and me going out, I'd be concerned. Instead, my pussy is practically throbbing.

"I'm sorry, another time, maybe?" I offer with a regrettable smile and a shrug.

Dillon blows out a breath as he rubs the back of his neck and nods.

"I get it. I like you a lot and I'd like to see where this goes when and if you're ready. I'm not giving up hope just yet. Until then, friends, yeah?"

I smile. "I'd like that."

"Good," he says as he glances at his watch. "If you'll excuse me, I have a conference call I have to hop on."

I wave goodbye as he makes his way down the hallway before turning to the eyes that have been practically drilling themselves into the side of my head. Atlas's jaw is clenched, his nostrils still flared as he crooks a finger to me. I silently stand and make my way inside his office before closing the door.

As soon as the door is shut, he's out of his seat in a flash. I startle for a moment and take a sidestep toward the glass floor-to-ceiling window beside me. Atlas matches me step for step as he practically chases me down, those brown eyes burrowing their way into me until my back is pressed against the window.

"What was that?" he asks lowly, his nose brushing against mine as he does.

My breath hitches as his minty breath takes up the space between us, his chest now plastered to mine and arms caging me in like an animal.

"Wh-hat was what?" I ask breathlessly because honestly, what did he just ask me? I couldn't tell you.

"I'm curious, Nevaeh. Why the fuck did another man have plans to take my woman out on a date this weekend?" he asks darkly, each syllable heavy with contempt.

"Because I wasn't your woman twenty hours ago when we made the plans," I answer honestly, causing Atlas's jaw to clench tightly.

"Goddammit, Andromeda! Don't fuck with me. You have been mine for longer than you realize, longer than I even realized. I thought we discussed this already."

"We did," I agree. "This morning. I haven't spoken to Dillon since then, now I have?"

"I heard him," he scoffs, bypassing my snark completely. "Heard that he isn't 'giving up hope.' Fucking prick."

I can't help but let a chuckle slip out of me at his outrage. His eyes snap up to mine, irritation filling them as he assesses me.

"What's so damn funny?"

"I like seeing you like this." I smirk.

"Like what?"

"Jealous, about me. Jealous another man wants to spend his time with me, date me, touch m—"

I don't get to finish my sentence before I am spun around, and my chest pressed against the glass. My skirt is suddenly bunched up around my waist, my panties ripped off my body like they were made of paper. Before I can ask him what he's doing I feel him push inside me, causing simultaneous groans to escape us both as he does.

Atlas doesn't waste a moment as he begins snapping his hips against me roughly.

"Oh god!" I moan as Atlas's fingers dig into my hips and presses my body harder against the window.

"You drive me fucking crazy, Neveah. You're mine, all fucking mine."

I whimper at his words, nodding my head slightly as I press my hands against the glass. I feel his thick hand run up my chest, wrapping around my throat before turning me to look up at him.

"Words, babygirl. Tell me you're mine."

"Of course I'm yours," I say breathily. "Don't I feel like yours?" I ask as I intentionally push back into him. I watch as his eyes practically roll to the back of his head as his grip on me tightens.

"Fuck, yes. Look down, Neveah. Look at all of those people below us, completely oblivious to how beautifully you squeeze my cock."

I do as he says, returning my gaze out to the window. Dozens of pedestrians are walking by, whether on their way to work or to run errands for the day. Everything below seems so mundane, so ordinary meanwhile I'm getting fucked against the floor-to-ceiling window in my boss's office by none other than my godfather.

"If I wasn't such a jealous fucking bastard I'd grace the world of the sight. But I am," Atlas says as his hand moves from my hip and slips around me to start rubbing tight circles against my clit.

"Thinking about another man just breathing the same air as you makes me murderous. If another man touched you, I would slaughter him and fuck you in his blood."

His words are horrifying, dirty, disturbing. So why the fuck am I getting wetter?

He continues to fuck me like he's trying to punish me, which I hate to break it to him, I'm loving this kind of punishment. Maybe I should talk about other men more often. I arch my back slightly, causing him to groan in pleasure.

"Fuck, yes. That's my good girl. Pop that pretty little cunt out for me. You're just a needy little thing, aren't you?"

"Yes," I gasp as his fingers rub against my clit faster.

I feel my pussy begin to throb and know that between the way he fucks and the way he talks, I won't have long.

"Yeah, you're needy for your godfather's cock. Can't get enough, can you babygirl?"

"I love my godfather's cock inside me," I agree as my hands brace against the glass.

"Fuck. That shouldn't be as hot as it is," he says as he takes the hand not strumming against my clit and slaps the side of my ass.

"This is your fault. It's your fault I'm like this, that we're like this. Your fault I can't go a fucking minute without thinking about this wet little cunt or that deep fucking throat. I wonder what else is nice and tight," he says as the hand on my ass trails a hot line to my ass, teasing the tight hole before applying just a bare amount of pressure.

"Have you ever been taken here?" he murmurs into my ear.

I shake my head against the glass. I've always been way too terrified to try it, despite Theo's begging and pleading over the years.

"Good. I can't wait to be the one to show you what it's like to be fucked in the ass nice and hard. You'll find out soon," he promises, a combination of fear and excitement running up my spine. Suddenly, Atlas's desk phone begins ringing. He curses as his pace quickens to nearly frantic.

"I can't miss that call. Come on my cock like a good girl, give me your orgasm, Nevaeh."

My pussy pulses and one more thrust against my G-spot is all it takes for me to shatter apart against the cool window in front of me. Atlas is quick to cover my mouth with his hand and muffle my shouts as I continue to pulse and squeeze his cock as he empties his release inside me.

In a flash, he has pulled out of me and is answering the phone.

"Yeah? Ah, Mr. Sunagel, so glad you got my message. Yes, the twentieth works for me," he says as he glances down at the shredded remnants of what were my panties.

I go to pick them up but he's faster than me, pocketing the mess of lace before giving me a dirty smirk. That's the second pair he's stolen from me. Prick. I feel the liquid between my thighs begin to spill down my leg and know I need to go clean myself up immediately especially when I have no panties.

"Just a moment," Atlas says into the phone as I begin walking toward the door.

He puts the phone on hold and crosses the room, cupping my face in his hands as he presses a kiss against my lips that instantly makes my knees buckle. He holds me up as he deepens the kiss before breaking away and resting his forehead against mine.

"You're so fucking perfect, Nevaeh. Too perfect."

"Hardly," I scoff as a blush rises in my cheeks.

"Unquestionably."

Atlas presses his lips to mine once more before smacking me on the ass and striding back over to his phone. I do my best to walk as normally as possible to the bathroom but the feeling of Atlas's cum running down my thighs doesn't do me any favors.

Chapter 27
Atlas

It's official. I've lost my goddamn mind, and I don't even want it back. It's been two weeks since Andromeda and I have been together, officially so. And every moment has felt like everything I never imagined I could have.

She's young, too young, honestly. It's complicated and messy and I have no doubt that we've got a hell of a road in front of us but I'm okay with that because the way I feel when she smiles at me, like I'm her whole world...it's unlike anything else.

When Andromeda stormed out of the office, the same day she told me she was done, I had to take a hard look at everything. I had to figure out if pushing her away, keeping her at arms distance out of responsibility and duty was worth losing her forever. Because I knew in that moment, that she was slipping through my fingers. I didn't know if I was allowed to hold on to her, if I'm being honest, I'm probably not. But I'm keeping her anyway.

We've already fallen into a little routine of sorts. We go to work, do our best to keep our hands off each other for those eight hours (and fail almost every day) before we head home where we make dinner together, maybe watch a movie or play some Scrabble and then spend the night getting lost in each other.

The sex is amazing, fucking out of this world. I can't even believe these words come to mind, even if it's just to myself, but my favorite part of every day has been what comes after. When we are spent and exhausted and she curls up into my arms like she was always meant to, before we drift off to sleep. She always falls asleep before me, and I can't help but watch as her soft body moves up and down softly as she slips off into her dreams. Dreams that look a lot more peaceful than her past ones. She told me that I take the bad dreams away and I have to admit, I don't think I've ever been prouder of anything in my life.

I just finish putting away the last dish when I come up behind Andromeda who is sitting at the island, her glasses perched on the end of her nose as she types away on her computer. She's deep into her first semester doing online classes and I'm so fucking proud of her dedication to it. Some kids might see it as an opportunity to slack off, but I swear she is working on a paper, studying or doing research like it's her full-time job. And the fact that she does all of that on top of an actual full-time internship that has pretty much morphed into a full-time job is nothing short of incredible.

Quietly, I make my way around the island, knowing she's too immersed in wrapping up her lit paper that isn't even due for another week as I come up behind her and snake my arms around her stomach.

She lets out a short, surprised gasp as she turns her face up to smile at me. I can't help but grin in return as her eyes lock with mine. I lean down to brush my lips against hers, my hand cupping underneath her chin to give me better access. The kiss starts off innocent but one swipe of her soft tongue against mine and my cock begins hardening in my sweats.

I tear my mouth away from hers as I run my nose along the length of her neck.

"Don't start something you can't finish, Nevaeh," I growl lowly.

"Who said anything about me not being able to finish you? In fact, from what I'm told, I excel in that category."

I scoff before squishing her cheeks together and capturing her lips once more. She melts into my touch as she meets me eagerly. Fuck. I can't get enough of this woman.

Without saying a word, I take a step around her before looping an arm underneath her thighs. I lift her with ease, not allowing her to break the kiss as I begin walking us out of the kitchen. I'm sure she expects me to carry her to bed but I have something better and closer in mind.

Reaching out blindly, I grab the back door handle before pushing it open. I cross the distance between us and the hot tub in record time before gently setting her down to her feet. When we break apart she looks up at me with dazed eyes but before she can speak I'm on my knees, peeling her leggings and panties off her smooth skin as I kiss my way down her thighs until I reach her ankles.

She wordlessly lifts her feet for me as I pull the clothes off her before skimming my hands up her sides, bunching her shirt up into my fists before slipping it up and over her head. She reaches behind her, undoing her bra and tossing it to the ground before setting her glasses down with it.

Suddenly, her hands are on me, pushing down my sweats as I whip my shirt up and over my head. The instant the cotton shirt hits the ground I'm bending down, lifting Andromeda over my shoulder and stepping up into the hot tub. The burn from the water scorches my skin instantly but it's not enough to slow me down.

We both let out matching hisses as the scalding water wraps around us before Andromeda settles into my lap. I crush my lips against hers before trailing kisses across her cheek, making my way down her neck as my hand reaches up to cup her breast. My thumb flicks over her pale pink nipple, causing her to moan in reaction. I smirk against her skin as I do it again and again.

"Atlas," she moans, my name on her lips sounding sweeter than any song as she arches into my hold.

"You like that, babygirl?" I rasp as I begin pinching and twisting her nipple.

She sinks her teeth into her bottom lip as her eyes close and she nods frantically.

"Eyes on me, Neveah. Let me see those pretty greens."

They fly open at that as I settle my hands over her hips and bring her down onto my cock. The water creates a lot of friction, and I can tell she is feeling it by the twisted-up look on her face.

"Shit. Atlas, I don't think it's going to fit," she whimpers.

I feel my head push just inside her entrance before a surge of pleasure zings up my spine.

"It'll fit," I grit out before snapping my hips up and burying myself deep.

She lets out a gasp, but I don't give her a chance to focus on the pain as I begin fucking her with no mercy. Goddamn, I could stay buried in this pussy for the rest of my life and I'd die a happy man.

Andromeda's hands rest on top of my shoulders as she begins bouncing on me like I'm her favorite ride, her head thrown back in pleasure as she chants, "Yes, oh. Fuck, yes." She's so beautiful like this, bathed in the moonlight, drenched in ecstasy. I feel her pussy spasm around my cock as she screams out her release.

When her moans quiet, she blinks her eyes blearily at me as I stand, lifting her with me before spinning on my heel. Andromeda's legs slip into the water as I release her, spinning her around before pushing on her lower back.

"Bend over for me, Neveah. Let me see that pretty pussy."

She does as I ask like the good girl she is, her pussy peeking out just under her perfect peach ass before I line myself up and push into her. Without the water in our way, I'm able to fuck her with a lot less resistance and a lot more pleasure. The hot tub sounded better in my head, but the way Andromeda feels wraps around my cock right now tells me this was still a good choice.

"You take me so good, babygirl," I praise as I run my hand along her spine as I keep my rhythm,

She whimpers in response, and I feel her begin to tighten on me again already. I can't help but smirk as my hand skates around to her stomach, dipping lower as I speak.

"Are you gonna come for me already, Neveah?"

"Maybe," she gasps as I thrust deeper, rubbing against her G-spot which causes her legs to buckle.

I pin my thighs against hers, keeping her in place as I continue to fuck her through it.

"So fucking responsive. So needy for me. You know how much I love it. Give me another. Give me one more," I demand.

Andromeda nods but doesn't say anything until I cup her cunt with my hand before rubbing the heel of my palm against her clit. It's just what she needs and the way her cunt practically cuts off my circulation sends me emptying myself inside her. My orgasm hits me like a freight train, my vision blurring momentarily as pleasure races up and down my spine.

"Jesus, Neveah," I growl as my grip on her tightens as I wring every ounce of pleasure I can out of myself and her before we both slow.

Rubbing my hand up and down her back I slowly pull out of her before pulling her to stand. Her hair is stuck to her forehead, her chest heaving as she looks up at me with a dazed glossy look that makes her eyes practically sparkle.

"You okay?" I ask.

"Better than." She smiles at me drunkenly.

A matching smile spreads across my own face. I'm totally and completely fucked when it comes to Andromeda Clarke.

Chapter 28
Andromeda

I'm finishing finalizing Atlas's schedule for the week when I get an instant message from him. I open the small window, doing my best to keep myself composed as I read it.

Atlas Kane: If you don't stop biting your lip like that, I'm going to spread you out naked across my desk.

I instantly release my lip, not even realizing I was biting the inside of it while I was working. I turn to look through the open door, sending Atlas a warning glance.

Andromeda Clarke: Don't type things like that. Anyone could see it!

Glancing over my shoulder, I watch Atlas smirk as he reads my message before he begins typing.

Atlas Kane: I don't give a damn. What the hell am I supposed to do when I've got literal perfection sitting just out of my reach?

I duck my head, doing my best to hide my smile as another message pings.

Atlas Kane: Come here.

Glancing over to him, I watch as he settles back into his chair, crooking his finger toward me in a way that has me locking my screen before standing and making my way to his office. I close the door on instinct because based on the look in Atlas's eyes, he doesn't want to go over his calendar right now.

"Come here, babygirl," he says as he pats his lap.

I go to him willingly, hesitating for a moment before I decide to straddle him. Heat flares in his gaze as his hands come to rest on my hips, gripping me tightly as he pulls me down until I'm flush against him.

"Hi," I say with a small smirk.

Atlas gives me half of a smile as he pulls my hips forward, forcing me to brush against his hard cock.

"Hello."

"You wanted to see me?" I ask, feigning innocence as I rock against him, causing his jaw to clench and his eyes to darken.

"Yes," he grits as he drags me over him again before one of his hands leaves my hip, trailing a line down my bare thigh and under my skirt. I feel his finger stroke against the damp fabric separating us before he hooks it to the side.

"I'm curious, Miss Clarke," he says lowly as he sinks a finger inside of me.

I gasp at the movement, gripping his shoulders tightly as he gently pushes in deeper.

"Do you dress like this intentionally? Do you wake up in the morning, slip on your tightest outfits just to drive me fucking crazy?" he asks as he slips another finger inside me, causing my eyes to roll into the back of my head as he continues his leisurely pace.

"Do you spend all morning thinking about new ways to torture me? Knowing that I can't resist your temptations. That I'm practically a sailor at sea and you're the captivating siren, luring me into my death?"

I let out a soft shuddered breath as his rhythm picked up.

"What a sweet death it would be, hmm?" I ask breathily.

Atlas leans forward, running his nose up the column of my neck as he gently inhales, his lips pressing against my pulse point ever so slightly as he speaks.

"So fucking sweet."

Atlas's thumb reaches up, brushing against my clit in smooth even circles that has my body quaking and my breath choppy.

"Fuck, don't stop," I beg.

Atlas grumbles low in his chest as he picks up speed.

"I'd rather die," he says as his fingers curl up, pressing against me in a way that sends me shattering apart in his arms. He holds me tight as I ride the waves of my orgasm before I practically collapse against him, allowing the smooth smell of his cologne to fill my senses.

"Such a good girl," Atlas murmurs against the top of my head before pressing a soft kiss to it.

Something in his words or maybe in his tone has a light feeling fluttering through me. I pull away to look at him, leaning down to brush my lips against his as his hand cups the back of my head to deepen the kiss. I grind my hips against him once more, causing him to groan into my mouth before I break the kiss.

Atlas's eyes open, disappointment heavy in them as he opens his mouth to speak when I slip out of his lap and sink down to my knees. Curiosity and excitement pass over his face as I reach for his belt, quickly undoing it along with his button and zipper until I'm able to pull his boxers and pants down. Atlas barely helps me, instead choosing to only lift his hips slightly as he watches me with rapt attention.

When I'm able to free his cock, I take it into my hand, stroking the entire length several times before looking up to him.

"Can I suck it?" I ask softly, knowing the doe eyes I'm giving him will drive him wild.

"Fuckkk," he groans as one of his hands reaches out to bury into the back of my hair. "You better," he says as he urges me forward, forcing me to take his cock all the way down my throat.

I do my best not to gag, taking several deep breaths through my nose as I come back up before pushing down again. I'm able to find an easy rhythm soon, my tongue running up and down the side of him, flicking against the head every time I come up.

"Goddammit, Nevaeh. Fuck. Just like that, babygirl. Keep sucking my cock like you were meant to."

His words of encouragement egg me on, pushing me to take him deeper as I continue. I feel Atlas's hips begin thrusting up slightly just as the sound of the door opens. My closed eyes fly open as I rip my mouth away from him, looking up at Atlas in panic. He isn't looking at me, though. Instead, he's focusing on whoever just walked in. I feel Atlas's hand on the back of my head push me down slightly, trying to keep me out of view as our intruder speaks.

"Hi, Mr. Kane. So, I got those reports back for you. Do you have time to go over them?" Cathy asks.

"Now isn't the best time," Atlas says calmly.

My racing heart rate settles slightly knowing that it's just Cathy. Probably the best-case scenario, honestly. A wicked idea crosses my mind, one that is most certainly playing with fire. As quietly as I can, I move my mouth back to Atlas, sticking out my tongue to run a long line up the length of him. I feel his grip on my hair tighten in warning, but it doesn't deter me as Cathy speaks.

"I promise it will take just a second," she says as I hear her take a seat.

Atlas sends a quick glance down to me, the look in his eyes as plain as day. It's a look that tells me to behave, to stay quiet. And I'll definitely do one of those things.

Covering the tip of his cock with my mouth, I slowly take him down my throat once again, doing my best to remain virtually silent as Cathy begins talking. I hear her ramble on about some forecasted number versus our current metrics but I'm not paying too much attention. I don't think Atlas is based on the way his punishing grip on my hair has turned to an encouraging rub, slightly pushing my head deeper and deeper each time.

The adrenaline I feel coursing through my veins is practically euphoric as I continue, reaching my hand out as I begin massaging his balls. I feel them tighten instantly at my touch as he lets out a choppy breath that he covers with a cough.

"Sounds great. Good work, Cathy," he says, his voice low and slightly breathy.

I can hear the suspicion in her voice as she speaks.

"Are you feeling okay, Mr. Kane? You don't look good."

Lowering myself until my lips are flush against his pelvis, I swallow once, causing my throat to constrict around him as he practically gasps out, "Never been better."

A smile forms against my lips at that. Something tells me that's the most honest statement he's ever made, and I take an immense amount of gratification in that. I swallow around him several more times in a row and I watch as he drops his forehead into his hand, his elbow resting against the desktop as he grunts out something that sounds like a rough cough. I feel his salty cum coat my tongue instantly, his balls draw up in my hand as he comes down my throat, his cock twitching as I drink him down.

"Okayyy," Cathy says slowly. "I have some cough drops at my desk if you need some?"

Atlas drops his hand, raising his head to look at her as he nods.

"Y-yes. That would be great, actually. Thank you, Cathy."

"No problem," she says as I hear her stand before the door shuts behind her.

As soon as she's gone, Atlas practically hauls me up off the floor and I'm suddenly bent over his desk. He rips my skirt up, exposing my bare ass as his hand comes down once, hard.

A muffled shout sounds from me as I bite my lip in pain.

"Do you think you're funny?" he asks as he leans over me, his mouth against my ear as his hand comes down, slapping against my ass once more.

This time I barely suppress the moan that escapes me. My pussy throbs at the contact, practically dripping down my thigh as his hand begins massaging the sensitive skin.

"You like it," I protest.

"Of course I did," Atlas scoffs as I wiggle my ass against him, poking out my pussy hoping he will get the hint.

I feel his hand slip down to where I need him most, his fingers lazily drawing a line over my soaked panties.

"Did that turn you on babygirl? You need to be filled up?"

"So bad," I practically whimper.

I feel him apply pressure, all that is separating us is that stupid scrap of lace before he pulls back and spanks my pussy. I gasp at the pleasure and pain mixture as Atlas speaks.

"Only good girls get to come, bad girls get spanked."

"Spank me again," I beg.

Atlas lets out a low chuckle as he shakes his head.

"You're one tap away from coming and it's gonna stay that way until we get home. I think a little lesson is what you need."

"Are you kidding me? You're edging me right now?" I practically snarl.

"Punishing you," Atlas corrects with a smug smirk.

Irritation builds inside me before I decide to take matters into my own hands, literally. Reaching down, I slip a finger inside me, using my other hand to rub against my clit.

"Nevaeh," Atlas admonishes but I'm so close a few more seconds is all it takes before I'm coming all over Atlas's mahogany desk.

I slowly stand, not able to hide my self-satisfied smirk as Atlas grasps my wrist, lifting my fingers up to his mouth before he sucks on them slowly, those deep brown eyes never leaving my own.

"We will be discussing this when we get home," he says in a tone that brokers no argument.

"Naked?" I test with a tilt of my head.

"Definitely," he growls before smacking me on my ass.

I can't help but giggle as I shimmy my skirt back into place and make my way out of the office. I'm just fixing my hair when Cathy comes from around the corner with a bag of cough drops.

"Oh, Drama. Perfect. Can you give this to Mr. Kane when you're done sucking him off?"

My eyes widen at her words, a million excuses that are all absolute trash coming to my mind before she gives me a wicked wink.

"Secret is safe with me."

"What are you talking about? There is no secret. What? What makes you think—"

"Wow. You're a terrible liar." She laughs. "I got you girl and I'm in full support. The boss is hot," she says with a nudge before making her way back to her desk.

I'm left standing there stunned in silence. If it was anyone besides Cathy, I'd be freaking out right now. For some reason though, I believe her. I don't think she would tell anyone because that's just not who she is. She's judgment-free and minds her business. So, I guess our secret is safe with her. Hopefully.

Chapter 29
Atlas

If every workday could be spent with Andromeda on her knees for me under my desk, I'd probably never leave the office. Unfortunately, that hasn't happened in almost a week and if I didn't have such a packed day, I'd call her in for a little midday refresher. It's been a long day and I think we could both use the release right now.

Things have been a little stressful lately, partially due to the work that has been looming over my head lately. From board meetings to conference calls to every other small thing that used to fall under Paul, I'm stretched too damn thin. I know it won't be long until I snap. The only thing keeping me halfway sane is Andromeda. Besides the obvious relief she brings me at home, she has shaped up to be an irreplaceable employee, not like I'm at all surprised.

We are currently on our way to a lunch meeting with Charles Abner and I already can't wait for it to be over. The guy is a pain in the ass to deal with on the best of days, but I don't like the way he looked at Andromeda the last time we met. I know his type. They are all the same. Let's hope he's smart enough to keep this lunch professional, otherwise he'll be walking out of here with a few less teeth in his head.

The valet opens my door and I make quick work of jogging around to Andromeda's side before opening her door for her. She's wearing a red blouse with a skintight black pencil skirt that leaves nothing to the imagination. As much as it drives me insane knowing other men are looking, lusting after what's mine, I can't deny that I love the access her skirts allow us during our mid-day fucks.

I press my hand to the small of her back as we step inside the restaurant, causing her to shoot me a soft smile over her shoulder as we are taken to our table. My heart beats harder in my chest at that smile as I follow just a step behind her so that I can keep my hand on her for just a little longer.

My good mood suddenly sours when I turn to see Abner watching us as we approach the table. Or should I say, watching her. I do my best to hide my irritation behind my bullshit professional smile but who's to say how convincing I actually am.

"What a pleasure it is to see you again, my dear," Charles leers as his eyes travel up and down Andromeda's body.

I see the strain in her smile as she nods at him before taking her seat. I offer my hand and a bullshit 'how are you doing' before taking my seat beside her. Casually slipping my hand underneath the tablecloth, I rest my palm on her knee and squeeze gently. I don't look at her and she doesn't turn to me but we both know the touch is enough to convey what I can't say right now.

I'm right here. Whatever you need, I'm here.

Abner and I talk business through lunch while Andromeda quietly takes notes. This project has been a pain in the ass, mainly because he is a pain in the ass, but our entire fourth quarter is heavily weighing on the completion of this project. So, I'm sitting here smiling like a dipshit while the asshole goes on and on about his private yacht.

"You know, I could take you out on it sometime," he directs to Andromeda. "We could have my chef come aboard. He will cook you the most divine Dungeness crab you've ever tasted. So succulent and juicy," he says with a lick of his lips while his eyes stay firmly trained on her cleavage.

My fist tightens into a ball on instinct.

Strike one, Abner.

"I'm afraid I'm not a fan of seafood," Andromeda says with a disappointed smile that couldn't be any faker.

Abner frowns at that. "Well, maybe you haven't had the right kind of seafood. I assure you. I provide nothing but the finest of things to all my guests. No one ever leaves unsatisfied," he says with a slow deliberate wink.

My jaw clenches as I try to steady my breathing.

Strike two.

Andromeda's polite smile fades as irritation takes over her face.

"I'm going to have to respectfully decline."

"My dear, you don't know what you're missing out on. I can open your eyes to so many new experiences," he says with a slimy smirk as he reaches out and brushes his fingers across the top of her hand resting on the table before she quickly yanks out of his grasp.

Strike three.

I shove back from my chair in an instant, rounding the table in three steps before I grab the fat sack of shit by his too-expensive shirt. I lift him up to stand before rearing back my right arm as I drive my fist into his bulging nose. Abner shouts in surprise as blood begins to pour down his face.

"What the fuck, Kane! You broke my goddamn nose!"

"I'll break more than that if you ever touch her again," I promise before shoving him to the ground where he crumples like a pathetic toddler.

Staff quickly rush over to us as a man who I think is supposed to be an acting manager comes up to me.

"Sir, I'm going to have to ask you to leave."

I laugh bitterly as I take a wad of cash out of my pocket and toss it onto the table before reaching my hand out for Andromeda. Her eyes are wide with concern as she cautiously takes my outstretched hand before standing.

"You're fired, Kane!" Abner shouts. "You won't get a dime of my money!"

"Don't want it," I shout over my shoulder before dragging Andromeda out of the restaurant.

When we get outside I give the valet my ticket and begin pacing, feeling the rush of adrenaline and rage pulse through me as I do.

"Atlas, what the hell just happened?" Andromeda practically shouts.

"He touched you," I gnash as I look up at her wide doe eyes.

"He touched my hand, which although repulsive, was not as obscene as you are making it out to be. You just lost the job that you've been working on for months, the one we have been depending on to meet our end-of-the-year goal. Hell, he could have you arrested! And for what? Because his sausage fingers touched the back of my hand for half a second?" she scolds.

I cross the distance between us and pull her into me, lowering my face to hers as I speak.

"It was half a second too long. You are mine, Andromeda. Mine to care for, mine to protect, mine to fuck and mine to touch. I'll burn the fucking world down before I let another man lay a finger on what's mine."

She shakes her head as she whispers under her breath, "You're a possessive psychopath."

I brush my lips against hers as the valet pulls up with my car before pulling away.

"Completely," I agree as I usher her toward the passenger side of the car.

Slowly, she eases into her seat before I slam the door shut and tip the valet as I climb into the car and peel out of there.

Andromeda is quiet for most of the way back before she finally speaks.

"That was stupid," she mutters under her breath as she looks out the window.

"What?"

"You hitting him, that was stupid. He's a prick, he's probably already called the cops. You'll go to jail for assault."

I shake my head as I maneuver into the office parking garage.

"Unlikely. I have a team of lawyers on retainer for this sort of thing. I'll call them when we get upstairs."

"And what if they can't get you out of this, Atlas? Then what?" she asks as she turns to me, her beautiful green eyes brimming with thick tears as her lip quivers.

I quickly park the car before turning to face her fully. The first tear slips down her cheek and I quickly swipe it away with my thumb as I cradle her face.

"Nevaeh, what's this really about?" I ask as softly as I can with a frown.

"You can't go to jail. If you're taken away then I'll have no one left. I need you, Atlas. I can't survive on my own. I need you," she cries as she closes her eyes and lets the tears free fall.

I quickly undo her seat belt before lifting her out of her seat and into my lap.

"Shhhh, babygirl. Breathe for me. I'm not going anywhere, you've got me. I'll never leave your side."

She sniffles as she lifts her head to look at me.

"You promise?"

"I promise. No one is taking me away from you, not when I just got you," I say as I squeeze her a little tighter.

Andromeda takes a shaky breath before nodding and resting her head into the crook of my neck.

"Do you want to take the rest of the day off? I'll start a lavender bubble bath for you. Light a couple candles? Open a bottle of wine?"

She turns her head to the side softly as some of the fear begins to recede in her eyes.

"Will you join me?"

My chest aches at the vulnerability tinging her words, like she's unsure. Like she thinks I even have it in me to deny her a single thing this world has to offer.

"Of course. Let me run upstairs and grab my laptop and I'll be right down, okay?"

"Okay," she says as she slowly climbs off my lap and back into her seat.

I lean over and press a quick kiss to her temple before opening my door.

"I'll be right back."

She tries to give me a smile but the long black streaks covering her otherwise flawless skin taint the effort. This is all because of Abner. If he would have just kept his fucking hands to himself, Andromeda wouldn't have had to spill a single tear.

Or maybe you could have just not hit him?

Nope. That was unavoidable.

When I get upstairs I give a rushed hello to Cathy as I walk into my office and grab my laptop. I'm just about ready to head out when a knock comes from my door.

"Hey," Dillon says as he takes a step inside. "How did everything with Abner go?"

"Not good. We lost the contract," I say as I slip my laptop into my messenger bag.

"What? What do you mean? How?" he asks, his accent thicker than normal as he rapidly fires off questions.

"Well, when I punched him in the middle of lunch, it put a bit of strain on our working relationship," I deadpan.

Dillon's mouth drops open in shock. I can't tell if it's because I punched Abner or because of my shitty attitude toward him. I'm still not done being pissed over the fact that he was interested in Andromeda, hell, probably still is. And he fucking kissed her, more than once. Last week I made her tell me every detail that happened between them so my overactive imagination could finally be put to rest.

I was furious to hear that she had made out with him in my fucking driveway, no less, but I took my frustration out on her body, and we were both near blissful by the end of it.

Fuck. I love that girl.

I freeze in place as my head trips over that word. Love? Do I love her? I mean, of course I do. She's my Nevaeh. I've loved her since the moment she was born. But am I in love with her?

"Why did you punch him? What happened?" Dillon balks, shaking me out of my quickly spiraling mind.

I look up at him, doing my best to wipe away any and all emotion as I speak.

"He touched Andromeda. He was making disgusting and lewd comments about the things he could show her before he touched her."

Dillon's shock turns to irritation as he narrows his eyes at me. He quickly turns around to see Andromeda's desk empty before looking back at me.

"Is she okay? Where is she?" he asks as he pulls out his phone, assumingly to text her.

"She's fine. She's downstairs. I'm taking her home for the day, she's pretty shaken up."

Dillon nods as he looks at me curiously, like he is piecing something together. Not liking being under his observant eyes I give him a nod as I walk past him.

"I'll see you tomorrow," I say briskly.

I'm four steps down the hallway when his voice calls out to me.

"I'm no idiot, Atlas."

Pausing in place, I glance over my shoulder just enough to see him standing in the hall with his arms crossed over his chest.

"I see the way you look at her, everyone does. If you're trying to be inconspicuous, it isn't working."

I don't respond, because what am I supposed to say to that? Instead, I make my way through the lobby and into the elevator before jamming the button. I know that we haven't been very careful. I know that I'm shit at hiding the way I see her, the way I look at her. I try but she's such a goddamn temptation, such a distraction. I can hardly keep my eyes off her. Dillon's statement doesn't sit well with me, it feels foreboding, like a warning of what's to come. I'm not exactly sure what that is but whatever it is, it doesn't feel good.

Chapter 30
Andromeda

We got out of the bath twenty minutes ago and after we dried off, Atlas went to his office to get some work done since we took the rest of the day off. I'm just getting ready to change out of my bathrobe and into some comfortable clothes when my phone starts ringing. I look down to see that it's a video chat from Theo, causing my stomach to instantly plummet.

Theo and I haven't spoken in a few weeks. Not since Atlas and I stopped dancing around each other. He's called me a few times, but I've been too nervous to call him back. It's not like my forehead has the tattoo "I'm sleeping with your father," Still, though. Theo knows me so well, too well, really.

Blowing out a deep breath I do my best to keep my tone even as I answer the call with a smile.

"Hey!" I smile a little too cheerily to be casual.

Theo's smile fills the screen as he lays down on what I assume is his bed, one arm behind his head as he holds his phone up in front of his face.

"Hey, Drama. Oh, shit. Did I interrupt your shower?" he asks as he glances at my robe.

I shake my head, keeping my smile in place. "No, I got out a bit ago. What's up?"

"I was just calling to check in, see if my dad was still being a fucking prick." Theo laughs.

I move from the dresser out into the hall and laugh before he speaks again.

"Is that my dad's room?"

My eyes widen at his words, I can practically feel them do so. Shit, shit, shit. Is it convincing if I tell him no? Probably not.

"Yeah, he let me use his shower." I shrug nonchalantly.

"Why? What's wrong with yours?" he asks with furrowed brows.

My brain stalls as I try to come up with something to say. Last time Theo and I spoke I had moved out and back to my house. Why wouldn't he think that I was still there?

"I don't know. The water won't get hot. I have to get it looked at."

Theo's confusion eases as he nods his head like that makes sense. Did it? I hope to god it did.

"Probably something to do with your hot water heater. Have you called a plumber?"

"Yeah," I lie. "They are supposed to come out tomorrow, here's hoping," I say with crossed fingers.

Crossed fingers, Andromeda? Really? Way to sell it.

"How's school?" I ask, desperate to change the topic to literally anything in the world as I slip out of Atlas's bedroom and into the hallway.

"Good." Theo nods. "I miss you. We haven't talked in a while, and I was hoping we were still okay."

"Yeah, of course. I miss you too." I smile genuinely for the first time since I answered.

"I can't wait to see you on Thanksgiving. I was hoping maybe before dinner we could go somewhere for a bit? Talk, maybe?"

My stomach twists at the cautious tone he uses. The slight hope tinging his words. I do my best to push it aside as I smile and nod.

"Sure. It'll be great to have you back in Brighton, like my big brother coming home," I say, doing my best to friend zone the hell out of him as casually as possible.

Theo tosses his head back and laughs before smirking at me.

"Drama baby, if you and I were brother and sister we would be in jail for the shit we've done together."

Well. That took a turn.

I laugh lightly, trying to play it off before I glance at the corner of my phone.

"Can I call you later? My grandma is calling me," I lie.

I'm getting better at this lying thing, I think.

"Sure. Call me tomorrow or something. Love ya."

I pause for a moment before I say, "Love ya too," and hang up.

Love ya? Theo hasn't said he loved me since he tried to get back together with me after we broke up. Then again he didn't say he loved me, he said love ya, which is different, right? Isn't it more casual? Friend-shippy? Oh god, it's been way too much of a day for all of this.

Heading back into Atlas's room, I slip on some yoga pants and a baggy T-shirt before throwing on my glasses and pulling out my laptop to get ahead on some assignments.

———

After I finally got dressed, I went out to find Atlas in the living room with two bags of Chinese food. I asked if he still needed to get more work done and he just shook his head and asked me to come eat. Once our food was spread out, Atlas put on one of the *Fast & The Furious* movies. Couldn't tell you which one, after the first two they are pretty much all the same.

Atlas is currently massaging the balls of my feet as I lay across the couch while we veg out. This is what I love about us. The sex is amazing, of course. No, scratch that. Electrifying. But as often as we tear each other's clothes off, we can also have moments like this too. Moments just for us, where we can touch and kiss and cuddle without fear that anyone will see or judge us.

Because let's be honest, even if no one knew who we were to each other in this town, they are still going to see an eighteen-year-old girl and a forty-one-year-old guy and think that it's wrong. People by nature are judgmental assholes, it's just the way it is. They don't get it and most probably never would and they don't have to. Atlas and I understand each other and that's what matters.

"So, I was thinking," Atlas says.

I turn to face him as I raise an eyebrow.

"Yeah? That sounds dangerous."

He rolls his eyes at me and pinches the bottom of my calf.

"Don't be a brat," he says on a chuckle. "What do you think about a little getaway? Nothing too extravagant, just a few days."

"When? Where?"

"Tomorrow. We can come back Sunday. That will give us four days just to ourselves. And I'm not telling you where, it's a surprise."

I lean up and scoot closer to him. "Well, color me intrigued. I'm in. I just caught up on my classes so I should be good through the weekend. What about work?"

"You're sleeping with the boss, remember? It comes with perks like last-minute vacation time being approved."

I shake my head and laugh as I shove his shoulder before leaning forward and pressing my lips against his.

"It sounds amazing. I'll go anywhere with you."

Atlas's eyes shine with a new emotion I haven't seen before. I can't quite name it. Excitement? Adoration? Love?

Yeah, right.

"I just thought that with everyone coming into town in a few weeks it's going to be hard to get any time together. I just want to be selfish with you for a little longer before I have to share you," he says softly.

"You never have to share me, Atlas." I smile. "I'm all yours."

"That's probably my favorite sentence in the English language," he says as he cups my face with his hand and smiles.

I nod before my smile falls slightly.

"Atlas, you know we won't be able to keep this from everyone for long, right?"

I watch as confliction contorts his face before he gives me a sad look and nods.

"I know, I don't want to either. I'm so proud to call you mine but—"

"Our families may not feel the same," I agree.

"Especially Theo." He grimaces.

"Or Alyssa," I sigh.

"And I'll be surprised if your grandpa doesn't kick my front teeth in. Can't say I'd blame him."

We are silent for a few moments, lost in our own heads before Atlas looks at me again.

"For a little longer? Just us?"

I nod in agreement. "Let's get through the holidays and then we can take it one step at a time."

And hope to god the people that matter most to us won't burn us at the stake for what we've done, what we continue to do, and what we plan on doing for a long time. Or, well, at least I plan on.

Chapter 31
Atlas

I lightly drum my fingers against the wheel as Neil Young plays from the speakers while we cruise down the road. Glancing over to the sleeping goddess in my passenger seat, I smirk to myself. I woke her up this morning at four and told her that we were getting an early start. Surprisingly, I wasn't greeted with an overwhelming amount of enthusiasm. She basically had only enough energy to brush her teeth, slip on a pair of yoga pants and a sweatshirt before she crawled back into bed.

I ended up scooping her up and carrying her to the car. Looking down at her peaceful sleeping face, I didn't mind a bit. Especially not when she buried her head into my chest, like she couldn't get close enough. My heart physically clenched at the action. I don't know what the hell I'm doing but all I know is that somewhere along the road she became my entire fucking world.

The coming weeks are going to be chaos for us. Paul's parents are still coming up for Thanksgiving just like they have every year since Emily and Paul got married. And based on the dozens of text messages that I've gotten from Alyssa this week alone she is coming to town too. Not to mention Theo will be home for Thanksgiving break. All of this adding up to absolutely zero alone time for Andromeda and me.

I know it's cowardice and maybe even selfish to want to keep our relationship a secret from those closest to us. But let's be honest, none of those conversations are going to go well. My son is going to hate me, Alyssa is going to hate us both and Paul's parents are going to be disappointed beyond belief in me, maybe in Andromeda too. We are finally in a good place, and I don't want to lose that. I know we will have to face the music sooner or later, just not right now. Right now it's our time and I plan on taking advantage of every single moment of it.

A soft cooing noise sounds from Andromeda as her beautiful eyes flutter open before taking in our surroundings. It's finally light out and she couldn't have chosen a better time to wake up, honestly. She gives me a soft smile that has a light feeling filling my chest before she looks out her window and her eyes widen to the size of saucers.

"Oh my god! San Francisco?" she gasps as we crest the middle of the Golden Gate Bridge.

"I wanted to take you somewhere special. Are you hungry? I was thinking we could grab some pancakes at Debbie's?"

"Yes! It feels like a lifetime since I've been there. I hope you brought some big bills in that wallet because I'm getting one of everything."

I chuckle as I reach out to take her hand in mine, placing a soft kiss against the back of it as I drive. She smiles at me before intertwining our fingers together as she looks out the window in awe, almost like she's never been here before, which isn't true. Maybe she's seeing things differently now, though. Things sure as hell have changed since the last time she came out here.

Everything has.

My hand unintentionally holds on a little tighter, as if she was about to be ripped out of my grasp. As if my grasp on her slender fingers is enough to brace us for the storm that is sure to come.

No. Not thinking about any of that, not this weekend.

Theo and I came with the Clarkes down here a couple of times over the years. We didn't make it a tradition like Paul and Em did, but I've been enough to know exactly where Andromeda's favorite breakfast spot is.

When we get there, she gets the widest grin as she proceeds to order enough to cover nearly the entire table, of course not forgetting the head-sized blueberry pancakes they are famous for. There is no way in hell this woman is going to eat all of this food. It's gonna be entertaining to see her try, though.

"You guys still doing alright?" the older waitress asks with a kind smile.

Andromeda nods as she pushes one of her four plates away from her and leans against the booth, cradling her stomach like she's about to be sick.

"It's wonderful, thank you, but for the love of god, why did you let me eat so much?" she says as her eyes come to me scoldingly.

I throw my hands up as I shake my head.

"Hey, I learned early on that it's never a man's place to comment on how much or little a woman eats."

The waitress lets out an amused laugh as she takes Andromeda's plates.

"No truer words have ever been spoken. Your boyfriend is right, sweetie."

I watch as Andromeda's cheeks pink at her words while I grin. I like the sound of it, but it feels a little bland. Andromeda and I are so much more than labels. She isn't just a girl I'm dating, and the title girlfriend doesn't seem to fit either. She's just...everything. My everything.

"Whenever you're ready," I say as I hold out my card to the waitress.

She smiles and nods as she grabs my plate and heads back to the kitchen. I notice that Andromeda is still blushing even when we are alone. I lean forward, resting my forearms against the table as I smirk.

"What?"

She glances at me before shaking her head. "Nothing. I just, no one has ever referred to me as your girlfriend before. I mean, am I? Is that what this is? Am I your girlfriend?"

I scoff before smiling at her as I lace our fingers together.

"Well, you sure as hell aren't anyone else's, are you, Neveah?"

She shakes her head as her smile grows before her eyes dart around the café and leans forward, brushing her lips against mine. It's soft, sweet, and over way too fucking quick for my liking before she is settling back into her seat.

Once we are done with breakfast we do a couple of touristy things that Andromeda begged for. I protested for all of five seconds until she turned those big puppy dog eyes on me and just like every other time, I was a goner.

Before we head to the hotel I have one more thing in mind. Wordlessly, I begin driving us in the direction of our destination. Andromeda talks enough for the both of us as I maneuver out of the city before turning off onto the familiar unmarked road. I know the instant she recognizes our surroundings because she immediately quiets as a heavy look crosses her face.

Maybe this was a bad idea. Maybe we should have spent our first vacation together making new memories, not rewriting old ones. I don't know. Something felt right about coming here, maybe to help her heal in a way. Maybe to help us both.

I put my car into park just before the gravel road turns to sand. We sit there in silence, both looking over the private little inlet of water that Paul and Emily discovered after their graduation road trip where they drove the entire 101.

"It looks different," Andromeda says softly under her breath.

I turn to see that she's staring out at the water as she continues to speak.

"It's not how I remember it. I couldn't tell you what's changed, but it just feels..."

"Wrong?" I ask gently.

Her head nods as she turns to face me, those big green gems of eyes shining with brimming tears. I reach my hand out and cup the side of her face before bringing her to meet my lips. She meets me instantly as her tongue gently strokes against mine. It's so soft, so passionate and I fucking revel in it.

She rests her forehead against mine as her eyes squeeze shut tightly.

"Hey," I say gently. "We can go. I don't want to upset you."

Shaking her head, she looks at me again with a sad smile this time.

"No, I want to be here. I don't want to go to places like this and only be reminded of the hurt. I want to remember the good, the happy. And if I can't remember it then I want to make it."

I smile softly at her as I nod. That I can do. Quickly, I hop out of the car before jogging around to her side. She looks up at me curiously as I reach inside to unbuckle her before scooping her up into my arms and tossing her over my shoulder.

"Atlas! What the hell are you doing?" she demands as I begin jogging toward the water.

"Atlas, this isn't funny!" her voice shouts as I pick up my pace.

"Don't you dare!" she shrieks as I get to the edge of the water and launch her into the air before she makes a loud splash into the water.

She always hated getting wet. Whether it was my pool or really any body of water, she always preferred to stay on dry land. And it's not because she isn't an excellent swimmer, I taught her myself. I'm chuckling to myself, waiting to be greeted with an angry little goddess but she doesn't come up.

Two more seconds pass by before panic sets in. I quickly rush into the water and dive down to look for her when a pair of hands comes up, resting on my shoulders before pushing me underwater. The water is colder than I anticipated, significantly colder. Nipping at my skin, the icy bite of the water sends a wave of shock through my body as I push up to break the surface despite the weight attempting to hold me down.

When I break through, I look over to see Andromeda smiling at me with a mischievous grin.

"What the fuck, Nevaeh! You can't play games like that. I thought you were hurt!" I shout.

She rolls her eyes as she comes over to wrap her legs around my torso.

"Good. That's what you get for tossing me in, Neanderthal. Now can we please get out of here before we die of hypothermia?"

I scoff and shake my head but do as she asks because I'm pretty sure I've already lost all circulation to my toes.

"Well, I did have a blanket and picnic packed for us, but I didn't plan on us both being soaking wet so close to sunset."

I feel her shiver in my arms before she looks up at me.

"You hate picnics."

I nod. They are ridiculous. Why do people think eating on the ground outside is fun or romantic in any way? We invented the table and chair for a reason.

"But you love them," I say with a shrug.

She smiles at me before she shivers again.

"Thank you, that means a lot. But this asshole threw me into the lake, and I need to get out of these wet clothes immediately."

"Now that I can get behind." I smirk.

I quickly grab the couple of towels that I brought from home and wrap one around each of us before starting up the car and heading toward our hotel.

Chapter 32
Andromeda

When we step inside the hotel, my mouth drops. Don't get me wrong, I know that Atlas is well off. My parents were definitely upper middle class as well so it's not like I haven't been to a nice hotel before. But I've never been to a hotel like *this* before.

There is literally a water fountain as the showpiece to the lobby. Large white pillars with what looks to be hand-carved details adorn each side of the receptionist desk and continue in a line through the building. My eyes wander up from the perfectly polished marble floors as they climb and climb to the vaulted ceiling with five of the largest chandeliers that I've ever seen.

"You're drooling, babygirl," Atlas teases as he slips his arm around my waist.

"This place is gorgeous. I can't even believe something like this exists."

He chuckles as we are greeted by an all-smiles receptionist, despite the fact that we look like drowned rats dripping tiny puddles through his lobby. Atlas gives him our information and only a minute later, he is handing us a set of keycards.

"You two will be on the thirty-second floor, if you need anything, please feel free to call us and we will do our best to accommodate.

Thank you so much for choosing The Aglaia. Enjoy your stay, Mr., and Mrs. Kane."

My heart flip flops at his words as Atlas thanks him and steers us toward the elevator, our bags in tow behind us. I thought that I was giddy when Mary at the diner called me Atlas's girlfriend but hearing someone call me Mrs. Kane has me ready to drop from a heart attack. I'm surprised we haven't faced more hesitance today.

Maybe it's because despite being forty-one, Atlas doesn't look a day over thirty-five and with my makeup applied just right, I can pass for twenty-two at least. I mean, that's still quite the age gap but no one seems to be looking at us twice. Is it really that easy? Could it be this simple? That we could just be together because we want to be? Because we can't imagine not being with the other and everyone will just be accepting and supportive? Wishful thinking, I suppose.

When we get to the thirty-second floor, Atlas gestures for me to step out first as we follow the room numbers until we reach ours. One tap of the key against the scanner and we are in, and oh my god is it gorgeous. The room has the same marble floors as the lobby, the same neutral but somehow elegant cream-colored walls and a mini chandelier hanging above the living room. My eyes trail over the suite to see a wet bar in the corner and a patio set on the balcony before coming to a set of french doors showcasing a pristinely made bed with rose petals and Ferrero Rocher's scattered across the top and several candles burning.

"It's cheesy," Atlas says as he sets down the bags and comes up behind me, looping his arms around my waist as he rests his face into my neck. "I thought it would be romantic, but it looks like a setup in a bad romance movie."

I turn my head to the side to look at him, shaking my head slightly.

"It's amazing."

His face softens at that as he smiles and presses a gentle kiss against the tip of my nose.

"Let's get you out of these wet clothes," Atlas suggests as he takes my hand in his and leads us toward the huge bathroom.

It's a wet bath style so there are no walls separating the shower from the rest of the room. There is just beautiful tile everywhere and a wrap-around bench in the corner adorned with various shampoo, body wash and other bottles.

Atlas reaches for the handle and turns the shower on, testing it after a moment before nodding as he looks to me. His hands wrap around the bottom of my shirt, my hoodie long forgotten in the car, thank God, because the way Atlas's eyes burn into my naked skin is a feeling unlike anything else.

His hands trail down my bare stomach before coming to the top of my jeans. His fingers make quick work of the buttons before peeling the soaked material away from my skin until all I'm left in is my bra and panties. I don't wait for him as I reach behind myself and undo my bra before tossing it to the side along with my panties. His eyes trace over me hungrily and a wave of confidence settles over me as I stand a little taller and let him get his fill.

It's not that I've ever been insecure about my body, but there is an inherent nature built into us that when we are naked we should hide ourselves, feel embarrassment. How can I do either of those things though, when Atlas is looking at me like I'm the most treasured thing he's ever laid eyes on?

He reaches behind himself and grabs his T-shirt with one hand before pulling it over his head and tossing it to the side. My eyes trace over his golden skin as he quickly undoes his belt and pushes his jeans and wet boxers to the floor. I don't care how many times we have slept together. I will never get over the fact that I have seen Atlas Kane naked, that I've been fucked by him in nearly every fathomable position.

Slowly, he moves first, taking my hand in his before pulling me into the stream of warm water. I let out an audible sigh of relief when the warmth of the water wraps around my skin. Atlas's hands are slow and rhythmic as they come behind me and begin massaging my muscles. I let out a groan in pleasure as he continues.

"Oh god, don't stop, please," I beg as he digs into my shoulders.

He lets out a rough chuckle as he places a soft kiss to the back of my shoulder.

"I'll do anything to keep hearing those sweet moans fall from your lips."

"You know exactly what to do to keep these moans falling from my lips, trust me."

One of his hands stops as it begins gliding down my naked skin while the other continues its work. I'm about to protest when his fingers brush against the seam of my thigh, encouraging me to spread my legs apart further. I slowly do, allowing him access to brush against my clit, just barely, but enough to have my legs nearly buckling.

"Do I, now?" Atlas rumbles teasingly. "Do I touch you just right, Nevaeh?" he asks when he brushes over me again.

"Yes," I gasp.

"Do you want me to keep rubbing you or does my dirty little girl want to play?"

My eyes flick over my shoulder to see him watching me with a predatory grin. The heat in my eyes must be answer enough for him because in the next moment, he is slipping a finger inside me. The water causes more friction than usual, similar to the other night in the hot tub. Despite how turned on I am right now. I wince slightly at the discomfort before it eases.

Atlas slowly moves in and out of me, like he isn't absolutely torturing me as he does. When I arch into him, he takes it as his cue and slips another finger inside. I let out a breathy moan as he begins working me over before his right hand drops from my shoulder and slowly runs down my spine before resting on my ass cheek.

"This fucking ass has been the main star in all of my dreams lately," he grumbles against the back of my shoulders.

"Are you gonna let me take you here, babygirl? Where no other man has ever been? Where no other man will ever be?" he asks as his hand begins running up and down the curve of my ass.

I hesitate for a moment as nerves take over. I've always been irrationally scared about it. I've just heard too many horror stories to have the desire to even try. Something about the way Atlas is so desperate, the way he wants to possess that part of me though has me nodding my head despite my nerves.

A satisfied growl emanates from his chest before he lifts me up into his arms, slaps the water off and carries me across the room, dumping me onto the bed without so much as a towel. I feel the silky comforter beneath me begin to soak but I couldn't care less right now when this Adonis of a man, no, this Atlas of a man is standing over me like he is two seconds away from losing all self-control.

"On your hands and knees, sweet girl," he says as he reaches down and strokes his cock slowly as if he can't help but touch himself as he watches me.

I do as I'm told and flip around so that I'm resting on my hands and knees when he comes up behind me. We've done it doggy style over a dozen times by now but nerves coil inside my stomach because I know this time is going to be different. Suddenly, a cool liquid hits my ass and I spin my head around to watch Atlas set a bottle of lube to the side.

I feel his fingers gather up the lube that is trying to run down my thighs before he rubs it over me. My hands have involuntarily gripped the sheets like a vice as I prepare for the intrusion but after a few seconds, I'm surprised that Atlas has done nothing more than run his fingers over me, never once putting enough pressure to even attempt to enter.

"Shhh," he coos gently as his hand comes to rub soothingly up and down my spine. "It'll hurt a lot more if you're tense. Relax for me, Neveah."

"Okay," I say with a heavy exhale. "I'll try."

"That's a good girl. Deep breaths. We're gonna start slow, okay?"

I nod just before I feel him apply pressure. It's slow and steady and though it's not the best feeling in the world, it's not nearly as painful as I thought it would be though either.

"You ready for more?" Atlas asks.

Nodding slowly, I take deep breaths as he pushes a second finger inside me. Fuck. Okay, a little uncomfortable now.

"You're doing so good," Atlas praises.

I can't lie that his words of encouragement help soothe something in me, allowing me to relax a little bit more. It takes a minute or so, but soon he is moving in and out of me, and the discomfort is completely gone, replaced with...pleasure?

A soft moan slips out before I even realize it as Atlas continues his pace. I feel his lips come down to kiss my spine as his mouth turns up into a smile.

"You like it, don't you? Does it feel good when I play with your ass, babygirl?"

"Y-yeah," I breathe out when he applies a little more pressure.

"That's good. I think you're ready for me now."

Atlas slowly removes his fingers from me until I'm left feeling almost empty. This time a warm liquid hits my ass and I glance back to see Atlas spitting on me in addition to the lube. Something about it has my pussy pulsing and my heart racing.

God, is there anything sexier than Atlas Kane?

"Alright, Nevaeh. Blow out a big breath when I tell you to; it's gonna help, okay?"

I nod as I feel his warm hands cup each of my hips, lifting me up higher and forcing me to drop onto my forearms instead of my hands as he arches my back up.

"Breathe out," he says, and I do so.

Instantly, I feel the head of Atlas's cock push against me before slipping inside. Pain envelops me, and I let out a small cry as he continues pushing inside until he is fully seated in me. My fists are balled up, my toes curled, and my face pinched in a grimace. Fuck. Okay this hurts, this sucks. Ow, fuck.

"Keep breathing, Nevaeh. Relax, or you're gonna suffocate my cock," he says through clenched teeth in a tone that indicates he wouldn't necessarily have a problem with that.

I do my best to relax and after a moment, Atlas withdraws slowly before pushing back in, moving his hips in extremely slow but rhythmic thrusts. Each one sends a pain through me but eventually, the pain begins to dull as a small amount of pleasure seeps in.

Reaching down, I take my hand and begin rubbing small circles over my clit, the extra stimulation helps distract me from the pain and relaxes me enough to even enjoy it. Moaning softly as I rub myself, I find my hips slowly thrusting along with Atlas, meeting him as I do.

"Fuck, yes. Touch that sweet little clit for me. I love watching you play with yourself," he rasps roughly.

His thrusts begin to come a little faster and a little deeper as he speaks.

"Your ass is the best thing I've ever felt, Neveah. And the fact that I'm the only man who will ever experience it?" he says before letting out a groan as he thrusts a little faster.

The pain is still there but it's much more tolerable now. I don't know if it's because I'm practically numb to it, I'm feeling so good from touching myself, or if Atlas's words are helping but either way, I arch into him more, ready to take all he is offering. I rub my clit faster as I let out another moan.

"You like having your tight little ass stuffed full of cock, don't you, babygirl? You love being filled up."

"Yes!" I gasp.

"I knew you'd love it. Good girls love being completely full," he says as his right hand moves from my hip to slap the side of my ass.

I jolt at the move, causing me to clench down on him which makes him let out a string of curse words before he does it again and again.

"Fuck. You squeeze my cock so good. No one has ever felt like you, no one ever could. I want to stay buried in your tight little hole forever. I want to fuck you until you pull the cum out of me and then use it to fuck you deeper."

"Atlas!" I gasp. "Shit!" I pant as I feel my orgasm build inside of me.

"I know, babygirl. I know how much you love that your godfather is fucking your ass right now. Have you been saving this for me, knowing no other man in the world could ever touch you like I can?"

At this point I can't even form a coherent thought, let alone speak it. I let out some grumbled strand of noises as I feel myself begin to fall over the edge. All it takes is one more slap to the side of the ass and a deep thrust from Atlas to send my orgasm crashing into me like a freight train.

I feel my pussy pulse as I come, my ass squeezing down on Atlas as a white-hot blinding feeling takes over me. My vision blurs as an orgasm like I have never experienced invades every inch of me, sending me into a screaming, shuddering mess.

Atlas follows me almost immediately, his cock pulsing and twitching inside me as his release begins to fill me up. When we are both spent, I collapse from my knees onto my stomach and Atlas does the same. He falls on top of me in a way that doesn't crush me but that ensures nearly every inch of us is touching right now. Our breaths are heavy and ragged, the room silent and calm before he speaks.

"I've never been in love before. Not a love like your parents had...but I've never loved anyone the way I love you, Nevaeh."

His voice is soft, almost vulnerable. It's a million times different than any tone I've ever heard Atlas use, ever. My heart begins to race as my stomach clenches. We've said we loved each other all our lives, obviously. Since we went down this road though, neither of us has said it. The lines were too blurred. There was already love there, but a different kind. Not this kind. But I feel it too. I feel it so deeply, so fundamentally that I know in this moment, I will never love another human being the way I love Atlas Kane.

"I love you, Atlas. Irrevocably."

Chapter 33
Andromeda

Our vacation went by way faster than either of us would have liked. After that first day, a solid seventy percent of our time was spent in our hotel room, and it was perfect. Something changed in us the day we said I love you. I had always felt this pull to Atlas, this closeness unlike anything I had ever experienced before. Those feelings pale in comparison to what I feel now, though.

We rarely go longer than a few minutes without touching each other in some way, I feel the desire to be near him almost constantly. He's like a drug and I'm desperate for another fix. I know that he feels the same. He's more tender with me now, caring. Before, our relationship could have been construed as purely physical, at least from an outsider's perspective. Now, though? There is no denying that this man is completely in love with me, and I him.

Which is going to make this weekend challenging as hell when our families come to town.

I'm in the break room getting myself and Atlas another cup of coffee when Dillon strides in. Since we got back from San Francisco, he has been traveling so we haven't really seen each other since last week. I give him a polite smile as I grab my mug before filling Atlas's up.

"Hey, how are you doing?" Dillon asks as he rinses out his cup in the sink.

"Good, how about you?"

"Not as good," he says on a sigh, his accent thick and low.

My eyebrows furrow as I look at him with worry.

"Why? What's going on?"

"It's been almost three months since we spent any time together, and I'll be honest, it's taking a toll on me," he says with a look of mock pain.

I snort and shake my head as I smile at him.

"You've been surviving so far. I think you'll be okay."

"Barely," he sighs, looking to his feet before glancing up to me with a smile. "How about we grab lunch?"

Lunch? Atlas said he was going to take me to lunch at this new Brazilian restaurant around the corner. No offense to Dillon but I would way rather have lunch with Atlas than him.

"Sorry, I already have lunch plans," I say with a shrug and a regrettable smile.

I'm almost out of the break room before his voice catches my attention.

"With the boss?"

I freeze in place before slowly looking over my shoulder to see Dillon watching me carefully, like he knows something. He couldn't, though. Could he? Shit. Shit. Shit. Reacting on instinct, I shake my head as I turn fully to face him.

"With Cathy, but she is pretty busy today. Where were you thinking?"

"There is this great little Brazilian restaurant down the road I've been wanting to try. I have a conference call at one thirty," he says as he looks at his watch. "Want to head out now?"

Fuckkk.

"Yeah." I smile tightly. "Let me just give the boss man his coffee before he gets all growly."

Dillon laughs as he dries off his coffee mug and walks with me.

"Yeah, no one wants that. Let me just grab my keys, and we can go, okay?" he asks as he veers off to his office.

I make it the rest of the way into Atlas's office when I see him frowning at his computer. It only takes him one second to notice that I'm in the room and his frown instantly gives way to a bright smile that warms me from my head to my toes. God, having this man's attention is like having the sun shine directly on you.

"There's my girl." He smiles as I walk over to his desk, placing his coffee cup in front of him as I lean down to quickly brush a kiss against his lips.

When I pull away, I know he instantly recognizes the tightness in my smile. His eyes flick back and forth between mine as his brows pinch together.

"What's wrong?"

I bite my lower lip before speaking.

"I can't make lunch today."

"Oh," he says, a twinge of disappointment but understanding in his tone. "Are you buried? It's okay if you don't finish everything today. I don't want you to work through your lunch break."

"No it's not that. Dillon asked me to lunch."

His eyes narrow on me, his body tightening to practical stone at just the mention of his name.

"Dillon?"

"Yeah. I told him I had plans, and he asked if they were with you. I think he knows about us, Atlas, or at least suspects. I didn't know what to do, so I said the plans were with Cathy and that I would go with him instead so he would drop it."

Atlas sits there for a moment, jaw clenched tightly as he shakes his head and stands up from his chair.

"I'm done with that fucker thinking he has a shot at what's mine. I'll make it very clear exactly who you belong to," he says as he rounds his desk.

"No!" I say as I rush in front of him, my hands on his chest to stop him. Unfortunately my attempt does nothing to stop him in his path.

"Atlas, you can't. This isn't the right time or place. We haven't even told our families yet! You can't be going around beating your chest like a caveman claiming me in the middle of the office."

He pauses at my words, his hand on the doorknob as he breathes heavily for several moments before he nods and takes a step away.

"You're right," he says as he turns to me and cups my face. The touch is a strange mixture of tender and possessive. An intoxicating combination that has my full attention on him.

"If he so much as lays a single finger on you, what I did to Abner will look like a love tap, understood?"

I nod. "He won't. We are just friends, he agreed."

He shakes his head as he looks down at me.

"Oh, my sweet little Nevaeh. You have no idea how devious a man can become when he sees something he wants. That's one of the things I love about you. You always try to see the good in everyone."

"I love you too," I say softly, causing his body to loosen as a touch of a smile lifts his lips.

He leans down to kiss me when a knock comes from the door. We spring apart just in time for Dillon to step inside. Looking around until his eyes land on me and then Atlas. His brows dip for a moment before his signature smile returns.

"You ready?" he asks me.

"Yeah, let me just grab my purse," I say as I step past Dillon.

"Do you have those plans I already asked for?" Atlas asks, quite possibly in the most disrespectful tone I've ever heard him use with any of his employees.

"Not yet. Since the whole Abner thing went to shit, there are some things I'm trying to move in," Dillon says back, with an almost equally disrespectful tone.

Atlas clearly picks up on it, and his chest inflates with a heavy inhale. I watch as he takes a step closer, no doubt ready to tear into Dillon. I quickly grab my purse and step next to Dillon to intervene, pulling on his jacket sleeve toward the hallway.

"Come on, don't want to make you late for your call later."

Atlas's eyes snap down to where my hand is touching Dillon, which makes me drop him as if he was on fire. Dillon nods, his eyes still on Atlas as he takes a step out of the doorway.

"Yeah, c'mon. Let's go get my girl fed."

Dillon spins on his heel so he misses the pure fire that fills Atlas's eyes, but I don't just before he steps inside his office and slams the door so hard the entire office reverberates.

Does Dillion have a death wish or something?

It's a quick drive to the little Brazilian place down the road and since I have only tried Brazilian food a few times, I let Dillon order for us. The food is amazing, and the place is so cute, I can tell it will be a lunchtime hot spot in no time. I'm finishing the last of my empanada when Dillon speaks.

"So, I heard what happened with Abner. I didn't know if it was okay to bring it up or not. Are you okay?"

My eyes flick up to him, a ball suddenly forming in my throat, or maybe it's the food. Either way, I'm speechless for a moment as I gather my thoughts. He knows what happened with Abner? That he barely touched my hand, and Atlas went all possessive caveman on him and broke his nose? No. He can't know that much.

"I'm fine. It wasn't a big deal." I shrug.

His brows furrow as he leans forward and touches my hand, similarly to how Abner did. Good thing Atlas isn't here, I guess.

"Yes, it was. Someone touched you without your permission. I'm glad the boss hit him because had I been there, he would have left with a whole lot more broken bones."

I think that was supposed to be sweet? Was it sweet? Kinda, I guess. Defending my honor and all. Even if Dillon is probably assuming Abner did something more inappropriate like pinched my ass.

"Thanks, he's a creep. I'm kind of relieved I won't have to sit at any more meetings with him."

At least that's the truth.

Dillon nods and lets out a sigh. "Yeah, but he was a rich creep. His project was going to set us up for the rest of the year and into the first quarter. Now, I don't know what we are going to pull off."

My brows furrow. "Is the company in trouble? I thought we were doing great?"

"Not in trouble per se. We are just in the middle or only beginning all of our projects right now. Nothing is close to being completed yet, and if we aren't closing jobs, we aren't getting paid."

I can't believe Atlas hasn't mentioned this.

"Well, what can I do to help?" I ask. "This was just as much my dad's company as it was Atlas's. If there is something I can do, I want to."

Dillon smiles as he shakes his head. "We will come through it, we always do, and Atlas is rich as sin. He just chooses not to flash it. We will be fine," he says as he squeezes my hand lightly.

Rich as sin? That seems like a bit of an exaggeration. I mean, he lived upper-middle class like my parents. He drives a nice car but nothing extravagant. Maybe Dillon's standard of rich is different than what I'm picturing.

Casually, I slip my hand out from under his. He looks a little hurt, but before he can say anything, the waitress brings us our check. Dillon smiles at her and gives her his card as I stand and gather up my purse and slip on my jacket.

"You ready to get back?" I ask, doing my best to avoid eye contact with him.

"Yeah, sure."

When Dillon gets his card back and leaves a tip, we head out the door and climb into his car. We don't say a word the entire way back, the tension so thick inside the car that you could practically choke on it.

We ride the elevator up in silence until we get to the top and step out.

"So, that was fun. I miss hanging out with you. We should do it more often. Friends do lunches and concerts all the time, right?" he asks as we walk past his office and toward my desk.

"Yeah, that's true. How was the concert? I bet it was amazing."

He shrugs. "I didn't end up going."

"What? Why not?"

He turns and stops when we get to my desk. "I didn't have anyone to go with. Felt lame going by myself."

"I'm sure you could have found someone to hold your interest for a night," I chuckle as I set down my purse and peel off my jacket.

I watch as he bites the inside of his lip for a moment as he shakes his head.

"That's the thing, someone is already holding my interest. I'm trying to give her time but it's pretty hard when she's all I can think about," he says, his accent rasping as he takes half a step closer to me.

"Dillon," I say softly as I take a small step backward, my ass bumping against my desk as I do.

"I know, you need time, love. I'm normally a very patient man. But with you? My strength is crumbling. I know what it feels like to have you in my arms, to taste your lips on mine. I'm trying to be patient, but god do I want you," he says as he leans forward, his lips ready to brush against mine and my back quite literally against the wall of my cubicle.

Before Dillon can kiss me, though, Atlas is yanking him backward by his neck. His hand wraps around Dillon's throat as he pins him to the glass wall of his office. Atlas's face is one of undiluted fury, whereas Dillon seems to almost have a small smirk on his face. What's wrong with him? Doesn't he realize he's about to get the shit kicked out of him?

"Don't you dare even think about touching her, you stupid motherfucker!" Atlas barks into his face.

"What's the matter, Atlas? Afraid of a little competition?" Dillon goads.

Oh fuck.

Atlas's hand squeezes tighter around Dillon's throat, causing his eyes to bulge for a moment as he does.

"There is no competition with you. She is mine, in every way, shape, and form, and if you so much as breathe in her direction again, I will fucking bury you."

Dillon nods quickly, his face turning from a bright red to a pale blue. Atlas drops his hand in an instant and turns his back on him, sending me a dark look as he makes his way into his office. Stopping only when Dillon speaks, or rasps, really.

"How do you think Paul would feel about that? You shagging his little girl? His best friend of all people. And let's not forget about your son. I'm assuming you haven't told him that as soon as he went off to college, you climbed on top of his girl?"

I flinch at the vulgar description he has given our relationship and go to defend myself as well as Atlas, but he is already there, turning on his heel and swinging. He delivers a punch right to Dillon's jaw that lands with a crunch. Dillon crumbles to the ground as he cradles his face with a pained groan. Atlas stands over him, his eyes cold and dark as he looks down at him.

"You're fired. Get the fuck out of my office and never come back."

Atlas reaches out and grabs my wrist before yanking me inside his office. I shut the door as soon as I pass the threshold and see Atlas begin to pace. His steps are jerky and angry as he mutters under his breath about Dillon being right.

"Atlas," I say softly, to which he ignores. "Atlas," I try again.

Still, he's pacing in that same line over and over again.

"Atlas!"

His eyes fly up to mine. I expect them to be wild and angry, filled with rage. Instead, they are filled with unshed tears and what looks like anguish. Tentatively, I take a few steps toward him until I've closed the distance before wrapping my arms around his back, resting my head against his chest. His arms come around me almost immediately, squeezing tightly as he does.

"Are you okay?" I ask softly.

"Of course not, Nevaeh. I just choked out an employee before I punched and fired him. I could get removed from the company for this, arrested. It was hard enough to keep Abner from going to the cops. I could lose everything I've ever worked for, and on top of it all, he's right.

"Paul would beat the living hell out of me for touching you. And Theo, fuck, he's probably going to try too. These are the kinds of things that happen when someone acts as selfishly and recklessly as I have."

His words are like physical blows, smashing against my already bruised and battered heart. My lower lip begins to wobble as I prepare myself for the final blow that destroys me. The one where guilt finally wins, and he tells me that it's over between us, for good.

Pulling back enough to see me, Atlas looks down, pure regret on his face, causing a tear to escape and run down my cheek.

"It's too late, though. I can't stop being selfish, I can't stop myself from having you. You're not just under my skin, you're in my veins. You're the air that I need to breathe. I should have never touched you, should have never wanted you. But I did, and I do. I regret wanting you, but I don't regret taking you."

Before I can respond, his lips come down to mine, crushing me in a brutally passionate kiss that feels like heaven and hell. It's a kiss that makes me feel like I can fly while also damning us both. I don't care, though. As long as I'm by his side, I'll gladly follow him to the depths of Tartarus.

Chapter 34
Andromeda

Atlas went to HR after he was able to calm down enough to do so. He explained everything down to him and me being together, Dillon trying to kiss me and him firing Dillon. He told them that he will be working from home until the board of directors makes their decision as to how to handle his position in the company going forward.

I'm physically sick to my stomach as we drive home. He's told me over and over that I'm worth it, that he would give it all up for me in a heartbeat, but it doesn't feel right. It feels like we finally got to a good place and now everything is spiraling.

When we pull up to the house, a muffled curse comes from Atlas as we see a very familiar car parked in the driveway.

"Theo's home," I murmur to myself.

"Yep," Atlas sighs.

We were expecting him to be home today which is why yesterday all of my stuff that had started to accumulate in Atlas's bedroom was moved back to my house. I had already planned to sleep over there tonight since Alyssa and my grandparents will be coming over bright and early for Thanksgiving tomorrow. Somehow in the chaos of today, though, I forgot. Nothing would have been nicer than to take a long bath with Atlas and get lost in each other, forget this train wreck of a day for a little while.

Oh well, I guess.

The front door opens, and a wide smile stretches across Theo's face when he sees me in the car. I can't help but smile back as I open the door and take a step out. He jogs over to me before scooping me up into his arms and spins me around like he's done a million times before.

When he sets me down, he squeezes me tightly one more time before looking at me, those bright blue eyes twinkling as he does.

"I've missed you so much, Drama. FaceTime is just not the same."

I nod. "I've missed you too."

His smile slowly slips as his brows furrow, and he wipes underneath my eye.

"Have you been crying?" he asks.

I quickly wipe my cheeks to see just a little bit of smudged mascara on my fingers as I do. I shake my head and come up with the first thing I can.

"It's just been a day. Tomorrow is Thanksgiving and I've never done a Thanksgiving dinner all by myself before."

Theo's concern washes away to sympathy as he nods, and his arms squeeze me a little tighter.

"I get that, but we are all here to help, okay?"

I smile softly and nod. "Okay."

He grins and presses a quick kiss to my cheek before he turns to face Atlas who is staring at us intently from the front of the car.

"Hey, Dad," Theo says as he walks over and gives him a quick hug.

Atlas claps Theo's back, his eyes still on me for a few moments before he pulls back to look at him.

"I'm glad you're home," Atlas says. "How are classes going?"

Theo's barely there smile vanishes in an instant as he shrugs and turns to face the door.

"They're fine. Glad the semester is over."

Atlas's brows furrow as he watches Theo walk off to the house without another word. He walks over to me, his eyes still on his son's retreating form before turning to me.

"What did I say wrong now?"

I give him a sympathetic shake of my head. "I can't speak for Theo,

Atlas. My guess, though, is that he just wants you to be happy that he's home. Not grilling him about his GPA as soon as you step out of the car."

"I wasn't," he defends. "He's been gone at school. I was asking how that was going. It's relevant."

I smile and let out a soft sigh. "I know but maybe Theo wants you to take an interest in his life outside of school."

"Andromeda, he's a full-time college student. He doesn't have time for anything besides school. What else could he be doing?" he asks as we make our way towards the house.

"I don't know. Maybe he met a girl?"

Atlas scoffs at that, causing me to give him the side eye.

"What?"

"He hasn't met a girl."

"Why do you say that?"

Atlas pauses before opening the door, lowering his voice just between us.

"Because I know my son, and the way that he still looks at you tells me he definitely hasn't found anyone else."

I wince at that, causing Atlas to let out a hollowed laugh.

"Yeah, my thoughts exactly."

Without another word, we step inside and find Theo sitting on the couch with a bowl of popcorn, watching a movie. Atlas looks at him like he wants to say something, to talk to him or connect, anything. But instead he seems to almost clam up before he starts walking toward the staircase.

"I got some stuff to take care of. You two order whatever you want for dinner," he says.

"K," Theo says absentmindedly as he stares at the screen.

I pause for a moment, wanting desperately to go check on Atlas but I know it will draw unnecessary attention to us. So, instead I step inside the living room and take a seat on the couch next to Theo.

"What are we watching?" I ask as I take a handful of popcorn.

"The newest Marvel movie, We can change it if you want," he says as he offers the remote.

I smile and shake my head. "This is perfect."

Theo smiles as he leans his head against the back of the couch and turns to look at me.

"So, how are you doing, Drama?"

"I'm good," I say with a nod. "How about you?"

"No, I mean, how are you actually doing? First real holiday without them. How are you holding up?"

My smile slowly falls as I consider his question. Until I said it on the fly in the driveway, I hadn't actually considered that yet, amazingly enough. I've been so busy with school and work and Atlas that I haven't had time to dwell on the fact. Wow, the first real holiday without Mom and Dad. An old yet familiar sharp pang tears through my chest at the thought. Fuck. I haven't felt this in months. The overwhelming grief ebbed long ago, and I thought it was gone altogether. I guess I was wrong.

"I'm okay, Theo. Thanks for checking," I say, my throat beginning to tighten with emotion and me not wanting anything to do with it.

"What about you?" I ask, hopefully smoothly changing topics. "What's new with you? How's the band? Girls? Tell me everything about college."

Theo shrugs. "Band is doing good. We've done some local gigs, nothing too crazy. What about you? Besides school and work? You seeing anyone?"

His tone is casual, not at all suspicious. So why do I break out into cold sweats at just the mention of the subject? Oh god, I don't think I'll ever be ready to tell Theo. Especially if he still isn't over us.

"I was," I admit. "I went on a couple dates with this guy from work."

"Who?" Theo asks a little too quickly to be casually interested.

Shit.

"Dillon—"

"Dillon Matthews?" Theo frowns. "I thought that was a one-time thing for Cathy's wedding?"

I shrug as Theo looks at me, almost bewildered.

"You actually dated him? He's like forty."

I roll my eyes at him as I shake my head. "He's thirty-one, and it didn't work out."

"No shit, you're eighteen, Drama. You're young and vibrant and beautiful and he is waiting to collect his AARP membership."

I can't help but laugh at that as I smack Theo's arm and crack up laughing.

"Oh my god, you're ridiculous. The age wasn't the problem. We were just better off as friends. Honestly, why do people get so hung up on age differences, anyway? Love is love, right?"

Theo shrugs. "I guess. It's just weird. Like those guys that go after women that are like half their age. I get why the guys are into the young women. I mean, they're hot. But why would the girls be into them? They are old, wrinkling, and probably can't get a hard-on without a little blue pill."

I do my best to keep my laughter in because Atlas has definitely never needed medication to get a hard-on. If anything, he might need something to make them stop. I swear to god that man is always horny.

Trust me, I'm not complaining. I fucking love it.

Shrugging, I choose to drop the topic as we focus on the movie. We watch it for a while before Theo speaks softly.

"I haven't dated anyone, not since you."

I raise an eyebrow as I glance at him out of the corner of my eye.

"Don't you mean Miranda?"

He winces at that and honestly, so do I. I thought I was over it, I mean, I am. I guess a little bit of hurt is still there, though.

"I'll never be able to say sorry enough for what I did, Andromeda. I have no excuses. I was a fucking idiot."

"Yeah, you were, but we've talked about it, Theo. It's okay. You were right, all we knew was each other. We owed it to ourselves to put that part of us to rest and explore the world around us."

"I guess. I should have talked to you, though."

"I agree," I nod. "But it's in the past. Let's not drag it up. I love you, Theo. Always will."

"I love you too. I just...I don't know how I'll ever be able to love anyone the way I loved you, the way I still love you."

Smiling softly, I nod as I rest my hand on his shoulder.

"You will, I promise. I was your first love, Theo, but not your epic love."

He watches me for a moment, seemingly contemplating that before lifting his arm for me. Normally, I would avoid the gesture, but something seems to almost pass between us. The final bit of closure I think we were both needing. Not closure for the sake of not being mad at each other during a difficult time. But genuine forgiveness and love for one another.

I lean against him as he wraps his arm around me in a completely platonic but comforting hold.

Chapter 35
Atlas

I stayed inside my office until Andromeda came upstairs to tell me that food was here. I needed to catch up on a few things and get them finalized in case the board decides to remove me after the holiday for what I did today. It's an unfortunate situation but I meant what I said to Andromeda earlier. I do regret wanting her, but taking her? Having her? I could never.

When I came downstairs, Andromeda and Theo were already eating at the kitchen island. Theo smiled at her when she spoke, but it wasn't the lustful gaze Dillon always gives her. It was more pure, loving. Andromeda hung out with us for a little bit after we ate before she decided to go home.

Surprising all of us, Theo asked if I wanted to hang out and catch up after dinner. I couldn't say yes fast enough. It's always killed me that Theo and my relationship became strained in his teenage years and on. I know that I can be hard on him at times, but it's just because I know he has so much potential.

What Andromeda said in the driveway has been sitting with me, though. When is the last time I asked Theo about how his life outside of school is going? Outside of his breakup with Andromeda or him dealing with the death of his godparents?

I grab two beers from the fridge before twisting the tops off and handing one to Theo. Normally, parents would be opposed to giving their underage kid alcohol. But I'm a firm believer that if these kids are old enough to vote and go to war, then they can have a beer.

"Drama seems good," he says as he takes a sip. "Better, at least. The last few times I've talked to her something seemed different. She didn't seem as...heavy, I guess."

I nod as I take a drink of my beer. "She's getting there, how about you?"

Theo shrugs. "I think it's easier for me than her, I mean, obviously. They weren't my biological parents—"

"They basically were," I correct.

Theo smiles sadly as he nods. "Yeah, but I'm away at school. Away from the memories, the routines. It wasn't until I pulled into the driveway and looked across the street that I remembered. Can you believe that? I actually forgot for a moment."

I nod. "I get it. It comes and goes in waves. I've found myself forgetting at times. It's hard. It will be for a while."

"Yeah, but I'm glad Drama is doing better. She deserves to be happy."

"And then some," I say, biting my tongue the moment it slips out.

A funny dip in Theo's face appears, and I switch the topic quickly.

"So, how have you been? Besides school?" I ask.

He almost seems surprised for a moment before he gives me the smallest smile as he eases back into his seat.

"I'm good. I joined a band."

His tone softens as he watches me warily like he is afraid of my reaction, but I can't imagine why.

I nod at him and smile.

"That's awesome. You're extremely talented, and you enjoy it. I'm glad you have that in your spare time."

He leans forward and rests his forearms on the island as he looks at me.

"Well, I've been thinking. If I didn't go to class, we could practice more, get out to more shows, more visibility. All we need is one solid show with a record label in the crowd and we'll be set. I could—"

"Whoa, whoa, whoa. Slow down. You want to drop out?"

The excitement in his eyes fades slowly as he leans up to sit a little taller.

"I've been thinking about it. School just isn't for me and—"

"Since when? You were a straight-A student all through high school, and if I remember correctly, you've maintained a 3.9 GPA in college. Those numbers definitely sound like someone who school *is* for them."

"Look, all I'm saying is that being an architect or a businessman or whatever isn't my dream. It's not what I want to do with my life."

"Then what do you want to do, Theo? Be a rock star? That's a great hobby, but it's not sustainable. You are twenty years old. You need to start being more responsible. When I was your age, I—"

"Fucked up and got a girl pregnant who had no interest in being a mom," he cuts in, a harshness I've never heard before in his tone as he speaks.

I clench my jaw as I think about Theo's mother while he continues to speak.

"Those are your mistakes, not mine. You had to be responsible because your choices led you there. I'm twenty, Dad. Not forty. It's okay for me to not want to settle down into a job with a high 401k match rate.

"It's okay for me to want to chase my dreams at least for a little while. If I'm not going to chase them now, then when? When I'm your age? You've lived your entire life for others and don't get me wrong, I appreciate the sacrifices you've made for me especially, but that's not what I want for myself. I don't want to wake up one day and realize that I never did anything for just me. That I never tried to go after something, even if I knew the chances weren't good. I don't want to be too afraid to live and too cowardly to admit it."

I'm speechless as I stare at him. It's clear these feelings have been building for a long time based on the weight that seems to almost visibly lift from his shoulders. He takes another long sip of his beer before setting it on the counter and standing up.

"You've had a great life, but it's not one I would choose. I'm gonna be my own person and I'd love my father to approve of that life, but it's happening either way."

Without another word, he turns and leaves the kitchen, his feet thumping upstairs before his door shuts with a hard thud. I look around the now-empty downstairs as I reflect on everything he said. It's nothing I didn't already know myself, but it hurts more to hear my son, of all people, voice the thoughts inside my head.

I drain the rest of my beer before throwing both bottles away and heading to bed. When I open the bedroom door, my heart sinks when I remember that I'll be sleeping alone tonight. It's been so long since I've slept alone, I couldn't even tell you when the last time was. Andromeda is my comfort, my obsession, my addiction. The thought of not having her in my bed where she belongs has me ready to storm across the street and slide into hers, at least for tonight.

I'm about ready to do just that when my phone buzzes in my pocket. I take it out and open the new text to see it's from the goddess herself.

Nevaeh: Are you and Theo still hanging out?
Me: No. We went to bed. It didn't end well.
Nevaeh: I'm sorry. Can I make your night any better?
I smile sadly as I type out my response.
Me: I can think of a few ways.

I stare at my phone for several minutes, waiting for her response, but it never comes. Maybe she fell asleep. Frustrated with this night, I toss my phone onto the side table and make my way into the bathroom to get ready for bed.

Stripping off my clothes except for my boxers, I brush my teeth before throwing my clothes into the laundry hamper as I head to bed. I only make it two steps before I freeze. Andromeda is sitting on my bed, cross-legged and smiling softly in a tiny pair of cotton shorts and a matching tank top. Her hair is pushed off to the side as she looks at me almost cautiously.

"I couldn't sleep without saying good night properly."

Thankful isn't enough of a word for the feeling I have right now. I cross the room in three steps before pushing Andromeda onto her back and climbing on top of her. She smiles at me as I press my lips against hers and run my hands over her tight and smooth body. God, her skin is fucking addicting. The silky smoothness is like butter under my fingertips.

My hands come down to the hem of her shorts as her back arches up, giving me access to pull them down. They slide off her skin along with her panties before she reaches up and yanks off her tank top, exposing her gorgeous tits to me. I bring a hand up to cup one while rubbing my thumb against her nipple. She makes a shuddering noise as I do before I cover it with my mouth.

Andromeda arches into my touch, digging her hand into my hair and urging me to continue. I twirl my tongue around her nipple before bringing my teeth out to gently nip at her. A sweet moan falls from her lips that I want to drown in. But then I remember that we aren't alone in this house right now.

My hand comes up and covers her mouth as my eyes look up at her, my mouth still ravaging her nipple as I do. The warning in my eyes must be clear enough because she nods against my hand quickly. Slowly, I remove my hand before dragging it against her silky skin until I rest it on her other breast, making sure to show it the amount of attention that I am giving the other one.

Andromeda is writhing underneath me, her body squirming, knuckles clenched into the sheets, and I haven't even played with her cunt yet. Fuck, she's so greedy for me. Almost as greedy as I am for her.

My lips move away from her nipple as I slowly begin trailing kisses over her torso and down to the seam of her thighs. I press a light kiss against the innermost part of her thigh before her legs fall open for me. I'm instantly greeted by the sight of her pretty pink cunt. Men around the world would drop to their knees in awe if they could see my babygirl spread open like this. They never will, though. She's mine until the day I die. Maybe even after that.

I don't waste another moment, desperate to taste her as her sweet flavor rolls over my tongue. Just one taste from her, and I'm letting out a deep growl of pleasure which causes her to gasp as my mouth vibrates gently against her. I do it again, earning another gasp that is a little louder this time. Hating that I have to pull away, I reluctantly lean up and look at her more seriously than before.

"You need to keep that sweet mouth quiet, Nevaeh, or we will have to stop. We aren't alone tonight."

She nods her head quickly as her eyes dart to the door, her thighs rubbing together as she does.

"Why does that turn me on?" she says quietly.

"What does?"

"The thought of someone on the other side of this wall. Someone potentially hearing us, catching us."

I shake my head as I blow out a breath.

"It would be fucking horrible," I say as my cock twitches in my boxers despite my words. The anticipation on her face does something to me. Those familiar green gems darkened with lust as they came up to me.

My hand slowly slips down, my fingers running through her cunt before pushing inside slowly. She gasps at the intrusion as her eyes stay on mine.

"Goddamn, you're so wet, babygirl. Does that turn you on? The idea of getting caught? You want someone to walk in and see your godfather finger fucking you?"

"So hot," she whimpers as her cunt squeezes my fingers.

"That's bad, Neveah. I thought you were my good girl but here you are having these naughty thoughts," I whisper hoarsely, my cock leaking precum as I continue working her over.

"I'm sorry," she moans softly as I rub against her G-spot.

"Don't apologize. Tell me more. I want all of your pleasure. What else?"

"I-I loved being pushed against the window in your office the other day," she pants. "I felt safe, I knew no one would look up but the thought that they could, and they would see me...see you fucking me..." she trails off as my other hand begins strumming against her clit.

"I liked it too, babygirl. You looked so beautiful at my mercy, kind of like you do now."

Her body is now squirming, toes wiggling and breathing choppy as she nods her head.

"Please, Atlas," she begs softly. "Make me come."

"Always," I promise as I change my angle, putting all of my focus on her G-spot and sending her over the edge.

She grabs a pillow and muffles her screams with it as her body convulses around me, her cunt soaking my fingers as I finger fuck her through her orgasm. When her shuddering slows, I spread her legs wider, flattening out my tongue as I begin licking her clean. I can't waste a drop. Not when it's her.

When I pull away, she grabs the back of my neck, pressing her lips to mine, her tongue eagerly seeking my own out as I pull off my boxers, finally freeing my cock. I reach down, stroking myself once before lining up to her as I push inside, never once removing my mouth from hers. She lets out a pleasured moan, and I do the same because, Christ, she feels like heaven.

Pulling away from her mouth, I trail my lips over her cheek and up her neck before resting on the shell of her ear.

"Give me one more, Neveah. Let me feel you squeeze my cock."

"Atlas," she whimpers as her pussy contracts as if on cue.

"That's it, such a good girl for me. Show me you missed me as much as I missed you."

"We were only apart for like an hour," she smiles as her hands wander up my back before digging into the back of my hair.

"An hour too long. Any second that I'm not buried inside you is a second wasted."

"True," she moans as she bridges her hips to meet my thrusts.

"Give me what I want, Neveah, what we both want," I encourage.

"I want you to cum with me," she whimpers as her heavy-lidded eyes flutter, a telltale sign that she is closer than she wants to be.

"I will, sweet girl. Give me what I need, and I'll fill this cunt to the brim."

"You always do. It's a miracle you haven't gotten me pregnant."

"Yet," I whisper darkly with a deep roll of my hips.

Her eyes fly open wide at that as her mouth parts slightly.

"You want to get me pregnant?"

"Of course I do. Seeing your belly round with my baby, knowing a piece of you and me together exists in this world." I shudder at the temptation of the ideas as I shake my head. "You better change the subject before I pitch your birth control in the garbage and knock you up right here and now."

"Wow," she whimpers, need thick in her voice.

"I don't think you understand, Neveah. I don't just love you. I'm obsessed with you. I'm addicted to you, and I never want to go to rehab."

"Please don't. Need me, love me," she begs as she squirms against me.

I pick up my pace, hiking her leg up and around my hip to fuck her deeper as I nod, cupping her cheek as I whisper against her lips.

"Always."

Somehow that is her undoing. Her mouth parts, ready to scream out her release before I capture it. My mouth devours hers, wringing out every ounce of pleasure I possibly can. One flick of her tongue against mine and it's no longer me in control. I'm the one on my knees for her, bowing at her altar as my own orgasm takes over.

When the pleasure fades and our breathing evens, I slowly lean back to sit between her thighs before taking my fingers and gathering up the leaking cum, pushing it back inside her where it belongs. I look up to see Andromeda's eyes darken with heat as I continue my mission. She doesn't know what she just did to me, what she just unleashed. She seemed too intrigued, too eager at the idea of having my baby in her. Our current situation be damned, that pill pack is going in the trash within the hour.

Soon.

I press a gentle kiss to the side of her thigh before I slip out of bed and turn the light off. When I lay back down, I pull the covers over us before tucking her into my side. We lay there in silence, that warm familiar feeling wrapping around me at just having her in my arms when her voice sounds.

"I should probably get back to the house."

I squeeze my arms around her tighter as if that will keep her here permanently.

"I know. Just let me hold you for a little longer."

Her mouth tips up into a smile against my bare chest as she nods softly.

Chapter 36
Andromeda

A soft tap wakes me up the next morning. It takes me a moment to realize that it isn't so much a tap but a knock. My eyes spring open seemingly at the same time that Atlas's does. The bedroom door begins opening, causing me to scramble underneath the blankets.

"Theo, what the fuck!" Atlas barks.

"Oh fuck. Sorry. I didn't know you had company, I just thought you overslept. I was gonna head over to Andromeda's and see if she needed help this morning."

My eyes widen as my heart begins thundering in my chest when Atlas quickly answers.

"Wait for me, we can bring her some breakfast. I'm sure she hasn't eaten, and no one wants to cook breakfast on Thanksgiving."

"Cool. I'll text her and see if she has any requests," Theo says as he turns on his heel and closes the door.

We wait another second or so before Atlas leaps out of bed and locks the door. He must have forgotten to lock it last night. Holy shit. My heart is hammering inside my chest and no matter how hard I try to get it under control, it won't stop.

Atlas blows out a deep breath, his back still against the door as if he can physically keep his son out of the room before he slowly makes his way over to me.

"Are you okay?"

"Yeah, nothing like a little shot of adrenaline to start the day," I joke hollowly.

Atlas lets out a short laugh as he scrubs his beard and nods. "Yeah."

"We have to tell him soon, Atlas. We clearly can't keep our distance from each other. So as much as it's going to be uncomfortable, I don't think we have much choice."

He runs his hands through his hair and nods.

"I know. After Thanksgiving, before he goes back to school, okay? We'll tell him for now. Then your family later?"

I nod. Probably best we don't drop the bombshell on everyone at once.

"I'm gonna get going. I'll get Theo out of the house as quickly as possible so you can get back over to your place. What time did you say Alyssa and your grandparents were coming?"

"Around ten."

Atlas glances down at his phone as his eyes widen. "It's nine fifty."

"Shit! Get him out of here," I say as I jump out of bed.

He nods as he rushes over to throw on a pair of sweats and a T-shirt before grabbing me for a brief but knee-buckling kiss and then he is out the door. I lock it just in case Theo decides to pop his head in here again. I refuse to even open it until I hear the car pull away and go down the road.

Trying to look as inconspicuous as possible, I make my way out of the house before walking across the street to my house and grab the hidden key before unlocking it. It's already ten in the morning and I haven't even started prepping for Thanksgiving dinner.

This is sure to be a shit show of a day.

I was just able to get out of the shower and slip on some clothes when Alyssa came barging into the house. She scoffed at me and couldn't believe that I hadn't started cooking yet but of course didn't offer to help when she noticed I was behind. Blaming her zodiac at this point is just not fair to all the other people out there unfortunate enough to share her signs. I'm honestly having a harder and harder time remembering why I used to look up to her. She's a self-centered lazy bitch. And I'm not just saying that because ever since she walked through that door an hour ago, she's been going on and on about *my* man.

"I'm gonna go over to his place and see if we can spend some alone time together," she says with a wink as she heads for the door, only stopping in her place when Theo and Atlas step inside.

"Oh, speak of the devil." She smirks as she walks up to Atlas and kisses his cheek.

Atlas lets her but his eyes flick to me apologetically immediately. Whatever. She's always done that. It's no big deal, I think to myself as I chop the celery for the stuffing with excessive aggression.

"I was just coming over to catch up," she says to Atlas before turning to Theo and scowling at him.

"I'm still not sure how I feel about you since you broke my baby niece's heart."

Huh. Maybe she does think about someone but herself, occasionally. Though in this case, her ire is unwanted.

Theo glances down at the floor, seemingly ashamed as he speaks.

"I know. I'll never forgive myself for it."

"Good," she says simply as she turns her attention back to Atlas. "So, what do you say? Can we go somewhere a little more private and catch up?"

Atlas's attention flicks to me briefly before giving Alyssa a tight smile.

"We actually came over to bring Andromeda some breakfast. Figured she wouldn't have had time to cook since she has dinner to worry about."

"Aww, you are so sweet, Atty," she coos, a nickname I know for a fact he detests. "It's probably for the best. This lazy bum slept in. She literally just put the turkey into the oven like ten minutes ago."

"I said it would be fine," I grit between clenched teeth. "I'm using a turkey bag. It seals in everything and cooks the turkey twice as fast."

"Whatever you say, Drama. All I'm saying is if it comes out under-done, don't expect anyone to eat it," Alyssa says with a roll of her eyes.

I feel myself gripping the knife extra tight before Theo walks over to me, a kind smile on his face as he offers me a bag from our local diner.

"Let me take over while you eat. We would have been over sooner, but Dad insisted on us letting you get a head start this morning before we inundated you. Looks like you could use some help though," he says as he glances around at my trainwreck of a kitchen.

"Thanks, Theo. I really appreciate it. I know a certain someone won't be helping today so I'll take anything I can get," I whisper lowly, causing Theo to laugh and nod.

I can feel Atlas's eyes suddenly on me without having to look. Alyssa's high-pitched laugh has me gritting my teeth as I open up the bag to see thick-cut french toast with all of the toppings you could wish for inside. I give Theo a grateful smile before I quickly dig in.

As I'm eating, I hear Atlas excuse himself, saying that he didn't get a chance to shower this morning and that he will be back over to help in a little bit. I also heard Alyssa offer some assistance in the shower, to which he politely but sternly declined. God, she is so desperate it's over-the-top pathetic.

Alyssa comes and sits next to me with a huff before looking down at my breakfast and wrinkling her nose.

"Sweetie, I say this because I care, but don't you think you should cut back on the carbs? I mean, french toast for breakfast and a whole Thanks-giving dinner for tonight? You won't have a fast metabolism forever."

I cut an irritated glare at her as I deliberately took a big bite.

"I'm eighteen, Alyssa. I'm not too concerned."

She rolls her eyes and shrugs her shoulders. "Whatever. What is with everyone today? You've been a total bitch ever since I got here, and Atlas acts like he isn't even interested in me anymore," she whines like a toddler as she crosses her arms over her chest.

Theo snorts as he continues cutting veggies for me. "Like he's ever been interested," he mutters loud enough for her to hear.

She sneers at him as she leans forward slightly.

"You're clearly out of the loop, Theo. We went out on a date last time I was in town. It was amazing, and we even got breakfast the next morning." She winks, totally leaving out the part where he didn't even kiss her and fucked me instead that night. Oh, right. She doesn't know that part. A vindictive part of me wishes she did.

"He hasn't been responding to any of my text messages lately, though. He used to always keep the conversation at least minimal and when I was in town before our date, I sent him some pictures and he told me that he liked what he saw. I don't get it."

"What?" I bite out sharper than I should have.

Alyssa's brows furrow as she looks at me. "What?"

"You sent him pictures? What kind of pictures?"

She rolls her eyes like I'm being stupid, but I need to hear her say it. I need to hear it come from her stupid big mouth.

"Of the naked variety, Andromeda," she scoffs. "Then the next day we went out on our date. He said he liked how big my tits were and how he couldn't wait to fuck them but now nothing."

"Jesus, that's my dad. Don't make me fucking puke," Theo spits with a look of disgust.

Not me, though. I just see red.

Shoving back my chair, I storm out of the house, despite Theo calling after me as I rush across the street and into Atlas's house. I barge into his room as he is slipping on a sweater and jeans. His eyes are surprised to see me before they fill with confusion. I don't slow down though until I am right in front of him before I rear my hand back and slap him across the face.

"You stupid fucking bastard!" I scream.

"Whoa! What the hell has gotten into you?"

"How could you fucking say those things! How could you sext with her when you were 'supposedly' falling for me?"

"Babygirl," he says cautiously, resting his hands on my shoulders. "Take a deep breath and tell me what you're talking about."

My chest is heaving with ragged breaths as anger burns in my veins.

"Alyssa just got done telling Theo and me all about how last time she was here, she sent you naked pictures and you told her that you liked them! Told her that you couldn't wait to titty fuck her, you son of a bitch!"

Realization seems to dawn on him before a flash of shame.

"Nevaeh, sweetheart. Take a deep breath and listen to me. I never said that. Yes, she sent me pictures, and yes, she asked me if I liked them. I was so fucked in the head over you I was desperate to do anything to get over you. I responded to her with a yes, hoping that it would distract me from you. It didn't, obviously, seeing as despite knowing everything she had to offer, I couldn't keep my mind off you for a second. Remember who I took to bed that night?"

"I don't care!" I snap. "I can't believe you looked at them."

"Babygirl, you know that I've been with other women before you. That's just it, though. Before you."

"I don't know about that. Alyssa sounds like she was during me," I snarl.

"Nevaeh, you know me better than that. You know us better than that," he says, his tone slightly disappointed as he frowns at me.

My temper starts to ease as I try to make sense of everything. The picture he is painting, though still pisses me off, is a much different one than Alyssa was portraying. The one Atlas describes aligns much more with the man I at least think him to be, but I'm still hesitant.

"I don't know what to believe. I don't like knowing that you've seen her naked. That you liked it."

"Do you know what it does to me knowing that my son has done the same with you?" Atlas asks with a tic in his jaw. "That he has...touched you," he grits. "That he stole your virginity when it was always supposed to be mine? It makes me irate. It makes me want to beat my own flesh and blood, Andromeda."

I swallow as I consider how that would feel if the roles were reversed. I guess it's slightly relieving to know that he's never touched her, even if he's seen her.

"She says that she's been texting you," I say with a lot less bite than I had previously.

He nods. "If it's a picture, which she has sent several since you and I have been together, I delete it immediately. If it's a message, I make sure it isn't life-threatening or pertaining to you before deleting it. Neveah, you are my whole world. I could never want another woman when I have you."

I still want to be mad, but his words make sense and I start to come to the realization that I may have acted like a jealous girlfriend, just a tiny bit.

"I'm sorry I slapped you," I say softly.

He shakes his head and gives me a sad smile.

"I deserved it. I should have never encouraged Alyssa's behavior. I just didn't know what to do. I didn't think I could have you, and I was a fucking idiot."

I nod my head in agreement which causes him to laugh. He leans down and cups both sides of my face before pressing a kiss against my lips. The rest of my anger and irritation slowly lifts away until he pulls back and rests his forehead to mine.

"Are we okay?"

I nod. "Yeah. Can you make things a little more clear with her, though. Tell her you are seeing someone or something?"

He cocks a brow at me. "Won't that look a little suspicious?"

I shrug. "I think it looks more suspicious that you were seemingly 'into her' last time she was here and now you are icing her out. It's just going to make her work harder for it. Besides, if she sits there all dinner long making goo-goo eyes at you I'm probably going to stab her."

Atlas smirks as he presses a kiss to the tip of my nose.

"I like it when you get jealous. It's fucking hot."

"Don't be an ass," I scoff as I shove away his chest.

He chuckles and nods as I take a step back. "Alright. I'm gonna get back and try to come up with some explanation as to why I stormed out of there like that."

"I'll be over soon, okay?"

I nod as he shoots me a wink before I turn and head down the stairs and back to my house.

Chapter 37
Andromeda

When I got back to the house, Alyssa was sitting on the couch watching something on the TV while Theo was peeling potatoes. His eyes snapped to me instantly, worry and maybe a tinge of suspicion in them as he watched me. I tried to act nonchalant, but his watchful gaze had me sweating bullets.

Thankfully, he didn't ask what that was all about or where I went, and I didn't volunteer the information. Atlas showed up shortly after and started working on the yams while Theo and I finished prepping the potatoes. Once Atlas was done, he asked Alyssa if they could step outside and talk. She was all too eager to do so, but within three minutes, she stormed into the house, fat crocodile tears pouring down her face as she stomped her way upstairs and slammed the guest bedroom door.

Atlas looked at me with a regretful shrug because he's too good of a guy to ever be okay with hurting anyone's feelings, even if it's for the best. Alyssa came down an hour or so later, seemingly all put back together in a nice sweater dress, makeup done to perfection, and her hair in big barrel curls. She looked stunning compared to me in my plain black sweater and my favorite pair of jeans. But when Theo wasn't looking, Atlas would casually touch my waist or brush my ass and that alone made me feel like the most desirable woman in the world.

Shortly after Alyssa came down from her temper tantrum, my

grandparents arrived. I practically threw myself into Grandpa Greg's arms while Grandma Jackie patted my back lovingly. I didn't realize how much I missed them until that moment. Grandpa Greg greeted Atlas like he was seeing his son after a long time apart because really that's how it is. My grandparents are the closest thing Atlas has to parents since his mother passed away. I could tell with how he hugged them both back that he missed them just as much as they missed him.

Grandma shooed the boys out of the kitchen, even though Theo offered to stay and help several times. She said she wanted to have some proper time with me and that he was sweet for trying, but he was ultimately in the way. I couldn't help but laugh at that. My grandma has always been a her way or the highway kind of woman. It used to drive my mom crazy.

A sad twinge hits me at the reminder. They aren't with us but today is the first time that this house has felt like a home in a long time. Everyone is off doing their own thing. Theo and Grandpa are watching football while Atlas is also trying to watch the game except he keeps getting interrupted by Alyssa's puppy dog eyes and her desperate attempts to get him to talk to her.

Am I going to have to slap the stupid out of her, because she honestly needs to get a fucking grip.

Atlas glances over at me several times, like he is checking on me. Each time I smile at him softly before resuming what I was working on. I don't miss the brief questioning glances my grandma gives me when she sees me smiling while mashing potatoes.

"So, how have you been doing, honey?" Grandma asks.

I look at her and smile. "Good. I just finished up my classes online this semester and have been working at Kane Designs."

She lifts an eyebrow as she nods and pulls the rolls from the oven where they were warming.

"Oh? What have you been doing there."

"Just typical admin work. I've been interning as Atlas's assistant, getting a feel for how everything works so that when I graduate, I can have experience on my resume."

"Well, that's good. Anywhere in particular you have your eyes on? Still wanting to be an architect?"

I nod and smile as Atlas interrupts us. "She better not say anywhere but Kane Designs. I don't know what we would do without her."

My grandma cuts him a look and smacks his hand when he tries to steal a roll.

"I'm sure you're capable of finding another assistant. My granddaughter is destined to be more than your lackey."

Atlas nods. "I agree. When the time comes, though, we would be lucky to have her as a junior architect."

"Really?" I ask.

Atlas gives me a soft look as he nods. "Of course. Paul helped me build the company from the ground up. It's your legacy. It wouldn't be right if you weren't a part of it."

My heart swells inside my chest at that. We never really talked about what life would look like a few years from now. Everything has been focused on one day at a time, and it works for us. But I can't say I hate the idea of a future where I get to work for a company that was as much my father's baby as Atlas's and then go home every night with the man of my dreams. Yeah, I don't hate that idea at all.

I don't realize that I am standing here smiling up at Atlas dreamily while he is doing the same to me until Grandma interrupts us.

"Well, I think we are ready. Atlas, be a dear and carry the turkey to the table. Gregory Clarke, get your butt in here and help carry all this food to the table."

I hear a loud creak from my dad's lazy boy as Grandpa calls out, "Yes, dear!"

Chuckling to myself, I grab what I can and make my way to the table. Once the table is set, Theo pulls out a chair for me before taking the seat next to mine. My grandpa took the head table next to me, and my grandma is in the other head seat. So that left Atlas and Alyssa sitting across from me and Theo.

Dinner is delicious, I'm proud of how great everything turned out and the turkey, much to Alyssa's obnoxious surprise, was cooked perfectly. Theo told some stories about college while Grandma and Grandpa reminisced about their days at school. We all avoided any and all topics about my parents, and I don't know about anyone else, but I was greatly appreciative of it.

Atlas had barely taken his eyes off me the entire meal, a soft sweet smile on his face permanently etched into his handsome features anytime our eyes would meet. Unfortunately, I think my grandma picked up on it a bit when she spoke next.

"So, Atlas, are you seeing anyone?"

He tenses just barely for a moment as he smiles and nods.

"I am."

Alyssa's face sours at that as she practically downs her entire glass of wine while Theo snorts.

"Yeah, caught him in the act with her this morning."

"Theodore!" Grandma admonishes. "That is not polite talk to be had at the dinner table."

Theo shoots me a wink that tells me he's not sorry at all before looking at Grandma.

"Sorry, Grandma Jackie."

"Well, who is she?" my grandma asks, her eyes coming to me just for a millisecond. It's enough to send my anxiety sky-high, though. Does she suspect? Of course she does. Why would she look at me otherwise? Oh god.

Alyssa leans forward like she couldn't be more interested to find this out herself. Probably to burn her house down because as I'm quickly realizing, Aunt Alyssa is a little fucking crazy when it comes to Atlas. He just laughs lightly and shakes his head, though.

"Too early to sic Mama Jackie on her, I'm afraid. When it becomes something more serious, I'll be sure to give you her full credentials."

Grandma seems semi-pleased with that response as she nods and takes a sip of her wine. My heart sinks slightly at his words, even if I know they are for show. Atlas must be able to tell because I feel his foot brush against mine underneath the table in the next moment. I smile softly before Alyssa speaks.

"Well, it's good not to settle down too fast. You always want to keep your options open," Alyssa says as her hand slips underneath the table before Atlas jolts in his seat and his body stiffens. He quickly reaches down and grabs what looks like her wrist before setting it back into her lap, which only causes her to do it again.

"Can I take anyone's plate?" I ask as I quickly stand up.

My grandpa offers up his for me, and I take the empty roll plate before grabbing my own. My body is shaking as I make my way to the sink before starting the water. The dishes are slick between my hands and as I angrily try to scrub one plate, it slips through my fingers. I try to catch it, but it ends up shattering apart in my hands, causing a sharp sting to rip through my palm.

"Shit," I hiss.

"Are you okay?" Atlas asks from behind me, dishes in his hands that he quickly abandons when he looks at my bleeding palm.

"I'm fine," I say as my hands continue to shake.

Atlas grabs a wad of paper towels and presses it to my cut before taking my wrist and dragging me into the bathroom.

"C'mon. I think there is a first-aid kit down here," he says as he kneels to the cabinet and begins fishing through everything.

When he finds the kit, he stands back up and pulls the paper towel away from my palm.

"It's not too deep. I don't think you'll need stitches. Let's just clean it and wrap it to be safe, though," he says as he takes an alcohol wipe and runs it over the angry red line. Once it's clean, he grabs some gauze and wraps my hand a few times before taping it.

"I hate it when she touches you," I whisper hoarsely.

"Trust me, I hate it too. The only woman I want touching me is you," he whispers lowly. Atlas presses a soft kiss against my open palm before giving me one of those breathtaking smiles that has my stomach fluttering with butterflies.

Licking his lips slowly, he glances out into the hallway before coming back to me, slipping his fingertips underneath my chin as he brushes his lips against mine. I can't help but melt into the touch, a sudden wave of reassurance rushing through me as he deepens the kiss. I know it sounds pathetic that I'm so quick to become insecure but how can you blame me? The odds are against us, by a lot, so I will take any reassurance that I can get.

My arms reach up to snake around his shoulders when a sound quickly brings me back to reality.

"OH MY GOD!" a high-pitched voice shrieks.

Atlas and I jump apart as my stomach drops.

Oh. Fuck.

Alyssa is staring at us, wide-eyed and mouth dropped as her head keeps whipping back and forth between the two of us. Minutes pass between us, or maybe it just feels like minutes until she finally speaks.

"You fucking BITCH!" she screams as she lunges for me.

I take a quick step back, and Atlas is thankfully able to intercept her as he holds her back, not by much though. She is going crazy, slapping him and screaming at the top of her lungs.

"My NIECE?! MY FUCKING NIECE?! I was always too young for you, but you can fuck my eighteen-year-old NIECE!"

"I knew it," Theo says lowly, his voice somehow unlike anything I've ever heard as he comes to stand in the hallway. His voice is calm, quiet, but deadly.

Alyssa gets one more slap across Atlas's face before she turns on her heel and runs down the hallway and up the stairs, bawling her head off the whole way. When she is gone, Theo is standing a few steps from Atlas, his fists balled at his sides, body nearly shaking with rage.

"I knew there was something going on with you two. I didn't want to believe it, but I could fucking feel it," Theo says, his composure slipping slightly as his voice quakes.

"Theo," Atlas says placatingly as he takes a few tentative steps toward him.

"She was the girl in your bed this morning, wasn't she? And you got me out of the house so she could sneak back home?"

"Just let me explain, son," Atlas tries again.

"Don't fucking call me that! I'm not your son because any semi-decent father would know better than to fuck the girl his son loves!" Theo roars before winding back and punching Atlas across the face.

Atlas is taken off guard, but Theo doesn't stop there as he charges him and swings again, causing Atlas to fall to the ground. Theo jumps on top of him to continue when Grandpa quickly comes up behind him and yanks Theo off.

"Calm down, Theo! Calm down! C'mon," he says as he drags Theo off to the formal living room on the other side of the house.

I kneel down beside Atlas to find his lip split and a bright red mark forming on his cheek.

"Oh god, Atlas. I'm so sorry!" I say as I cup his face gently.

"Not your fault, babygirl."

"It's both of your faults," my grandma scolds with her arms crossed over her chest. "Atlas Kane, I am so mad at you right now I can't even look at you. Go talk to your son right now."

"Not sure he wants to talk to me, Jackie."

"Well too damn bad! Let him punch you again if that's what he needs. You fucked up, now be a grown-up and go fix it."

Atlas hangs his head in shame for a moment before he nods, standing up to his full height with my help. He gives me a regretful look as he turns and heads down the way Grandpa and Theo went. Tears begin falling down my cheeks as I watch him go as the realization washes over me that both of our lives quite literally just imploded.

"Don't sit there feeling sorry for yourself, Drama. You did this to yourself. What were you thinking?" she asks with a shake of her head.

"I love him, Grandma," I say with a watery frown.

"Jesus," she says on an exhale as she closes her eyes and opens her arms up.

I don't hesitate to walk into them as I begin to cry harder as she rubs my back.

"Anyone with two eyes can see that, sweetheart. I'm worried about you, though. I'm worried for both of you. What would your parents say if they were alive? They wouldn't approve and you know that. He's been like a second father to you."

"It doesn't feel that way. He's always felt like...more."

She winces at that, like the words turn her stomach before blowing out a heavy breath.

"You two bonded, right? Ever since your parents passed, he's been there for you, and you've been there for him?"

I nod as I pull away to look at her, wiping underneath my eyes as I do.

"That's good that you've had each other to support one another, but this is about more than you two. As you can see, this involves a lot of people, and on top of that, this isn't healthy. Set aside the extreme age difference and rather unusual...dynamic. You aren't coping with the loss of your parents, sweetheart. Neither of you are. You're burying the pain, using each other to numb it."

She lets out a sympathetic sigh as she brushes away my tears.

"Be honest with me. Have you even been to their graves since the funeral?"

I hesitate, guilt beginning to gnaw at me from the reminder as I slowly shake my head.

"You chose to ignore the pain instead of dealing with it. You found the first thing that you could lose yourself in and latched on. And it looks like Atlas did the same. I know you feel like you are in love, but it's the grief talking. If you choose to continue...whatever is going on here, then you have to wait until you have properly coped and started healing, in a healthy way."

Her words are like a punch straight to my chest. I don't know what to say to her because I don't know how to feel about it all. I know that I've been pushing the pain away, but I didn't fall for Atlas because I needed a distraction. I fell for him because he's...him. I know that there is at least some slight truth to her words, though. Truth in the fact that I haven't been coping, haven't been healing. I've just been surviving, perfectly sheltered in my little Atlas cocoon.

What about him? Is the only reason he fell for me because he was grieving? Hurting? Was I just an outlet? A way to escape reality for a little while? After all, what kind of a future could we genuinely have? We're like two lost souls, bound together in grief and pain. Does that make us soul mates, though? I know what I feel but...what if Grandma is right?

Taking a shaky step backward, I take another and another before I turn and run for the back door. When I throw it open, I find that it's down pouring outside, but that doesn't stop me. I begin sprinting. Stretching my legs out as far as I can, pumping my arms as hard as I can while I do my best to outrun the pain beginning to seep into me like an ugly decay.

Streets pass by in a blur, but it feels like I can't run fast enough. With each step, the ache in my chest splinters, spreading to every inch of my body. When I can't take anymore, I fall to my knees, sopping wet grass soaking my knees as I let out a gut-wrenching sob. It hurts so bad, so much worse than even that first day. The months and months of built-up grief have finally boiled over, and I swear, I think I'm going to die from it.

My eyes are blurred, my body drenched as I slowly lift my head to see the words scrawled in front of my face.

Here lies Emily Clarke & Brian Clarke.
Beloved parents, siblings, children and best friends.

Another sob that more likely resembles a scream wretches out of me as I shout into the black sky. It hurts so much. The pain, the heartache, the loss. It's more than I can bear. I can't fight it anymore. I don't have it in me.

Chapter 38
Atlas

"Get the fuck away from me!" Theo shouts as he paces the Clarke's formal living room.

"Theo, please. Let me explain," I say defeatedly.

His eyes are wild as he turns to me, Greg seemingly ready to jump in between us if it comes to that again.

"Oh, you want to explain? Okay. Go ahead, *Dad*. Explain. I'm all fucking ears to understand how you can justify fucking my girlfriend."

"Ex-girlfriend," I correct tightly, though I don't know why. The look of outrage on my son's face sure as hell tells me that small detail doesn't matter.

"Are you sure about that? Sure you weren't fucking her behind my back while I was away at college?" he snarls.

"I can promise, the only person in yours and Andromeda's relationship that was unfaithful was you."

That harsh dose of reality seems to bring him back down to earth at least momentarily. Shaking his head roughly, he runs his fingers through his hair as he tilts his head up to the ceiling.

"I don't get how this even happened! I get that you wanted to fuck her, she's beautiful and smart and *young*. What I don't get is why the hell she fucked you. I swear to fucking god, if you forced her, I will—"

"Don't even finish that sentence, Theodore Paul Kane. Everything that is and has ever been between Andromeda and I is completely consensual."

"I'd like to hear that from her myself," he says as he goes to pass me and walk down the hall where we left Andromeda and Jackie.

I step in front of him, blocking his path which causes him to shove me away.

"You will not be speaking to her when you are this worked up. Calm down, now."

"Fuck you! You don't control her or me. You think she actually loves you? That she could fall for someone like you? Age aside, you're a fucking prick. A fact she verbalized regularly on our calls. Age included, you're fucking disgusting," he sneers.

I do my best to not let his words affect me but coming from my son of all people, I can't deny they sting.

"Enough fighting," Jackie says as she rushes into the room. "She's gone."

"Who?" Theo and I voice at the same time.

"Andromeda," she says as her eyes begin to water. "We were talking, and she just ran out of the house. She didn't even have a coat on and it's pouring outside."

I'm moving before she can even finish speaking as I grab my keys and head for the door. I glance to my right to see Theo doing the same.

"I'll check the house. If she isn't there, I'll start driving," he says without looking at me as he opens the front door and jogs across the street.

"Atlas!" Jackie calls out before I step outside.

I turn around only to be met with a sharp slap to the cheek. I wince at the impact before Jackie wraps me up in a tight hug.

"I love you like a son, but I don't approve of this thing between you and my granddaughter."

I open my mouth to tell her that, respectfully, I don't give a shit, but she continues speaking.

"I think I know where she is going. Their graves," she says solemnly.

My stomach drops at that. I sure as hell hope she's wrong. The graveyard is at least two miles away and if she is running the entire way in the rain, she will be practically hypothermic by the time she gets there. I nod my understanding before running across the street to my car, hopping in as I watch Theo leave the house and sprint to his car. He turns left out of the driveway toward town while I turn right toward the graveyard.

I get there in minutes, throwing my car into park in the middle of the parking lot as I sprint toward the graves that I could find blindfolded. Though I don't know how I remember the way so well. Like Andromeda, I haven't been back since their funeral.

When I get to their row, I stop in place as I see a dark form huddled in front of their grave. My heart cracks as I see my sweet Nevaeh so still, so lifeless. I rush toward her, bending down in front of her before scooping her up into my arms. Her eyes look up at me, but it's as if she isn't actually seeing me. I press my fingers to her neck to feel her pulse. It's there but weak, and it scares the living shit out of me.

"Babygirl, it's me. What happened?"

"I miss them," she croaks, her voice raspy and raw.

My stomach twists as I stand with her in my arms, doing my best to shield her from the rain.

"Me too."

Turning on my heel, I rush us to the car before speeding the entire way home. When I get there, I lift her out of the car just as Theo drives past the house before stopping in the middle of the road when he sees me. He quickly parks next to me as he rushes up to us.

"What the fuck happened? Where was she? Has she been outside this whole time?"

I nod as I jog toward the front door. Theo runs ahead of me and quickly unlocks the door before opening it for me. I take the stairs two steps at a time as I push into my bathroom. Theo starts up the shower as I set Andromeda down on the ground and begin undoing her shoes.

"Not too hot, Theo. We need to bring her temp up slowly."

"I'm not an idiot," he grits through clenched teeth as I peel off her sopping socks.

Theo bends down to help me, lifting the bottom of her sweater before I stop him with a glare.

"Get your fucking hands off her."

Theo rolls his eyes as he stands up and crosses his arms over his chest.

"It's nothing I haven't seen before."

I bite on my tongue until I draw blood. It's the better option as opposed to going off on him for reminding me of one of many things I try to forget daily. Theo turns around, probably more so out of respect for Andromeda than me as I lift her sweater up and over her head. She shivers against me, but her eyes remain cold, and her mouth closed.

Slowly, I stand her up so I can take her jeans off, but she collapses almost instantly.

"Shit," I say as I grab her before she can fall.

Theo is there in a flash as he bends down to undo her jeans, looking away the entire time as he pulls them down and off her. I decide to keep her panties and bra on for her sake as I walk us into the lukewarm shower. Andromeda lets out a soft gasp when the water hits her, but other than that, she just stays leaned up against me.

Little by little, Theo turns up the water when I nod my head. We do this until we are finally completely out of hot water. When we turn the shower off, Theo is there with a large towel that I quickly wrap around Andromeda as I scoop her up and carry her to my bed.

Stepping away for a moment, I shuck off my wet clothes and slip on a fresh pair of boxers before grabbing a T-shirt of mine for Andromeda. I quickly slip it over her head until she is fully covered before I reach behind her and take off her wet bra and panties.

I tuck her under the covers as Theo tosses her wet clothes into the laundry hamper before I climb in next to her, pulling her onto my chest to help keep her warm. Theo pauses at her side, looking down at her with a sad shake of his head as he brushes a piece of hair out of her face before his eyes come up to me, filled with pain and what looks like hate.

"This is all your fault."

I'm not sure if it's the way he looks at me, his words, or a combination, but it takes my breath away as my son steps out of the room, shutting the door with a sharp thud. I blow out a breath, doing my best to keep my emotions at bay, but today has my strength weakening. Andromeda clings to me tighter, and it causes a small part of me to ease before she makes a soft cooing sound and cuddles into me deeper.

I reach my fingers out to her neck and am so thankful to feel her pulse is a hell of a lot stronger than it was when I found her. I take some peace where I can in knowing that I have my girl safe in my arms. It's about all I can say for this shit show of a day.

Happy fucking Thanksgiving, everyone.

———

Feeling that the space next to me is empty, I immediately shoot upright. My eyes quickly look around for Andromeda, softening when I see her sitting at the edge of the bed, fully dressed in some clothes she must have forgotten to move back to her place as she stares at her hands.

"Nevaeh? How are you feeling?" I ask as I sit up a little more.

She looks up from her hands before facing me with a watery smile.

"Babygirl," I whisper as I cross the space between us, cupping her face gently as I look into her pain-drenched eyes.

"What happened last night? What were you thinking running out in the rain like that? You don't know what seeing you like that did to me."

"I'm sorry," she rasps. "I-I don't really know. I needed to see them. I've been avoiding it for too long."

"I would have driven you," I say gently.

"Our world was kind of imploding around us, Atlas. I didn't exactly have the time or brain capacity to ask for a ride," she says with a humorless laugh.

I nod as I bring her hand up to mine and press a kiss against it.

"I thought I could bury the pain, Atlas. But it hurts more than ever," she chokes out as she clutches her chest.

I wrap my arms around her tightly as I rock her back and forth.

"I know. It's okay to hurt. We'll get through this together. I promise."

She only sobs harder at that, and something unspoken suddenly has the hairs on the back of my neck standing up as I turn her to face me fully.

"Babygirl, I know yesterday wasn't what we talked about or pictured when telling everyone. But they will come around. We are going to make it through this. I can face anything as long as I have you by my side."

She doesn't respond for a moment. For several moments, actually. The silence sends an unnerving feeling seeping into my stomach before she finally speaks.

"My grandma thinks that we are using each other to block out the pain, numb it. She thinks the reason that we got together in the first place is because we were each other's crutch, a distraction to get lost in."

I begin to shake my head, knowing that none of that is true, not even for even an ounce of it as she continues speaking after a shuddered breath.

"A-and, I think she might be right."

My heart plummets, to my stomach, to the floor, to the very surface of the earth. It keeps falling and falling until I feel a sickening crack inside myself from her words.

"I-I think I need some time. I think we need some time."

"Time?" I rasp hoarsely, hating how vulnerable I sound. I don't have it in me to act tough right now though, not when my heart is physically fucking breaking.

"It's been easier for me to lose myself in you than to accept everything that has changed in my life, everything that my life has become. I need time away from you to properly grieve, to heal. To move on the right way this time. I never want to feel like I did last night again, and it starts with recognizing that the coping mechanism I've been using is not what's best for me."

I lick my lips as I nod, doing my best to keep a level head. Okay, it's not that bad. She just needs some space to process everything properly. I can give her that.

"Whatever you need, Nevaeh. I'm here for you. Anything you need," I say.

"I can't work for Kane Designs anymore," she says, delivering another blow to my already aching chest.

I swallow over the thick lump forming in my throat as I nod.

"The job will be there for you when you are ready, any job you want."

"If you are still the CEO at that point, that is," she points out.

Shit, yeah. I guess so.

"And I'm switching to in-person classes at OSU. I already emailed the admissions office and asked if I could start in January."

"You've been busy this morning," I say, attempting to lighten the mood but failing miserably as she stares at me with watery eyes and a wobbling lower lip.

"I'm sorry," she whispers.

I shake my head as I cup both sides of her face tightly, keeping her eyes on me as I speak.

"Don't be. I'm not giving up on us, Nevaeh. You take what time you need, all the time you need. When you are ready, I will be right here waiting. I know a good thing when I see it. So, I'm holding on with both fucking hands."

She gives me a sad smile as she nods.

"Can I still talk to you? Visit once in a while?" I ask.

She shakes her head sadly as a tear rolls down her cheek.

"It would probably be easier if you didn't."

Disappointment takes up a permanent residence inside my chest where my heart used to be before it fell to the earth's core.

"Well, when can I see you again? A month?"

"Atlas," she sighs. "I need more time than that, a year, at least."

A year? Unacceptable. I don't think I'd physically survive a year of not seeing her. Not even once? Fuck no.

"End of the semester," I counter. "And then I'm coming for you."

"Atlas—" she begins to argue before I silence her with a kiss.

She doesn't pull away, but she doesn't exactly engage as I press my lips against hers, pouring every promise and vow possible into this one kiss. When I pull away, I rest my forehead against hers like I've always done as I whisper to her.

"One semester, Nevaeh, and then I'm coming for my girl."

"Okay," she whispers softly. "But you never know, you could meet someone by then, move on."

I shake my head before she can even finish such a ridiculous sentence.

"Never. There is only you. There has only ever been you."

Chapter 39
Andromeda

Five Months Later

Despite the time away from Atlas, the heavy—near debilitating—feeling in my chest has yet to subside. Sometimes I hate myself for insisting on not having any contact with him. He abided by my wish of no contact for about a month. Christmas morning I woke up to a text message from him and a horribly wrapped present. It was a new iPad, similar to the one he uses for work, a Golden Gate Bridge charm for my bracelet and a T-shirt of his.

I know I should have ignored the presents, that would have been the healthy thing to do. Instead, I took it all inside and slept in that shirt every day for the last five months, in between washes of course.

Thankfully, I was able to be admitted to in-person classes at OSU. It was pretty easy to fall into a routine and though I mostly have been keeping to myself, I have made a few semi-close acquaintances.

I see Theo around campus every now and then, but we aren't exactly on speaking terms. When I first got to campus, he helped show me around and took me to lunch where he told me that he would always love me but felt betrayed by me and his dad and that he needed time to forgive me. I didn't blame him for feeling that way at all, and still don't.

In the time that I've been here, I've also been seeing a therapist,

Marissa. She has been amazingly patient with me from day one, when we literally just sat in silence for fifty minutes inside her office. Little by little over the months, we have broached the topics of my parents, the accident, and Atlas.

That last one is still kind of sore for me. Especially when my therapist agreed that from the information I was giving her, it seems our relationship was based on survival and desperation to have someone to lean on. She voiced what I already knew. We were toxic together, unintentionally so, with the best intentions for one another, but toxic, nonetheless.

The end of the semester is drawing near, and I know Atlas is expecting to come for me, for us. To pick up right where we left off. And the largest part of me wants that too, more than anything. The time apart hasn't made me love him any less. It's only helped me see our situation more clearly.

But I've just been offered an amazing opportunity, once in a lifetime, really. The offer has been sitting on my dorm room desk for weeks now and the deadline is tonight. There has been one thing truly holding me back. One person. Taking in a deep breath, I blow it out as I focus on what Marissa and I talked about in our last session. About how I need to consider what's best for me before deciding what's best for others. It was a session Atlas and his bleeding heart probably could have benefited from.

Without letting myself hesitate another moment, I click send, accepting the offer, officially sealing my fate, and hoping to god that one day Atlas will find it in himself to forgive me.

Chapter 40
Atlas

I've been keeping tabs on Andromeda. I know, it's wrong. She asked me for space, and I should have respected that. To be fair, I mostly did, except for Christmas but how could I not at least try to reach out to her on Christmas? She didn't respond to my text or present, not that I was too surprised. I really thought that she would have responded on her birthday, though. I sent her another charm for her bracelet and a note, telling her that I was counting down the days until the end of the semester. I expected a text, maybe even a call, but I was met with silence.

None of that matters anymore, though. What does matter is that today is the last day of spring semester.

It's over and I'm here for you, babygirl.

I'm walking through the OSU campus, weaving in and out of students and faculty, all overly eager to get the hell out of here for the summer as I make my way toward her dorm room. Like I said, I've been keeping tabs on her. It really wasn't all that hard. A few winks and eloquent words about how I wanted to check in on my goddaughter and I was walking out with a building name and room number.

A lanky kid holds open the dorm building door for me, and I tip my head in thanks as I slip inside. The small box in my front pocket is weighing heavy with each step I take. Another charm to add to her growing collection. Something special just for her, just for us.

When I find her room, I take a deep breath before knocking. It's been a long six months. Some days I didn't know how the hell I was going to make it this long without seeing or even speaking to her.

Despite my utter shock, the board of directors didn't have me removed from Kane Designs. I guess while they didn't agree with my methods of putting Dillon in his place, harassment of an employee of any kind was not tolerated and they let me off on a probationary period. So, at least I've had work to bury myself in since my son won't speak to me, and my girl told me she needed space. God, I sound like a sad fucking sack.

The door opens and my heart begins pounding with excitement, but it thuds almost to a complete halt as a girl with red hair and brown eyes stands in front of me. She raises an eyebrow at me as she looks me up and down.

"Can I help you?"

"Yes, I'm looking for Andromeda?"

She furrows her brows before shaking her head. "Oh, she left like a week ago."

The polite smile on my face begins to fall as I look at this girl in front of me with utter confusion.

"I'm sorry? Left?"

"Yeah." She shrugs. "She finished early or whatever. She was a total nerd, always studying. Already headed home for the summer, I guess."

"Alright," I say, still completely confused. "Thanks, I guess."

The girl shrugs again and slams the door closed as I stumble away from it, still not fully comprehending what is going on. Andromeda has been home for a week? Impossible. I would have seen her car there. No one has been in the Clarke home since she left for school in January.

Worry begins to set in. What if something happened? What if there was an accident? She's been gone for an entire week? I storm out of the dorm only to run into my son. His eyes widen as he looks at me with furrowed brows.

"Dad? What are you doing here?"

"Have you seen Andromeda? Where is she? When was the last time you saw her?"

"Whoa, whoa. Chill out. What are you talking about?" he asks.

"She isn't here," I say as I quickly begin pacing, pulling out my phone and calling her. Of course, I'm immediately sent to voice mail. I try again but same thing, and again, same thing.

"Fuck fuck fuck fuck," I mutter as I continue pacing.

"What the hell is going on?" Theo asks.

"Andromeda!" I snap. "The love of my fucking life is missing. I told her I was coming for her. I told her that when the semester was over, I was coming here. I'm fucking here, but she isn't! Her roommate said that she left a week ago! A week, Theo. She's been missing for an entire week!"

"Calm down, let me try her," Theo says as he pulls out his phone and starts dialing.

"It won't work!" I stress. "Her phone is going straight to voice mail. I'm telling you. Something—"

"Hello?" Theo asks, causing me to freeze in place. "Hey, where are you? I wanted to see you before I left campus."

He pauses for a moment, confusion filling his face before responding.

"What do you mean, you're not in Oregon? Are you back home in Brighton?"

Another pause.

"Well, then where are you? You're starting to freak me out."

He stands there, seemingly listening to her before he blows out a breath and nods his head.

"Okay, yeah, fine. Call me soon, okay? If you need anything, day or night, you call me."

He nods. "Okay, yeah. Talk to you later."

With that, he pockets his phone as I stare at him expectantly.

"Well?" I ask.

"She said she isn't here or in Brighton."

"Well, then, where the hell is she, Theo?"

He shrugs as he runs his fingers through his hair.

"She wouldn't say. All she said was that she was safe and would call me when she could later."

"Did she say anything about me?" I ask, not giving a shit how desperate I sound.

He nods with a sympathetic look. "She told me not to tell you that I've spoken to her. She said that it's best this way."

"Best? Best for who!" I shout.

"I don't know, Dad," he says with his hands raised in surrender. "That's all she said. I'm...sorry."

"So...she's just gone?" I ask, the words tasting foreign on my tongue. It doesn't make sense. None of this makes sense.

"Yeah, I guess so." He shrugs before turning on his heel and heading in the direction he was originally going without another word.

A fog settles over me as I slowly make my way to the parking lot. I don't remember getting there, nor do I remember the entire drive home. It's only when I'm parked in my driveway, looking up at the empty house in front of me, that reality begins to sink in. She left, so I don't know where and she didn't even say goodbye. Didn't even do me the courtesy of telling me to my face. The love of my life is gone without a trace, and I don't know how to begin to process that shit.

Chapter 41
Atlas

I wake up the next morning on the couch, my head pounding, my mouth dry and an empty bottle of bourbon on the floor beside me. The beating inside my skull confirms I drank what was left of that bottle before passing out down here. I was going to go to bed, but it felt so... empty in there.

Pushing myself to sit up, I lean my elbows onto my knees as I begin massaging my temples. A confusing fog is settled over me, making things hard to sort out. Like how I was able to drive hours in a daze, not really able to grasp anything as my mind raced with possibilities.

How could Andromeda just leave like that? Where did she go? Who is she with? Does she miss me as much as I miss her?

Obviously not, or she wouldn't have left.

For a moment, I let that really sink in, and it feels as if a thousand razor blades are being dug into my skin at once. No, something has to be wrong. She wouldn't just leave like this. She wouldn't just disappear into thin air after she *knew* I was coming for her. Coming for us.

Forcing myself to my feet, I only sway slightly as I gain my bearings and go in search of my phone. I need to make some calls. Someone will be able to help me find her. I'm not just going to roll over and let her slip through my fingers like this. She needs to come home, she needs to be with me, and I'll do whatever it takes to bring her back.

It's been a week since I left for OSU, ready to pick up my girl and start this next chapter of our story together, a week since I came back empty-handed, my heart a mangled mess from the fallout. I've hardly slept, I've been avoiding eating until it's absolutely necessary and I've assigned all of my tasks to Garrett, Dillon's replacement. He's a smart man with a good eye. I have no doubt he's doing just fine. Even if he wasn't though, I wouldn't give a shit.

For seven days I've done nearly everything I can think of in tracking down Andromeda Clarke, and for all seven of those days, I've come up empty-handed. I called the school, gave them some bullshit story about how I lost contact with her and needed to reach her, see if she gave them any information or something. Obviously my story wasn't convincing enough because the woman told me that information was confidential and told me to stop calling or she'd contact the police.

I've called Greg and Jackie. They both had some choice words for me when I did, but they were both shocked to hear I had no clue where Andromeda had disappeared to. I guess they haven't really heard from her since Thanksgiving.

After them, I made my way down the list of Andromeda's friends from high school, which admittedly wasn't a very long list. None of them had spoken to her since high school graduation, so they were no help.

Theo was the logical avenue I needed to wear down. It was a tough situation though, seeing as he still hated me for my relationship with her in the first place, and I can't even blame him. I'm a shitty father though because him telling me that he was disgusted with me and disappointed in her didn't stop me from begging him for any information he had on her.

"You think even if I knew, I would tell you? She specifically asked me not to tell you that I had spoken to her. What kind of message does that send your dad? To me, that sounds like she wants nothing to do with you and you need to walk away with what little pride you have left. If she wanted you, she would have been there. But she wasn't."

Recalling Theo's words from the other day stings more than I'd ever be able to admit out loud. I don't allow myself to focus on those thoughts for too long. There has to be more to this. I know it. She loves me, loves me like I love her. She's the air that I breathe, the blood running in my veins. Being away from her is physically fucking painful and I know she feels the same. She has to.

Right?

———

It's been a month since Andromeda seemingly dropped off the face of the planet, and I'm starting to really worry. Finding her has practically become my obsession. From the moment my eyes open to the second my body begins shutting down from lack of sleep, my mind is on her. I've all but hired a private investigator at this point in finding her.

I waiver daily on it and with the lack of sleep, the absence of food in my daily diet and the frequency I'm going to the gym to burn off the constant adrenaline, I'm wondering why the hell I don't do it already. I have the money, more money than I could probably spend in my lifetime, if I'm honest. I don't live a lavish lifestyle because I don't need one to be happy. But I'd spend every goddamn cent of that money to hold her in my arms one last time.

My legs burn as they stretch out, eating up the never-ending distance of the treadmill. I'm just in the garage today since I didn't feel like leaving the house, but I knew I needed to run. Ever since I've known Andromeda has been gone, an almost buzzing feeling has taken up permanent residence under my skin. It makes it impossible for me to do hardly anything. The only time it fades is when I run, which is how I've found myself on mile number six for this morning's impromptu workout.

My shirt is damp with cold sweats, my breathing heaving and labored as my extremities shake with weakness. I can feel myself growing dizzy as my stomach begins to turn, but I push through it when an image of Andromeda's bright eyes pops into my head. Fuck, how has it been nearly seven months since I've seen those eyes? In person, at least, I've practically become glued to the pictures of her on my phone.

I know what people must think of me, or at least what they would think if they knew how bad I'm spiraling. I don't care, though. She's not just any woman. She's *the* woman, *my* woman. And she's out there somewhere instead of by my side. My love and affection for her have only grown and my obsession to find her has become my reason to live.

A familiar feeling aches inside me, and I jump off the treadmill and lean my head over into the garbage can across the garage seconds later, emptying my stomach. As I expel my body of whatever useless things are inside of me, I feel a hand on my back, patting gently before I wipe my mouth with the back of my sweatshirt.

Glancing up, I'm surprised to find Theo watching me with furrowed brows. I haven't seen him since that day at OSU. We have talked a little. Mainly me checking to see if he'd heard from Andromeda and him either ignoring me or telling me no, though I'm certain he isn't telling the truth.

Theo shakes his head disappointedly as he looks at me.

"You look like shit."

A mirthless laugh escapes me as I stand up a little taller. My legs quake at the move but I try not to let it show.

"I feel like shit."

He stares at me silently for several seconds before he blows out a breath.

"Dad, this isn't healthy. You sounded rough on the phone, but I didn't expect...this," he says as he gestures to me.

I frown at his words. I get that he walked in on me puking, but I don't look all that bad, all things considered. I don't look like how I feel on the inside at least. Like I'm a fucking gutted man, walking around aimlessly, searching for the love of his life who doesn't want to be found.

"You gotta let her go," Theo continues.

"I did," I grit through suddenly clenched teeth. "I gave her space. I let her go off to college for a semester and then we were supposed to start over. It was supposed to be our time."

Theo lets out a hollow laugh.

"Do you hear yourself? You 'let' her go to college? You're not her keeper. You had no say in that. That was Drama's decision and so is this. She left to take care of herself, and I suggest you do the same. You're broken, Dad. Maybe you don't see it, but I'll bet anything you can feel it. Andromeda is broken too. She's just trying to do the right thing and heal herself. I think you should do the same."

Chapter 42
Atlas

The blue and gray carpet stares at me, mocking my presence, an endless amount of about times ringing out through the room. Or maybe it's just in my head. I honestly don't know anymore.

I never thought I'd ever be caught dead in a place like this. I'm stronger than this, I don't need it.

You do, though.

What Theo said resonated with me. I'm *broken*. At first, I was offended. How could he even think that when all my life I've done everything I could not to break? Not to give up, to persevere no matter what hand I was dealt.

I've never felt broken, never felt empty. Just seven months ago, I felt like the most fulfilled man in the world. I had everything I could have ever wanted and then it all crumbled apart faster than I could put it back together. I didn't even get the chance to fix it. In one moment, it was just gone.

"Atlas," a man about my age calls out from the doorway, causing me to stand and make my way over to him.

I reach out my hand and shake his as he ushers me into the room before gesturing toward either of the couches inside. I opt for the closest one to the door just in case I decide this is all actual bullshit and want to leave before I sit down, doing my best to relax but my muscles are not fully allowing that to happen.

"I'm Chris. It's nice to meet you," he says as he sits down in his chair facing me, grabbing a small notepad as he does.

I nod. "Nice to meet you too."

Chris smiles softly as he tilts his head to the side slightly.

"So, tell me what brought you here today?"

I open my mouth to speak when the words die on my tongue. What a loaded fucking question. There is such an uncomfortability to being vulnerable with a complete stranger. Why does anyone think it's a good idea to spill my deepest and darkest thoughts and feelings to this guy? What's he going to do? Wave a magic wand and make all my problems disappear? Unlikely.

The urge to leave is stronger than ever, the pain from my past and even my present is beginning to weigh on my chest like a brick house and suddenly, I can't breathe. Closing my eyes, I do my best to catch my breath when a pair of bright-green eyes pops into my head. It takes milliseconds for my brain to conjure her face. Her small pert nose, those full lips, her flawless skin accompanied by that flowing golden hair that I could tangle my hair in for hours.

A pain runs through my chest at the sight of her, yet I never want to open my eyes. I don't want to let the image of her fade or disappear altogether.

This is for her. I need to be full if I'm ever going to have a chance at getting my girl back and I guess it starts here. Reluctantly, I open my eyes, hoping my angel will visit me in my dreams tonight as the image of her slips away and I'm greeted with Chris, watching me with a patient smile. I swallow roughly as a million thoughts race around in my head, all begging to be released aloud.

For Nevaeh and maybe a little bit for me too.

———

My hand begins to cramp up as I finish today's letter. As soon as the stroke of the pen makes its final mark, my hand celebrates with a charley horse as I drop the pen and apply pressure. It's amazing how out of practice we have become with handwriting these days. Everything is on computers or cell phones, and rarely ink and a blank piece of paper. It's practically obsolete, or at least that's what I thought at first.

Chris and I unburied a lot that first session, more than I even knew was there. We started back to my childhood, cliché, but it's where he wanted to start, and he's the professional, so I went with it. It took daily sessions for a week just to get to the point in my life where my mom died, and it was more exhausting than it sounds.

Eventually we broached the topic of how I met Em and Paul, how I got Theo's mom pregnant and how she split on us when he was a baby. I was surprised at how easy those sessions were. The ones where I was telling stories or lessons we all learned through childhood, though I could hardly bring myself to use Andromeda's name for most of those sessions. It felt too...out of place. She would always be that little girl, but it's like she also became a completely separate entity. A new woman re-birthed in the ashes of her pain and sorrow. A woman that completely owns my heart and soul.

I was anticipating judgment when we finally got to Andromeda a few weeks ago. I'd been seeing Chris for a little over four months, and I'd successfully managed to avoid one of the most difficult things that I've ever faced. But in true therapist fashion, he seemed to know I was hiding something, keeping it close to chest. So when he spoke her name for the first time, asking what my relationship with her is like, it was like all of the oxygen was sucked out of the room.

It took several minutes before I decided the hell with it and told him everything. How our feelings changed seemingly on a dime. How the love I've always felt for her morphed and twisted into something deeper, something all-consuming. And then how she broke me, left without a trace with simple instructions to my son not to let me know where she is. That session fucking sucked.

Chris took it all in stride, if he has an opinion or judgment on the issue, I wouldn't know. He keeps things very cut and dry, asking what I feel in response to those things, how I'm coping with yet another abandonment in my life. I never thought that I had abandonment issues,

Chris says that's not what I'm supposed to call them, but I can't stand all of the fancy terms he tries to create to explain why I am the way I am.

Honestly, right after that session, I almost quit. Therapy wasn't helping. It was only bringing out the hurt, in full force this time. Until he gave me some homework. He told me to go home and write a letter to Andromeda. When I got visibly irritated by his request and reminded him that I don't have her address, he raised his hand gently and told me to write it to her anyway, then put it in a drawer and leave it there.

I told him I could write it out in an email or something, but he insisted on me doing it on a piece of paper. He said that it was different and if I trusted him, I'd see for myself. Almost out of spite, I decided to try it and I hate to admit it, but he was right.

At first, I just stared at the blank page in front of me, so many words dying to be inked against the crisp white paper. Then, I remembered Chris told me to start with the basics, so I did. I wrote about how I woke up that morning, like all of the other mornings reaching for her, because even though it's been close to a year since I've seen her, she still meets me in my dreams every night.

I wrote about what happened at work, how the traffic was fucking maddening and how I almost missed my appointment with Chris because of it. I wanted to write more, but I had covered the page front to back and decided to put it in the drawer. Something washed over me in that moment. Something akin to relief, even if she would never read the letters, for a moment, it felt as if I were able to write all of those things. Like now that it's been written, it's out there in the universe and she knows it now.

Chris was proud of me and encouraged me to keep writing to anyone I wanted about anything I wanted. Over the last few months, I've written letters to my mom, my deadbeat dad, Jackie and Greg, Emily and Paul, even Theo. There is so much I have to say to so many people, so much I didn't realize I needed to say. Regardless of what I felt needed to be written to who that day, the constant is that I've written one to Andromeda every day without fail. It helps and I feel closer to her for it, even if that's not our reality anymore.

Chapter 43
Theo

Drama has been gone for over a year now. I never would have imagined that I'd go that long without seeing her, ever. I mean, I guess technically, I see her. We FaceTime nearly every day. Still, it's definitely not the same.

"You're so fucking tan," I say with a shake of my head as I lean back into the seat of my car.

"Well that's what happens when you're out in this sun all day like I am," she teases as she rolls over onto her back on the beach.

"Guess so," I say on a yawn.

"You need to go to bed. It's like three in the morning your time," she says.

I shake my head as I open my eyes a little wider.

"No, it's good. It was just a long night. We fucking killed it, though."

"Knew you would." She smiles. "I live-streamed your last gig. You guys have this energy, I can feel it through the screen. You'll be picked up before you know it."

"You think?"

"Well, you will at least. Your lead singer is...different."

I bark out a laugh as I scrub a hand through my hair. That's one way to put it. Andromeda laughs for a few seconds before it slowly eases, her eyes growing distant as she stares off-screen.

"Drama?" I ask with slightly furrowed brows.

She snaps back to look at me, seemingly forcing her eyes wider and her smile brighter.

"You good?"

Quickly, she nods but I watch her thickly swallow. Usually I don't ask, mainly because I know what puts that look on her face. It's only ever one thing. My dad.

"Thinking about him again?" I ask.

"Who?" she questions with a frown that has me rolling my eyes.

"Okay, so we're just gonna play dumb here?"

Her frown slips as she shrugs her shoulders. "I'm fine, Theo."

"Are you?" I challenge. "I'm not so sure, Drama. It's been a year since you left OSU. You picked up and ran away halfway around the world and you still haven't been able to outrun your feelings. So, give it to me straight. Are you actually okay?"

"I left for school, Theo. You know that. I couldn't pass up this opportunity."

"Are you okay?" I repeat, slower this time.

She stares at me for a while, so long I'd think the screen froze if I didn't see her chest slowly moving with her breaths.

"I want to be," she whispers softly, something in her whisper cracking my heart.

"Fuck, Drama. I hate that you're so far away."

"I've told you to come out and visit me anytime."

My tongue begins playing with my lip ring, an unintentional habit these days as I mull over her offer more than ever before.

"I'll see what I can do."

"Really?" she asks, her eyes lighting up as she does.

"Yeah, just make sure your hot friends are there." I smirk.

Andromeda groans. "Please don't lead them on. Between your flirtations and practically full body tattoos, they are both halfway in love with you already."

I waggle my eyebrows as I give her a wink.

"The feeling is mutual."

Andromeda groans as she runs a hand through her hair.

"Alright, time for bed for you. I'll talk to you soon."

I laugh lightly as I nod. "Love ya."

"Love ya too," she says before ending the call.

Sitting in my dad's driveway for one more second, I blow out a breath before getting out of the car. Now that I graduated, I've been pretty much throwing myself into the band. I know we're close to making it. We just need the right show. It's why we are going on a self-scheduled tour in a few weeks.

I've been thinking about getting my own place in town but honestly, I'm worried about leaving my dad alone. He's been doing better, a lot better than working out until he pukes, avoiding food altogether, and practically living at the office. But I don't know if his good is the same as other people. He's like a ghost of the man he used to be, and I hate to say it, but I think Drama is in the same boat.

They are more alike than they probably realize. Both burying their pain, putting on a show, ignoring the elephant in the room. Despite them both being in therapy, looks like they haven't learned much. Or maybe I'm just being an asshole.

When I make my way inside, I instantly notice my dad on the couch. He's passed out cold, his phone on the floor. Bending down, I pick it up to put it on the coffee table when the screen has me pausing.

A picture of Andromeda and him fills the screen. Not sure when this was taken, it's a picture of them in the car. Andromeda smiles widely at the camera while my dad smiles at her. It's weird for me to see them like that. My ex-girlfriend and my dad coupled up like that. Instead of making me furious like it would have to see this picture a year or so ago, it makes me kinda bummed. Because I don't think I've seen a smile like that on either of their faces in a long ass time.

Chapter 44
Atlas

When I wake up, the first thing I see is my living room TV. The next is the fireplace to its right and the coffee table with my phone on it. Fuck, I must have fallen asleep down here. My back is gonna hate me for that today.

"Morning," a voice says, catching me off guard to my left.

Theo is standing there with his arms crossed, a cup of coffee in his hand as he looks at me.

"Hey, morning. When did you get in last night?" I ask as I sit up fully.

"Around three." He shrugs.

"And you're already up?" I laugh. "Don't you need sleep, kid?"

"Eh, sleep when you're dead."

I roll my eyes at him but chuckle anyway. I still feel Theo staring at me, causing me to glance up to him. My brows furrow at the look on his face.

"What?"

He rolls his lips together, seemingly contemplating his next words before he speaks.

"I talked to Drama last night."

My heart instantly leaps inside my chest, as my pulse begins thundering inside my veins. I do my best to keep my cool, but a million thoughts race in my head. How is she? Is she okay? Did something happen? Where is she? Does she miss me like I miss her?

"Oh yeah?" I ask, my posture rigid, my attention ready to eat up any morsel he has to give about her. I'm practically desperate for it and I don't even care how pathetic that makes me.

Theo nods slowly, silently. So silent I almost think that was all he had to say. Before I can snap at him for dangling something like that in my face, though, he opens his mouth.

"She's, uh...she's not doing great."

My stomach drops in an instant, and I'm to my feet.

"What happened? Is she hurt? What can I do? I—"

"Easy, easy," he says with a hand raised.

"Physically, she's fine, but she..."

He trails off like his words don't mean life or death for me in this moment. Or at least that's how it feels. I feel like I'm on the verge of a fucking coronary if my son doesn't spit it out.

"Different," he finally says.

"Different?" I question.

He nods.

"Okay. Is it a bad different?"

Theo shrugs.

"Jesus, Theo. Can you say something of consequence, please?"

"Do you still love her?" he asks, seemingly out of the blue.

I turn my head away, not ready to start this morning off with a fight between me and my son. That's how this conversation always seems to go. I know that the hurt will never truly be gone, but he's chosen to forgive me, and I'll never be able to express how thankful I am for that. But the one rift we always seem to come across is that I'll never lie about how I feel about Andromeda.

"You already know the answer to that," I say a little softer than before.

"Then why haven't you hounded me lately? That was all you ever used to do. Have you given up on her?"

My head whips back to him. "Never," I say quickly. "But it was affecting our relationship, and that wasn't fair of me. You're upholding her trust, and that's something I could never be upset with you for."

Theo nods as he looks down at his cup of coffee.

"What would you say if I told you I might be willing to break her trust?"

My body practically lurches forward before I stop myself, my breathing quickening as I stare at my son intently. If this is a joke or something, I'm going to be so fucking pissed.

"I'd say that probably doesn't make you a very good friend, but there has to be a reason you're willing to all of the sudden."

"She's not happy. Not like she clearly was when she was with you. Not when she was here, in Brighton."

"Where is she, Theo?" I ask carefully, worried the familiar question will set him off or set our relationship back.

"She's gonna kill me," he whispers under his breath as he shakes his head.

I take a step closer to him, reaching out to grab him by the shoulder. I squeeze him gently, causing him to look up at me.

"Where is she?"

He blows out a deep breath as he looks up at the ceiling before his eyes come back to me.

"Ever been to Greece?"

Chapter 45
Andromeda

"Andromeda, hurry up!" Sophia calls out from the other side of my dorm room door.

I quickly toss my cell phone, wallet, and keys into my purse before slipping my sandals on. When I open the door, she and Aster are standing there not so patiently waiting for me. They are both wearing mini tanks and cargo pants that look so effortlessly put together while I'm in a plain white T-shirt and a pair of jean shorts. If I've learned anything during my year of living abroad, it's that nearly every European is born with an inherent fashion sense that must have skipped over eighty-nine percent of America.

"What's the rush?" I laugh as we start walking through the hall.

"Aster is starving and won't stop complaining," Sophia says with a mock eye roll.

Aster huffs her irritation as she begins snapping at Sophia in Greek. I've picked up quite a bit living here, I'm nowhere near fluent but I know enough to understand that Aster is saying some not-so-sweet things to her childhood best friend right now.

I met both of them on my first day here. I'm not sure if it was meant to be or they took pity on the out-of-place American. Either way though, they practically adopted me into their friendship, and we've been inseparable ever since. I can talk to them like no one else, mainly because they know everything about me, and I do mean everything. From my parents to Theo to Atlas, the poor girls have endured the endless saga of Andromeda Clarke's life, down to every painful detail. The fact that through it all they gave me nothing but love and support meant everything, and I knew they were my forever people.

Sometimes I can't believe I've been away from the US for so long, from Brighton for so long. It was hard at first, despite Sophia and Aster's best efforts. There were a lot of long nights in the beginning. Those first six months at OSU without Atlas hurt so much, though. I woke up nearly every night searching for him, only to find the other side of my bed empty and cold. I was healing from the trauma of my parent's death, but I wasn't even close to healing over the trauma of losing Atlas. I could have held true to our agreement, been there waiting for him when the semester was over like we said. I could have even still taken the exchange program and told him about it, he would have been thrilled for me. We could have made it work.

Could we have, though? I wasn't so sure at the time.

Six months of separation between Atlas and I, and life still hadn't gone back to normal. Theo wasn't talking to either of us. Alyssa told me she hated my guts and would never forgive me for stealing the man she loves. My grandparents still stayed in contact with me at least but every time I spoke to them I could hear the disappointment always lurking beneath the surface of their words.

At the end of the day, Atlas and I could have gotten back together, and we would have been happy, but we would have been the only ones happy. I guess it just didn't feel right at the time, though looking back, some days I wonder what would have happened if I would have called him. If I would have stayed.

Playing the what-if game never got anyone anywhere, though. At least that's what my therapist said. When I was going to Oregon State I was seeing a therapist and was beginning to work through my issues, where I quickly learned my work wasn't done. I've continued seeing someone in Athens and she helped more than I could ever verbalize. I still get the occasional PTSD-fueled nightmare, but I have developed some really solid coping mechanisms that help me through them. I adore my therapist and she agreed to continue our sessions on the phone, which I'm thankful for.

When I left for Athens, I considered having the house back in Brighton rented out. I mean, it was just sitting there empty, and I wasn't even in the country. But when I made the call and spoke to a property management company it just felt too...weird. Having strangers use my home as their own, creating new memories over my family's old ones. Call me sentimental or maybe even stupid, but I just couldn't do it. So for the last year it's sat there empty, waiting for me to return. Though, if I'm honest, I don't know if I ever want to return. I mean, what do I have back there to return to anyway?

The only person I even stay in contact with these days is Theo, and he's already coming to visit me later this week, which I'm so unbelievably excited for. Though, I'm not sure I'm ready for whatever rift Theo will no doubt cause between Sophia and Aster because both of my friends have the hots for my ex-boyfriend. I can't help but chuckle at that as we make our way out of the dorm and onto the city street. It's fairly busy in this part of town, especially on a Saturday, and Aster's favorite restaurant is just up the road, so it's not too bad of a walk.

My phone begins ringing in my purse, and I quickly fish it out before smiling as I glance at the screen.

"Hey, I was just thinking about you. How are you doing?" I ask Theo.

"Don't hate me," he says instantly, a deep exhale escaping him that has my nerves instantly on edge.

"What? Why would I hate you? What's wrong."

"Just don't hate me. I did it for you. For both of you," he says, avoiding my questions completely.

I stop in my tracks, my brows furrowed as I speak.

"Theo, what are you—"

My words die on my tongue, the air in my lungs is stolen right then and there, and my heart rate drops to a dangerously low level. Or maybe it's dangerously high. Right now, I can't tell if it's beating out of my chest or barely pumping.

Slowly, my brain tries to process this apparition in front of me. Obviously, it's some weird kind of self-induced delusion. There is no way I'm seeing what I'm actually seeing, right? There is no way Atlas Kane is striding toward me, a black box tucked under his arm, a sharp contrast to his crisp white dress shirt and slate gray slacks. I don't have to wonder if he sees me because his eyes have been on me since the moment I noticed him like I'm his single mission. Like I'm his only focus.

"Drama? Hello?" Theo says from the phone, but I can't bother to respond to him as his father eats up the distance between me and him until we are practically toe to toe.

My hand drops to my side, hitting end on my call as I stare up at Atlas. He looks the same, yet different. There is a touch more gray at his temples than I remember, maybe a few more fine lines. He looks just how I always remembered him, though all of my memories always had a smile on his face, and though the look he is giving me isn't a bad one, it's definitely not that breathtaking Atlas smile I used to be spoiled rotten with.

"Uh, you lost?" Aster asks Atlas, ever the blunt one.

Atlas ignores her as his eyes trace over me, like he's categorizing every detail possible.

"Nevaeh," he breathes out, my name on his lips like a whispered prayer. It does something to me, my stomach flipping at the three simple syllables.

"Atlas," I respond in an almost equally breathy tone.

I hear the soft gasps from behind Atlas coming from Aster and Sophia before their feet shuffle down the road a bit, assumingly to give us some privacy.

"W-what are you doing here?" I ask after a moment.

His heavy gaze doesn't leave mine for a few seconds as he takes another half of a step toward me, his cologne an assault of so many memories wrapping me up like a cocoon.

"I think I should be asking you that."

His tone surprisingly holds no heat, no judgment. Just a simple fact, and honestly, it's valid.

"I-I go to school here," I stutter.

Atlas nods. "Theo told me."

Theo. Duh, of course. Why would he tell him, though? Now of all times? I can't go further down that train of thought though because Atlas is claiming my attention once again.

"You look so beautiful. You're like a walking dream," he says with a shake of his head like he can't believe I'm really standing in front of him right now.

"You too...the dream part. And the beautiful part too, I guess. You're probably the most beautiful man I've ever seen."

Atlas's mouth twitches with the start of a smirk as he dips his head once in acknowledgment. I always wondered what would happen if I ran into Atlas again. What I would say, what I wouldn't. Would I apologize or be proud for taking charge of my emotional needs? Now that I'm faced with the moment, though, I freeze. Unable to move, unable to breathe.

"I've missed you, babygirl. So fucking much," he says vulnerably.

I swallow roughly, doing my best to choke down the words "me too."

Your circumstances still haven't changed, Andromeda. No amount of time will ever change your circumstances. It's one thing to fall for your godfather, your parents' best friend, your ex-boyfriend's dad, however you want to categorize it. It's another thing entirely to try to create a long-lasting relationship that was built on the rubble and ruin of our imploded lives.

Our relationship was hot and heavy and dizzying with passion because it was shot with an exceedingly high dose of pain, grief, and adrenaline. It wasn't love, not the true kind. At least not from him. It couldn't be, you know? That's the conclusion I've come to, at least. Even if I don't one hundred percent believe it, it tapers the sting when I think of him.

"What are you doing here, Atlas?" I ask again, my voice stronger this time.

I can tell that he notices my change of tone instantly, but he doesn't visibly react. Instead he just stares at me for several more seconds before he speaks.

"I came for my girl."

My stomach flips despite how much I tell it not to.

"I'm not your girl, Atlas. I never really was. I was just—"

"Please, don't finish that sentence. Please don't cheapen what we had by whatever slanderous statement you were about to make. You were my girl. You still are my girl too. I'm just here to bring you home now."

"Home?" I ask with furrowed brows.

Atlas nods as if it were that simple. As if we can just forget this last year and a half apart hasn't changed everything.

"To Brighton, to me. I can't do it without you anymore, Nevaeh. I don't want to. I...I need you, babygirl. I need you back."

"Brighton isn't my home, Atlas. Not anymore, and that was a lot of I sentences back-to-back. What about what I want? What I need?"

"You can have it, whatever you want, it's yours. I'll lay the world at your feet, Nevaeh. All you have to do is ask."

I do my best to ignore the sharp pang in my chest at his words. I close my eyes and swallow, shaking my head before looking back at him.

"We don't *fit*, Atlas. We weren't good together. We were toxic, using each other to outrun the grief, practically hiding from it. How am I supposed to believe any of it was real and not just a coping mechanism?"

"Because it was, Nevaeh," he says as he finally closes the remaining distance between us, his hand going to the back of my hair and tipping my head up to meet his gaze.

"I loved you with everything I fucking was, everything I am. I still do."

He pauses for a moment before dropping my hair, grabbing my hand to rest over his heart, his chocolate eyes drilling me into place as he speaks.

"Do you feel this? Do you feel how hard my heart is beating just at the sight of you?"

Slowly, I nod my head because his heart does feel like a jackhammer in the moment.

"I haven't felt that in almost two years. I haven't felt anything remotely close to that because my soulmate picked up and left the country without so much as a word. When you left, you took a piece of me with you, and standing in front of you now, remembering how full I felt with you. There is no way you will ever convince me that what we had wasn't the most real, authentic relationship that I will ever experience."

Now my heart is the one beating out of its chest. So many emotions swirl inside of me I don't even know where to begin. The familiar high I feel when I'm around him almost sways me, almost.

"Look, Atlas, you've been doing fine without me. And I'm doing fine too. Maybe it's just easier if we continue the path we're on."

Desperation fills his eyes as he shakes his head, his fingers tightening around my hand. He opens his mouth but clamps it shut as he looks at the ground and shakes his head. When his eyes return to mine, he lets go of my hand and reaches for the small box that is still tucked underneath his arm.

"Here, these are for you."

Slowly, I take the box, inspecting it before looking up at him.

"What is it?"

"My therapist suggested writing letters as a way to work through stuff. I kinda got in to it and...those are for you."

"Letters for me?" I parrot.

He shrugs. "I never knew if I'd see you again, but I hoped I would. I hoped I would get the chance to give them to you, tell you how much I've missed you and how I'll never stop loving you."

I swallow thickly, my words getting stuck in my throat before he smiles sadly, cupping my face so delicately it's like his fingers ghost over my skin.

"I'll be at the Electra Metropolis until Thursday. My number is the same. If you need anything, day or night, I'll be here."

I nod, mainly because I don't know what to say. He watches me for several seconds before leaning forward, pressing his lips against my forehead in something that feels deeper than just a simple kiss. It stirs my aching heart, twisting my stomach and stalling my breath.

"Having you in any measure of time was the greatest pleasure of my life," he whispers against my skin before slowly pulling back.

I don't realize that my eyes are closed until I force them open, watching as Atlas's form retreats down the road the way he came. The sight hurts, hurts more than I want it to, more than it should.

Aster and Sophie come seemingly out of nowhere, both rapid-firing questions, asking me what he's doing here, if I'm okay. I don't answer them, though. Instead, I look down at the box clasped in my hands, my fingers tracing over the waxy material.

Without a word, I turn on my heel, heading back toward my dorm. Thankfully, the girls don't follow me. I need space. Space to think, to process and maybe shed a few tears because the emotion currently choking me is ready to boil over.

Chapter 46
Andromeda

I've been staring at that black box in front of me for I don't know how long. I don't know why I'm nervous to open them. They are just letters. And obviously there is something inside them that Atlas wants me to see, otherwise, he wouldn't have given them to me, right?

My curiosity wins overall, and my fingers reach out to open the top. When I set it to the side, my lips part as my eyes widen. When he said letters, I pictured a dozen or so. The large pile of white paper practically spilling out of the box is unbelievable.

Not knowing where to start or what to do with all of these, I grab the one on top and notice that it's dated nearly seven months ago. He held on to this letter for seven months? My fingertips skim over the smooth, crisp paper, instantly noticing the Kane Designs gold letterhead at the top before I find Atlas's near-perfect penmanship below.

Andromeda,

I'm not sure what I'm supposed to say. I've never written a letter I had no intention of giving before, but Chris says that it'll help, and right now, I'll try just about anything.

I miss you. So much. I miss you so much it fucking hurts. There are days I wake up, and I hate you for leaving the way you did, vanishing between my fingers before I realized that I needed to hold on tighter, because I would have. I would have held on to you with my last dying breath given the chance. That's not what you wanted though, and I'm starting to accept that. Kind of.

Work isn't the same without you. Home isn't the same without you. Life is just...dull, less vibrant, less meaningful. Fucking hell, I sound like every cheesy rom-com movie you ever made me watch right now, but fuck if it isn't all true.

I wish I knew where you were. Not even for the fact that I want to be by your side, but I want to know you're okay. For my own eyes to see. Theo won't tell me anything. Only that you are safe and healing. I may be selfish in my own pain but hearing that you are healing yourself makes it worth it.

I know that you thought that what we had was just a reaction of our circumstances, that it wasn't real. You're typically right about a lot of things, but this time you missed the mark by a lot.

I've loved you since the day you were born. Since the day you opened your sweet bright-green eyes and stared straight into my soul. I had the extreme honor and privilege to watch you grow, falter, and transform into the amazing woman that I know you are today.

Somewhere along that way, lines were blurred, feelings shifted, and before I knew it, I wasn't just on my knees, I was on my face for you, ready to worship the altar of you. You're my deity, my goddess, my Nevaeh. Our relationship hurt some people, and as selfish as it is to say, the only person I regret hurting is you. Because I did something, right? I had to have. Otherwise, you wouldn't have run from me, from us. You would have stayed. You would have braved the storm by my side. So please, Nevaeh, put me out of my misery and tell me what I did. I know I never should have had you, and maybe that was reason enough, but I hope you know, given the chance, given the choice, you would be right by my side right now, kept safe, protected, and loved always.

I know this will never make it to you, mainly because I'm starting to lose hope that I'll ever see you again. Fuck, just writing those words breaks my goddamn heart. They just can't be true. Please tell me they aren't true, Nevaeh. Because a life without you, that's not a life I want to fathom.

. . .

Water droplets begin dotting the page, blurring some of the ink, I try to dab at what I can, but it continues splattering across the page until I realize that they are coming from me. I feel the hot tracks of the tears down my cheeks as I set the letter to the side, my heart cracked wide and hurting as I sob into my hands.

Why does he have to be so perfect? Why does he have to say all of the right things when I don't have a choice? Doesn't he get that if he was anyone else in the entire world, things would be different? How dare he come out here, disrupt my happiness, my peace. I was doing just fine without him. At least, I thought I was. If I'm honest though, maybe I just became numb to it all. Is this how I'm supposed to feel? These raw, visceral emotions that practically consume me? I haven't felt anything like this in over a year. Maybe that was the point, though.

Not being able to help myself, I reach for the next letter, devouring his every word, inhaling his I love yous and consuming his pain that practically bleeds through the page. One by one, I read through the letters he wrote me, if the dates are accurate, every single day for the last seven months.

My tears have practically dried up, my throat raw and hoarse, and I reach for the last letter. It has a date of yesterday with a single sentence.

I'm coming for you, Nevaeh.

Something about those words is like a balm over my exposed pain, soothing the sharp jagged edges that have poked and prodded at my already battered heart. Slowly, I set it to the side, slumping back into my seat as I look out the window to notice that it's already night. I've been here for hours, learning more about Atlas Kane than I ever have before. I feel like I've seen into his mind, felt his heart and before I can register what I'm doing, I'm grabbing my purse and heading out the door.

When I step outside, the chilled night air biting me as I do, I run. My legs stretch out in long even strides as I eat up the distance between Atlas and me. I run until my lungs burn, until my legs quake and my shirt is practically soaked through with sweat. I run until I'm out front of the Electra Metropolis.

My steps don't falter as I step inside the posh hotel, walking up to the concierge desk.

"What room is Atlas Kane staying in?" I ask briskly.

The concierge furrows his brows as he looks at me before a look of understanding dawns on his face.

"What is your name, miss?" he asks, his accent thick as he begins rifling through some papers.

"Andromeda Clarke. I need to—"

"Perfect. Room 3205. Here is your key, Miss Clarke. Have a wonderful stay."

I'm stunned momentarily as he hands me a room key, but I'm not stupid enough to question him. I take the key and turn toward the elevators, stepping into the first one I can find before pressing the thirty-second-floor button. Adrenaline from my high and maybe from this day, in general, has my heart rate racing as the elevator dings and the doors open. I blow out a shaky breath before I follow the hall down until I find his room. I contemplate knocking but I have a key in my hand. It was obviously left for me for a reason, right?

Inserting the key, my stomach flips as the locking mechanism sounds, unlocking it for me as I step inside. The room is nice, spacious and crisp with bright-white and deep-blue accents practically everywhere you look. My eyes categorize the room, noticing a single suitcase in the corner and a few discarded clothes. A few steps farther in and I hear the faint sound of water running. I follow it like a moth to a flame, like a beacon calling me home.

When I step inside the tiled bathroom, my heart thuds as I see Atlas in the open-style shower, all hard lines, tanned and toned to perfection. His head is resting against the shower wall, his hands dug into his hair as his chest rises and falls.

I open my mouth to speak, but nothing more than a croaked sound comes out. It's barely audible, but it's enough to get Atlas's attention. His head is shooting up, whipping around over his shoulder before his eyes land on me. In an instant, he pushes away from the wall and walks straight toward me, not at all deterred by the fact that he's naked or dripping water everywhere.

He eats up the distance between us, his large hands coming up to cup the back of my head, forcing my eyes to his as he searches my face almost frantically.

"You're here," he whispers softly, almost in awe. "Does that mean…" he trails off, not even finishing his sentence. He doesn't need to, though. I know what he's saying, what he's thinking, and I'm nodding before he can say more.

His face crumples with what looks like undiluted relief causing fresh tears to spring to my eyes as he crushes his mouth to mine. His tongue licks against the seam of my lips, demanding entrance that I grant willingly. It's like his hands are suddenly everywhere. Touching every inch of me in seconds as if he needed to assure himself that this was real, that I am real.

My arms move up to wrap around his neck, holding on for dear life because I know that if he lets go, if he pushes me away, this will be the end of life as I know it. Thankfully, he does neither of those things.

Instead, his hands make quick work of undoing my jeans, stripping them off my legs along with my panties before he reaches for the hem of my shirt. I unclasp my bra in the same moment and before I can even blink, I'm lifted into his arms, carried into the shower as if I was light as a feather. I feel the moment my back hits the cold stoned wall followed by the warm stream of the shower. The entire time never breaking my kiss with Atlas. I'm fairly certain we'd both rather die of suffocation than ever stop.

I feel him line up to me before his cock pushes inside me. The feeling has me gasping into his mouth, my fingernails digging into his back as my legs wrap around his lower back so I can get just a little closer to him. It's never enough with Atlas, it never is.

His mouth moves away from mine, only to begin peppering my neck as his hips begin thrusting.

"Atlas," I gasp as my eyes roll into the back of my head.

"Fucking hell, my name sounds like heaven on your lips, Nevaeh. Say it again," he practically begs.

I bring my gaze down to him as he pistons himself into me faster and harder than before.

"Atlas," I moan again, moving in sync with him as his cock pushes deeper into me.

"That's my good fucking girl," he practically growls.

"I missed you," I whimper as his pace becomes practically feral.

His wild eyes come up to my own, one of his hands lifting to cup my cheek as he does.

"I barely fucking existed without you. Promise me I'll never have to do it again. Promise me I'll never have to let you go."

"Never," I say with a shake of my head.

He rests his forehead against mine as he blows out a breath before nodding.

"Thank god, now be a good girl and come on my cock. I've missed you too fucking much to last much longer."

Atlas adjusts his angle, rubbing my G-spot in just the right way to make me shatter apart in his arms. I scream and shake as one of the most intense orgasms of my life tears through me, causing literal tears to run down my face from the sheer impact of it all.

I feel Atlas's cum coat me in the next moment, a satisfied groan escaping his mouth as his grip on me becomes near punishing. He only pauses for a moment before he readjusts his hold on me and begins walking us out of the bathroom.

The next thing I know, my back is dropping against the bed and Atlas is dropping to his knees.

"What are you doing?" I ask, practically in a daze.

"I need to taste you," he says as he peels my legs open, baring myself completely to him.

"You can't. You just finished in me."

Atlas scoffs, holding my eyes with his own as he leans down slowly, sticking out his tongue and licking one long line through me. The image and act combined sends a pleasured shiver running through my body. He does it again and again before letting out a satisfied groan.

"We taste so good together, babygirl."

I feel his fingers dip inside me before pulling back out and brushing against my lips.

"Open," he says.

I do as I'm told instantly, the unique taste spreading across my tongue as I suck Atlas's fingers clean.

"Fuck," he grunts before reaching down to fist his cock.

Atlas continues stroking himself as he puts his face back between my thighs, devouring me like I'm his favorite meal. His tongue rapidly strokes against my clit, causing another orgasm to violently rip through me. I reach down and tangle my hand down into his hair, forcing him against me harder as I grind against his face.

When my orgasm subsides, I watch as Atlas stands, his hand still grasping his cock as he strokes himself up and down.

"So good for me. Now give me one more, babygirl."

"Atlas, I—"

Without another word, he shoves his way inside me, causing my mouth to open on a gasp and my head to tilt back. I feel Atlas's hand wrap around my throat in the next moment, commanding my attention and obedience as my eyes come back to his.

"There's my girl. Goddammit, you're so fucking beautiful," he says, punctuating his statement with his savage thrusts.

"So-so are you," I gasp as his other hand reaches for my left thigh, hiking it up and around his hip as he pounds into me at a deeper angle. "So fucking handsome."

"I love you, Nevaeh. So much. Too much."

His words, combined with the way he perfectly works over my body, has me already trembling. Is it possible for someone to come three times in less than ten minutes? Because I think I'm about to break that record to bits.

"I love you," I say, Atlas spanking my ass almost like in encouragement. "So much," I continue. "I couldn't stop thinking about you."

"You shouldn't have left, Nevaeh. You knew where I was. You knew how to find me. Same can't be said," he says as he spanks my ass again, causing my pussy to throb in reaction.

"I shouldn't even let you come. Only good girls get to come. Do you think you deserve to?" he asks.

"P-probably not," I agree, though my voice is drenched in desperation that he will take mercy on me.

"Good girl. You know you broke my fucking heart. You know I should run far and wide, never letting you get the chance to hurt me like that again."

Tears begin to well up in my eyes again as I nod softly, the words hurting too much to agree aloud. He bends down slightly, his hand putting more pressure on my throat as he comes nose to nose with me.

"You also know that I'd rather take a thousand knives to my heart before I ever lived a day without you again. Come for me, Nevaeh."

Relief flows through me at his words, and as if my body was at his will, I come, hard. Blindingly so. I feel Atlas squeeze my throat harder, sending a dizzy high rushing through me as my lungs beg for oxygen while my body shakes and shudders through my release.

Atlas follows right along, his cock throbbing inside me as he fills me up once again. I watch his muscles strain, his body quaking before he collapses on top of me. We lay there for several seconds, existing in the warm and fuzzy haze of the post-orgasmic bliss. It won't last forever, but in this moment, life feels pretty fucking perfect.

Slowly, Atlas eases off of me, sitting back on his heels in between my open thighs. I expect him to get up and get a cloth or something since that was typically always our ritual. Instead, he skims his fingers against my thigh before coming to my pussy, gathering up the leaking cum and pushing it back inside me. His movements are too fast or hard. They are an almost calming rhythm as he pushes both of our cum back inside me, making sure not to miss a single drop.

"What are you doing?" I ask breathily, my chest heaving as I gasp for air.

"Planning our future, babygirl."

I can't help but laugh at that, though the look on his face tells me he's not joking.

"The implant in my arm makes that a little difficult, Atlas."

His brows furrow a look of distaste clouding his face.

"We need to get that removed immediately."

"I'm twenty years old. We most definitely do not."

"Well, I'm forty-two years old, and I want my baby inside you as soon as possible."

I scoff at him though I can't deny his words send a fluttering inside me.

"One day. Maybe," I say softly.

"Definitely," he says before leaning forward and pressing a kiss to my lips.

Epilogue

Atlas

One Year Later

My hands shake as I fasten my suit jacket. Fuck. I've never been more goddamn nervous in my entire life. A heavy knock comes from the wooden door as Theo pops his head inside.

"You ready?"

Blowing out a breath, I nod as I turn to face my son.

"How do I look?"

"Old."

I let out a rough chuckle as I walked up to him and put him in a headlock. He's quick to slip out of it though before doing the same to me. I tap his arm before he chuckles and shoves me away. Fuck, maybe forty-three is getting old. Or maybe these twenty-three-year-olds are just spryer than I remember being.

Theo and I walk out of the dressing room before making our way through the old cathedral church. Andromeda and I aren't overly religious, but she insisted that we get married in this church since it is the oldest functioning church in all of Athens. She knew her mom would have loved it and honestly, when have I ever been able to tell Andromeda no to anything?

After that day in the hotel, I ended up staying in Greece indefinitely. There was no way in hell I was leaving her behind, and Andromeda's program was extended for another two years. She wasn't sure if she should accept but I practically filed the reapplication for her.

The interim CEO for Kane Designs has become more permanent than I had originally planned, but I couldn't care less. I have more than enough to support both of us comfortably for the rest of our lives. I love my job, and I'm sure once Andromeda graduates, we will return home. For now, I'm happy to just be with her.

After that night, we spent the entire weekend talking about our time apart. We spoke about how we grew as individuals, how we both sought out help, and what it did for us. I will never say that I'm thankful for the time we spent apart, but Andromeda seems more full, more fulfilled and for that, I have no complaints.

Theo has probably been our biggest supporter, which I suppose shouldn't have been as surprising as it was. If it wasn't for him, I probably would still be wallowing in my own misery back in Brighton. I knew that Andromeda and Theo had kept in touch over the years, and I'm glad that she had him to lean on when I couldn't be there.

Andromeda's grandparents were also a little more accepting of us being together again than either of us anticipated. After several long phone calls, they told us that as long as we were happy, that was all that mattered.

Alyssa, on the other hand, we rightfully haven't spoken to in years now. I'll never forgive her for the vile things she said to Andromeda shortly after Thanksgiving. I blocked her a number of years ago, and I'm thankful for it. Psycho bitch can stay as far away from me and my fiancée for the rest of our lives for all I care. Well, wife here in a few minutes.

Fuck. I can't even believe it. I'm getting married. To Andromeda. Definitely never saw this coming. We had only been back together for two months before I got down on one knee. She asked me if I was crazy, to which I answered most definitely, before she said yes, tackled me, and slid the ring onto her finger herself.

So here we are, me and Theo, anxiously waiting for my bride to walk down the aisle. For Andromeda Nevaeh Clarke to officially become mine, though as I remind her often, she's always been mine.

The processional music begins to play as Aster and Sophia walk down the aisle. They are both very sweet girls who seem to have their eyes on Theo. Based on the way Theo is looking at both of them, I'd say he feels the same. My rock star son in the making already has the womanizing down to an art. Though he knows that if he ever hurts one of Andromeda's friends, she will no doubt castrate him.

In the crowd are a few colleagues from work that Andromeda has become close with as well as Sophia and Aster's families whom Andromeda and I have spent a lot of time with. They are all extremely welcoming to me, and they feel like a second family. I see Jackie in the crowd, staring up at me warmly. I smile at her warmly as she gives me a teary-eyed nod.

When Sophia and Aster stand to the left of the aisle, the music changes before Greg steps into view, a glowing white vision taking his arm as they begin walking down the aisle. I'm in awe. I know my jaw is on the floor, I know tears are welling up in my eyes and I don't give a damn. Theo claps my shoulder tightly as he leans into my side with a smile.

"She looks beautiful," he says lowly.

He's got that right, but beautiful doesn't come close to describing my soon-to-be bride. She's stunning, perfection. Andromeda glides down the altar in a gauzy dress with long sleeves that leave the front of her arms bare as she holds a candy bouquet in front of her since she to this day still hates flowers. She looks like a Greek goddess. My goddess.

She smiles widely at me, and I can't help but do the same. My eyes snag on the now bulky charm bracelet around her wrist as I smile. One charm in particular stands out. One that I've been holding on to for two years. I gave it to her after we got home from the graveyard, a present that was long overdue. A charm with the Andromeda galaxy and the Atlas constellation interwoven, just like they were always meant to be. Or at least in my opinion.

When she reaches the altar, I hold out my hand for her, and she takes it immediately, practically leaping away from Greg as she does. He shakes his head before winking at me and slapping me on my shoulder before making his way to his seat. Andromeda and I smile at each other as the priest begins talking about love and why we are here today. I hardly hear a word he says, too lost in those deep emerald eyes to care about anything around me except for her.

I'm still in shock when she slides the ring onto my finger before I do the same. I can't believe it, this goddess, this angel, is all for me. It's the greatest gratification I've ever felt in my life.

Thank you!

Phew. How are you doing? You good? I'm not sure if I am. This book was a RIDE to write. It's so different from my usual work and I have to tell you, I'm obsessed. Thank you so much for taking the time to read Gratify, I hope you loved it!

If you want more, make sure you check out my other books!

Gallows Hill Series—a dark academia reverse harem
Damnation (Prequel)
Deceit
Descent
Demise

Standalones
Graves—an MFM stalker romance
Deliverance—an FF secret society romance (spin-off from Gallows Hill)
Gratify—a forbidden age gap
Jagged Harts—an MMA enemies to lovers

The ONS Series—interconnected forbidden romances
One Night Seduction
One Night Scandal - Coming Soon

Acknowledgments

To my alphas, Skarlet and Courtney, I'm so thankful for you. Being an alpha is a difficult task, dealing with me is a whole other beast entirely. Thank you for taking the rough bones of this book and helping me uncover it. You stood by my side in some of my lowest points during this book and raised me even higher on the highs. I don't deserve you but am so freaking thankful for you.

To my betas, Cathy, DeAnna, Sheyla, Thalia, Elena, and Lynds, I adore you all. Each one of you is so incredibly invaluable, and I can honestly say I would not be the writer I am today without you all. From the feedback you give to the absolutely unhinged DMs I get from you while you're reading, you know exactly who I'm talking to, I'm so grateful to have you all!

To my amazing editor, Ellie. I am so thankful for you as an editor and a friend! Thank you so much for transforming this book into the polished finished project that I couldn't be more proud to share. I appreciate you more than you know.

To my ARC and Street Team, thank you all for being my nonstop hype crew! Every single post, share and comment means everything. I'm overwhelmed with the absolute love you all show not only my books but me as well. Thank you for allowing me to drag you onto this crazy train through the Taylorverse (See, it's totally becoming a thing.)

To my readers, I adore every single one of you. Thank you for reading my books, for leaving a review, and for supporting me in the best way possible. I may be a new to you author and if so, thank you for taking a chance on the perpetually sarcastic (but biasedly super funny) indie author. To those of you who have already binged my backlist, and this is your latest read of my books, I could never thank you enough for your support. Every page read, every book picked up is quite literally changing my life, and I hope, at moments, it changes yours too.

All of my love!